CARNACKI

THE COMPLETE INVESTIGATIONS AND OTHER STRANGE PHENOMA

CURIOUS MATTER ANTHOLOGY PRESENTS

WILLIAM HOPE HODGSON

EDITED BY
JONATHAN PEZZA

ILLUSTRATED BY
ONI

About the Author

William Hope Hodgson was born on November 15, 1877, in the small Essex village of Blackmore End, near Finchingfield, England. Born into a family of twelve children, three of whom died in infancy, young "Hope" was the second son of the Reverend Samuel Hodgson, an Anglican clergyman with radical biblical interpretations that frequently put him at odds with church hierarchy. His mother, Lissie Sarah Brown, bore the considerable burden of managing this large, constantly relocating family as the Reverend moved from parish to parish throughout Hope's early years.

The Hodgson family moved almost yearly during Hope's first thirteen years, shuttling between Yorkshire, Nottinghamshire, London, Kent, Essex, and Ireland. In 1887 when the family was sent as missionaries to convert the Catholics in Ardrahan, County Galway, Ireland. The bleak landscape of Western Ireland, with its treacherous bogs and hostile atmosphere, would later inspire the nightmarish bog creatures in Hodgson's work "The House on the Borderland".

Unhappy and rebellious, Hope repeatedly attempted to run away from home before age thirteen, invariably heading toward his obsession: the sea.

Hope's fascination with maritime life finally succeeded after his father died of throat cancer in 1891, cutting short his formal education. With assistance from his uncle, the fourteen-year-old William indentured himself as a cabin boy aboard an merchant wind-jammer on August 28, 1891.

The reality of seafaring life proved brutally harsh. Hodgson later recalled the defining incident: "Being a little chap with a very ordinary physique, I had the misfortune to serve under a second mate of the worst possible type. He was brutal... I summoned sufficient courage to retaliate and 'went for him'. It was all the world like a fight between a mastiff and a terrier, for he was powerful and knew how to punish. Of course, I took a merciless thrashing..."

This incident launched Hodgson's lifelong obsession with physical culture and bodybuilding, but more importantly for his literary development, it established the foundational theme that would run through all his supernatural fiction: the necessity of courage when facing overwhelming forces. His protagonists, from the unnamed narrator of "The House on the Borderland" to Carnacki himself, would embody this principle of standing firm against seeminglty insurmountable odds through the search for, and emplolyment of practical knowledge and need to overcome fear.

Despite harsh conditions, Hodgson proved himself an exceptional seaman, earning his third mate's certificate and the Royal Humane Society's award for diving into shark-infested waters to rescue his ship's first mate. His eight years at sea provided him with authentic maritime knowledge that would lend unparalleled realism to his horror fiction. More crucially, these experiences taught him that the ocean was both sublime and terrifying—a lesson that would inform his creation of the Sargasso Sea stories and the oceanic imagery that pervades even his landlocked supernatural tales.

Standing just 5 feet 4½ inches tall and weighing 150 pounds, Hodgson had transformed his compact frame into a powerhouse through scientific exercise. His measurements were impressive for any era: 42½-inch expanded chest, 15-inch biceps, 12½-inch forearms, and a 28½-inch waist. His feats of strength included a 112-pound one-arm press (holding two 56-pound dumbbells in one hand) and partial deadlifts exceeding 500 pounds. These achievements weren't merely vanity; they represented his methodical approach to overcoming physical limitations through scientific study and relentless practice.

Settling in Blackburn, England, Hodgson opened his "School of Physical Culture" in 1899 at Ainsworth Street. The local newspaper praised the facility as having "absolutely nothing wanting" in terms of equipment, describing it as covering 1,200 square feet with "a large roomy theatre for exercises and drills, comfortable and cosy dressing and other ante-rooms, with shower baths, &c." Among his clients were members of the Blackburn police force, who undoubtedly benefited from his practical approach to physical conditioning.

Hodgson advertised himself as "the inventor and teacher of a system that will cure indigestion," demonstrating his understanding of the connection between physical fitness and overall health. His approach combined scientific methodology with practical application, reflecting the same analytical mind that would later construct intricate supernatural mysteries for his detective Carnacki.

It was during this period that Hodgson achieved his most famous feat outside literature: against the legendary escape artist Harry Houdini. When Houdini performed his show challenging people to bind him anyway they saw fit at Blackburn's Palace Theatre in October 1902, Hodgson accepted the dare with characteristic boldness. Using his anatomical knowledge, he bound Houdini so effectively that the escape artist took one hour and forty minutes to free himself, suffering bloody welts in the process.

Houdini later complained that he had "never been so brutally treated" in fourteen years of performing. The incident generated considerable controversy, with accusations that Hodgson had deliberately injured Houdini and jammed the locks of his handcuffs.

Hodgson wasn't shy about publicity. In another notable stunt, he rode a bicycle down a street so steep it had stairs, an event covered in the local paper. These theatrical demonstrations of physical prowess served both to promote his business and satisfy his need for public recognition—a desire that would later drive his literary ambitions.

When his fitness business proved financially unsustainable, Hodgson turned to writing with the same determination as all his previous endeavors. His first published story, "The Goddess of Death" (1904), established many of the themes that would define his writing career: exotic settings, supernatural revenge, and the consequences of tampering with forces beyond human understanding.

What distinguished Hodgson from his contemporaries was his fascination with contemporary scientific discoveries and their potential applications to supernatural investigation. The late Victorian and Edwardian periods witnessed revolutionary scientific breakthroughs that captivated the public imagination: Wilhelm Röntgen's discovery of X-rays in 1895, Guglielmo Marconi's wireless telegraphy experiments beginning in 1894, and Sir William Crookes's investigations into electrical discharges in vacuum tubes. These discoveries probed that invisible forces existed beyond what we could see or touch that were powerful enough to penetrate matter and transmit information across vast distances—concepts that he would brilliantly incorporate into his supernatural fiction.

The breakthrough came in 1906 with "From the Tideless Sea," the first of his legendary Sargasso Sea stories. These tales created Hodgson's most enduring contribution to popular mythology: his vision of the Sargasso Sea as a supernatural graveyard of ships. Critics immediately recognized the power contained withing his stories, with one proclaiming the work possessed "unusual dramatic power"

Hodgson transformed the real Sargasso Sea into something far more sinister wasteland populated by monstrous creatures and serving as what scholar Timothy S. Murphy calls "a distinctly supernatural 'borderland'" where natural and supernatural realms blur into sinister murkiness. This concept of "borderlands"—spaces between known and unknown, human and inhuman—would become fundamental to weird fiction and appear prominently in the Carnacki stories.

Between 1910 and 1912, Hodgson created Thomas Carnacki, "the

Ghost-Finder," revolutionizing both detective fiction and supernatural horror through his innovative integration of contemporary scientific theory with traditional occult investigation. The six original Carnacki stories appeared in *The Idler* magazine, setting the template that continues to permeate paranormal investigators in fiction today.

Scholar Luciano Boi comments in his essay on the use of scientific discoveries on literature, "In the stories of Carnacki, a fictional supernatural detective, we find several references to new scientific discoveries of the early 20th century". Unlike Arthur Conan Doyle's Sherlock Holmes, who invariably revealed supernatural manifestations as fraudulent, Carnacki existed in a world where the supernatural was genuinely real and terrifying. This innovation was crucial to the development of weird fiction—Hodgson refused the comfortable Victorian assumption that reason could explain everything."

Hodgson's masterstroke was Carnacki's "Electric Pentacle," a device that exemplified his synthesis of scientific knowledge with supernatural protection. As Boi notes, "The 'electric pentacle' is a device invented by Hodgson for his character to protect himself from supernatural forces, ghosts or monsters. The device consists of a series of wires and glowing vacuum tubes, a realistic portrait of electric technology in early 20th century".

The Electric Pentacle represented Hodgson's sophisticated understanding of contemporary electrical science. Carnacki explains: "I came across Professor Garder's 'Experiments with a Medium.' When they surrounded the Medium with a current, in vacuum, he lost his power - almost as if it cut him off from the Immaterial. That made me think a lot; and that is how I came to make the Electric Pentacle... I connected up the battery, and the next instant the pale blue glare from the intertwining vacuum tubes shone out".

The devices Hodgson invents for his stories was scientifically plausible for its era, and unlike the works of Jules Verne and other contemporary writers who depicted technology that was pure fantasy, Hodgson based his merger of occult and science on real world concepts that at the time were cutting edge. The blue glow, for example, came from mercury discharge tubes, which were already available when Hodgson wrote the stories. The protective principle drew from actual experiments with electrical fields and vacuum tubes that scientists like Crookes were conducting. Hodgson's genius lay in extrapolating from real science to validate the supernatural beyond simple belief and superstition.

Hodgson's fascination with contemporary technology extended beyond the Electric Pentacle to encompass the full range of late Victorian and Edwardian scientific breakthroughs. Scholar Luciano Boi identifies specific examples: "Let us remember that Guglielmo Marconi made the first experiment of a transatlantic wireless communication in 1901," just nine years before Hodgson began writing the Carnacki stories. Hodgson extrapolated from these discoveries to imagine supernatural entities that could communicate across dimensional barriers. His "Outer Monstrosities" in the Carnacki stories operate according to quasi-scientific principles, using methods that parallel wireless transmission.

Similarly, Röntgen's discovery of X-rays in 1895 demonstrated that invisible radiation could penetrate solid matter. This revelation that matter was not impermeable to invisible forces provided a scientific foundation for Hodgson's supernatural entities that could manifest through apparently solid barriers. Contemporary experiments with radioactivity, conducted by scientists like Marie and Pierre Curie, revealed that matter itself could spontaneously emit invisible energy. These discoveries suggested that the boundary between matter and energy was more fluid than previously imagined.

These wondrous expansions in humanity's understanding of the natural world provided the inspiration that Hodgson masterfully wove into his tales and grounding them in a sense of realism that helped make them truly terrifying.

Hodgson's innovations extended beyond these technological themes into the writing technique itself. Hodgson employed what scholar Timothy S. Murphy in his book *William Hope Hodgson and the Rise of Weird* calls "decognitive narration," narrative that takes scientific rationality as an object of suspicion rather than triumphant certainty." This uncertainty is employed to enhance the immersion of the reader, putting them directly into the mindset of the characters as a psychological tool.

Immersion as a means to evoke a deep reading response seems to be at the heart of many of Hodgson's choices. In "The Night Land," Hodgson invents a pseudo-archaic language that forces readers to experience the same disorientation that characters feel when confronting the unknown. William Hope Hodgson scholar Nigel Brown defends these techniques, the archaic style "adds a patina of gravitas to the story" and creates "a tension... between dramatic engagement and stylistic alienation that is part of the uniqueness of this book".

This linguistic experimentation reflected Hodgson's belief that encountering truly alien phenomena would require new forms of expression. Like scientists developing new terminology to describe previously unknown phenomena, Hodgson created specialized vocabularies for supernatural investigation. His "Sigsand Manuscript" and references to "Ab-Natural" versus "Supernatural" entities demonstrate systematic categorization reminiscent of scientific classification.

The impact of Hodgson's scientific approach to supernatural fiction gained recognition from the genre's most influential writers. H.P. Lovecraft extensively praised his work in multiple letters, writing to Robert Barlow in 1934: "Have also read 3 weird books by William Hope Hodgson... In some respects they have a peculiar & magnificent power—an ability to suggest realms & dimensions just out of reach & sieges by hellish legions the nameless from unsuspected, fathomless abysses of night. 'The House On The Borderland' has a breath-taking cosmic reach"

Clark Ashton Smith, another master of weird fiction, wrote of Hodgson: "William Hope Hodgson surely merits a place with the very few that inform their treatment of such themes with a sense of authenticity". Smith particularly admired how Hodgson's maritime experience lent genuine credibility to his fantastic elements.

Terry Pratchett, the beloved fantasy author, acknowledged Hodgson's profound influence on his literary development, calling "The House on the Borderland" "the Big Bang in my private universe as a science fiction and fantasy reader and, later, writer".

Contemporary filmmaker Guillermo del Toro has praised Hodgson's scientific approach to horror, specifically citing "A Voice in the Night" as inspiration for the Japanese horror film "Matango," proving that Hodgson's legacy is still permeating literature and media more than a century after his death.

When World War I erupted in 1914, Hodgson demonstrated characteristic courage by immediately enlisting. Commissioned as a second lieutenant in the Royal Artillery on July 3, 1915, he notably refused naval service despite his extensive maritime experience.

His war letters reveal how combat experience was influencing his literary vision with continued scientific precision. Writing to his mother from the front, Hodgson described the battlefield landscape in terms that echoed his fiction: "My God! talk about a Lost World— talk about the end of the World; talk about the 'Night Land', it is all here, not more than two hundred odd miles from where you sit infinitely remote... If I live and come somehow out of this... what a book I shall write if my old 'ability' with the pen has not forsaken me".

This passage suggests Hodgson was preparing to apply his approach to supernatural fiction to the unprecedented technological horror of modern warfare. The tragic irony is that he would never get the chance. On April 17, 1918, Lieutenant William Hope Hodgson volunteered for forward observation duty on Mont Kemmel near Ypres. Two days later, on April 19, 1918, he and a signaler suffered a direct hit from a German artillery shell. He was forty years old, killed just months before the war's end.

His commanding officer wrote: "Of his courage I can give no

praise that is high enough. He was always volunteering for any dangerous duty... I myself am deeply grieved, having lost a real, true friend and a splendid officer".

Hodgson's death represented the loss of a revolutionary voice that was only at the beginning of his literary journey. Even so, his influence continues to shape speculative fiction today.

Modern scholars recognize Hodgson as the bridge between Victorian supernatural fiction to modern supernatural horror and science-fiction. Many of his scientifically-grounded tropes are now the established background machinery of genre fiction._From John Wyndham's "The Day of the Triffids" to James S.A. Corey's Expanse books, from "The Matrix" films to Mike Carey's "The Girl with All the Gifts," Hodgson's scientific approach to cosmic horror appears throughout modern genre fiction. His integration of authentic scientific knowledge with supernatural speculation established a template that remains vital.

The tragic question that haunts Hodgson studies is what scientific and literary achievements might have emerged had he survived the war. At his death, Hodgson had been concentrating on adventure stories and serial characters, but his battlefield letter suggests he was preparing for a major literary evolution incorporating his wartime experience. One can only speculate how Hodgson may have integrated the coming tectonic shifts in global politics, technology, and culture into his further works. The literary possibilities are tantalizing.

William Hope Hodgson lived intensely in his brief forty years, creating literary innovations that continue influencing writers more than a century after his death. His synthesis of authentic scientific knowledge with cosmic imagination established new forms of weird fiction that transcended his age while speaking directly to contemporary concerns about science, technology, and humanity's place in the cosmos.

The stories in this collection represent more than historical curiosities, they are living documents of a writer who dared to peer beyond the borderlands of human experience into the vast, scientifically comprehensible yet terrifying cosmos beyond. Hodgson's greatest achievement was demonstrating that effective horror comes not from gothic conventions but from science revealing our position as vulnerable beings.

The great tragedy is that we can only imagine what further literary innovations this remarkable writer might have achieved. But perhaps that mystery is fitting for a man who spent his career exploring the unknown.

BOOK ONE
THE COMPLETE INVESTIGATIONS OF THOMAS CARNACKI

CHAPTER I

GATEWAY OF THE MONSTER

I n response to Carnacki's usual card of invitation to have dinner and listen to a story, I arrived promptly at 427, Cheyne Walk, to find the three others who were always invited to these happy little times, there before me. Five minutes later, Carnacki, Arkright, Jessop, Taylor, and I were all engaged in the "pleasant occupation" of dining.

"You've not been long away, this time," I remarked, as I finished my soup; forgetting momentarily Carnacki's dislike of being asked even to skirt the borders of his story until such time as he was ready. Then he would not stint words.

"That's all," he replied, with brevity; and I changed the subject, remarking that I had been buying a new gun, to which piece of news he gave an intelligent nod, and a smile which I think showed a genuinely good-humored appreciation of my intentional changing of the conversation.

Later, when dinner was finished, Carnacki snugged himself comfortably down in his big chair, along with his pipe, and began his story, with very little circumlocution:—

"As Dodgson was remarking just now, I've only been away a short time, and for a very good reason too—I've only been away a short distance. The exact locality I am afraid I must not tell you; but it is less than twenty miles from here; though, except for changing a name, that won't spoil the story. And it is a story too! One of the most extraordinary things ever I have run against.

"I received a letter a fortnight ago from a man I must call Anderson, asking for an appointment. I arranged a time, and when he came, I found that he wished me to investigate and see whether I could not clear up a long-standing and well—too well—authenticated case of what he termed 'haunting.' He gave me very full particulars, and, finally, as the case seemed to present something unique, I decided to take it up.

"Two days later, I drove to the house late in the afternoon. I found it a very old place, standing quite alone in its own grounds. Anderson had left a letter with the butler, I found, pleading excuses for his absence, and leaving the whole house at my disposal for my investigations. The butler evidently knew the object of my visit, and I questioned him pretty thoroughly during dinner, which I had in rather lonely state. He is an old and privileged servant, and had the history of the Grey Room exact in detail. From him I learned more particulars regarding two things that Anderson had mentioned in but a casual manner. The first was that the door of the Grey Room would be heard in the dead of night to open, and slam heavily, and this even though the butler knew it was locked, and the key on the bunch in his pantry. The second was that the bedclothes would always be found torn off the bed, and hurled in a heap into a corner.

"But it was the door slamming that chiefly bothered the old butler. Many and many a time, he told me, had he lain awake and just got shivering with fright, listening; for sometimes the door would be slammed time after time—thud! thud! thud!—so that sleep was impossible.

"From Anderson, I knew already that the room had a history extending back over a hundred and fifty years. Three people had been strangled in it—an ancestor of his and his wife and child. This is authentic, as I had taken very great pains to discover; so that you can imagine it was with a feeling I had a striking case to investigate that I went upstairs after dinner to have a look at the Grey Room.

"Peter, the old butler, was in rather a state about my going, and assured me with much solemnity that in all the twenty years of his service, no one had ever entered that room after nightfall. He begged me, in quite a fatherly way, to wait till the morning, when there would be no danger, and then he could accompany me himself.

"Of course, I smiled a little at him, and told him not to bother. I explained that I should do no more than look 'round a bit, and, perhaps, affix a few seals. He need not fear; I was used to that sort of thing. But he shook his head when I said that.

"'There isn't many ghosts like ours, sir,' he assured me, with mournful pride. And, by Jove! he was right, as you will see.

"I took a couple of candles, and Peter followed with his bunch of keys. He unlocked the door; but would not come inside with me. He was evidently in a fright, and he renewed his request that I would put off my examination until daylight. Of course, I laughed at him again, and told him he could stand sentry at the door, and catch anything that came out.

"'It never comes outside, sir,' he said, in his funny, old, solemn manner. Somehow, he managed to make me feel as if I were going to have the 'creeps' right away. Anyway, it was one to him, you know.

"I left him there, and examined the room. It is a big apartment, and well furnished in the grand style, with a huge four-poster, which stands with its head to the end wall. There were two candles on the mantelpiece, and two on each of the three tables that were in the room. I lit the lot, and after that, the room felt a little less inhumanly dreary; though, mind you, it was quite fresh, and well kept in every way.

"After I had taken a good look 'round, I sealed lengths of baby ribbon across the windows, along the walls, over the pictures, and over the fireplace and the wall closets. All the time, as I worked, the butler stood just without the door, and I could not persuade him to enter; though I jested him a little, as I stretched the ribbons, and went here and there about my work. Every now and again, he would say:—'You'll excuse me, I'm sure, sir; but I do wish you would come out, sir. I'm fair in a quake for you.'

"I told him he need not wait; but he was loyal enough in his way to what he considered his duty. He said he could not go away and leave me all alone there. He apologized; but made it very clear that I did not realize the danger of the room; and I could see, generally, that he was in a pretty frightened state. All the same, I had to make the room so that I should know if anything material entered it; so I asked him not to bother me, unless he really heard or saw something. He was beginning to get on my nerves, and the 'feel' of the room was bad enough, without making it any nastier.

"For a time further, I worked, stretching ribbons across the floor, and sealing them, so that the merest touch would have broken them, were anyone to venture into the room in the dark with the intention of playing the fool. All this had taken me far longer than I had antici-pated; and, suddenly, I heard a clock strike eleven. I had taken off my coat soon after commencing work; now, however, as I had practically made an end of all that I intended to do, I walked across to the settee, and picked it up. I was in the act of getting into it, when the old butler's voice (he had not said a word for the last hour) came sharp and frightened:—'Come out, sir, quick! There's something going to happen!' Jove! but I jumped, and then, in the same moment, one of the candles on the table to the left went out. Now whether it was the wind, or what, I do not know; but, just for a moment, I was enough startled to make a run for the door; though I am glad to say that I pulled up, before I reached it. I simply could not bunk out, with the butler standing there, after having, as it were, read him a sort of lesson on 'bein' brave, y'know.' So I just turned right 'round, picked up the two candles off the mantelpiece, and walked across to the table near the bed. Well, I saw nothing. I blew out the candle that was still alight; then I went to those on the two tables, and blew them out. Then, outside of the door, the old man called again:—'Oh! sir, do be told! Do be told!'

"'All right, Peter,' I said, and by Jove, my voice was not as steady as I should have liked! I made for the door, and had a bit of work not to start running. I took some thundering long strides, as you can imagine. Near the door, I had a sudden feeling that there was a cold wind in the room. It was almost as if the window had been suddenly opened a little. I got to the door, and the old butler gave back a step, in a sort of instinctive way. 'Collar the candles, Peter!' I said, pretty sharply, and shoved them into his hands. I turned, and caught the handle, and slammed the door shut, with a crash. Somehow, do you know, as I did so, I thought I felt something pull back on it; but it must have been only fancy. I turned the key in the lock, and then again, double-locking the door. I felt easier then, and set-to and sealed the door. In addition, I put my card over the keyhole, and sealed it there; after which I pocketed the key, and went downstairs —with Peter; who was nervous and silent, leading the way. Poor old beggar! It had not struck me until that moment that he had been enduring a considerable strain during the last two or three hours.

"About midnight, I went to bed. My room lay at the end of the corridor upon which opens the door of the Grey Room. I counted the doors between it and mine, and found that five rooms lay between. And I am sure you can understand that I was not sorry. Then, just as I was beginning to undress, an idea came to me, and I took my candle and sealing wax, and sealed the doors of all five rooms. If any door slammed in the night, I should know just which one.

"I returned to my room, locked the door, and went to bed. I was waked suddenly from a deep sleep by a loud crash somewhere out in the passage. I sat up in bed, and listened, but heard nothing. Then I lit my candle. I was in the very act of lighting it when there came the bang of a door being violently slammed, along the corridor. I jumped out of bed, and got my revolver. I unlocked the door, and went out into the passage, holding my candle high, and keeping the pistol ready. Then a queer thing happened. I could not go a step toward the Grey Room. You all know I am not really a cowardly chap. I've gone into too many cases connected with ghostly things, to be accused of that; but I tell you I funked it; simply funked it, just like any blessed kid. There was something precious unholy in the air that night. I ran back into my bedroom, and shut and locked the door. Then I sat on the bed all night, and listened to the dismal thudding of a door up the corridor. The sound seemed to echo through all the house.

"Daylight came at last, and I washed and dressed. The door had not slammed for about an hour, and I was getting back my nerve again. I felt ashamed of myself; though, in some ways it was silly; for when you're meddling with that sort of thing, your nerve is bound to go, sometimes. And you just have to sit quiet and call yourself a coward until daylight. Sometimes it is more than just cowardice, I fancy. I believe at times it is something warning you, and fighting for you. But, all the same, I always feel mean and miserable, after a time like that.

"When the day came properly, I opened my door, and, keeping my revolver handy, went quietly along the passage. I had to pass the head of the stairs, along the way, and who should I see coming up, but the old butler, carrying a cup of coffee. He had merely tucked his nightshirt into his trousers, and he had an old pair of carpet slippers on.

"'Hullo, Peter!' I said, feeling suddenly cheerful; for I was as glad as any lost child to have a live human being close to me. 'Where are you off to with the refreshments?'

"The old man gave a start, and slopped some of the coffee. He stared up at me, and I could see that he looked white and done-up. He came on up the stairs, and held out the little tray to me. 'I'm very thankful indeed, sir, to see you safe and well,' he said. 'I feared, one time, you might risk going into the Grey Room, sir. I've lain awake all night, with the sound of the Door. And when it came light, I thought I'd make you a cup of coffee. I knew you would want to look at the seals, and somehow it seems safer if there's two, sir.'

"'Peter,' I said, 'you're a brick. This is very thoughtful of you.' And I drank the coffee. 'Come along,' I told him, and handed him back the tray. 'I'm going to have a look at what the Brutes have been up to. I simply hadn't the pluck to in the night.'

"'I'm very thankful, sir,' he replied. 'Flesh and blood can do nothing, sir, against devils; and that's what's in the Grey Room after dark.'

"I examined the seals on all the doors, as I went along, and found them right; but when I got to the Grey Room, the seal was broken; though the card, over the keyhole, was untouched. I ripped it off, and unlocked the door, and went in, rather cautiously, as you can imagine; but the whole room was empty of anything to frighten one, and there was heaps of light. I examined all my seals, and not a single one was disturbed. The old butler had followed me in, and, suddenly, he called out:—'The bedclothes, sir!'

"I ran up to the bed, and looked over; and, surely, they were lying in the corner to the left of the bed. Jove! you can imagine how queer I felt. Something had been in the room. I stared for a while, from the bed, to the clothes on the floor. I had a feeling that I did not want to touch either. Old Peter, though, did not seem to be affected that way. He went over to the bed coverings, and was going to pick them up, as, doubtless, he had done every day these twenty years back; but I stopped him. I wanted nothing touched, until I had finished my examination. This, I must have spent a full hour over, and then I let Peter straighten up the bed; after which we went out, and I locked the door; for the room was getting on my nerves.

"I had a short walk, and then breakfast; after which I felt more my own man, and so returned to the Grey Room, and, with Peter's help, and one of the maids, I had everything taken out of the room, except the bed—even the very pictures. I examined the walls, floor and ceiling then, with probe, hammer and magnifying glass; but found nothing suspicious. And I can assure you, I began to realize, in very truth, that some incredible thing had been loose in the room during the past night. I sealed up everything again, and went out, locking and sealing the door, as before.

"After dinner, Peter and I unpacked some of my stuff, and I fixed up my camera and flashlight opposite to the door of the Grey Room, with a string from the trigger of the flashlight to the door. Then, you see, if the door were really opened, the flashlight would blare out, and there would be, possibly, a very queer picture to examine in the morning. The last thing I did, before leaving, was to uncap the lens; and after that I went off to my bedroom, and to bed; for I intended to be up at midnight; and to ensure this, I set my little alarm to call me; also I left my candle burning.

"The clock woke me at twelve, and I got up and into my dressing gown and slippers. I shoved my revolver into my right side-pocket, and opened my door. Then, I lit my darkroom lamp, and withdrew the slide, so that it would give a clear light. I carried it up the corridor, about thirty feet, and put it down on the floor, with the open side away from me, so that it would show me anything that might approach along the dark passage. Then I went back, and sat in the doorway of my room, with my revolver handy, staring up the passage toward the place where I knew my camera stood outside the door of the Grey Room.

"I should think I had watched for about an hour and a half, when, suddenly, I heard a faint noise, away up the corridor. I was immediately conscious of a queer prickling sensation about the back of my head, and my hands began to sweat a little. The following instant, the whole end of the passage flicked into sight in the abrupt glare of the flashlight. There came the succeeding darkness, and I peered nervously up the corridor, listening tensely, and trying to find what lay beyond the faint glow of my dark-lamp, which now seemed ridiculously dim by contrast with the tremendous blaze of the flash-power.... And then, as I stooped forward, staring and listening, there came the crashing thud of the door of the Grey Room. The sound seemed to fill the whole of the large corridor, and go echoing hollowly through the house. I tell you, I felt horrible—as if my bones were water. Simply beastly. Jove! how I did stare, and how I listened. And then it came again—thud, thud, thud, and then a silence that was almost worse than the noise of the door; for I kept fancying that some awful thing was stealing upon me along the corridor. And then, suddenly, my lamp was put out, and I could not see a yard before me. I realized all at once that I was doing a very silly thing, sitting there, and I jumped up. Even as I did so, I thought I heard a sound in the passage, and quite near me. I made one backward spring into my room, and slammed and locked the door. I sat on my bed, and stared at the door. I had my revolver in my hand; but it seemed an abominably useless thing. I felt that there was something the other side of that door. For some unknown reason I knew it was pressed up against the door, and it was soft. That was just what I thought. Most extraordinary thing to think.

"Presently I got hold of myself a bit, and marked out a pentacle hurriedly with chalk on the polished floor; and there I sat in it almost until dawn. And all the time, away up the corridor, the door of the Grey Room thudded at solemn and horrid intervals. It was a miserable, brutal night.

"When the day began to break, the thudding of the door came gradually to an end, and, at last, I got hold of my courage, and went along the corridor in the half light to cap the lens of my camera. I can tell you, it took some doing; but if I had not done so my photograph would have been spoilt, and I was tremendously keen to save it. I got back to my room, and then set-to and rubbed out the five-pointed star in which I had been sitting.

"Half an hour later there was a tap at my door. It was Peter with my coffee. When I had drunk it, we both went along to the Grey Room. As we went, I had a look at the seals on the other doors; but they were untouched. The seal on the door of the Grey Room was broken, as also was the string from the trigger of the flashlight; but the card over the keyhole was still there. I ripped it off, and opened the door. Nothing unusual was to be seen until we came to the bed; then I saw that, as on the previous day, the bedclothes had been torn off, and hurled into the left-hand corner, exactly where I had seen them before. I felt very queer; but I did not forget to look at all the seals, only to find that not one had been broken.

"Then I turned and looked at old Peter, and he looked at me, nodding his head.

"'Let's get out of here!' I said. 'It's no place for any living human to enter, without proper protection.'

"We went out then, and I locked and sealed the door, again.

"After breakfast, I developed the negative; but it showed only the door of the Grey Room, half opened. Then I left the house, as I wanted to get certain matters and implements that might be necessary to life; perhaps to the spirit; for I intended to spend the coming night in the Grey Room.

"I got back in a cab, about half-past five, with my apparatus, and this, Peter and I carried up to the Grey Room, where I piled it carefully in the center of the floor. When everything was in the room, including a cat which I had brought, I locked and sealed the door, and went toward the bedroom, telling Peter I should not be down for dinner. He said, 'Yes, sir,' and went downstairs, thinking that I was going to turn in, which was what I wanted him to believe, as I knew he would have worried both me and himself, if he had known what I intended.

"But I merely got my camera and flashlight from my bedroom, and hurried back to the Grey Room. I locked and sealed myself in, and set to work, for I had a lot to do before it got dark.

"First, I cleared away all the ribbons across the floor; then I carried the cat—still fastened in its basket—over toward the far wall, and left it. I returned then to the center of the room, and measured out a space twenty-one feet in diameter, which I swept with a 'broom of hyssop.' About this, I drew a circle of chalk, taking care never to step over the circle. Beyond this I smudged, with a bunch of garlic, a broad belt right around the chalked circle, and when this was complete, I took from among my stores in the center a small jar of a certain water. I broke away the parchment, and withdrew the stopper. Then, dipping my left forefinger in the little jar, I went 'round the circle again, making upon the floor, just within the line of chalk, the Second Sign of the Saaamaaa Ritual, and joining each Sign most carefully with the left-handed crescent. I can tell you, I felt easier when this was done, and the 'water circle' complete. Then, I unpacked some more of the stuff that I had brought, and placed a lighted candle in the 'valley' of each Crescent. After that, I drew a Pentacle, so that each of the five points of the defensive star touched the chalk circle. In the five points of the star I placed five portions of the bread, each wrapped in linen, and in the five 'vales,' five opened jars of the water I had used to make the 'water circle.' And now I had my first protective barrier complete.

"Now, anyone, except you who know something of my methods of investigation, might consider all this a piece of useless and foolish superstition; but you all remember the Black Veil case, in which I believe my life was saved by a very similar form of protection, whilst Aster, who sneered at it, and would not come inside, died. I got the idea from the Sigsand MS., written, so far as I can make out, in the 14th century. At first, naturally, I imagined it was just an expression of the superstition of his time; and it was not until a year later that it occurred to me to test his 'Defense,' which I did, as I've just said, in that horrible Black Veil business. You know how that turned out. Later, I used it several times, and always I came through safe, until that Moving Fur case. It was only a partial 'defense' therefore, and I nearly died in the pentacle. After that I came across Professor Garder's 'Experiments with a Medium.' When they surrounded the Medium with a current, in vacuum, he lost his power—almost as if it cut him off from the Immaterial. That made me think a lot; and that is how I came to make the Electric Pentacle, which is a most marvelous 'Defense' against certain manifestations. I used the shape of the defensive star for this protection, because I have, personally, no doubt at all but that there is some extraordinary virtue in the old magic figure. Curious thing for a Twentieth Century man to admit, is it not? But, then, as you all know, I never did, and never will, allow myself to be blinded by the little cheap laughter. I ask questions, and keep my eyes open.

"In this last case I had little doubt that I had run up against a supernatural monster, and I meant to take every possible care; for the danger is abominable.

"I turned-to now to fit the Electric Pentacle, setting it so that each of its 'points' and 'vales' coincided exactly with the 'points' and 'vales' of the drawn pentagram upon the floor. Then I connected up the battery, and the next instant the pale blue glare from the inter-twining vacuum tubes shone out.

"I glanced about me then, with something of a sigh of relief, and realized suddenly that the dusk was upon me, for the window was grey and unfriendly. Then 'round at the big, empty room, over the double barrier of electric and candle light. I had an abrupt, extraordinary sense of weirdness thrust upon me—in the air, you know; as it were, a sense of something inhuman impending. The room was full of the stench of bruised garlic, a smell I hate.

"I turned now to the camera, and saw that it and the flashlight were in order. Then I tested my revolver, carefully, though I had little thought that it would be needed. Yet, to what extent materialization of an ab-natural creature is possible, given favorable conditions, no one can say; and I had no idea what horrible thing I was going to see, or feel the presence of. I might, in the end, have to fight with a mate-rialized monster. I did not know, and could only be prepared. You see, I never forgot that three other people had been strangled in the bed close to me, and the fierce slamming of the door I had heard myself. I had no doubt that I was investigating a dangerous and ugly case.

"By this time, the night had come; though the room was very light with the burning candles; and I found myself glancing behind me, constantly, and then all 'round the room. It was nervy work waiting for that thing to come. Then, suddenly, I was aware of a little, cold wind sweeping over me, coming from behind. I gave one great nerve-thrill, and a prickly feeling went all over the back of my head. Then I hove myself 'round with a sort of stiff jerk, and stared straight against that queer wind. It seemed to come from the corner of the room to the left of the bed—the place where both times I had found the heap of tossed bedclothes. Yet, I could see nothing unusual; no opening—nothing!...

"Abruptly, I was aware that the candles were all a-flicker in that unnatural wind.... I believe I just squatted there and stared in a horribly frightened, wooden way for some minutes. I shall never be able to let you know how disgustingly horrible it was sitting in that vile, cold wind! And then, flick! flick! flick! all the candles 'round the outer barrier went out; and there was I, locked and sealed in that room, and with no light beyond the weakish blue glare of the Electric Pentacle.

"A time of abominable tenseness passed, and still that wind blew upon me; and then, suddenly, I knew that something stirred in the corner to the left of the bed. I was made conscious of it, rather by some inward, unused sense than by either sight or sound; for the pale, short-radius glare of the Pentacle gave but a very poor light for seeing by. Yet, as I stared, something began slowly to grow upon my sight—a moving shadow, a little darker than the surrounding shadows. I lost the thing amid the vagueness, and for a moment or two I glanced swiftly from side to side, with a fresh, new sense of impending danger. Then my attention was directed to the bed. All the covering's were being drawn steadily off, with a hateful, stealthy sort of motion. I heard the slow, dragging slither of the clothes; but I could see nothing of the thing that pulled. I was aware in a funny, subconscious, introspective fashion that the 'creep' had come upon me; yet that I was cooler mentally than I had been for some minutes; sufficiently so to feel that my hands were sweating coldly, and to shift my revolver, half-consciously, whilst I rubbed my right hand dry upon my knee; though never, for an instant, taking my gaze or my attention from those moving clothes.

"The faint noises from the bed ceased once, and there was a most intense silence, with only the sound of the blood beating in my head. Yet, immediately afterward, I heard again the slurring of the bedclothes being dragged off the bed. In the midst of my nervous tension I remembered the camera, and reached 'round for it; but without looking away from the bed. And then, you know, all in a moment, the whole of the bed coverings were torn off with extraordinary violence, and I heard the flump they made as they were hurled into the corner.

"There was a time of absolute quietness then for perhaps a couple of minutes; and you can imagine how horrible I felt. The bedclothes had been thrown with such savageness! And, then again, the brutal unnaturalness of the thing that had just been done before me!

"Abruptly, over by the door, I heard a faint noise—a sort of crickling sound, and then a pitter or two upon the floor. A great nervous thrill swept over me, seeming to run up my spine and over the back of my head; for the seal that secured the door had just been broken. Something was there. I could not see the door; at least, I mean to say that it was impossible to say how much I actually saw, and how much my imagination supplied. I made it out, only as a continuation of the grey walls.... And then it seemed to me that something dark and indistinct moved and wavered there among the shadows.

"Abruptly, I was aware that the door was opening, and with an effort I reached again for my camera; but before I could aim it the door was slammed with a terrific crash that filled the whole room with a sort of hollow thunder. I jumped, like a frightened child. There seemed such a power behind the noise; as though a vast, wanton Force were 'out.' Can you understand?

"The door was not touched again; but, directly afterward, I heard the basket, in which the cat lay, creak. I tell you, I fairly pringled all along my back. I knew that I was going to learn definitely whether whatever was abroad was dangerous to Life. From the cat there rose suddenly a hideous caterwaul, that ceased abruptly; and then—too late—I snapped off the flashlight. In the great glare, I saw that the basket had been overturned, and the lid was wrenched open, with the cat lying half in, and half out upon the floor. I saw nothing else, but I was full of the knowledge that I was in the presence of some Being or Thing that had power to destroy.

"During the next two or three minutes, there was an odd, noticeable quietness in the room, and you much remember I was half-blinded, for the time, because of the flashlight; so that the whole place seemed to be pitchy dark just beyond the shine of the Pentacle. I tell you it was most horrible. I just knelt there in the star, and whirled 'round, trying to see whether anything was coming at me.

"My power of sight came gradually, and I got a little hold of myself; and abruptly I saw the thing I was looking for, close to the 'water circle.' It was big and indistinct, and wavered curiously, as though the shadow of a vast spider hung suspended in the air, just beyond the barrier. It passed swiftly 'round the circle, and seemed to probe ever toward me; but only to draw back with extraordinary jerky movements, as might a living person if they touched the hot bar of a grate.

"'Round and 'round it moved, and 'round and 'round I turned. Then, just opposite to one of the Vales' in the pentacles, it seemed to pause, as though preliminary to a tremendous effort. It retired almost beyond the glow of the vacuum light, and then came straight toward me, appearing to gather form and solidity as it came. There seemed a vast, malign determination behind the movement, that must succeed. I was on my knees, and I jerked back, falling on to my left hand, and hip, in a wild endeavor to get back from the advancing thing. With my right hand I was grabbing madly for my revolver, which I had let slip. The brutal thing came with one great sweep straight over the garlic and the 'water circle,' almost to the vale of the pentacle. I believe I yelled. Then, just as suddenly as it had swept over, it seemed to be hurled back by some mighty, invisible force.

"It must have been some moments before I realized that I was safe; and then I got myself together in the middle of the pentacles, feeling horribly gone and shaken, and glancing 'round and 'round the barrier; but the thing had vanished. Yet, I had learnt something, for I knew now that the Grey Room was haunted by a monstrous hand.

"Suddenly, as I crouched there, I saw what had so nearly given the monster an opening through the barrier. In my movements within the pentacle I must have touched one of the jars of water; for just where the thing had made its attack the jar that guarded the 'deep' of the 'vale' had been moved to one side, and this had left one of the 'five doorways' unguarded. I put it back, quickly, and felt almost safe again, for I had found the cause, and the 'defense' was still good. And I began to hope again that I should see the morning come in. When I saw that thing so nearly succeed, I had an awful, weak, overwhelming feeling that the 'barriers' could never bring me safe through the night against such a Force. You can understand?

"For a long time I could not see the hand; but, presently, I thought I saw, once or twice, an odd wavering, over among the shadows near the door. A little later, as though in a sudden fit of malignant rage, the dead body of the cat was picked up, and beaten with dull, sickening blows against the solid floor. That made me feel rather queer.

"A minute afterward, the door was opened and slammed twice with tremendous force. The next instant the thing made one swift, vicious dart at me, from out of the shadows. Instinctively, I started sideways from it, and so plucked my hand from upon the Electric Pentacle, where—for a wickedly careless moment—I had placed it. The monster was hurled off from the neighborhood of the pentacles; though—owing to my inconceivable foolishness—it had been enabled for a second time to pass the outer barriers. I can tell you, I shook for a time, with sheer funk. I moved right to the center of the pentacles again, and knelt there, making myself as small and compact as possible.

"As I knelt, there came to me presently, a vague wonder at the two 'accidents' which had so nearly allowed the brute to get at me. Was I being influenced to unconscious voluntary actions that endangered me? The thought took hold of me, and I watched my every movement. Abruptly, I stretched a tired leg, and knocked over one of the jars of water. Some was spilled; but, because of my suspicious watchfulness, I had it upright and back within the vale while yet some of the water remained. Even as I did so, the vast, black, half-materialized hand beat up at me out of the shadows, and seemed to leap almost into my face; so nearly did it approach; but for the third time it was thrown back by some altogether enormous, overmastering force. Yet, apart from the dazed fright in which it left me, I had for a moment that feeling of spiritual sickness, as if some delicate, beautiful, inward grace had suffered, which is felt only upon the too near approach of the ab-human, and is more dreadful, in a strange way, than any physical pain that can be suffered. I knew by this more of the extent and closeness of the danger; and for a long time I was simply cowed by the butt-headed brutality of that Force upon my spirit. I can put it no other way.

"I knelt again in the center of the pentacles, watching myself with more fear, almost, than the monster; for I knew now that, unless I guarded myself from every sudden impulse that came to me, I might simply work my own destruction. Do you see how horrible it all was?

"I spent the rest of the night in a haze of sick fright, and so tense that I could not make a single movement naturally. I was in such fear that any desire for action that came to me might be prompted by the Influence that I knew was at work on me. And outside of the barrier that ghastly thing went 'round and 'round, grabbing and grabbing in the air at me. Twice more was the body of the dead cat molested. The second time, I heard every bone in its body scrunch and crack. And all the time the horrible wind was blowing upon me from the corner of the room to the left of the bed.

"Then, just as the first touch of dawn came into the sky, that unnatural wind ceased, in a single moment; and I could see no sign of the hand. The dawn came slowly, and presently the wan light filled all the room, and made the pale glare of the Electric Pentacle look more unearthly. Yet, it was not until the day had fully come, that I made any attempt to leave the barrier, for I did not know but that there was some method abroad, in the sudden stopping of that wind, to entice me from the pentacles.

"At last, when the dawn was strong and bright, I took one last look 'round, and ran for the door. I got it unlocked, in a nervous and clumsy fashion, then locked it hurriedly, and went to my bedroom, where I lay on the bed, and tried to steady my nerves. Peter came, presently, with the coffee, and when I had drunk it, I told him I meant to have a sleep, as I had been up all night. He took the tray, and went out quietly, and after I had locked my door I turned in properly, and at last got to sleep.

"I woke about midday, and after some lunch, went up to the Grey Room. I switched off the current from the Pentacle, which I had left on in my hurry; also, I removed the body of the cat. You can understand I did not want anyone to see the poor brute. After that, I made a very careful search of the corner where the bedclothes had been thrown. I made several holes, and probed, and found nothing. Then it occurred to me to try with my instrument under the skirting. I did so, and heard my wire ring on metal. I turned the hook end that way, and fished for the thing. At the second go, I got it. It was a small object, and I took it to the window. I found it to be a curious ring, made of some greying material. The curious thing about it was that it was made in the form of a pentagon; that is, the same shape as the inside of the magic pentacle, but without the 'mounts,' which form the points of the defensive star. It was free from all chasing or engraving.

"You will understand that I was excited, when I tell you that I felt sure I held in my hand the famous Luck Ring of the Anderson family; which, indeed, was of all things the one most intimately connected with the history of the haunting. This ring was handed on from father to son through generations, and always—in obedience to some ancient family tradition—each son had to promise never to wear the ring. The ring, I may say, was brought home by one of the

Crusaders, under very peculiar circumstances; but the story is too long to go into here.

"It appears that young Sir Hulbert, an ancestor of Anderson's, made a bet, in drink, you know, that he would wear the ring that night. He did so, and in the morning his wife and child were found strangled in the bed, in the very room in which I stood. Many people, it would seem, thought young Sir Hulbert was guilty of having done the thing in drunken anger; and he, in an attempt to prove his innocence, slept a second night in the room. He also was strangled. Since then, as you may imagine, no one has ever spent a night in the Grey Room, until I did so. The ring had been lost so long, that it had become almost a myth; and it was most extraordinary to stand there, with the actual thing in my hand, as you can understand.

"It was whilst I stood there, looking at the ring, that I got an idea. Supposing that it were, in a way, a doorway—You see what I mean? A sort of gap in the world-hedge. It was a queer idea, I know, and probably was not my own, but came to me from the Outside. You see, the wind had come from that part of the room where the ring lay. I thought a lot about it. Then the shape—the inside of a pentacle. It had no 'mounts,' and without mounts, as the Sigsand MS. has it: —'Thee mownts wych are thee Five Hills of safetie. To lack is to gyve pow'r to thee daemon; and surelie to fayvor the Evill Thynge.' You see, the very shape of the ring was significant; and I determined to test it.

"I unmade the pentacle, for it must be made afresh and around the one to be protected. Then I went out and locked the door; after which I left the house, to get certain matters, for neither 'yarbs nor fyre nor waier' must be used a second time. I returned about seven thirty, and as soon as the things I had brought had been carried up to the Grey Room, I dismissed Peter for the night, just as I had done the evening before. When he had gone downstairs, I let myself into the room, and locked and sealed the door. I went to the place in the center of the room where all the stuff had been packed, and set to work with all my speed to construct a barrier about me and the ring.

"I do not remember whether I explained it to you. But I had reasoned that, if the ring were in any way a 'medium of admission,' and it were enclosed with me in the Electric Pentacle, it would be, to express it loosely, insulated. Do you see? The Force, which had visible expression as a Hand, would have to stay beyond the Barrier which separates the Ab from the Normal; for the 'gateway' would be removed from accessibility.

"As I was saying, I worked with all my speed to get the barrier completed about me and the ring, for it was already later than I cared to be in that room 'unprotected.' Also, I had a feeling that there would be a vast effort made that night to regain the use of the ring. For I had the strongest conviction that the ring was a necessity to materialization. You will see whether I was right.

"I completed the barriers in about an hour, and you can imagine something of the relief I felt when I felt the pale glare of the Electric Pentacle once more all about me. From then, onward, for about two hours, I sat quietly, facing the corner from which the wind came. About eleven o'clock a queer knowledge came that something was near to me; yet nothing happened for a whole hour after that. Then, suddenly, I felt the cold, queer wind begin to blow upon me. To my astonishment, it seemed now to come from behind me, and I whipped 'round, with a hideous quake of fear. The wind met me in the face. It was blowing up from the floor close to me. I stared down, in a sickening maze of new frights. What on earth had I done now! The ring was there, close beside me, where I had put it. Suddenly, as I stared, bewildered, I was aware that there was something queer about the ring—funny shadowy movements and convolutions. I looked at them, stupidly. And then, abruptly, I knew that the wind was blowing up at me from the ring. A queer indistinct smoke became visible to me, seeming to pour upward through the ring, and mix with the moving shadows. Suddenly, I realized that I was in more than any mortal danger; for the convoluting shadows about the ring were taking shape, and the death-hand was forming within the Pentacle. My Goodness! do you realize it! I had brought the 'gateway' into the pentacles, and the brute was coming through—pouring into the material world, as gas might pour out from the mouth of a pipe.

"I should think that I knelt for a moment in a sort of stunned fright. Then, with a mad, awkward movement, I snatched at the ring, intending to hurl it out of the Pentacle. Yet it eluded me, as though some invisible, living thing jerked it hither and thither. At last, I gripped it; yet, in the same instant, it was torn from my grasp with incredible and brutal force. A great, black shadow covered it, and rose into the air, and came at me. I saw that it was the Hand, vast and nearly perfect in form. I gave one crazy yell, and jumped over the Pentacle and the ring of burning candles, and ran despairingly for the door. I fumbled idiotically and ineffectually with the key, and all the time I stared, with a fear that was like insanity, toward the Barriers. The hand was plunging toward me; yet, even as it had been unable to pass into the Pentacle when the ring was without, so, now that the ring was within, it had no power to pass out. The monster was chained, as surely as any beast would be, were chains riveted upon it.

"Even then, I got a flash of this knowledge; but I was too utterly shaken with fright, to reason; and the instant I managed to get the key turned, I sprang into the passage, and slammed the door with a crash. I locked it, and got to my room somehow; for I was trembling so that I could hardly stand, as you can imagine. I locked myself in, and managed to get the candle lit; then I lay down on my bed, and kept quiet for an hour or two, and so I got steadied.

"I got a little sleep, later; but woke when Peter brought my coffee. When I had drunk it I felt altogether better, and took the old man along with me whilst I had a look into the Grey Room. I opened the door, and peeped in. The candles were still burning, wan against the daylight; and behind them was the pale, glowing star of the Electric Pentacle. And there, in the middle, was the ring ... the gateway of the monster, lying demure and ordinary.

"Nothing in the room was touched, and I knew that the brute

had never managed to cross the Pentacles. Then I went out, and locked the door.

"After a sleep of some hours, I left the house. I returned in the afternoon in a cab. I had with me an oxy-hydrogen jet, and two cylinders, containing the gases. I carried the things into the Grey Room, and there, in the center of the Electric Pentacle, I erected the little furnace. Five minutes later the Luck Ring, once the 'luck,' but now the 'bane,' of the Anderson family, was no more than a little solid splash of hot metal."

Carnacki felt in his pocket, and pulled out something wrapped in tissue paper. He passed it to me. I opened it, and found a small circle of greyish metal, something like lead, only harder and rather brighter.

"Well?" I asked, at length, after examining it and handing it 'round to the others. "Did that stop the haunting?"

Carnacki nodded. "Yes," he said. "I slept three nights in the Grey Room, before I left. Old Peter nearly fainted when he knew that I meant to; but by the third night he seemed to realize that the house was just safe and ordinary. And, you know, I believe, in his heart, he hardly approved."

CARNACKI STOOD up and began to shake hands. "Out you go!" he said, genially. And presently we went, pondering, to our various homes.

THE HOUSE AMONG THE LAURELS

"This is a curious yarn that I am going to tell you," said Carnacki, as after a quiet little dinner we made ourselves comfortable in his cozy dining room.

"I have just got back from the West of Ireland," he continued. "Wentworth, a friend of mine, has lately had rather an unexpected legacy, in the shape of a large estate and manor, about a mile and a half outside of the village of Korunton. This place is named Gannington Manor, and has been empty a great number of years; as you will find is almost always the case with Houses reputed to be haunted, as it is usually termed.

"It seems that when Wentworth went over to take possession, he found the place in very poor repair, and the estate totally uncared for, and, as I know, looking very desolate and lonesome generally. He went through the big house by himself, and he admitted to me that it had an uncomfortable feeling about it; but, of course, that might be nothing more than the natural dismalness of a big, empty house, which has been long uninhabited, and through which you are wandering alone.

"When he had finished his look 'round, he went down to the

village, meaning to see the one-time Agent of the Estate, and arrange for someone to go in as caretaker. The Agent, who proved by the way to be a Scotchman, was very willing to take up the management of the Estate once more; but he assured Wentworth that they would get no one to go in as caretaker; and that his—the Agent's—advice was to have the house pulled down, and a new one built.

"This, naturally, astonished my friend, and, as they went down to the village, he managed to get a sort of explanation from the man. It seems that there had been always curious stories told about the place, which in the early days was called Landru Castle, and that within the last seven years there had been two extraordinary deaths there. In each case they had been tramps, who were ignorant of the reputation of the house, and had probably thought the big empty place suitable for a night's free lodging. There had been absolutely no signs of violence to indicate the method by which death was caused, and on each occasion the body had been found in the great entrance hall.

"By this time they had reached the inn where Wentworth had put up, and he told the Agent that he would prove that it was all rubbish about the haunting, by staying a night or two in the Manor himself. The death of the tramps was certainly curious; but did not prove that any supernatural agency had been at work. They were but isolated accidents, spread over a large number of years by the memory of the villagers, which was natural enough in a little place like Korunton. Tramps had to die some time, and in some place, and it proved nothing that two, out of possibly hundreds who had slept in the empty house, had happened to take the opportunity to die under shelter.

"But the Agent took his remark very seriously, and both he and Dennis the landlord of the inn, tried their best to persuade him not to go. For his 'sowl's sake,' Irish Dennis begged him to do no such thing; and because of his 'life's sake,' the Scotchman was equally in earnest.

"It was late afternoon at the time, and as Wentworth told me, it was warm and bright, and it seemed such utter rot to hear those two talking seriously about the impossible. He felt full of pluck, and he made up his mind he would smash the story of the haunting, at once by staying that very night, in the Manor. He made this quite clear to them, and told them that it would be more to the point and to their credit, if they offered to come up along with him, and keep him company. But poor old Dennis was quite shocked, I believe, at the suggestion; and though Tabbit, the Agent, took it more quietly, he was very solemn about it.

"It seems that Wentworth did go; and though, as he said to me, when the evening began to come on, it seemed a very different sort of thing to tackle.

"A whole crowd of the villagers assembled to see him off; for by this time they all knew of his intention. Wentworth had his gun with him, and a big packet of candles; and he made it clear to them all that it would not be wise for anyone to play any tricks; as he intended to shoot 'at sight.' And then, you know, he got a hint of how serious they considered the whole thing; for one of them came up to him, leading a great bullmastiff, and offered it to him, to take to keep him company. Wentworth patted his gun; but the old man who owned the dog shook his head and explained that the brute might warn him in sufficient time for him to get away from the castle. For it was obvious that he did not consider the gun would prove of any use.

"Wentworth took the dog, and thanked the man. He told me that, already, he was beginning to wish that he had not said definitely that he would go; but, as it was, he was simply forced to. He went through the crowd of men, and found suddenly that they had all turned in a body and were keeping him company. They stayed with him all the way to the Manor, and then went right over the whole place with him.

"It was still daylight when this was finished; though turning to dusk; and, for a while, the men stood about, hesitating, as if they felt ashamed to go away and leave Wentworth there all alone. He told me that, by this time, he would gladly have given fifty pounds to be going back with them. And then, abruptly, an idea came to him. He suggested that they should stay with him, and keep him company through the night. For a time they refused, and tried to persuade him to go back with them; but finally he made a proposition that got home to them all. He planned that they should all go back to the inn, and there get a couple of dozen bottles of whisky, a donkey-load of turf and wood, and some more candles. Then they would come back, and make a great fire in the big fire-place, light all the candles, and put them 'round the place, open the whisky and make a night of it. And, by Jove! he got them to agree.

"They set off back, and were soon at the inn, and here, whilst the donkey was being loaded, and the candles and whisky distributed, Dennis was doing his best to keep Wentworth from going back; but he was a sensible man in his way, for when he found that it was no use, he stopped. You see, he did not want to frighten the others from accompanying Wentworth.

"'I tell ye, sorr,' he told him, ''tis of no use at all, thryin' ter reclaim ther castle. 'Tis curst with innocent blood, an' ye'll be betther pullin' it down, an' buildin' a fine new wan. But if ye be intendin' to shtay this night, kape the big dhoor open whide, an' watch for the bhlood-dhrip. If so much as a single dhrip falls, don't shtay though all the gold in the worrld was offered ye.'

"Wentworth asked him what he meant by the blood-drip.

"'Shure,' he said, ''tis the bhlood av thim as ould Black Mick 'way back in the ould days kilt in their shlape. 'Twas a feud as he pretendid to patch up, an' he invited thim—the O'Haras they was—siventy av thim. An' he fed thim, an' shpoke soft to thim, an' thim thrustin' him, sthayed to shlape with him. Thin, he an' thim with him, sharted in an' mhurdered thim wan an' all as they slep'. 'Tis from me father's grandfather ye have the sthory. An' sence thin 'tis death to any, so they say, to pass the night in the castle whin the bhlood-dhrip comes. 'Twill put out candle an' fire, an' thin in the darkness the Virgin Herself would be powerless to protect ye.'

"Wentworth told me he laughed at this; chiefly because, as he put it:—'One always must laugh at that sort of yarn, however it makes you feel inside.' He asked old Dennis whether he expected him to believe it.

"'Yes, sorr,' said Dennis, 'I do mane ye to b'lieve it; an' please God, if ye'll b'lieve, ye may be back safe befor' mornin'.' The man's serious simplicity took hold of Wentworth, and he held out his hand. But, for all that, he went; and I must admire his pluck.

"THERE WERE NOW about forty men, and when they got back to the Manor—or castle as the villagers always call it—they were not long in getting a big fire going, and lighted candles all 'round the great hall. They had all brought sticks; so that they would have been a pretty formidable lot to tackle by anything simply physical; and, of course, Wentworth had his gun. He kept the whisky in his own charge; for he intended to keep them sober; but he gave them a good strong tot all 'round first, so as to make things seem cheerful; and to get them yearning. If you once let a crowd of men like that grow silent, they begin to think, and then to fancy things.

"The big entrance door had been left wide open, by his orders; which shows that he had taken some notice of Dennis. It was a quiet night, so this did not matter, for the lights kept steady, and all went on in a jolly sort of fashion for about three hours. He had opened a second lot of bottles, and everyone was feeling cheerful; so much so that one of the men called out aloud to the ghosts to come out and show themselves. And then, you know a very extraordinary thing happened; for the ponderous main door swung quietly and steadily to, as though pushed by an invisible hand, and shut with a sharp click.

"Wentworth stared, feeling suddenly rather chilly. Then he remembered the men, and looked 'round at them. Several had ceased their talk, and were staring in a frightened way at the big door; but the great number had never noticed, and were talking and yarning.

He reached for his gun, and the following instant the great bullmastiff set up a tremendous barking, which drew the attention of the whole company.

"The hall I should tell you is oblong. The south wall is all windows; but the north and east have rows of doors, leading into the house, whilst the west wall is occupied by the great entrance. The rows of doors leading into the house were all closed, and it was toward one of these in the north wall that the big dog ran; yet he would not go very close; and suddenly the door began to move slowly open, until the blackness of the passage beyond was shown. The dog came back among the men, whimpering, and for a minute there was an absolute silence.

"Then Wentworth went out from the men a little, and aimed his gun at the doorway.

"'Whoever is there, come out, or I shall fire,' he shouted; but nothing came, and he blazed forth both barrels into the dark. As though the report had been a signal, all the doors along the north and east walls moved slowly open, and Wentworth and his men were staring, frightened into the black shapes of the empty doorways.

"Wentworth loaded his gun quickly, and called to the dog; but the brute was burrowing away in among the men; and this fear on the dog's part frightened Wentworth more, he told me, than anything. Then something else happened. Three of the candles over in the corner of the hall went out; and immediately about half a dozen in different parts of the place. More candles were put out, and the hall had become quite dark in the corners.

"The men were all standing now, holding their clubs, and crowded together. And no one said a word. Wentworth told me he felt positively ill with fright. I know the feeling. Then, suddenly, something splashed on to the back of his left hand. He lifted it, and looked. It was covered with a great splash of red that dripped from his fingers. An old Irishman near to him, saw it, and croaked out in a quavering voice:—'The bhlood-dhrip!' When the old man called out, they all looked, and in the same instant others felt it upon them. There were frightened cries of:—'The bhlood-dhrip! The bhlood-dhrip!' And then, about a dozen candles went out simultaneously, and the hall was suddenly dark. The dog let out a great, mournful howl, and there was a horrible little silence, with everyone standing rigid. Then the tension broke, and there was a mad rush for the main door. They wrenched it open, and tumbled out into the dark; but something slammed it with a crash after them, and shut the dog in; for Wentworth heard it howling as they raced down the drive. Yet no one had the pluck to go back to let it out, which does not surprise me.

"Wentworth sent for me the following day. He had heard of me in connection with that Steeple Monster Case. I arrived by the night mail, and put up with Wentworth at the inn. The next day we went up to the old Manor, which certainly lies in rather a wilderness; though what struck me most was the extraordinary number of laurel bushes about the house. The place was smothered with them; so that the house seemed to be growing up out of a sea of green laurel. These, and the grim, ancient look of the old building, made the place look a bit dank and ghostly, even by daylight.

"The hall was a big place, and well lit by daylight; for which I was not sorry. You see, I had been rather wound-up by Wentworth's yarn. We found one rather funny thing, and that was the great bullmastiff, lying stiff with its neck broken. This made me feel very serious; for it showed that whether the cause was supernatural or not, there was present in the house some force exceedingly dangerous to life.

"Later, whilst Wentworth stood guard with his shotgun, I made an examination of the hall. The bottles and mugs from which the men had drunk their whisky were scattered about; and all over the place were the candles, stuck upright in their own grease. But in the somewhat brief and general search, I found nothing; and decided to begin my usual exact examination of every square foot of the place—not only of the hall, in this case, but of the whole interior of the castle.

. . .

"I SPENT THREE UNCOMFORTABLE WEEKS, searching; but without result of
any kind. And, you know, the care I take at this period is extreme; for
I have solved hundreds of cases of so-called 'hauntings' at this early
stage, simply by the most minute investigation, and the keeping of a
perfectly open mind. But, as I have said, I found nothing. During the
whole of the examination, I got Wentworth to stand guard with his
loaded shotgun; and I was very particular that we were never caught
there after dusk.

"I decided now to make the experiment of staying a night in the
great hall, of course 'protected.' I spoke about it to Wentworth; but
his own attempt had made him so nervous that he begged me to do
no such thing. However, I thought it well worth the risk, and I
managed in the end to persuade him to be present.

"With this in view, I went to the neighboring town of Gaunt, and
by an arrangement with the Chief Constable I obtained the services
of six policemen with their rifles. The arrangement was unofficial, of
course, and the men were allowed to volunteer, with a promise of
payment.

"When the constables arrived early that evening at the inn, I gave
them a good feed; and after that we all set out for the Manor. We had
four donkeys with us, loaded with fuel and other matters; also two
great boarhounds, which one of the police led. When we reached the
house, I set the men to unload the donkeys; whilst Wentworth and I
set-to and sealed all the doors, except the main entrance, with tape
and wax; for if the doors were really opened, I was going to be sure of
the fact. I was going to run no risk of being deceived by ghostly
hallucination, or mesmeric influence.

"By the time that this was done, the policemen had unloaded the
donkeys, and were waiting, looking about them, curiously. I set two
of them to lay a fire in the big grate, and the others I used as I
required them. I took one of the boarhounds to the end of the hall
furthest from the entrance, and there I drove a staple into the floor,

to which I tied the dog with a short tether. Then, 'round him, I drew upon the floor the figure of a Pentacle, in chalk. Outside of the Pentacle, I made a circle with garlic. I did exactly the same thing with the other hound; but over more in the northeast corner of the big hall, where the two rows of doors make the angle.

"When this was done, I cleared the whole center of the hall, and put one of the policemen to sweep it; after which I had all my apparatus carried into the cleared space. Then I went over to the main door and hooked it open, so that the hook would have to be lifted out of the hasp, before the door could be closed. After that, I placed lighted candles before each of the sealed doors, and one in each corner of the big room; and then I lit the fire. When I saw that it was properly alight, I got all the men together, by the pile of things in the center of the room, and took their pipes from them; for, as the Sigsand MS. has it:—'Theyre must noe lyght come from wythin the barryier.' And I was going to make sure.

"I got my tape measure then, and measured out a circle thirty-three feet in diameter, and immediately chalked it out. The police and Wentworth were tremendously interested, and I took the opportunity to warn them that this was no piece of silly mumming on my part; but done with a definite intention of erecting a barrier between us and any ab-human thing that the night might show to us. I warned them that, as they valued their lives, and more than their lives it might be, no one must on any account whatsoever pass beyond the limits of the barrier that I was making.

"After I had drawn the circle, I took a bunch of the garlic, and smudged it right 'round the chalk circle, a little outside of it. When this was complete, I called for candles from my stock of material. I set the police to lighting them, and as they were lit, I took them, and sealed them down on the floor, just within the chalk circle, five inches apart. As each candle measured approximately one inch in diameter, it took sixty-six candles to complete the circle; and I need hardly say that every number and measurement has a significance.

"Then, from candle to candle I took a 'gayrd' of human hair, entwining it alternately to the left and to the right, until the circle was completed, and the ends of the hair shod with silver, and pressed into the wax of the sixty-sixth candle.

"It had now been dark some time, and I made haste to get the 'Defense' complete. To this end, I got the men well together, and began to fit the Electric Pentacle right around us, so that the five points of the Defensive Star came just within the Hair Circle. This did not take me long, and a minute later I had connected up the batteries, and the weak blue glare of the intertwining vacuum tubes shone all around us. I felt happier then; for this Pentacle is, as you all know, a wonderful 'Defense.' I have told you before, how the idea came to me, after reading Professor Garder's 'Experiments with a Medium.' He found that a current, of a certain number of vibrations, in vacuo, 'insulated' the medium. It is difficult to suggest an explanation non-technically, and if you are really interested you should read Carder's lecture on 'Astral Vibrations Compared with Matero-involuted Vibrations below the Six-Billion Limit.'

"As I stood up from my work, I could hear outside in the night a constant drip from the laurels, which as I have said, come right up around the house, very thick. By the sound, I knew that a 'soft' rain had set in; and there was absolutely no wind, as I could tell by the steady flames of the candles.

"I stood a moment or two, listening, and then one of the men touched my arm, and asked me in a low voice, what they should do. By his tone, I could tell that he was feeling something of the strangeness of it all; and the other men, including Wentworth, were so quiet that I was afraid they were beginning to get shaky.

"I set-to, then, and arranged them with their backs to one common center; so that they were sitting flat upon the floor, with their feet radiating outward. Then, by compass, I laid their legs to the eight chief points, and afterward I drew a circle with chalk around them; and opposite to their feet, I made the Eight Signs of the Saaa-maaa Ritual. The eighth place was, of course, empty; but ready for me to occupy at any moment; for I had omitted to make the Sealing

Sign to that point, until I had finished all my preparations, and could enter the Inner Star.

"I took a last look 'round the great hall, and saw that the two big hounds were lying quietly, with their noses between their paws. The fire was big and cheerful, and the candles before the two rows of doors, burnt steadily, as well as the solitary ones in the corners. Then I went 'round the little star of men, and warned them not to be frightened whatever happened; but to trust to the 'Defense'; and to let nothing tempt or drive them to cross the Barriers. Also, I told them to watch their movements, and to keep their feet strictly to their places. For the rest, there was to be no shooting, unless I gave the word.

"And now at last, I went to my place, and, sitting down, made the Eighth sign just beyond my feet. Then I arranged my camera and flashlight handy, and examined my revolver.

"Wentworth sat behind the First Sign, and as the numbering went 'round reversed, that put him next to me on my left. I asked him, in a low voice, how he felt; and he told me, rather nervous; but that he felt confidence in my knowledge and was resolved to go through with the matter, whatever happened.

"We settled down to wait. There was no talking, except that, once or twice, the police bent toward one another, and whispered odd remarks concerning the hall, that appeared queerly audible in the intense silence. But in a while there was not even a whisper from anyone, and only the monotonous drip, drip of the quiet rain without the great entrance, and the low, dull sound of the fire in the big fireplace.

"It was a queer group that we made sitting there, back to back, with our legs starred outward; and all around us the strange blue glow of the Pentacle, and beyond that the brilliant shining of the great ring of lighted candles. Outside of the glare of the candles, the large empty hall looked a little gloomy, by contrast, except where the lights shone before the sealed doors, and the blaze of the big fire made a good honest mass of flame. And the feeling of mystery! Can you picture it all?

"It might have been an hour later that it came to me suddenly that I was aware of an extraordinary sense of dreeness, as it were, come into the air of the place. Not the nervous feeling of mystery that had been with us all the time; but a new feeling, as if there were something going to happen any moment.

"Abruptly, there came a slight noise from the east end of the hall, and I felt the star of men move suddenly. 'Steady! Keep steady!' I shouted, and they quietened. I looked up the hall, and saw that the dogs were upon their feet, and staring in an extraordinary fashion toward the great entrance. I turned and stared, also, and felt the men move as they craned their heads to look. Suddenly, the dogs set up a tremendous barking, and I glanced across to them, and found they were still 'pointing' for the big doorway. They ceased their noise just as quickly, and seemed to be listening. In the same instant, I heard a faint chink of metal to my left, that set me staring at the hook which held the great door wide. It moved, even as I looked. Some invisible thing was meddling with it. A queer, sickening thrill went through me, and I felt all the men about me, stiffen and go rigid with intensity. I had a certainty of something impending: as it might be the impression of an invisible, but overwhelming, Presence. The hall was full of a queer silence, and not a sound came from the dogs. Then I saw the hook slowly raised from out of its hasp, without any visible thing touching it. Then a sudden power of movement came to me. I raised my camera, with the flashlight fixed, and snapped it at the door. There came the great blare of the flashlight, and a simultaneous roar of barking from the two dogs.

"The intensity of the flash made all the place seem dark for some moments, and in that time of darkness, I heard a jingle in the direction of the door, and strained to look. The effect of the bright light passed, and I could see clearly again. The great entrance door was being slowly closed. It shut with a sharp snick, and there followed a long silence, broken only by the whimpering of the dogs.

"I turned suddenly, and looked at Wentworth. He was looking at me.

"'Just as it did before,' he whispered.

"'Most extraordinary,' I said, and he nodded and looked 'round, nervously.

"The policemen were pretty quiet, and I judged that they were feeling rather worse than Wentworth; though, for that matter, you must not think that I was altogether natural; yet I have seen so much that is extraordinary, that I daresay I can keep my nerves steady longer than most people.

"I looked over my shoulder at the men, and cautioned them, in a low voice, not to move outside of the Barriers, whatever happened; not even though the house should seem to be rocking and about to tumble on to them; for well I knew what some of the great Forces are capable of doing. Yet, unless it should prove to be one of the cases of the more terrible Saiitii Manifestation, we were almost certain of safety, so long as we kept to our order within the Pentacle.

"Perhaps an hour and a half passed, quietly, except when, once in a way, the dogs would whine distressfully. Presently, however, they ceased even from this, and I could see them lying on the floor with their paws over their noses, in a most peculiar fashion, and shivering visibly. The sight made me feel more serious, as you can understand.

"Suddenly, the candle in the corner furthest from the main door, went out. An instant later, Wentworth jerked my arm, and I saw that the candle before one of the sealed doors had been put out. I held my camera ready. Then, one after another, every candle about the hall was put out, and with such speed and irregularity, that I could never catch one in the actual act of being extinguished. Yet, for all that, I took a flashlight of the hall in general.

"There was a time in which I sat half-blinded by the great glare of the flash, and I blamed myself for not having remembered to bring a pair of smoked goggles, which I have sometimes used at these times. I had felt the men jump, at the sudden light, and I called out loud to them to sit quiet, and to keep their feet exactly to their proper places.

My voice, as you can imagine, sounded rather horrid and frightening in the great room, and altogether it was a beastly moment.

"Then, I was able to see again, and I stared here and there about the hall; but there was nothing showing unusual; only, of course, it was dark now over in the corners.

"Suddenly, I saw that the great fire was blackening. It was going out visibly, as I looked. If I said that some monstrous, invisible, impossible creature sucked the life from it, I could best explain the way the light and flame went out of it. It was most extraordinary to watch. In the time that I watched it, every vestige of fire was gone from it, and there was no light outside of the ring of candles around the Pentacle.

"The deliberateness of the thing troubled me more than I can make clear to you. It conveyed to me such a sense of a calm Deliberate Force present in the hall: The steadfast intention to 'make a darkness' was horrible. The extent of the Power to affect the Material was horrible. The extent of the Power to affect the Material was now the one constant, anxious questioning in my brain. You can understand?

"Behind me, I heard the policemen moving again, and I knew that they were getting thoroughly frightened. I turned half 'round, and told them, quietly but plainly, that they were safe only so long as they stayed within the Pentacle, in the position in which I had put them. If they once broke, and went outside of the Barrier, no knowledge of mine could state the full extent of the dreadfulness of the danger.

"I steadied them up, by this quiet, straight reminder; but if they had known, as I knew, that there is no certainty in any 'Protection,' they would have suffered a great deal more, and probably have broken the 'Defense,' and made a mad, foolish run for an impossible safety.

"Another hour passed, after this, in an absolute quietness. I had a sense of awful strain and oppression, as though I were a little spirit in the company of some invisible, brooding monster of the unseen world, who, as yet, was scarcely conscious of us. I leant across to Wentworth, and asked him in a whisper whether he had a feeling as if something were in the room. He looked very pale, and his eyes kept always on the move. He glanced just once at me, and nodded; then stared away 'round the hall again. And when I came to think, I was doing the same thing.

"Abruptly, as though a hundred unseen hands had snuffed them, every candle in the Barrier went dead out, and we were left in a darkness that seemed, for a little, absolute; for the light from the Pentacle was too weak and pale to penetrate far across the great hall.

"I tell you, for a moment, I just sat there as though I had been frozen solid. I felt the 'creep' go all over me, and seem to stop in my brain. I felt all at once to be given a power of hearing that was far beyond the normal. I could hear my own heart thudding most extraordinarily loud. I began, however, to feel better, after a while; but I simply had not the pluck to move. You can understand?

"Presently, I began to get my courage back. I gripped at my camera and flashlight, and waited. My hands were simply soaked with sweat. I glanced once at Wentworth. I could see him only dimly. His shoulders were hunched a little, his head forward; but though it was motionless, I knew that his eyes were not. It is queer how one knows that sort of thing at times. The police were just as silent. And thus a while passed.

"A sudden sound broke across the silence. From two sides of the room there came faint noises. I recognized them at once, as the breaking of the sealing-wax. The sealed doors were opening. I raised the camera and flashlight, and it was a peculiar mixture of fear and courage that helped me to press the button. As the great flare of light lit up the hall I felt the men all about me jump. The darkness fell like a clap of thunder, if you can understand, and seemed tenfold. Yet, in the moment of brightness, I had seen that all the sealed doors were wide open.

"Suddenly, all around us, there sounded a drip, drip, drip, upon the floor of the great hall. I thrilled with a queer, realizing emotion, and a sense of a very real and present danger—imminent. The 'blood-drip' had commenced. And the grim question was now whether the Barriers could save us from whatever had come into the huge room.

"Through some awful minutes the 'blood-drip' continued to fall in an increasing rain; and presently some began to fall within the Barriers. I saw several great drops splash and star upon the pale glowing intertwining tubes of the Electric Pentacle; but, strangely enough, I could not trace that any fell among us. Beyond the strange horrible noise of the 'drip,' there was no other sound. And then, abruptly, from the boarhound over in the far corner, there came a terrible yelling howl of agony, followed instantly by a sickening, breaking noise, and an immediate silence. If you have ever, when out shooting, broken a rabbit's neck, you will know the sound—in miniature! Like lightning, the thought sprang into my brain:—IT has crossed the Pentacle. For you will remember that I had made one about each of the dogs. I thought instantly, with a sick apprehension, of our own Barriers. There was something in the hall with us that had passed the Barrier of the Pentacle about one of the dogs. In the awful succeeding silence, I positively quivered. And suddenly, one of the men behind me, gave out a scream, like any woman, and bolted for the door. He fumbled, and had it open in a moment. I yelled to the others not to move; but they followed like sheep, and I heard them kick the candles flying, in their panic. One of them stepped on the Electric Pentacle, and smashed it, and there was an utter darkness. In an instant, I realized that I was defenseless against the powers of the Unknown World, and with one savage leap I was out of the useless Barriers, and instantly through the great doorway, and into the night. I believe I yelled with sheer funk.

"The men were a little ahead of me, and I never ceased running, and neither did they. Sometimes, I glanced back over my shoulder; and I kept glancing into the laurels which grew all along the drive. The beastly things kept rustling, rustling in a hollow sort of way, as though something were keeping parallel with me, among them. The rain had stopped, and a dismal little wind kept moaning through the grounds. It was disgusting.

"I caught Wentworth and the police at the lodge gate. We got outside, and ran all the way to the village. We found old Dennis up, waiting for us, and half the villagers to keep him company. He told us that he had known in his 'sowl' that we should come back, that is, if we came back at all; which is not a bad rendering of his remark.

"Fortunately, I had brought my camera away from the house— possibly because the strap had happened to be over my head. Yet, I did not go straight away to develop; but sat with the rest of the bar, where we talked for some hours, trying to be coherent about the whole horrible business.

"LATER, however, I went up to my room, and proceeded with my photography. I was steadier now, and it was just possible, so I hoped, that the negatives might show something.

"On two of the plates, I found nothing unusual: but on the third, which was the first one that I snapped, I saw something that made me quite excited. I examined it very carefully with a magnifying glass; then I put it to wash, and slipped a pair of rubber overshoes over my boots.

"The negative had showed me something very extraordinary, and I had made up my mind to test the truth of what it seemed to indicate, without losing another moment. It was no use telling anything to Wentworth and the police, until I was certain; and, also, I believed that I stood a greater chance to succeed by myself; though, for that matter, I do not suppose anything would have taken them up to the Manor again that night.

"I took my revolver, and went quietly downstairs, and into the dark. The rain had commenced again; but that did not bother me. I walked hard. When I came to the lodge gates, a sudden, queer instinct stopped me from going through, and I climbed the wall into the park. I kept away from the drive, and approached the building through the dismal, dripping laurels. You can imagine how beastly it was. Every time a leaf rustled, I jumped.

"I made my way 'round to the back of the big house, and got in through a little window which I had taken note of during my search; for, of course, I knew the whole place from roof to cellars. I went silently up the kitchen stairs, fairly quivering with funk; and at the top, I went to the left, and then into a long corridor that opened, through one of the doorways we had sealed, into the big hall. I looked up it, and saw a faint flicker of light away at the end; and I tiptoed silently toward it, holding my revolver ready. As I came near to the open door, I heard men's voices, and then a burst of laughing. I went on, until I could see into the hall. There were several men there, all in a group. They were well dressed, and one, at least, I saw was armed. They were examining my 'Barriers' against the Supernatural, with a good deal of unkind laughter. I never felt such a fool in my life.

"It was plain to me that they were a gang of men who had made use of the empty Manor, perhaps for years, for some purpose of their own; and now that Wentworth was attempting to take possession, they were acting up the traditions of the place, with the view of driving him away, and keeping so useful a place still at their disposal. But what they were, I mean whether coiners, thieves, inventors, or what, I could not imagine.

"Presently, they left the Pentacle, and gathered 'round the living boarhound, which seemed curiously quiet, as though it were half-drugged. There was some talk as to whether to let the poor brute live, or not; but finally they decided it would be good policy to kill it. I saw two of them force a twisted loop of rope into its mouth, and the two bights of the loop were brought together at the back of the hound's neck. Then a third man thrust a thick walking-stick through the two loops. The two men with the rope, stooped to hold the dog, so that I could not see what was done; but the poor beast gave a sudden awful howl, and immediately there was a repetition of the uncomfortable breaking sound, I had heard earlier in the night, as you will remember.

"The men stood up, and left the dog lying there, quiet enough now, as you may suppose. For my part, I fully appreciated the calculated remorselessness which had decided upon the animal's death, and the cold determination with which it had been afterward executed so neatly. I guessed that a man who might get into the 'light' of those particular men, would be likely to come to quite as uncomfortable an ending.

"A minute later, one of the men called out to the rest that they should 'shift the wires.' One of the men came toward the doorway of the corridor in which I stood, and I ran quickly back into the darkness of the upper end. I saw the man reach up, and take something from the top of the door, and I heard the slight, ringing jangle of steel wire.

"When he had gone, I ran back again, and saw the men passing, one after another, through an opening in the stairs, formed by one of the marble steps being raised. When the last man had vanished, the slab that made the step was shut down, and there was not a sign of the secret door. It was the seventh step from the bottom, as I took care to count: and a splendid idea; for it was so solid that it did not ring hollow, even to a fairly heavy hammer, as I found later.

"There is little more to tell. I got out of the house as quickly and quietly as possible, and back to the inn. The police came without any coaxing, when they knew the 'ghosts' were normal flesh and blood. We entered the park and the Manor in the same way that I had done. Yet, when we tried to open the step, we failed, and had finally to smash it. This must have warned the haunters; for when we descended to a secret room which we found at the end of a long and narrow passage in the thickness of the walls, we found no one.

"The police were horribly disgusted, as you can imagine; but for my part, I did not care either way. I had 'laid the ghost,' as you might say, and that was what I set out to do. I was not particularly afraid of being laughed at by the others; for they had all been thoroughly 'taken in'; and in the end, I had scored, without their help.

"We searched right through the secret ways, and found that

there was an exit, at the end of a long tunnel, which opened in the side of a well, out in the grounds. The ceiling of the hall was hollow, and reached by a little secret stairway inside of the big staircase. The 'blood-drip' was merely colored water, dropped through the minute crevices of the ornamented ceiling. How the candles and the fire were put out, I do not know; for the haunters certainly did not act quite up to tradition, which held that the lights were put out by the 'blood-drip.' Perhaps it was too difficult to direct the fluid, without positively squirting it, which might have given the whole thing away. The candles and the fire may possibly have been extinguished by the agency of carbonic acid gas; but how suspended, I have no idea.

"The secret hiding paces were, of course, ancient. There was also, did I tell you? a bell which they had rigged up to ring, when anyone entered the gates at the end of the drive. If I had not climbed the wall, I should have found nothing for my pains; for the bell would have warned them had I gone in through the gateway."

"What was on the negative?" I asked, with much curiosity.

"A picture of the fine wire with which they were grappling for the hook that held the entrance door open. They were doing it from one of the crevices in the ceiling. They had evidently made no preparations for lifting the hook. I suppose they never thought that anyone would make use of it, and so they had to improvise a grapple. The wire was too fine to be seen by the amount of light we had in the hall; but the flashlight 'picked it out.' Do you see?

"The opening of the inner doors was managed by wires, as you will have guessed, which they unshipped after use, or else I should soon have found them, when I made my search.

"I think I have now explained everything. The hound was killed, of course, by the men direct. You see, they made the place as dark as possible, first. Of course, if I had managed to take a flashlight just at that instant, the whole secret of the haunting would have been exposed. But Fate just ordered it the other way."

"And the tramps?" I asked.

"Oh, you mean the two tramps who were found dead in the Manor," said Carnacki. "Well, of course it is impossible to be sure, one way or the other. Perhaps they happened to find out something, and were given a hypodermic. Or it is just as probable that they had come to the time of their dying, and just died naturally. It is conceivable that a great many tramps had slept in the old house, at one time or another."

Carnacki stood up, and knocked out his pipe. We rose also, and went for our coats and hats.

"Out you go!" said Carnacki, genially, using the recognized formula. And we went out on to the Embankment, and presently through the darkness to our various homes.

CHAPTER 3
THE WHISTLING ROOM

Carnacki shook a friendly fist at me as I entered, late. Then he opened the door into the dining room, and ushered the four of us—Jessop, Arkright, Taylor and myself—in to dinner.

We dined well, as usual, and, equally as usual, Carnacki was pretty silent during the meal. At the end, we took our wine and cigars to our usual positions, and Carnacki—having got himself comfortable in his big chair—began without any preliminary:—

"I have just got back from Ireland, again," he said. "And I thought you chaps would be interested to hear my news. Besides, I fancy I shall see the thing clearer, after I have told it all out straight. I must tell you this, though, at the beginning—up to the present moment, I have been utterly and completely 'stumped.' I have tumbled upon one of the most peculiar cases of 'haunting'—or devilment of some sort—that I have come against. Now listen.

"I have been spending the last few weeks at Iastrae Castle, about twenty miles northeast of Galway. I got a letter about a month ago from a Mr. Sid K. Tassoc, who it seemed had bought the place lately, and moved in, only to find that he had bought a very peculiar piece of property.

"When I got there, he met me at the station, driving a jaunting car, and drove me up to the castle, which, by the way, he called a 'house shanty.' I found that he was 'pigging it' there with his boy brother and another American, who seemed to be half-servant and half-companion. It seems that all the servants had left the place, in a body, as you might say, and now they were managing among themselves, assisted by some day-help.

"The three of them got together a scratch feed, and Tassoc told me all about the trouble whilst we were at table. It is most extraordinary, and different from anything that I have had to do with; though that Buzzing Case was very queer, too.

"Tassoc began right in the middle of his story. 'We've got a room in this shanty,' he said, 'which has got a most infernal whistling in it; sort of haunting it. The thing starts any time; you never know when, and it goes on until it frightens you. All the servants have gone, as you know. It's not ordinary whistling, and it isn't the wind. Wait till you hear it.'

"'We're all carrying guns,' said the boy; and slapped his coat pocket.

"'As bad as that?' I said; and the older boy nodded. 'It may be soft,' he replied; 'but wait till you've heard it. Sometimes I think it's some infernal thing, and the next moment, I'm just as sure that someone's playing a trick on me.'

"'Why?' I asked. 'What is to be gained?'

"'You mean,' he said, 'that people usually have some good reason for playing tricks as elaborate as this. Well, I'll tell you. There's a lady in this province, by the name of Miss Donnehue, who's going to be my wife, this day two months. She's more beautiful than they make them, and so far as I can see, I've just stuck my head into an Irish hornet's nest. There's about a score of hot young Irishmen been courting her these two years gone, and now that I'm come along and cut them out, they feel raw against me. Do you begin to understand the possibilities?'

"'Yes,' I said. 'Perhaps I do in a vague sort of way; but I don't see how all this affects the room?'

"'Like this,' he said. 'When I'd fixed it up with Miss Donnehue, I looked out for a place, and bought this little house shanty. Afterward, I told her—one evening during dinner, that I'd decided to tie up here. And then she asked me whether I wasn't afraid of the whistling room. I told her it must have been thrown in gratis, as I'd heard nothing about it. There were some of her men friends present, and I saw a smile go 'round. I found out, after a bit of questioning, that several people have bought this place during the last twenty-odd years. And it was always on the market again, after a trial.

"'Well, the chaps started to bait me a bit, and offered to take bets after dinner that I'd not stay six months in the place. I looked once or twice to Miss Donnehue, so as to be sure I was "getting the note" of the talkee-talkee; but I could see that she didn't take it as a joke, at all. Partly, I think, because there was a bit of a sneer in the way the men were tackling me, and partly because she really believes there is something in this yarn of the Whistling Room.

"'However, after dinner, I did what I could to even things up with the others. I nailed all their bets, and screwed them down hard and safe. I guess some of them are going to be hard hit, unless I lose; which I don't mean to. Well, there you have practically the whole yarn.'

"'Not quite,' I told him. 'All that I know, is that you have bought a castle with a room in it that is in some way "queer," and that you've been doing some betting. Also, I know that your servants have got frightened and run away. Tell me something about the whistling?'

"'Oh, that!' said Tassoc; 'that started the second night we were in. I'd had a good look 'round the room, in the daytime, as you can understand; for the talk up at Arlestrae—Miss Donnehue's place—had made me wonder a bit. But it seems just as usual as some of the other rooms in the old wing, only perhaps a bit more lonesome. But that may be only because of the talk about it, you know.

"'The whistling started about ten o'clock, on the second night, as

I said. Tom and I were in the library, when we heard an awfully queer whistling, coming along the East Corridor—The room is in the East Wing, you know.

"'That's that blessed ghost!' I said to Tom, and we collared the lamps off the table, and went up to have a look. I tell you, even as we dug along the corridor, it took me a bit in the throat, it was so beastly queer. It was a sort of tune, in a way; but more as if a devil or some rotten thing were laughing at you, and going to get 'round at your back. That's how it makes you feel.

"'When we got to the door, we didn't wait; but rushed it open; and then I tell you the sound of the thing fairly hit me in the face. Tom said he got it the same way—sort of felt stunned and bewildered. We looked all 'round, and soon got so nervous, we just cleared out, and I locked the door.

"'We came down here, and had a stiff peg each. Then we got fit again, and began to think we'd been nicely had. So we took sticks, and went out into the grounds, thinking after all it must be some of these confounded Irishmen working the ghost-trick on us. But there was not a leg stirring.

"'We went back into the house, and walked over it, and then paid another visit to the room. But we simply couldn't stand it. We fairly ran out, and locked the door again. I don't know how to put it into words; but I had a feeling of being up against something that was rottenly dangerous. You know! We've carried our guns ever since.

"'Of course, we had a real turn out of the room next day, and the whole house place; and we even hunted 'round the grounds; but there was nothing queer. And now I don't know what to think; except that the sensible part of me tells me that it's some plan of these Wild Irishmen to try to take a rise out of me.'

"'Done anything since?' I asked him.

"'Yes,' he said—'watched outside of the door of the room at nights, and chased 'round the grounds, and sounded the walls and floor of the room. We've done everything we could think of; and it's beginning to get on our nerves; so we sent for you.'

"By this, we had finished eating. As we rose from the table, Tassoc suddenly called out:—'Ssh! Hark!'

"We were instantly silent, listening. Then I heard it, an extraordinary hooning whistle, monstrous and inhuman, coming from far away through corridors to my right.

"'By G—d!' said Tassoc; 'and it's scarcely dark yet! Collar those candles, both of you, and come along.'

"In a few moments, we were all out of the door and racing up the stairs. Tassoc turned into a long corridor, and we followed, shielding our candles as we ran. The sound seemed to fill all the passage as we drew near, until I had the feeling that the whole air throbbed under the power of some wanton Immense Force—a sense of an actual taint, as you might say, of monstrosity all about us.

"Tassoc unlocked the door; then, giving it a push with his foot, jumped back, and drew his revolver. As the door flew open, the sound beat out at us, with an effect impossible to explain to one who has not heard it—with a certain, horrible personal note in it; as if in there in the darkness you could picture the room rocking and creaking in a mad, vile glee to its own filthy piping and whistling and hooning. To stand there and listen, was to be stunned by Realization. It was as if someone showed you the mouth of a vast pit suddenly, and said:—That's Hell. And you knew that they had spoken the truth. Do you get it, even a little bit?

"I stepped back a pace into the room, and held the candle over my head, and looked quickly 'round. Tassoc and his brother joined me, and the man came up at the back, and we all held our candles high. I was deafened with the shrill, piping hoon of the whistling; and then, clear in my ear, something seemed to be saying to me: —'Get out of here—quick! Quick! Quick!'

"As you chaps know, I never neglect that sort of thing. Sometimes it may be nothing but nerves; but as you will remember, it was just such a warning that saved me in the 'Grey Dog' Case, and in the 'Yellow Finger' Experiments; as well as other times. Well, I turned sharp 'round to the others: 'Out!' I said. 'For God's sake, out quick.' And in an instant I had them into the passage.

"There came an extraordinary yelling scream into the hideous whistling, and then, like a clap of thunder, an utter silence. I slammed the door, and locked it. Then, taking the key, I looked 'round at the others. They were pretty white, and I imagine I must have looked that way too. And there we stood a moment, silent.

"'Come down out of this, and have some whisky,' said Tassoc, at last, in a voice he tried to make ordinary; and he led the way. I was the back man, and I know we all kept looking over our shoulders. When we got downstairs, Tassoc passed the bottle 'round. He took a drink, himself, and slapped his glass down on to the table. Then sat down with a thud.

"'That's a lovely thing to have in the house with you, isn't it!' he said. And directly afterward:—'What on earth made you hustle us all out like that, Carnacki?'

"'Something seemed to be telling me to get out, quick,' I said. 'Sounds a bit silly, superstitious, I know; but when you are meddling with this sort of thing, you've got to take notice of queer fancies, and risk being laughed at.'

"I told him then about the 'Grey Dog' business, and he nodded a lot to that. 'Of course,' I said, 'this may be nothing more than those would-be rivals of yours playing some funny game; but, personally, though I'm going to keep an open mind, I feel that there is something beastly and dangerous about this thing.'

"We talked for a while longer, and then Tassoc suggested billiards, which we played in a pretty half-hearted fashion, and all the time cocking an ear to the door, as you might say, for sounds; but none came, and later, after coffee, he suggested early bed, and a thorough overhaul of the room on the morrow.

"My bedroom was in the newer part of the castle, and the door opened into the picture gallery. At the East end of the gallery was the entrance to the corridor of the East Wing; this was shut off from the gallery by two old and heavy oak doors, which looked rather odd and quaint beside the more modern doors of the various rooms.

"When I reached my room, I did not go to bed; but began to unpack my instrument trunk, of which I had retained the key. I intended to take one or two preliminary steps at once, in my investigation of the extraordinary whistling.

"Presently, when the castle had settled into quietness, I slipped out of my room, and across to the entrance of the great corridor. I opened one of the low, squat doors, and threw the beam of my pocket searchlight down the passage. It was empty, and I went through the doorway, and pushed-to the oak behind me. Then along the great passageway, throwing my light before and behind, and keeping my revolver handy.

"I had hung a 'protection belt' of garlic 'round my neck, and the smell of it seemed to fill the corridor and give me assurance; for, as you all know, it is a wonderful 'protection' against the more usual Aeiirii forms of semi-materialization, by which I supposed the whistling might be produced; though, at that period of my investigation, I was quite prepared to find it due to some perfectly natural cause; for it is astonishing the enormous number of cases that prove to have nothing abnormal in them.

"In addition to wearing the necklet, I had plugged my ears loosely with garlic, and as I did not intend to stay more than a few minutes in the room, I hoped to be safe.

"WHEN I REACHED THE DOOR, and put my hand into my pocket for the key, I had a sudden feeling of sickening funk. But I was not going to back out, if I could help it. I unlocked the door and turned the handle. Then I gave the door a sharp push with my foot, as Tassoc had done, and drew my revolver, though I did not expect to have any use for it, really.

"I shone the searchlight all 'round the room, and then stepped inside, with a disgustingly horrible feeling of walking slap into a waiting Danger. I stood a few seconds, waiting, and nothing happened, and the empty room showed bare from corner to corner. And then, you know, I realized that the room was full of an abominable silence; can you understand that? A sort of purposeful silence, just as sickening as any of the filthy noises the Things have power to make. Do you remember what I told you about that 'Silent Garden' business? Well, this room had just that same malevolent silence—the beastly quietness of a thing that is looking at you and not seeable itself, and thinks that it has got you. Oh, I recognized it instantly, and I whipped the top off my lantern, so as to have light over the whole room.

"Then I set-to, working like fury, and keeping my glance all about me. I sealed the two windows with lengths of human hair, right across, and sealed them at every frame. As I worked, a queer, scarcely perceptible tenseness stole into the air of the place, and the silence seemed, if you can understand me, to grow more solid. I knew then that I had no business there without 'full protection'; for I was practically certain that this was no mere Aeiirii development; but one of the worst forms, as the Saiitii; like that 'Grunting Man' case—you know.

"I finished the window, and hurried over to the great fireplace. This is a huge affair, and has a queer gallows-iron, I think they are called, projecting from the back of the arch. I sealed the opening with seven human hairs—the seventh crossing the six others.

"Then, just as I was making an end, a low, mocking whistle grew in the room. A cold, nervous pricking went up my spine, and 'round my forehead from the back. The hideous sound filled all the room with an extraordinary, grotesque parody of human whistling, too gigantic to be human—as if something gargantuan and monstrous made the sounds softly. As I stood there a last moment, pressing down the final seal, I had no doubt but that I had come across one of those rare and horrible cases of the Inanimate reproducing the functions of the Animate, I made a grab for my lamp, and went quickly to the door, looking over my shoulder, and listening for the thing that I expected. It came, just as I got my hand upon the handle—a squeal of incredible, malevolent anger, piercing through the low hooning of the whistling. I dashed out, slamming the door and locking it. I leant a little against the opposite wall of the corridor, feeling rather funny; for it had been a narrow squeak.... 'Theyr be noe sayfetie to be gained bye gayrds of holieness when the monyster hath pow'r to speak throe woode and stoene.' So runs the passage in the Sigsand MS., and I proved it in that 'Nodding Door' business. There is no protection against this particular form of monster, except, possibly, for a fractional period of time; for it can reproduce itself in, or take to its purpose, the very protective material which you may use, and has the power to 'forme wythine the pentycle'; though not immediately. There is, of course, the possibility of the Unknown Last Line of the Saaa-maaa Ritual being uttered; but it is too uncertain to count upon, and the danger is too hideous; and even then it has no power to protect for more than 'maybee fyve beats of the harte,' as the Sigsand has it.

"Inside of the room, there was now a constant, meditative, hooning whistling; but presently this ceased, and the silence seemed worse; for there is such a sense of hidden mischief in a silence.

"After a little, I sealed the door with crossed hairs, and then cleared off down the great passage, and so to bed.

"For a long time I lay awake; but managed eventually to get some sleep. Yet, about two o'clock I was waked by the hooning whistling of the room coming to me, even through the closed doors. The sound was tremendous, and seemed to beat through the whole house with a presiding sense of terror. As if (I remember thinking) some monstrous giant had been holding mad carnival with itself at the end of that great passage.

"I got up and sat on the edge of the bed, wondering whether to go along and have a look at the seal; and suddenly there came a thump on my door, and Tassoc walked in, with his dressing gown over his pajamas.

"'I thought it would have waked you, so I came along to have a talk,' he said. 'I can't sleep. Beautiful! Isn't it!'

"'Extraordinary!' I said, and tossed him my case.

"He lit a cigarette, and we sat and talked for about an hour; and all the time that noise went on, down at the end of the big corridor.

"Suddenly, Tassoc stood up:—

"'Let's take our guns, and go and examine the brute,' he said, and turned toward the door.

"'No!' I said. 'By Jove—no! I can't say anything definite, yet; but I believe that room is about as dangerous as it well can be.'

"'HAUNTED—REALLY HAUNTED?' he asked, keenly and without any of his frequent banter.

"I told him, of course, that I could not say a definite yes or no to such a question; but that I hoped to be able to make a statement, soon. Then I gave him a little lecture on the False Re-Materialization of the Animate-Force through the Inanimate-Inert. He began then to see the particular way in the room might be dangerous, if it were really the subject of a manifestation.

"About an hour later, the whistling ceased quite suddenly, and Tassoc went off again to bed. I went back to mine, also, and eventually got another spell of sleep.

"In the morning, I went along to the room. I found the seals on the door intact. Then I went in. The window seals and the hair were all right; but the seventh hair across the great fireplace was broken. This set me thinking. I knew that it might, very possibly, have snapped, through my having tensioned it too highly; but then, again, it might have been broken by something else. Yet, it was scarcely possible that a man, for instance, could have passed between the six unbroken hairs; for no one would ever have noticed them, entering the room that way, you see; but just walked through them, ignorant of their very existence.

"I removed the other hairs, and the seals. Then I looked up the chimney. It went up straight, and I could see blue sky at the top. It was a big, open flue, and free from any suggestion of hiding places, or corners. Yet, of course, I did not trust to any such casual examination, and after breakfast, I put on my overalls, and climbed to the very top, sounding all the way; but I found nothing.

"Then I came down, and went over the whole of the room—floor, ceiling, and walls, mapping them out in six-inch squares, and sounding with both hammer and probe. But there was nothing abnormal.

"Afterward, I made a three-weeks search of the whole castle, in the same thorough way; but found nothing. I went even further, then; for at night, when the whistling commenced, I made a microphone test. You see, if the whistling were mechanically produced, this test would have made evident to me the working of the machinery, if there were any such concealed within the walls. It certainly was an up-to-date method of examination, as you must allow.

"Of course, I did not think that any of Tassoc's rivals had fixed up any mechanical contrivance; but I thought it just possible that there had been some such thing for producing the whistling, made away back in the years, perhaps with the intention of giving the room a reputation that would ensure its being free of inquisitive folk. You see what I mean? Well, of course, it was just possible, if this were the case, that someone knew the secret of the machinery, and was utilizing the knowledge to play this devil of a prank on Tassoc. The microphone test of the walls would certainly have made this known to me, as I have said; but there was nothing of the sort in the castle; so that I had practically no doubt at all now, but that it was a genuine case of what is popularly termed 'haunting.'

"All this time, every night, and sometimes most of each night, the hooning whistling of the Room was intolerable. It was as if an intelligence there knew that steps were being taken against it, and piped and hooned in a sort of mad, mocking contempt. I tell you, it was as extraordinary as it was horrible. Time after time, I went along —tiptoeing noiselessly on stockinged feet—to the sealed door (for I always kept the Room sealed). I went at all hours of the night, and often the whistling, inside, would seem to change to a brutally malignant note, as though the half-animate monster saw me plainly through the shut door. And all the time the shrieking, hooning whistling would fill the whole corridor, so that I used to feel a precious lonely chap, messing about there with one of Hell's mysteries.

"And every morning, I would enter the room, and examine the different hairs and seals. You see, after the first week, I had stretched parallel hairs all along the walls of the room, and along the ceiling; but over the floor, which was of polished stone, I had set out little, colorless wafers, tacky-side uppermost. Each wafer was numbered, and they were arranged after a definite plan, so that I should be able to trace the exact movements of any living thing that went across the floor.

"You will see that no material being or creature could possibly have entered that room, without leaving many signs to tell me about it. But nothing was ever disturbed, and I began to think that I should have to risk an attempt to stay the night in the room, in the Electric Pentacle. Yet, mind you, I knew that it would be a crazy thing to do; but I was getting stumped, and ready to do anything.

"Once, about midnight, I did break the seal on the door, and have a quick look in; but, I tell you, the whole Room gave one mad yell, and seemed to come toward me in a great belly of shadows, as if the walls had bellied in toward me. Of course, that must have been fancy. Anyway, the yell was sufficient, and I slammed the door, and locked it, feeling a bit weak down my spine. You know the feeling.

"And then, when I had got to that state of readiness for anything, I made something of a discovery. It was about one in the morning, and I was walking slowly 'round the castle, keeping in the soft grass. I had come under the shadow of the East Front, and far above me, I could hear the vile, hooning whistle of the Room, up in the darkness of the unlit wing. Then, suddenly, a little in front of me, I heard a man's voice, speaking low, but evidently in glee:—

"'By George! You Chaps; but I wouldn't care to bring a wife home in that!' it said, in the tone of the cultured Irish.

"Someone started to reply; but there came a sharp exclamation, and then a rush, and I heard footsteps running in all directions. Evidently, the men had spotted me.

"For a few seconds, I stood there, feeling an awful ass. After all, they were at the bottom of the haunting! Do you see what a big fool it made me seem? I had no doubt but that they were some of Tassoc's rivals; and here I had been feeling in every bone that I had hit a real, bad, genuine Case! And then, you know, there came the memory of hundreds of details, that made me just as much in doubt again. Anyway, whether it was natural, or ab-natural, there was a great deal yet to be cleared up.

"I told Tassoc, next morning, what I had discovered, and through the whole of every night, for five nights, we kept a close watch 'round the East Wing; but there was never a sign of anyone prowling about; and all the time, almost from evening to dawn, that grotesque whistling would hoon incredibly, far above us in the darkness.

"On the morning after the fifth night, I received a wire from here, which brought me home by the next boat. I explained to Tassoc that I was simply bound to come away for a few days; but told him to keep up the watch 'round the castle. One thing I was very careful to do, and that was to make him absolutely promise never to go into the Room, between sunset and sunrise. I made it clear to him that we knew nothing definite yet, one way or the other; and if the room were what I had first thought it to be, it might be a lot better for him to die first, than enter it after dark.

"When I got here, and had finished my business, I thought you chaps would be interested; and also I wanted to get it all spread out clear in my mind; so I rung you up. I am going over again to-morrow, and when I get back, I ought to have something pretty extraordinary to tell you. By the way, there is a curious thing I forgot to tell you. I tried to get a phonographic record of the whistling; but it simply produced no impression on the wax at all. That is one of the things that has made me feel queer, I can tell you. Another extraordinary thing is that the microphone will not magnify the sound—will not even transmit it; seems to take no account of it, and acts as if it were nonexistent. I am absolutely and utterly stumped, up to the present. I am a wee bit curious to see whether any of your dear clever heads can make daylight of it. I cannot—not yet."

He rose to his feet.

"Good night, all," he said, and began to usher us out abruptly, but without offence, into the night.

A fortnight later, he dropped each of us a card, and you can imagine that I was not late this time. When we arrived, Carnacki took us straight into dinner, and when we had finished, and all made ourselves comfortable, he began again, where he had left off:—

"Now just listen quietly; for I have got something pretty queer to tell you. I got back late at night, and I had to walk up to the castle, as I had not warned them that I was coming. It was bright moonlight; so that the walk was rather a pleasure, than otherwise. When I got there, the whole place was in darkness, and I thought I would take a walk 'round outside, to see whether Tassoc or his brother was keeping watch. But I could not find them anywhere, and concluded that they had got tired of it, and gone off to bed.

"As I returned across the front of the East Wing, I caught the hooning whistling of the Room, coming down strangely through the stillness of the night. It had a queer note in it, I remember—low and constant, queerly meditative. I looked up at the window, bright in the moonlight, and got a sudden thought to bring a ladder from the stable yard, and try to get a look into the Room, through the window.

"With this notion, I hunted 'round at the back of the castle, among the straggle of offices, and presently found a long, fairly light ladder; though it was heavy enough for one, goodness knows! And I thought at first that I should never get it reared. I managed at last, and let the ends rest very quietly against the wall, a little below the sill of the larger window. Then, going silently, I went up the ladder.

Presently, I had my face above the sill and was looking in alone with the moonlight.

"Of course, the queer whistling sounded louder up there; but it still conveyed that peculiar sense of something whistling quietly to itself—can you understand? Though, for all the meditative lowness of the note, the horrible, gargantuan quality was distinct—a mighty parody of the human, as if I stood there and listened to the whistling from the lips of a monster with a man's soul.

"And then, you know, I saw something. The floor in the middle of the huge, empty room, was puckered upward in the center into a strange soft-looking mound, parted at the top into an ever changing hole, that pulsated to that great, gentle hooning. At times, as I watched, I saw the heaving of the indented mound, gap across with a queer, inward suction, as with the drawing of an enormous breath; then the thing would dilate and pout once more to the incredible melody. And suddenly, as I stared, dumb, it came to me that the thing was living. I was looking at two enormous, blackened lips, blistered and brutal, there in the pale moonlight....

"Abruptly, they bulged out to a vast, pouting mound of force and sound, stiffened and swollen, and hugely massive and clean-cut in the moon-beams. And a great sweat lay heavy on the vast upper-lip. In the same moment of time, the whistling had burst into a mad screaming note, that seemed to stun me, even where I stood, outside of the window. And then, the following moment, I was staring blankly at the solid, undisturbed floor of the room—smooth, polished stone flooring, from wall to wall; and there was an absolute silence.

"You can picture me staring into the quiet Room, and knowing what I knew. I felt like a sick, frightened kid, and wanted to slide quietly down the ladder, and run away. But in that very instant, I heard Tassoc's voice calling to me from within the Room, for help, help. My God! but I got such an awful dazed feeling; and I had a vague, bewildered notion that, after all, it was the Irishmen who had got him in there, and were taking it out of him. And then the call came again, and I burst the window, and jumped in to help him. I had a confused idea that the call had come from within the shadow of the great fireplace, and I raced across to it; but there was no one there.

"'Tassoc!' I shouted, and my voice went empty-sounding 'round the great apartment; and then, in a flash, I knew that Tassoc had never called. I whirled 'round, sick with fear, toward the window, and as I did so, a frightful, exultant whistling scream burst through the Room. On my left, the end wall had bellied-in toward me, in a pair of gargantuan lips, black and utterly monstrous, to within a yard of my face. I fumbled for a mad instant at my revolver; not for it, but myself; for the danger was a thousand times worse than death. And then, suddenly, the Unknown Last Line of the Saaamaaa Ritual was whispered quite audibly in the room. Instantly, the thing happened that I have known once before. There came a sense as of dust falling continually and monotonously, and I knew that my life hung uncertain and suspended for a flash, in a brief, reeling vertigo of unseeable things. Then that ended, and I knew that I might live. My soul and body blended again, and life and power came to me. I dashed furiously at the window, and hurled myself out head-foremost; for I can tell you that I had stopped being afraid of death. I crashed down on to the ladder, and slithered, grabbing and grabbing; and so came some way or other alive to the bottom. And there I sat in the soft, wet grass, with the moonlight all about me; and far above, through the broken window of the Room, there was a low whistling.

"That is the chief of it. I was not hurt, and I went 'round to the front, and knocked Tassoc up. When they let me in, we had a long yarn, over some good whisky—for I was shaken to pieces—and I explained things as much as I could, I told Tassoc that the room would have to come down, and every fragment of it burned in a blast-furnace, erected within a pentacle. He nodded. There was nothing to say. Then I went to bed.

"We turned a small army on to the work, and within ten days, that lovely thing had gone up in smoke, and what was left was calcined, and clean.

"It was when the workmen were stripping the paneling, that I got hold of a sound notion of the beginnings of that beastly development. Over the great fireplace, after the great oak panels had been torn down, I found that there was let into the masonry a scrollwork of stone, with on it an old inscription, in ancient Celtic, that here in this room was burned Dian Tiansay, Jester of King Alzof, who made the Song of Foolishness upon King Ernore of the Seventh Castle.

"When I got the translation clear, I gave it to Tassoc. He was tremendously excited; for he knew the old tale, and took me down to the library to look at an old parchment that gave the story in detail. Afterward, I found that the incident was well-known about the countryside; but always regarded more as a legend than as history. And no one seemed ever to have dreamt that the old East Wing of Iastrae Castle was the remains of the ancient Seventh Castle.

"From the old parchment, I gathered that there had been a pretty dirty job done, away back in the years. It seems that King Alzof and King Ernore had been enemies by birthright, as you might say truly; but that nothing more than a little raiding had occurred on either side for years, until Dian Tiansay made the Song of Foolishness upon King Ernore, and sang it before King Alzof; and so greatly was it appreciated that King Alzof gave the jester one of his ladies, to wife.

"Presently, all the people of the land had come to know the song, and so it came at last to King Ernore, who was so angered that he made war upon his old enemy, and took and burned him and his castle; but Dian Tiansay, the jester, he brought with him to his own place, and having torn his tongue out because of the song which he had made and sung, he imprisoned him in the Room in the East Wing (which was evidently used for unpleasant purposes), and the jester's wife, he kept for himself, having a fancy for her prettiness.

"But one night, Dian Tiansay's wife was not to be found, and in the morning they discovered her lying dead in her husband's arms, and he sitting, whistling the Song of Foolishness, for he had no longer the power to sing it.

"Then they roasted Dian Tiansay, in the great fireplace—probably from that selfsame 'galley-iron' which I have already mentioned. And until he died, Dian Tiansay ceased not to whistle the Song of Foolishness, which he could no longer sing. But afterward, 'in that room' there was often heard at night the sound of something whistling; and there 'grew a power in that room,' so that none dared to sleep in it. And presently, it would seem, the King went to another castle; for the whistling troubled him.

"There you have it all. Of course, that is only a rough rendering of the translation of the parchment. But it sounds extraordinarily quaint. Don't you think so?"

"Yes," I said, answering for the lot. "But how did the thing grow to such a tremendous manifestation?"

"One of those cases of continuity of thought producing a positive action upon the immediate surrounding material," replied Carnacki. "The development must have been going forward through centuries, to have produced such a monstrosity. It was a true instance of Saiitii manifestation, which I can best explain by likening it to a living spiritual fungus, which involves the very structure of the aether-fiber itself, and, of course, in so doing, acquires an essential control over the 'material substance' involved in it. It is impossible to make it plainer in a few words."

"What broke the seventh hair?" asked Taylor.

But Carnacki did not know. He thought it was probably nothing but being too severely tensioned. He also explained that they found out that the men who had run away, had not been up to mischief; but had come over secretly, merely to hear the whistling, which, indeed, had suddenly become the talk of the whole countryside.

"One other thing," said Arkright, "have you any idea what governs the use of the Unknown Last Line of the Saaamaaa Ritual? I know, of course, that it was used by the Ab-human Priests in the

Incantation of Raaaee; but what used it on your behalf, and what made it?"

"You had better read Harzan's Monograph, and my Addenda to it, on Astral and Astral Co-ordination and Interference," said Carnacki. "It is an extraordinary subject, and I can only say here that the human vibration may not be insulated from the astral (as is always believed to be the case, in interferences by the Ab-human), without immediate action being taken by those Forces which govern the spinning of the outer circle. In other words, it is being proved, time after time, that there is some inscrutable Protective Force constantly intervening between the human soul (not the body, mind you,) and the Outer Monstrosities. Am I clear?"

"Yes, I think so," I replied. "And you believe that the Room had become the material expression of the ancient Jester—that his soul, rotten with hatred, had bred into a monster—eh?" I asked.

"Yes," said Carnacki, nodding, "I think you've put my thought rather neatly. It is a queer coincidence that Miss Donnehue is supposed to be descended (so I have heard since) from the same King Ernore. It makes one think some curious thoughts, doesn't it? The marriage coming on, and the Room waking to fresh life. If she had gone into that room, ever ... eh? It had waited a long time. Sins of the fathers. Yes, I've thought of that. They're to be married next week, and I am to be best man, which is a thing I hate. And he won his bets, rather! Just think, if ever she had gone into that room. Pretty horrible, eh?"

He nodded his head, grimly, and we four nodded back. Then he rose and took us collectively to the door, and presently thrust us forth in friendly fashion on the Embankment and into the fresh night air.

"Good night," we all called back, and went to our various homes. If she had, eh? If she had? That is what I kept thinking.

CHAPTER 4

THE HORSE OF THE INVISIBLE

I had that afternoon received an invitation from Carnacki. When I reached his place I found him sitting alone. As I came into the room he rose with a perceptibly stiff movement and extended his left hand. His face seemed to be badly scarred and bruised and his right hand was bandaged. He shook hands and offered me his paper, which I refused. Then he passed me a handful of photographs and returned to his reading.

Now, that is just Carnacki. Not a word had come from him and not a question from me. He would tell us all about it later. I spent about half an hour looking at the photographs which were chiefly "snaps" (some by flashlight) of an extraordinarily pretty girl; though in some of the photographs it was wonderful that her prettiness was so evident for so frightened and startled was her expression that it was difficult not to believe that she had been photographed in the presence of some imminent and overwhelming danger.

The bulk of the photographs were of interiors of different rooms and passages and in every one the girl might be seen, either full length in the distance or closer, with perhaps little more than a hand or arm or portion of the head or dress included in the photograph. All of these had evidently been taken with some definite aim that did not have for its first purpose the picturing of the girl, but obviously of her surroundings and they made me very curious, as you can imagine.

Near the bottom of the pile, however, I came upon something definitely extraordinary. It was a photograph of the girl standing abrupt and clear in the great blaze of a flashlight, as was plain to be seen. Her face was turned a little upward as if she had been frightened suddenly by some noise. Directly above her, as though half-formed and coming down out of the shadows, was the shape of a single enormous hoof.

I examined this photograph for a long time without understanding it more than that it had probably to do with some queer case in which Carnacki was interested. When Jessop, Arkright and Taylor came in Carnacki quietly held out his hand for the photographs which I returned in the same spirit and afterward we all went in to dinner. When we had spent a quiet hour at the table we pulled our chairs 'round and made ourselves snug and Carnacki began:

"I've been North," he said, speaking slowly and painfully between puffs at his pipe. "Up to Hisgins of East Lancashire. It has been a pretty strange business all 'round, as I fancy you chaps will think, when I have finished. I knew before I went, something about the 'horse story,' as I have heard it called; but I never thought of it coming my way, somehow. Also I know now that I never considered it seriously—in spite of my rule always to keep an open mind. Funny creatures, we humans!

"Well, I got a wire asking for an appointment, which of course told me that there was some trouble. On the date I fixed old Captain Hisgins himself came up to see me. He told me a great many new details about the horse story; though naturally I had always known the main points and understood that if the first child were a girl, that girl would be haunted by the Horse during her courtship.

"It is, as you can see already, an extraordinary story and though I have always known about it, I have never thought it to be anything more than an old-time legend, as I have already hinted. You see, for seven generations the Hisgins family have had men children for their first-born and even the Hisginses themselves have long considered the tale to be little more than a myth.

"To come to the present, the eldest child of the reigning family is a girl and she has been often teased and warned in jest by her friends and relations that she is the first girl to be the eldest for seven generations and that she would have to keep her men friends at arm's length or go into a nunnery if she hoped to escape the haunting. And this, I think, shows us how thoroughly the tale had grown to be considered as nothing worthy of the least serious thought. Don't you think so?

"Two months ago Miss Hisgins became engaged to Beaumont, a young Naval Officer, and on the evening of the very day of the engagement, before it was even formally announced, a most extraordinary thing happened which resulted in Captain Hisgins making the appointment and my ultimately going down to their place to look into the thing.

"From the old family records and papers that were entrusted to me I found that there could be no possible doubt that prior to something like a hundred and fifty years ago there were some very extraordinary and disagreeable coincidences, to put the thing in the least emotional way. In the whole of the two centuries prior to that date there were five first-born girls out of a total of seven generations of the family. Each of these girls grew up to maidenhood and each became engaged, and each one died during the period of engagement, two by suicide, one by falling from a window, one from a 'broken heart' (presumably heart failure, owing to sudden shock through fright). The fifth girl was killed one evening in the park 'round the house; but just how, there seemed to be no exact knowledge; only that there was an impression that she had been kicked by a horse. She was dead when found. Now, you see, all of these deaths might be attributed in a way—even the suicides—to natural causes, I mean as distinct from supernatural. You see? Yet, in every case the maidens had undoubtedly suffered some extraordinary and terrifying experiences during their various courtships for in all of the records there was mention either of the neighing of an unseen horse or of the sounds of an invisible horse galloping, as well as many other peculiar and quite inexplicable manifestations. You begin to understand now, I think, just how extraordinary a business it was that I was asked to look into.

"I gathered from one account that the haunting of the girls was so constant and horrible that two of the girls' lovers fairly ran away from their ladyloves. And I think it was this, more than anything else, that made me feel that there had been something more in it than a mere succession of uncomfortable coincidences.

"I got hold of these facts before I had been many hours in the house and after this I went pretty carefully into the details of the thing that happened on the night of Miss Hisgins's engagement to Beaumont. It seems that as the two of them were going through the big lower corridor, just after dusk and before the lamps had been lighted, there had been a sudden, horrible neighing in the corridor, close to them. Immediately afterward Beaumont received a tremendous blow or kick which broke his right forearm. Then the rest of the family and the servants came running to know what was wrong. Lights were brought and the corridor and, afterward, the whole house searched, but nothing unusual was found.

"You can imagine the excitement in the house and the half incredulous, half believing talk about the old legend. Then, later, in the middle of the night the old Captain was waked by the sound of a great horse galloping 'round and 'round the house.

"Several times after this both Beaumont and the girl said that they had heard the sounds of hoofs near to them after dusk, in several of the rooms and corridors.

"Three nights later Beaumont was waked by a strange neighing in the nighttime seeming to come from the direction of his sweetheart's bedroom. He ran hurriedly for her father and the two of them raced to her room. They found her awake and ill with sheer terror, having been awakened by the neighing, seemingly close to her bed.

"The night before I arrived, there had been a fresh happening and they were all in a frightfully nervy state, as you can imagine.

"I spent most of the first day, as I have hinted, in getting hold of details; but after dinner I slacked off and played billiards all the evening with Beaumont and Miss Hisgins. We stopped about ten o'clock and had coffee and I got Beaumont to give me full particulars about the thing that had happened the evening before.

"He and Miss Hisgins had been sitting quietly in her aunt's boudoir whilst the old lady chaperoned them, behind a book. It was growing dusk and the lamp was at her end of the table. The rest of the house was not yet lit as the evening had come earlier than usual.

"Well, it seems that the door into the hall was open and suddenly the girl said: 'H'sh! what's that?'

"They both listened and then Beaumont heard it—the sound of a horse outside of the front door.

"'Your father?' he suggested, but she reminded him that her father was not riding.

"Of course they were both ready to feel queer, as you can suppose, but Beaumont made an effort to shake this off and went into the hall to see whether anyone was at the entrance. It was pretty dark in the hall and he could see the glass panels of the inner draft door, clear-cut in the darkness of the hall. He walked over to the glass and looked through into the drive beyond, but there nothing in sight.

"He felt nervous and puzzled and opened the inner door and went out on to the carriage-circle. Almost directly afterward the great hall door swung to with a crash behind him. He told me that he had a sudden awful feeling of having been trapped in some way—that is how he put it. He whirled 'round and gripped the door handle, but something seemed to be holding it with a vast grip on the other side. Then, before he could be fixed in his mind that this was so, he was able to turn the handle and open the door.

"He paused a moment in the doorway and peered into the hall, for he had hardly steadied his mind sufficiently to know whether he was really frightened or not. Then he heard his sweetheart blow him a kiss out of the greyness of the big, unlit hall and he knew that she had followed him from the boudoir. He blew her a kiss back and stepped inside the doorway, meaning to go to her. And then, suddenly, in a flash of sickening knowledge he knew that it was not his sweetheart who had blown him that kiss. He knew that something was trying to tempt him alone into the darkness and that the girl had never left the boudoir. He jumped back and in the same instant of time he heard the kiss again, nearer to him. He called out at the top of his voice: 'Mary, stay in the boudoir. Don't move out of the boudoir until I come to you.' He heard her call something in reply from the boudoir and then he had struck a clump of a dozen or so matches and was holding them above his head and looking 'round the hall. There was no one in it, but even as the matches burned out there came the sounds of a great horse galloping down the empty drive.

"Now you see, both he and the girl had heard the sounds of the horse galloping; but when I questioned more closely I found that the aunt had heard nothing, though it is true she is a bit deaf, and she was further back in the room. Of course, both he and Miss Hisgins had been in an extremely nervous state and ready to hear anything. The door might have been slammed by a sudden puff of wind owing to some inner door being opened; and as for the grip on the handle, that may have been nothing more than the snick catching.

"With regard to the kisses and the sounds of the horse galloping, I pointed out that these might have seemed ordinary enough sounds, if they had been only cool enough to reason. As I told him, and as he knew, the sounds of a horse galloping carry a long way on the wind so that what he had heard might have been nothing more than a horse being ridden some distance away. And as for the kiss, plenty of quiet noises—the rustle of a paper or a leaf—have a somewhat similar sound, especially if one is in an overstrung condition and imagining things.

"I finished preaching this little sermon on commonsense versus hysteria as we put out the lights and left the billiard room. But neither Beaumont nor Miss Hisgins would agree that there had been any fancy on their parts.

"We had come out of the billiard room by this time and were going along the passage and I was still doing my best to make both of them see the ordinary, commonplace possibilities of the happening, when what killed my pig, as the saying goes, was the sound of a hoof in the dark billiard room we had just left.

"I felt the 'creep' come on me in a flash, up my spine and over the back of my head. Miss Hisgins whooped like a child with the whooping cough and ran up the passage, giving little gasping screams. Beaumont, however, ripped 'round on his heels and jumped back a couple of yards. I gave back too, a bit, as you can understand.

"'There it is,' he said in a low, breathless voice. 'Perhaps you'll believe now.'

"'There's certainly something,' I whispered, never taking my gaze off the closed door of the billiard room.

"'H'sh!' he muttered. 'There it is again.'

"There was a sound like a great horse pacing 'round and 'round the billiard room with slow, deliberate steps. A horrible cold fright took me so that it seemed impossible to take a full breath, you know the feeling, and then I saw we must have been walking backward for we found ourselves suddenly at the opening of the long passage.

"We stopped there and listened. The sounds went on steadily with a horrible sort of deliberateness, as if the brute were taking a sort of malicious gusto in walking about all over the room which we had just occupied. Do you understand just what I mean?

"Then there was a pause and a long time of absolute quiet except for an excited whispering from some of the people down in the big hall. The sound came plainly up the wide stairway. I fancy they were gathered 'round Miss Hisgins, with some notion of protecting her.

"I should think Beaumont and I stood there, at the end of the passage for about five minutes, listening for any noise in the billiard room. Then I realized what a horrible funk I was in and I said to him: 'I'm going to see what's there.'

"'So'm I,' he answered. He was pretty white, but he had heaps of pluck. I told him to wait one instant and I made a dash into my bedroom and got my camera and flashlight. I slipped my revolver into my right-hand pocket and a knuckle-duster over my left fist, where it was ready and yet would not stop me from being able to work my flashlight.

"Then I ran back to Beaumont. He held out his hand to show me that he had his pistol and I nodded, but whispered to him not to be too quick to shoot, as there might be some silly practical joking at work, after all. He had got a lamp from a bracket in the upper hall which he was holding in the crook of his damaged arm, so that we had a good light. Then we went down the passage toward the billiard room and you can imagine that we were a pretty nervous couple.

"All this time there had not been a sound, but abruptly when we were within perhaps a couple of yards of the door we heard the sudden clumping of a hoof on the solid parquet floor of the billiard room. In the instant afterward it seemed to me that the whole place shook beneath the ponderous hoof falls of some huge thing, coming toward the door. Both Beaumont and I gave back a pace or two, and then realized and hung on to our courage, as you might say, and waited. The great tread came right up to the door and then stopped and there was an instant of absolute silence, except that so far as I was concerned, the pulsing in my throat and temples almost deafened me.

"I dare say we waited quite half a minute and then came the

further restless clumping of a great hoof. Immediately afterward the sounds came right on as if some invisible thing passed through the closed door and the ponderous tread was upon us. We jumped, each of us, to our side of the passage and I know that I spread myself stiff against the wall. The clungk clunck, clungk clunck, of the great hoof falls passed right between us and slowly and with deadly deliberateness, down the passage. I heard them through a haze of blood beats in my ears and temples and my body was extraordinarily rigid and pringling and I was horribly breathless. I stood for a little time like this, my head turned so that I could see up the passage. I was conscious only that there was a hideous danger abroad. Do you understand?

"And then, suddenly, my pluck came back to me. I was aware that the noise of the hoof beats sounded near the other end of the passage. I twisted quickly and got my camera to bear and snapped off the flashlight. Immediately afterward, Beaumont let fly a storm of shots down the passage and began to run, shouting: 'It's after Mary. Run! Run!'

"He rushed down the passage and I after him. We came out on the main landing and heard the sound of a hoof on the stairs and after that, nothing. And from thence onward, nothing.

"Down below us in the big hall I could see a number of the household 'round Miss Hisgins, who seemed to have fainted and there were several of the servants clumped together a little way off, staring up at the main landing and no one saying a single word. And about some twenty steps up the stairs was the old Captain Hisgins with a drawn sword in his hand where he had halted, just below the last hoof sound. I think I never saw anything finer than the old man standing there between his daughter and that infernal thing.

"I daresay you can understand the queer feeling of horror I had at passing that place on the stairs where the sounds had ceased. It was as if the monster were still standing there, invisible. And the peculiar thing was that we never heard another sound of the hoof, either up or down the stairs.

"After they had taken Miss Hisgins to her room I sent word that I should follow, so soon as they were ready for me. And presently, when a message came to tell me that I could come any time, I asked her father to give me a hand with my instrument box and between us we carried it into the girl's bedroom. I had the bed pulled well out into the middle of the room, after which I erected the electric pentacle 'round the bed

"Then I directed that lamps should be placed 'round the room, but that on no account must any light be made within the pentacle; neither must anyone pass in or out. The girl's mother I had placed within the pentacle and directed that her maid should sit without, ready to carry any message so as to make sure that Mrs. Hisgins did not have to leave the pentacle. I suggested also that the girl's father should stay the night in the room and that he had better be armed.

"When I left the bedroom I found Beaumont waiting outside the door in a miserable state of anxiety. I told him what I had done and explained to him that Miss Hisgins was probably perfectly safe within the 'protection'; but that in addition to her father remaining the night in the room, I intended to stand guard at the door. I told him that I should like him to keep me company, for I knew that he could never sleep, feeling as he did, and I should not be sorry to have a companion. Also, I wanted to have him under my own observation, for there was no doubt but that he was actually in greater danger in some ways than the girl. At least, that was my opinion and is still, as I think you will agree later.

"I asked him whether he would object to my drawing a pentacle 'round him for the night and got him to agree, but I saw that he did not know whether to be superstitious about it or to regard it more as a piece of foolish mumming; but he took it seriously enough when I gave him some particulars about the Black Veil case, when young Aster died. You remember, he said it was a piece of silly superstition and stayed outside. Poor devil!

"The night passed quietly enough until a little while before dawn when we both heard the sounds of a great horse galloping 'round and 'round the house just as old Captain Hisgins had described it. You can imagine how queer it made me feel and directly afterward, I heard someone stir within the bedroom. I knocked at the door, for I was uneasy, and the Captain came. I asked whether everything was right; to which he replied yes, and immediately asked me whether I had heard the galloping, so that I knew he had heard them also. I suggested that it might be well to leave the bedroom door open a little until the dawn came in, as there was certainly something abroad. This was done and he went back into the room, to be near his wife and daughter.

"I had better say here that I was doubtful whether there was any value in the 'Defense' about Miss Hisgins, for what I term the 'personal sounds' of the manifestation were so extraordinarily material that I was inclined to parallel the case with that one of Harford's where the hand of the child kept materializing within the pentacle and patting the floor. As you will remember, that was a hideous business.

"Yet, as it chanced, nothing further happened and so soon as daylight had fully come we all went off to bed.

"Beaumont knocked me up about midday and I went down and made breakfast into lunch. Miss Hisgins was there and seemed in very fair spirits, considering. She told me that I had made her feel almost safe for the first time for days. She told me also that her cousin, Harry Parsket, was coming down from London and she knew that he would do anything to help fight the ghost. And after that she and Beaumont went out into the grounds to have a little time together.

"I had a walk in the grounds myself and went 'round the house, but saw no traces of hoof marks and after that I spent the rest of the day making an examination of the house, but found nothing.

"I MADE an end of my search before dark and went to my room to dress for dinner. When I got down the cousin had just arrived and I found him one of the nicest men I have met for a long time. A chap with a tremendous amount of pluck, and the particular kind of man I like to have with me in a bad case like the one I was on. I could see that what puzzled him most was our belief in the genuineness of the haunting and I found myself almost wanting something to happen, just to show him how true it was. As it chanced, something did happen, with a vengeance.

"Beaumont and Miss Hisgins had gone out for a stroll just before the dusk and Captain Hisgins asked me to come into his study for a short chat whilst Parsket went upstairs with his traps, for he had no man with him.

"I had a long conversation with the old Captain in which I pointed out that the 'haunting' had evidently no particular connection with the house, but only with the girl herself and that the sooner she was married, the better as it would give Beaumont a right to be with her at all times and further than this, it might be that the manifestations would cease if the marriage were actually performed.

"The old man nodded agreement to this, especially to the first part and reminded me that three of the girls who were said to have been 'haunted' had been sent away from home and met their deaths whilst away. And then in the midst of our talk there came a pretty frightening interruption, for all at once the old butler rushed into the room, most extraordinarily pale:

"'Miss Mary, sir! Miss Mary, sir!' he gasped. 'She's screaming ... out in the Park, sir! And they say they can hear the Horse—'

"The Captain made one dive for a rack of arms and snatched down his old sword and ran out, drawing it as he ran. I dashed out and up the stairs, snatched my camera-flashlight and a heavy revolver, gave one yell at Parsket's door: 'The Horse!' and was down and into the grounds.

"Away in the darkness there was a confused shouting and I caught the sounds of shooting, out among the scattered trees. And then, from a patch of blackness to my left, there burst suddenly an infernal gobbling sort of neighing. Instantly I whipped 'round and snapped off the flashlight. The great light blazed out momentarily, showing me the leaves of a big tree close at hand, quivering in the night breeze, but I saw nothing else and then the ten-fold blackness came down upon me and I heard Parsket shouting a little way back to know whether I had seen anything.

"THE NEXT INSTANT he was beside me and I felt safer for his company, for there was some incredible thing near to us and I was momentarily blind because of the brightness of the flashlight. 'What was it? What was it?' he kept repeating in an excited voice. And all the time I was staring into the darkness and answering, mechanically, 'I don't know. I don't know.'

"There was a burst of shouting somewhere ahead and then a shot. We ran toward the sounds, yelling to the people not to shoot; for in the darkness and panic there was this danger also. Then there came two of the game-keepers racing hard up the drive with their lanterns and guns; and immediately afterward a row of lights dancing toward us from the house, carried by some of the men-servants.

"As the lights came up I saw we had come close to Beaumont. He was standing over Miss Hisgins and he had his revolver in his hand. Then I saw his face and there was a great wound across his forehead. By him was the Captain, turning his naked sword this way and that, and peering into the darkness; a little behind him stood the old butler, a battle-axe from one of the arm stands in the hall in his hands. Yet there was nothing strange to be seen anywhere.

"We got the girl into the house and left her with her mother and Beaumont, whilst a groom rode for a doctor. And then the rest of us, with four other keepers, all armed with guns and carrying lanterns, searched 'round the home park. But we found nothing.

"When we got back we found that the doctor had been. He had bound up Beaumont's wound, which luckily was not deep, and ordered Miss Hisgins straight to bed. I went upstairs with the

Captain and found Beaumont on guard outside of the girl's door. I asked him how he felt and then, so soon as the girl and her mother were ready for us, Captain Hisgins and I went into the bedroom and fixed the pentacle again 'round the bed. They had already got lamps about the room and after I had set the same order of watching as on the previous night, I joined Beaumont outside of the door.

"Parsket had come up while I had been in the bedroom and between us we got some idea from Beaumont as to what had happened out in the Park. It seems that they were coming home after their stroll from the direction of the West Lodge. It had got quite dark and suddenly Miss Hisgins said: 'Hush!' and came to a stand-still. He stopped and listened, but heard nothing for a little. Then he caught it—the sound of a horse, seemingly a long way off, galloping toward them over the grass. He told the girl that it was nothing and started to hurry her toward the house, but she was not deceived, of course. In less than a minute they heard it quite close to them in the darkness and they started running. Then Miss Hisgins caught her foot and fell. She began to scream and that is what the butler heard. As Beaumont lifted the girl he heard the hoofs come thudding right at him. He stood over her and fired all five chambers of his revolver right at the sounds. He told us that he was sure he saw something that looked like an enormous horse's head, right upon him in the light of the last flash of his pistol. Immediately afterward he was struck a tremendous blow which knocked him down and then the Captain and the butler came running up, shouting. The rest, of course, we knew.

"About ten o'clock the butler brought us up a tray, for which I was very glad, as the night before I had got rather hungry. I warned Beaumont, however, to be very particular not to drink any spirits and I also made him give me his pipe and matches. At midnight I drew a pentacle 'round him and Parsket and I sat one on each side of him, outside the pentacle, for I had no fear that there would be any mani-festation made against anyone except Beaumont or Miss Hisgins.

"After that we kept pretty quiet. The passage was lit by a big lamp at each end so that we had plenty of light and we were all armed, Beaumont and I with revolvers and Parsket with a shotgun. In addition to my weapon I had my camera and flashlight.

"Now and again we talked in whispers and twice the Captain came out of the bedroom to have a word with us. About half-past one we had all grown very silent and suddenly, about twenty minutes later, I held up my hand, silently, for there seemed to be a sound of galloping out in the night. I knocked on the bedroom door for the Captain to open it and when he came I whispered to him that we thought we heard the Horse. For some time we stayed listening, and both Parsket and the Captain thought they heard it; but now I was not so sure, neither was Beaumont. Yet afterward, I thought I heard it again.

"I told Captain Hisgins I thought he had better go into the bedroom and leave the door a little open and this he did. But from that time onward we heard nothing and presently the dawn came in and we all went very thankfully to bed.

"When I was called at lunchtime I had a little surprise, for Captain Hisgins told me that they had held a family council and had decided to take my advice and have the marriage without a day's more delay than possible. Beaumont was already on his way to London to get a special License and they hoped to have the wedding next day.

"This pleased me, for it seemed the sanest thing to be done in the extraordinary circumstances and meanwhile I should continue my investigations; but until the marriage was accomplished, my chief thought was to keep Miss Hisgins near to me.

"After lunch I thought I would take a few experimental photographs of Miss Hisgins and her surroundings. Sometimes the camera sees things that would seem very strange to normal human eyesight.

"With this intention and partly to make an excuse to keep her in my company as much as possible, I asked Miss Hisgins to join me in my experiments. She seemed glad to do this and I spent several hours with her, wandering all over the house, from room to room and whenever the impulse came I took a flashlight of her and the room or corridor in which we chanced to be at the moment.

"After we had gone right through the house in this fashion, I asked her whether she felt sufficiently brave to repeat the experiments in the cellars. She said yes, and so I rooted out Captain Hisgins and Parsket, for I was not going to take her even into what you might call artificial darkness without help and companionship at hand.

"When we were ready we went down into the wine cellar, Captain Hisgins carrying a shotgun and Parsket a specially prepared background and a lantern. I got the girl to stand in the middle of the cellar whilst Parsket and the Captain held out the background behind her. Then I fired off the flashlight, and we went into the next cellar where we repeated the experiment.

"Then in the third cellar, a tremendous, pitch-dark place, something extraordinary and horrible manifested itself. I had stationed Miss Hisgins in the center of the place, with her father and Parsket holding the background as before. When all was ready and just as I pressed the trigger of the 'flash,' there came in the cellar that dreadful, gobbling neighing that I had heard out in the Park. It seemed to come from somewhere above the girl and in the glare of the sudden light I saw that she was staring tensely upward, but at no visible thing. And then in the succeeding comparative darkness, I was shouting to the Captain and Parsket to run Miss Hisgins out into the daylight.

"This was done instantly and I shut and locked the door afterward making the First and Eighth signs of the Saaamaaa Ritual opposite to each post and connecting them across the threshold with a triple line.

"In the meanwhile Parsket and Captain Hisgins carried the girl to her mother and left her there, in a half fainting condition whilst I stayed on guard outside of the cellar door, feeling pretty horrible for I knew that there was some disgusting thing inside, and along with this feeling there was a sense of half ashamedness, rather miserable, you know, because I had exposed Miss Hisgins to the danger.

"I had got the Captain's shotgun and when he and Parsket came down again they were each carrying guns and lanterns. I could not possibly tell you the utter relief of spirit and body that came to me when I heard them coming, but just try to imagine what it was like, standing outside of that cellar. Can you?

"I remember noticing, just before I went to unlock the door, how white and ghastly Parsket looked and the old Captain was grey-looking and I wondered whether my face was like theirs. And this, you know, had its own distinct effect upon my nerves, for it seemed to bring the beastliness of the thing crashing down on to me in a fresh way. I know it was only sheer will power that carried me up to the door and made me turn the key.

"I paused one little moment and then with a nervy jerk sent the door wide open and held my lantern over my head. Parsket and the Captain came one on each side of me and held up their lanterns, but the place was absolutely empty. Of course, I did not trust to a casual look of this kind, but spent several hours with the help of the two others in sounding every square foot of the floor, ceiling and walls.

"Yet, in the end I had to admit that the place itself was absolutely normal and so we came away. But I sealed the door and outside, opposite each doorpost I made the First and Last signs of the Saaamaaa Ritual, joined them as before, with a triple line. Can you imagine what it was like, searching that cellar?

"When we got upstairs I inquired very anxiously how Miss Hisgins was and the girl came out herself to tell me that she was all right and that I was not to trouble about her, or blame myself, as I told her I had been doing.

"I felt happier then and went off to dress for dinner and after that was done, Parsket and I took one of the bathrooms to develop the negatives that I had been taking. Yet none of the plates had anything to tell us until we came to the one that was taken in the cellar.

Parsket was developing and I had taken a batch of the fixed plates out into the lamplight to examine them.

"I had just gone carefully through the lot when I heard a shout from Parsket and when I ran to him he was looking at a partly-developed negative which he was holding up to the red lamp. It showed the girl plainly, looking upward as I had seen her, but the thing that astonished me was the shadow of an enormous hoof, right above her, as if it were coming down upon her out of the shadows. And you know, I had run her bang into that danger. That was the thought that was chief in my mind.

"As soon as the developing was complete I fixed the plate and examined it carefully in a good light. There was no doubt about it at all, the thing above Miss Hisgins was an enormous, shadowy hoof. Yet I was no nearer to coming to any definite knowledge and the only thing I could do was to warn Parsket to say nothing about it to the girl for it would only increase her fright, but I showed the thing to her father for I considered it right that he should know.

"That night we took the same precaution for Miss Hisgins's safety as on the two previous nights and Parsket kept me company; yet the dawn came in without anything unusual having happened and I went off to bed.

"When I got down to lunch I learnt that Beaumont had wired to say that he would be in soon after four; also that a message had been sent to the Rector. And it was generally plain that the ladies of the house were in a tremendous fluster.

"Beaumont's train was late and he did not get home until five, but even then the Rector had not put in an appearance and the butler came in to say that the coachman had returned without him as he had been called away unexpectedly. Twice more during the evening the carriage was sent down, but the clergyman had not returned and we had to delay the marriage until the next day.

"That night I arranged the 'Defense' 'round the girl's bed and the Captain and his wife sat up with her as before. Beaumont, as I expected, insisted on keeping watch with me and he seemed in a curiously frightened mood; not for himself, you know, but for Miss Hisgins. He had a horrible feeling he told me, that there would be a final, dreadful attempt on his sweetheart that night.

"This, of course, I told him was nothing but nerves; yet really, it made me feel very anxious; for I have seen too much not to know that under such circumstances a premonitory conviction of impending danger is not necessarily to be put down entirely to nerves. In fact, Beaumont was so simply and earnestly convinced that the night would bring some extraordinary manifestation that I got Parsket to rig up a long cord from the wire of the butler's bell, to come along the passage handy.

"To the butler himself I gave directions not to undress and to give the same order to two of the footmen. If I rang he was to come instantly, with the footmen, carrying lanterns and the lanterns were to be kept ready lit all night. If for any reason the bell did not ring and I blew my whistle, he was to take that as a signal in the place of the bell.

"After I had arranged all these minor details I drew a pentacle about Beaumont and warned him very particularly to stay within it, whatever happened. And when this was done, there was nothing to do but wait and pray that the night would go as quietly as the night before.

"We scarcely talked at all and by about one a.m. we were all very tense and nervous so that at last Parsket got up and began to walk up and down the corridor to steady himself a bit. Presently I slipped off my pumps and joined him and we walked up and down, whispering occasionally for something over an hour, until in turning I caught my foot in the bell cord and went down on my face; but without hurting myself or making a noise.

"When I got up Parsket nudged me.

"'Did you notice that the bell never rang?' he whispered.

"'Jove!' I said, 'you're right.'

"'Wait a minute,' he answered. 'I'll bet it's only a kink somewhere in the cord.' He left his gun and slipped along the passage and taking the top lamp, tiptoed away into the house, carrying Beaumont's revolver ready in his right hand. He was a plucky chap, I remember thinking then, and again, later.

"Just then Beaumont motioned to me for absolute quiet. Directly afterward I heard the thing for which he listened—the sound of a horse galloping, out in the night. I think that I may say I fairly shivered. The sound died away and left a horrible, desolate, eerie feeling in the air, you know. I put my hand out to the bell cord, hoping Parsket had got it clear. Then I waited, glancing before and behind.

"Perhaps two minutes passed, full of what seemed like an almost unearthly quiet. And then, suddenly, down the corridor at the lighted end there sounded the clumping of a great hoof and instantly the lamp was thrown with a tremendous crash and we were in the dark. I tugged hard on the cord and blew the whistle; then I raised my snapshot and fired the flashlight. The corridor blazed into brilliant light, but there was nothing, and then the darkness fell like thunder. I heard the Captain at the bedroom door and shouted to him to bring out a lamp, quick; but instead something started to kick the door and I heard the Captain shouting within the bedroom and then the screaming of the women. I had a sudden horrible fear that the monster had got into the bedroom, but in the same instant from up the corridor there came abruptly the vile, gobbling neighing that we had heard in the park and the cellar. I blew the whistle again and groped blindly for the bell cord, shouting to Beaumont to stay in the Pentacle, whatever happened. I yelled again to the Captain to bring out a lamp and there came a smashing sound against the bedroom door. Then I had my matches in my hand, to get some light before that incredible, unseen Monster was upon us.

"The match scraped on the box and flared up dully and in the same instant I heard a faint sound behind me. I whipped 'round in a kind of mad terror and saw something in the light of the match—a monstrous horse-head close to Beaumont.

"'Look out, Beaumont!' I shouted in a sort of scream. 'It's behind you!'

"The match went out abruptly and instantly there came the huge bang of Parsket's double-barrel (both barrels at once), fired evidently single-handed by Beaumont close to my ear, as it seemed. I caught a momentary glimpse of the great head in the flash and of an enormous hoof amid the belch of fire and smoke seeming to be descending upon Beaumont. In the same instant I fired three chambers of my revolver. There was the sound of a dull blow and then that horrible, gobbling neigh broke out close to me. I fired twice at the sound. Immediately afterward something struck me and I was knocked backward. I got on to my knees and shouted for help at the top of my voice. I heard the women screaming behind the closed door of the bedroom and was dully aware that the door was being smashed from the inside, and directly afterward I knew that Beaumont was struggling with some hideous thing near to me. For an instant I held back, stupidly, paralyzed with funk and then, blindly and in a sort of rigid chill of goose flesh I went to help him, shouting his name. I can tell you, I was nearly sick with the naked fear I had on me. There came a little, choking scream out of the darkness, and at that I jumped forward into the dark. I gripped a vast, furry ear. Then something struck me another great blow knocking me sick. I hit back, weak and blind and gripped with my other hand at the incredible thing. Abruptly I was dimly aware of a tremendous crash behind me and a great burst of light. There were other lights in the passage and a noise of feet and shouting. My hand-grips were torn from the thing they held; I shut my eyes stupidly and heard a loud yell above me and then a heavy blow, like a butcher chopping meat and then something fell upon me.

"I was helped to my knees by the Captain and the butler. On the floor lay an enormous horse-head out of which protruded a man's trunk and legs. On the wrists were fixed great hoofs. It was the monster. The Captain cut something with the sword that he held in his hand and stooped and lifted off the mask, for that is what it was. I saw the face then of the man who had worn it. It was Parsket. He had a bad wound across the forehead where the Captain's sword had bit through the mask. I looked bewilderedly from him to Beaumont, who was sitting up, leaning against the wall of the corridor. Then I stared at Parsket again.

"'By Jove!' I said at last, and then I was quiet for I was so ashamed for the man. You can understand, can't you? And he was opening his eyes. And you know, I had grown so to like him.

"And then, you know, just as Parsket was getting back his wits and looking from one to the other of us and beginning to remember, there happened a strange and incredible thing. For from the end of the corridor there sounded suddenly, the clumping of a great hoof. I looked that way and then instantly at Parsket and saw a horrible fear in his face and eyes. He wrenched himself 'round, weakly, and stared in mad terror up the corridor to where the sound had been, and the rest of us stared, in a frozen group. I remember vaguely half sobs and whispers from Miss Hisgins's bedroom, all the while that I stared frightenedly up the corridor.

"The silence lasted several seconds and then, abruptly there came again the clumping of the great hoof, away at the end of the corridor. And immediately afterward the clungk, clunk—clungk, clunk of mighty hoofs coming down the passage toward us.

"Even then, you know, most of us thought it was some mechanism of Parsket's still at work and we were in the queerest mixture of fright and doubt. I think everyone looked at Parsket. And suddenly the Captain shouted out:

"'Stop this damned fooling at once. Haven't you done enough?'

"For my part, I was now frightened for I had a sense that there was something horrible and wrong. And then Parsket managed to gasp out:

"'It's not me! My God! It's not me! My God! It's not me.'

"And then, you know, it seemed to come home to everyone in an instant that there was really some dreadful thing coming down the passage. There was a mad rush to get away and even old Captain Hisgins gave back with the butler and the footmen. Beaumont fainted outright, as I found afterward, for he had been badly mauled.

I just flattened back against the wall, kneeling as I was, too stupid and dazed even to run. And almost in the same instant the ponderous hoof falls sounded close to me and seeming to shake the solid floor as they passed. Abruptly the great sounds ceased and I knew in a sort of sick fashion that the thing had halted opposite to the door of the girl's bedroom. And then I was aware that Parsket was standing rocking in the doorway with his arms spread across, so as to fill the doorway with his body. Parsket was extraordinarily pale and the blood was running down his face from the wound in his forehead; and then I noticed that he seemed to be looking at something in the passage with a peculiar, desperate, fixed, incredibly masterful gaze. But there was really nothing to be seen. And suddenly the clungk, clunk—clungk, clunk recommenced and passed onward down the passage. In the same moment Parsket pitched forward out of the doorway on to his face.

"There were shouts from the huddle of men down the passage and the two footmen and the butler simply ran, carrying their lanterns, but the Captain went against the side-wall with his back and put the lamp he was carrying over his head. The dull tread of the Horse went past him, and left him unharmed and I heard the monstrous hoof falls going away and away through the quiet house and after that a dead silence.

"Then the Captain moved and came toward us, very slow and shaky and with an extraordinarily grey face.

"I crept toward Parsket and the Captain came to help me. We turned him over and, you know, I knew in a moment that he was dead; but you can imagine what a feeling it sent through me.

"I looked at the Captain and suddenly he said:

"'That—That—That—' and I know that he was trying to tell me that Parsket had stood between his daughter and whatever it was that had gone down the passage. I stood up and steadied him, though I was not very steady myself. And suddenly his face began to work and he went down on to his knees by Parsket and cried like some shaken child. Then the women came out of the doorway of the bedroom and I turned away and left him to them, whilst I over to Beaumont.

"That is practically the whole story and the only thing that is left to me is to try to explain some of the puzzling parts, here and there.

"Perhaps you have seen that Parsket was in love with Miss Hisgins and this fact is the key to a good deal that was extraordinary. He was doubtless responsible for some portions of the 'haunting'; in fact I think for nearly everything, but, you know, I can prove nothing and what I have to tell you is chiefly the result of deduction.

"In the first place, it is obvious that Parsket's intention was to frighten Beaumont away and when he found that he could not do this, I think he grew so desperate that he really intended to kill him. I hate to say this, but the facts force me to think so.

"I am quite certain that it was Parsket who broke Beaumont's arm. He knew all the details of the so-called 'Horse Legend,' and got the idea to work upon the old story for his own end. He evidently had some method of slipping in and out of the house, probably through one of the many French windows, or possibly he had a key to one or two of the garden doors, and when he was supposed to be away, he was really coming down on the quiet and hiding somewhere in the neighborhood.

"The incident of the kiss in the dark hall I put down to sheer nervous imaginings on the part of Beaumont and Miss Hisgins, yet I must say that the sound of the horse outside of the front door is a little difficult to explain away. But I am still inclined to keep to my first idea on this point, that there was nothing really unnatural about it

"The hoof sounds in the billiard room and down the passage were done by Parsket from the floor below by bumping up against the paneled ceiling with a block of wood tied to one of the window hooks. I proved this by an examination which showed the dents in the woodwork.

"The sounds of the horse galloping 'round the house were possibly made also by Parsket, who must have had a horse tied up in the plantation nearby, unless, indeed, he made the sounds himself, but I do not see how he could have gone fast enough to produce the illusion. In any case, I don't feel perfect certainty on this point. I failed to find any hoof marks, as you remember.

"The gobbling neighing in the park was a ventriloquial achievement on the part of Parsket and the attack out there on Beaumont was also by him, so that when I thought he was in his bedroom, he must have been outside all the time and joined me after I ran out of the front door. This is almost probable. I mean that Parsket was the cause, for if it had been something more serious he would certainly have given up his foolishness, knowing that there was no longer any need for it. I cannot imagine how he escaped being shot, both then and in the last mad action of which I have just told you. He was enormously without fear of any kind for himself as you can see.

"The time when Parsket was with us, when we thought we heard the Horse galloping 'round the house, we must have been deceived. No one was very sure, except, of course, Parsket, who would naturally encourage the belief.

"The neighing in the cellar is where I consider there came the first suspicion into Parsket's mind that there was something more at work than his sham haunting. The neighing was done by him in the same way that he did it in the park; but when I remember how ghastly he looked I feel sure that the sounds must have had some infernal quality added to them which frightened the man himself. Yet, later, he would persuade himself that he had been getting fanciful. Of course, I must not forget that the effect upon Miss Hisgins must have made him feel pretty miserable.

"Then, about the clergyman being called away, we found afterward that it was a bogus errand, or, rather, call and it is apparent that Parsket was at the bottom of this, so as to get a few more hours in which to achieve his end and what that was, a very little imagination will show you; for he had found that Beaumont would not be frightened away. I hate to think this, but I'm bound to. Anyway, it is obvious that the man was temporarily a bit off his normal balance. Love's a queer disease!

"Then, there is no doubt at all but that Parsket left the cord to the butler's bell hitched somewhere so as to give him an excuse to slip away naturally to clear it. This also gave him the opportunity to remove one of the passage lamps. Then he had only to smash the other and the passage was in utter darkness for him to make the attempt on Beaumont.

"In the same way, it was he who locked the door of the bedroom and took the key (it was in his pocket). This prevented the Captain from bringing a light and coming to the rescue. But Captain Hisgins broke down the door with the heavy fender curb and it was his smashing the door that sounded so confusing and frightening in the darkness of the passage.

"The photograph of the monstrous hoof above Miss Hisgins in the cellar is one of the things that I am less sure about. It might have been faked by Parsket, whilst I was out of the room, and this would have been easy enough, to anyone who knew how. But, you know, it does not look like a fake. Yet, there is as much evidence of probability that it was faked, as against; and the thing is too vague for an examination to help to a definite decision so that I will express no opinion, one way or the other. It is certainly a horrible photograph.

"And now I come to that last, dreadful thing. There has been no further manifestation of anything abnormal so that there is an extraordinary uncertainty in my conclusions. If we had not heard those last sounds and if Parsket had not shown that enormous sense of fear the whole of this case could be explained in the way in which I have shown. And, in fact, as you have seen, I am of the opinion that almost all of it can be cleared up, but I see no way of going past the thing we heard at the last and the fear that Parsket showed.

"His death—no, that proves nothing. At the inquest it was described somewhat untechnically as due to heart spasm. That is normal enough and leaves us quite in the dark as to whether he died because he stood between the girl and some incredible thing of monstrosity.

"The look on Parsket's face and the thing he called out when he heard the great hoof sounds coming down the passage seem to show that he had the sudden realization of what before then may have been nothing more than a horrible suspicion. And his fear and appreciation of some tremendous danger approaching was probably more keenly real even than mine. And then he did the one fine, great thing!"

"And the cause?" I said. "What caused it?"

Carnacki shook his head.

"God knows," he answered, with a peculiar, sincere reverence. "If that thing was what it seemed to be one might suggest an explanation which would not offend one's reason, but which may be utterly wrong. Yet I have thought, though it would take a long lecture on Thought Induction to get you to appreciate my reasons, that Parsket had produced what I might term a kind of 'induced haunting,' a kind of induced simulation of his mental conceptions to his desperate thoughts and broodings. It is impossible to make it clearer in a few words."

"But the old story!" I said. "Why may not there have been something in that?"

"There may have been something in it," said Carnacki. "But I do not think it had anything to do with this. I have not clearly thought out my reasons, yet; but later I may be able to tell you why I think so."

"And the marriage? And the cellar—was there anything found there?" asked Taylor.

"Yes, the marriage was performed that day in spite of the tragedy," Carnacki told us. "It was the wisest thing to do considering the things that I cannot explain. Yes, I had the floor of that big cellar up, for I had a feeling I might find something there to give me some light. But there was nothing.

"You know, the whole thing is tremendous and extraordinary. I shall never forget the look on Parsket's face. And afterward the disgusting sounds of those great hoofs going away through the quiet house."

Carnacki stood up.

"Out you go!" he said in friendly fashion, using the recognized formula.

And we went presently out into the quiet of the Embankment, and so to our homes.

CHAPTER 5

THE SEARCHER OF THE END HOUSE

It was still evening, as I remember, and the four of us, Jessop, Arkright, Taylor and I, looked disappointedly at Carnacki, where he sat silent in his great chair.

We had come in response to the usual card of invitation, which—as you know—we have come to consider as a sure prelude to a good story; and now, after telling us the short incident of the Three Straw Platters, he had lapsed into a contented silence, and the night not half gone, as I have hinted.

However, as it chanced, some pitying fate jogged Carnacki's elbow, or his memory, and he began again, in his queer level way:—

"The 'Straw Platters' business reminds me of the 'Searcher' Case, which I have sometimes thought might interest you. It was some time ago, in fact a deuce of a long time ago, that the thing happened; and my experience of what I might term 'curious' things was very small at that time.

"I was living with my mother when it occurred, in a small house just outside of Appledorn, on the South Coast. The house was the last of a row of detached cottage villas, each house standing in its own garden; and very dainty little places they were, very old, and most of them smothered in roses; and all with those quaint old leaded windows, and doors of genuine oak. You must try to picture them for the sake of their complete niceness.

"Now I must remind you at the beginning that my mother and I had lived in that little house for two years; and in the whole of that time there had not been a single peculiar happening to worry us.

"And then, something happened.

"It was about two o'clock one morning, as I was finishing some letters, that I heard the door of my mother's bedroom open, and she came to the top of the stairs, and knocked on the banisters.

"'All right, dear,' I called; for I suppose she was merely reminding me that I should have been in bed long ago; then I heard her go back to her room, and I hurried my work, for fear she should lie awake, until she heard me safe up to my room.

"When I was finished, I lit my candle, put out the lamp, and went upstairs. As I came opposite the door of my mother's room, I saw that it was open, called good night to her, very softly, and asked whether I should close the door. As there was no answer, I knew that she had dropped off to sleep again, and I closed the door very gently, and turned into my room, just across the passage. As I did so, I experienced a momentary, half-aware sense of a faint, peculiar, disagreeable odor in the passage; but it was not until the following night that I realized I had noticed a smell that offended me. You follow me? It is so often like that—one suddenly knows a thing that really recorded itself on one's consciousness, perhaps a year before.

"The next morning at breakfast, I mentioned casually to my mother that she had 'dropped off,' and I had shut the door for her. To my surprise, she assured me she had never been out of her room. I reminded her about the two raps she had given upon the banister; but she still was certain I must be mistaken; and in the end I teased her, saying she had grown so accustomed to my bad habit of sitting up late, that she had come to call me in her sleep. Of course, she denied this, and I let the matter drop; but I was more than a little puzzled, and did not know whether to believe my own explanation, or to take the mater's, which was to put the noises down to the mice, and the open door to the fact that she couldn't have properly latched it, when she went to bed. I suppose, away in the subconscious part of me, I had a stirring of less reasonable thoughts; but certainly, I had no real uneasiness at that time.

"THE NEXT NIGHT there came a further development. About two thirty a.m., I heard my mother's door open, just as on the previous night, and immediately afterward she rapped sharply, on the banister, as it seemed to me. I stopped my work and called up that I would not be long. As she made no reply, and I did not hear her go back to bed, I had a quick sense of wonder whether she might not be doing it in her sleep, after all, just as I had said.

"With the thought, I stood up, and taking the lamp from the table, began to go toward the door, which was open into the passage. It was then I got a sudden nasty sort of thrill; for it came to me, all at once, that my mother never knocked, when I sat up too late; she always called. You will understand I was not really frightened in any way; only vaguely uneasy, and pretty sure she must really be doing the thing in her sleep.

"I went quickly up the stairs, and when I came to the top, my mother was not there; but her door was open. I had a bewildered sense though believing she must have gone quietly back to bed, without my hearing her. I entered her room and found her sleeping quietly and naturally; for the vague sense of trouble in me was sufficiently strong to make me go over to look at her.

"When I was sure that she was perfectly right in every way, I was still a little bothered; but much more inclined to think my suspicion correct and that she had gone quietly back to bed in her sleep, without knowing what she had been doing. This was the most reasonable thing to think, as you must see.

"And then it came to me, suddenly, that vague, queer, mildewy smell in the room; and it was in that instant I became aware I had smelt the same strange, uncertain smell the night before in the passage.

"I was definitely uneasy now, and began to search my mother's room; though with no aim or clear thought of anything, except to assure myself that there was nothing in the room. All the time, you know, I never expected really to find anything; only my uneasiness had to be assured.

"In the middle of my search my mother woke up, and of course I had to explain. I told her about her door opening, and the knocks on the banister, and that I had come up and found her asleep. I said nothing about the smell, which was not very distinct; but told her that the thing happening twice had made me a bit nervous, and possibly fanciful, and I thought I would take a look 'round, just to feel satisfied.

"I have thought since that the reason I made no mention of the smell, was not only that I did not want to frighten my mother, for I was scarcely that myself; but because I had only a vague half-knowledge that I associated the smell with fancies too indefinite and peculiar to bear talking about. You will understand that I am able now to analyze and put the thing into words; but then I did not even know my chief reason for saying nothing; let alone appreciate its possible significance.

"It was my mother, after all, who put part of my vague sensations into words:

"'What a disagreeable smell!' she exclaimed, and was silent a moment, looking at me. Then:—'You feel there's something wrong?' still looking at me, very quietly but with a little, nervous note of questioning expectancy.

"'I don't know,' I said. 'I can't understand it, unless you've really been walking about in your sleep.'

"'The smell,' she said.

"'Yes,' I replied. 'That's what puzzles me too. I'll take a walk through the house; but I don't suppose it's anything.'

"I lit her candle, and taking the lamp, I went through the other bedrooms, and afterward all over the house, including the three underground cellars, which was a little trying to the nerves, seeing that I was more nervous than I would admit.

"Then I went back to my mother, and told her there was really nothing to bother about; and, you know, in the end, we talked ourselves into believing it was nothing. My mother would not agree that she might have been sleepwalking; but she was ready to put the door opening down to the fault of the latch, which certainly snicked very lightly. As for the knocks, they might be the old warped wood-work of the house cracking a bit, or a mouse rattling a piece of loose plaster. The smell was more difficult to explain; but finally we agreed that it might easily be the queer night smell of the moist earth, coming in through the open window of my mother's room, from the back garden, or—for that matter—from the little churchyard beyond the big wall at the bottom of the garden.

"And so we quietened down, and finally I went to bed, and to sleep.

"I think this is certainly a lesson on the way we humans can delude ourselves; for there was not one of these explanations that my reason could really accept. Try to imagine yourself in the same circumstances, and you will see how absurd our attempts to explain the happenings really were.

"In the morning, when I came down to breakfast, we talked it all over again, and whilst we agreed that it was strange, we also agreed that we had begun to imagine funny things in the backs of our minds, which now we felt half ashamed to admit. This is very strange when you come to look into it; but very human.

"And then that night again my mother's door was slammed once more just after midnight. I caught up the lamp, and when I reached her door, I found it shut. I opened it quickly, and went in, to find my mother lying with her eyes open, and rather nervous; having been waked by the bang of the door. But what upset me more than anything, was the fact that there was a disgusting smell in the passage and in her room.

"Whilst I was asking her whether she was all right, a door slammed twice downstairs; and you can imagine how it made me feel. My mother and I looked at one another; and then I lit her candle, and taking the poker from the fender, went downstairs with the lamp, beginning to feel really nervous. The cumulative effect of so many queer happenings was getting hold of me; and all the apparently reasonable explanations seemed futile.

"The horrible smell seemed to be very strong in the downstairs passage; also in the front room and the cellars; but chiefly in the passage. I made a very thorough search of the house, and when I had finished, I knew that all the lower windows and doors were properly shut and fastened, and that there was no living thing in the house, beyond our two selves. Then I went up to my mother's room again, and we talked the thing over for an hour or more, and in the end came to the conclusion that we might, after all, be reading too much into a number of little things; but, you know, inside of us, we did not believe this.

"Later, when we had talked ourselves into a more comfortable state of mind, I said good night, and went off to bed; and presently managed to get to sleep.

"In the early hours of the morning, whilst it was still dark, I was waked by a loud noise. I sat up in bed, and listened. And from down-stairs, I heard:—bang, bang, bang, one door after another being slammed; at least, that is the impression the sounds gave to me.

"I jumped out of bed, with the tingle and shiver of sudden fright on me; and at the same moment, as I lit my candle, my door was pushed slowly open; I had left it unlatched, so as not to feel that my mother was quite shut off from me.

"'Who's there?' I shouted out, in a voice twice as deep as my natural one, and with a queer breathlessness, that sudden fright so often gives one. 'Who's there?'

"Then I heard my mother saying:—

"'It's me, Thomas. Whatever is happening downstairs?'

"She was in the room by this, and I saw she had her bedroom

poker in one hand, and her candle in the other. I could have smiled at her, had it not been for the extraordinary sounds downstairs.

"I got into my slippers, and reached down an old sword bayonet from the wall; then I picked up my candle, and begged my mother not to come; but I knew it would be little use, if she had made up her mind; and she had, with the result that she acted as a sort of rear-guard for me, during our search. I know, in some ways, I was very glad to have her with me, as you will understand.

"By this time, the door slamming had ceased, and there seemed, probably because of the contrast, to be an appalling silence in the house. However, I led the way, holding my candle high, and keeping the sword bayonet very handy. Downstairs we found all the doors wide open; although the outer doors and the windows were closed all right. I began to wonder whether the noises had been made by the doors after all. Of one thing only were we sure, and that was, there was no living thing in the house, beside ourselves, while every-where throughout the house, there was the taint of that disgusting odor.

"Of course it was absurd to try to make believe any longer. There was something strange about the house; and as soon as it was daylight, I set my mother to packing; and soon after breakfast, I saw her off by train.

"Then I set to work to try to clear up the mystery. I went first to the landlord, and told him all the circumstances. From him, I found that twelve or fifteen years back, the house had got rather a curious name from three or four tenants; with the result that it had remained empty a long while; in the end he had let it at a low rent to a Captain Tobias, on the one condition that he should hold his tongue, if he saw anything peculiar. The landlord's idea—as he told me frankly—was to free the house from these tales of 'something queer,' by keeping a tenant in it, and then to sell it for the best price he could get.

"However, when Captain Tobias left, after a ten years' tenancy, there was no longer any talk about the house; so when I offered to take it on a five years' lease, he had jumped at the offer. This was the whole story; so he gave me to understand. When I pressed him for details of the supposed peculiar happenings in the house, all those years back, he said the tenants had talked about a woman who always moved about the house at night. Some tenants never saw anything; but others would not stay out the first month's tenancy.

"One thing the landlord was particular to point out, that no tenant had ever complained about knockings, or door slamming. As for the smell, he seemed positively indignant about it; but why, I don't suppose he knew himself, except that he probably had some vague feeling that it was an indirect accusation on my part that the drains were not right.

"In the end, I suggested that he should come down and spend the night with me. He agreed at once, especially as I told him I intended to keep the whole business quiet, and try to get to the bottom of the curious affair; for he was anxious to keep the rumor of the haunting from getting about.

"About three o'clock that afternoon, he came down, and we made a thorough search of the house, which, however, revealed nothing unusual. Afterward, the landlord made one or two tests, which showed him the drainage was in perfect order; after that we made our preparations for sitting up all night.

"First, we borrowed two policemen's dark lanterns from the station nearby, and where the superintendent and I were friendly, and as soon as it was really dusk, the landlord went up to his house for his gun. I had the sword bayonet I have told you about; and when the landlord got back, we sat talking in my study until nearly midnight.

"Then we lit the lanterns and went upstairs. We placed the lanterns, gun and bayonet handy on the table; then I shut and sealed the bedroom doors; afterward we took our seats, and turned off the lights.

"From then until two o'clock, nothing happened; but a little after two, as I found by holding my watch near the faint glow of the closed lanterns, I had a time of extraordinary nervousness; and I bent toward the landlord, and whispered to him that I had a queer feeling something was about to happen, and to be ready with his lantern; at the same time I reached out toward mine. In the very instant I made this movement, the darkness which filled the passage seemed to become suddenly of a dull violet color; not, as if a light had been shone; but as if the natural blackness of the night had changed color. And then, coming through this violet night, through this violet-colored gloom, came a little naked Child, running. In an extraordinary way, the Child seemed not to be distinct from the surrounding gloom; but almost as if it were a concentration of that extraordinary atmosphere; as if that gloomy color which had changed the night, came from the Child. It seems impossible to make clear to you; but try to understand it.

"The Child went past me, running, with the natural movement of the legs of a chubby human child, but in an absolute and inconceivable silence. It was a very small Child, and must have passed under the table; but I saw the Child through the table, as if it had been only a slightly darker shadow than the colored gloom. In the same instant, I saw that a fluctuating glimmer of violet light outlined the metal of the gun-barrels and the blade of the sword bayonet, making them seem like faint shapes of glimmering light, floating unsupported where the tabletop should have shown solid.

"Now, curiously, as I saw these things, I was subconsciously aware that I heard the anxious breathing of the landlord, quite clear and labored, close to my elbow, where he waited nervously with his hands on the lantern. I realized in that moment that he saw nothing; but waited in the darkness, for my warning to come true.

"Even as I took heed of these minor things, I saw the Child jump to one side, and hide behind some half-seen object that was certainly nothing belonging to the passage. I stared, intently, with a most extraordinary thrill of expectant wonder, with fright making goose flesh of my back. And even as I stared, I solved for myself the less important problem of what the two black clouds were that hung over a part of the table. I think it very curious and interesting, the double working of the mind, often so much more apparent during times of stress. The two clouds came from two faintly shining shapes, which I knew must be the metal of the lanterns; and the things that looked black to the sight with which I was then seeing, could be nothing else but what to normal human sight is known as light. This phenomenon I have always remembered. I have twice seen a somewhat similar thing; in the Dark Light Case and in that trouble of Maetheson's, which you know about.

"Even as I understood this matter of the lights, I was looking to my left, to understand why the Child was hiding. And suddenly, I heard the landlord shout out:—'The Woman!' But I saw nothing. I had a disagreeable sense that something repugnant was near to me, and I was aware in the same moment that the landlord was gripping my arm in a hard, frightened grip. Then I was looking back to where the Child had hidden. I saw the Child peeping out from behind its hiding place, seeming to be looking up the passage; but whether in fear I could not tell. Then it came out, and ran headlong away, through the place where should have been the wall of my mother's bedroom; but the Sense with which I was seeing these things, showed me the wall only as a vague, upright shadow, unsubstantial. And immediately the child was lost to me, in the dull violet gloom. At the same time, I felt the landlord press back against me, as if something had passed close to him; and he called out again, a hoarse sort of cry:—'The Woman! The Woman!' and turned the shade clumsily from off his lantern. But I had seen no Woman; and the passage showed empty, as he shone the beam of his light jerkily to and fro; but chiefly in the direction of the doorway of my mother's room.

"He was still clutching my arm, and had risen to his feet; and now, mechanically and almost slowly, I picked up my lantern and turned on the light. I shone it, a little dazedly, at the seals upon the doors; but none were broken; then I sent the light to and fro, up and down the passage; but there was nothing; and I turned to the land-lord, who was saying something in a rather incoherent fashion. As my light passed over his face, I noted, in a dull sort of way, that he was drenched with sweat.

"Then my wits became more handleable, and I began to catch the drift of his words:—'Did you see her? Did you see her?' he was saying, over and over again; and then I found myself telling him, in quite a level voice, that I had not seen any Woman. He became more coherent then, and I found that he had seen a Woman come from the end of the passage, and go past us; but he could not describe her, except that she kept stopping and looking about her, and had even peered at the wall, close beside him, as if looking for something. But what seemed to trouble him most, was that she had not seemed to see him at all. He repeated this so often, that in the end I told him, in an absurd sort of way, that he ought to be very glad she had not. What did it all mean? was the question; somehow I was not so frightened, as utterly bewildered. I had seen less then, than since; but what I had seen, had made me feel adrift from my anchorage of Reason.

"What did it mean? He had seen a Woman, searching for something. I had not seen this Woman. I had seen a Child, running away, and hiding from Something or Someone. He had not seen the Child, or the other things—only the Woman. And I had not seen her. What did it all mean?

"I had said nothing to the landlord about the Child. I had been too bewildered, and I realized that it would be futile to attempt an explanation. He was already stupid with the thing he had seen; and not the kind of man to understand. All this went through my mind as we stood there, shining the lanterns to and fro. All the time, intermingled with a streak of practical reasoning, I was questioning myself, what did it all mean? What was the Woman searching for; what was the Child running from?

"Suddenly, as I stood there, bewildered and nervous, making random answers to the landlord, a door below was violently slammed, and directly I caught the horrible reek of which I have told you.

"'There!' I said to the landlord, and caught his arm, in my turn. 'The Smell! Do you smell it?'

"He looked at me so stupidly that in a sort of nervous anger, I shook him.

"'Yes,' he said, in a queer voice, trying to shine the light from his shaking lantern at the stair head.

"'Come on!' I said, and picked up my bayonet; and he came, carrying his gun awkwardly. I think he came, more because he was afraid to be left alone, than because he had any pluck left, poor beggar. I never sneer at that kind of funk, at least very seldom; for when it takes hold of you, it makes rags of your courage.

"I led the way downstairs, shining my light into the lower passage, and afterward at the doors to see whether they were shut; for I had closed and latched them, placing a corner of a mat against each door, so I should know which had been opened.

"I saw at once that none of the doors had been opened; then I threw the beam of my light down alongside the stairway, in order to see the mat I had placed against the door at the top of the cellar stairs. I got a horrid thrill; for the mat was flat! I paused a couple of seconds, shining my light to and fro in the passage, and holding fast to my courage, I went down the stairs.

"As I came to the bottom step, I saw patches of wet all up and down the passage. I shone my lantern on them. It was the imprint of a wet foot on the oilcloth of the passage; not an ordinary footprint, but a queer, soft, flabby, spreading imprint, that gave me a feeling of extraordinary horror.

"Backward and forward I flashed the light over the impossible marks and saw them everywhere. Suddenly I noticed that they led to each of the closed doors. I felt something touch my back, and glanced 'round swiftly, to find the landlord had come close to me, almost pressing against me, in his fear.

"'It's all right,' I said, but in a rather breathless whisper, meaning to put a little courage into him; for I could feel that he was shaking through all his body. Even then as I tried to get him steadied enough to be of some use, his gun went off with a tremendous bang. He jumped, and yelled with sheer terror; and I swore because of the shock.

"'Give it to me, for God's sake!' I said, and slipped the gun from his hand; and in the same instant there was a sound of running steps up the garden path, and immediately the flash of a bull's-eye lantern upon the fan light over the front door. Then the door was tried, and directly afterward there came a thunderous knocking, which told me a policeman had heard the shot.

"I went to the door, and opened it. Fortunately the constable knew me, and when I had beckoned him in, I was able to explain matters in a very short time. While doing this, Inspector Johnstone came up the path, having missed the officer, and seeing lights and the open door. I told him as briefly as possible what had occurred, and did not mention the Child or the Woman; for it would have seem too fantastic for him to notice. I showed him the queer, wet footprints and how they went toward the closed doors. I explained quickly about the mats, and how that the one against the cellar door was flat, which showed the door had been opened.

"The inspector nodded, and told the constable to guard the door at the top of the cellar stairs. He then asked the hall lamp to be lit, after which he took the policeman's lantern, and led the way into the front room. He paused with the door wide open, and threw the light all 'round; then he jumped into the room, and looked behind the door; there was no one there; but all over the polished oak floor, between the scattered rugs, went the marks of those horrible spreading footprints; and the room permeated with the horrible odor.

"The inspector searched the room carefully, and then went into the middle room, using the same precautions. There was nothing in the middle room, or in the kitchen or pantry; but everywhere went the wet footmarks through all the rooms, showing plainly wherever there were woodwork or oilcloth; and always there was the smell.

"The inspector ceased from his search of the rooms, and spent a minute in trying whether the mats would really fall flat when the doors were open, or merely ruckle up in a way as to appear they had been untouched; but in each case, the mats fell flat, and remained so.

"'Extraordinary!' I heard Johnstone mutter to himself. And then he went toward the cellar door. He had inquired at first whether there were windows to the cellar, and when he learned there was no way out, except by the door, he had left this part of the search to the last.

"As Johnstone came up to the door, the policeman made a motion of salute, and said something in a low voice; and something in the tone made me flick my light across him. I saw then that the man was very white, and he looked strange and bewildered.

"'What?' said Johnstone impatiently. 'Speak up!'

"'A woman come along 'ere, sir, and went through this 'ere door,' said the constable, clearly, but with a curious monotonous intonation that is sometimes heard from an unintelligent man.

"'Speak up!' shouted the inspector.

"'A woman come along and went through this 'ere door,' repeated the man, monotonously.

"The inspector caught the man by the shoulder, and deliberately sniffed his breath.

"'No!' he said. And then sarcastically:—'I hope you held the door open politely for the lady.'

"'The door weren't opened, sir,' said the man, simply.

"'Are you mad—' began Johnstone.

"'No,' broke in the landlord's voice from the back. Speaking steadily enough. 'I saw the Woman upstairs.' It was evident that he had got back his control again.

"'I'm afraid, Inspector Johnstone,' I said, 'that there's more in this than you think. I certainly saw some very extraordinary things upstairs.'

"The inspector seemed about to say something; but instead, he turned again to the door, and flashed his light down and 'round about the mat. I saw then that the strange, horrible footmarks came straight up to the cellar door; and the last print showed under the door; yet the policeman said the door had not been opened.

"And suddenly, without any intention, or realization of what I was saying, I asked the landlord:—

"'What were the feet like?'

"I received no answer; for the inspector was ordering the constable to open the cellar door, and the man was not obeying. Johnstone repeated the order, and at last, in a queer automatic way, the man obeyed, and pushed the door open. The loathsome smell beat up at us, in a great wave of horror, and the inspector came backward a step.

"'My God!' he said, and went forward again, and shone his light down the steps; but there was nothing visible, only that on each step showed the unnatural footprints.

"The inspector brought the beam of the light vividly on the top step; and there, clear in the light, there was something small, moving. The inspector bent to look, and the policeman and I with him. I don't want to disgust you; but the thing we looked at was a maggot. The policeman backed suddenly out of the doorway:

"'The churchyard,' he said, '... at the back of the 'ouse.'

"'Silence!' said Johnstone, with a queer break in the word, and I knew that at last he was frightened. He put his lantern into the doorway, and shone it from step to step, following the footprints down into the darkness; then he stepped back from the open doorway, and we all gave back with him. He looked 'round, and I had a feeling that he was looking for a weapon of some kind.

"'Your gun,' I said to the landlord, and he brought it from the front hall, and passed it over to the inspector, who took it and ejected the empty shell from the right barrel. He held out his hand for a live cartridge, which the landlord brought from his pocket. He loaded the gun and snapped the breech. He turned to the constable:—

"'Come on,' he said, and moved toward the cellar doorway.

"'I ain't comin', sir,' said the policeman, very white in the face.

"With a sudden blaze of passion, the inspector took the man by the scruff and hove him bodily down into the darkness, and he went downward, screaming. The inspector followed him instantly, with his lantern and the gun; and I after the inspector, with the bayonet ready. Behind me, I heard the landlord.

"At the bottom of the stairs, the inspector was helping the policeman to his feet, where he stood swaying a moment, in a bewildered fashion; then the inspector went into the front cellar, and his man followed him in stupid fashion; but evidently no longer with any thought of running away from the horror.

"We all crowded into the front cellar, flashing our lights to and fro. Inspector Johnstone was examining the floor, and I saw that the footmarks went all 'round the cellar, into all the corners, and across the floor. I thought suddenly of the Child that was running away from Something. Do you see the thing that I was seeing vaguely?

"We went out of the cellar in a body, for there was nothing to be found. In the next cellar, the footprints went everywhere in that queer erratic fashion, as of someone searching for something, or following some blind scent.

"In the third cellar the prints ended at the shallow well that had been the old water supply of the house. The well was full to the brim, and the water so clear that the pebbly bottom was plainly to be seen, as we shone the lights into the water. The search came to an abrupt end, and we stood about the well, looking at one another, in an absolute, horrible silence.

"Johnstone made another examination of the footprints; then he shone his light again into the clear shallow water, searching each inch of the plainly seen bottom; but there was nothing there. The cellar was full of the dreadful smell; and everyone stood silent, except for the constant turning of the lamps to and fro around the cellar.

"The inspector looked up from his search of the well, and nodded quietly across at me, with his sudden acknowledgment that our belief was now his belief, the smell in the cellar seemed to grow more dreadful, and to be, as it were, a menace—the material expression that some monstrous thing was there with us, invisible.

"'I think—' began the inspector, and shone his light toward the stairway; and at this the constable's restraint went utterly, and he ran for the stairs, making a queer sound in his throat.

"The landlord followed, at a quick walk, and then the inspector and I. He waited a single instant for me, and we went up together, treading on the same steps, and with our lights held backward. At the top, I slammed and locked the stair door, and wiped my forehead, and my hands were shaking.

"The inspector asked me to give his man a glass of whisky, and then he sent him on his beat. He stayed a short while with the landlord and me, and it was arranged that he would join us again the following night and watch the Well with us from midnight until daylight. Then he left us, just as the dawn was coming in. The landlord and I locked up the house, and went over to his place for a sleep.

"In the afternoon, the landlord and I returned to the house, to make arrangements for the night. He was very quiet, and I felt he was to be relied on, now that he had been 'salted,' as it were, with his fright of the previous night.

"We opened all the doors and windows, and blew the house through very thoroughly; and in the meanwhile, we lit the lamps in the house, and took them into the cellars, where we set them all about, so as to have light everywhere. Then we carried down three chairs and a table, and set them in the cellar where the well was sunk. After that, we stretched thin piano wire across the cellar, about nine inches from the floor, at such a height that it should catch anything moving about in the dark.

"When this was done, I went through the house with the landlord, and sealed every window and door in the place, excepting only the front door and the door at the top of the cellar stairs.

"Meanwhile, a local wire-smith was making something to my order; and when the landlord and I had finished tea at his house, we went down to see how the smith was getting on. We found the thing complete. It looked rather like a huge parrot's cage, without any bottom, of very heavy gage wire, and stood about seven feet high and was four feet in diameter. Fortunately, I remembered to have it made longitudinally in two halves, or else we should never have got it through the doorways and down the cellar stairs.

"I told the wire-smith to bring the cage up to the house so he could fit the two halves rigidly together. As we returned, I called in at an ironmonger's, where I bought some thin hemp rope and an iron rack pulley, like those used in Lancashire for hauling up the ceiling clothes racks, which you will find in every cottage. I bought also a couple of pitchforks.

"'We shan't want to touch it,' I said to the landlord; and he nodded, rather white all at once.

"As soon as the cage arrived and had been fitted together in the cellar, I sent away the smith; and the landlord and I suspended it over the well, into which it fitted easily. After a lot of trouble, we managed to hang it so perfectly central from the rope over the iron pulley, that when hoisted to the ceiling and dropped, it went every time plunk into the well, like a candle-extinguisher. When we had it finally arranged, I hoisted it up once more, to the ready position, and made the rope fast to a heavy wooden pillar, which stood in the middle of the cellar.

"By ten o'clock, I had everything arranged, with the two pitch-forks and the two police lanterns; also some whisky and sandwiches. Underneath the table I had several buckets full of disinfectant.

"A little after eleven o'clock, there was a knock at the front door, and when I went, I found Inspector Johnstone had arrived, and brought with him one of his plainclothes men. You will understand how pleased I was to see there would be this addition to our watch; for he looked a tough, nerveless man, brainy and collected; and one I should have picked to help us with the horrible job I felt pretty sure we should have to do that night.

"When the inspector and the detective had entered, I shut and locked the front door; then, while the inspector held the light, I sealed the door carefully, with tape and wax. At the head of the cellar stairs, I shut and locked that door also, and sealed it in the same way.

"As we entered the cellar, I warned Johnstone and his man to be careful not to fall over the wires; and then, as I saw his surprise at my arrangements, I began to explain my ideas and intentions, to all of which he listened with strong approval. I was pleased to see also that the detective was nodding his head, as I talked, in a way that showed he appreciated all my precautions.

"As he put his lantern down, the inspector picked up one of the pitchforks, and balanced it in his hand; he looked at me, and nodded.

"'The best thing,' he said. 'I only wish you'd got two more.'

"Then we all took our seats, the detective getting a washing stool from the corner of the cellar. From then, until a quarter to twelve, we talked quietly, whilst we made a light supper of whisky and sandwiches; after which, we cleared everything off the table, excepting the lanterns and the pitchforks. One of the latter, I handed to the inspector; the other I took myself, and then, having set my chair so as to be handy to the rope which lowered the cage into the well, I went 'round the cellar and put out every lamp.

"I groped my way to my chair, and arranged the pitchfork and the dark lantern ready to my hand; after which I suggested that everyone should keep an absolute silence throughout the watch. I asked, also, that no lantern should be turned on, until I gave the word.

"I put my watch on the table, where a faint glow from my lantern made me able to see the time. For an hour nothing happened, and everyone kept an absolute silence, except for an occasional uneasy movement.

"About half-past one, however, I was conscious again of the same extraordinary and peculiar nervousness, which I had felt on the previous night. I put my hand out quickly, and eased the hitched rope from around the pillar. The inspector seemed aware of the movement; for I saw the faint light from his lantern, move a little, as if he had suddenly taken hold of it, in readiness.

"A minute later, I noticed there was a change in the color of the night in the cellar, and it grew slowly violet tinted upon my eyes. I glanced to and fro, quickly, in the new darkness, and even as I looked, I was conscious that the violet color deepened. In the direction of the well, but seeming to be at a great distance, there was, as it were, a nucleus to the change; and the nucleus came swiftly toward us, appearing to come from a great space, almost in a single moment. It came near, and I saw again that it was a little naked Child, running, and seeming to be of the violet night in which it ran.

"The Child came with a natural running movement, exactly as I described it before; but in a silence so peculiarly intense, that it was as if it brought the silence with it. About half-way between the well and the table, the Child turned swiftly, and looked back at something invisible to me; and suddenly it went down into a crouching attitude, and seemed to be hiding behind something that showed vaguely; but there was nothing there, except the bare floor of the cellar; nothing, I mean, of our world.

"I could hear the breathing of the three other men, with a wonderful distinctness; and also the tick of my watch upon the table seemed to sound as loud and as slow as the tick of an old grandfather's clock. Someway I knew that none of the others saw what I was seeing.

"Abruptly, the landlord, who was next to me, let out his breath with a little hissing sound; I knew then that something was visible to him. There came a creak from the table, and I had a feeling that the inspector was leaning forward, looking at something that I could not see. The landlord reached out his hand through the darkness, and fumbled a moment to catch my arm:—

"'The Woman!' he whispered, close to my ear. 'Over by the well.'

"I stared hard in that direction; but saw nothing, except that the violet color of the cellar seemed a little duller just there.

"I looked back quickly to the vague place where the Child was hiding. I saw it was peering back from its hiding place. Suddenly it rose and ran straight for the middle of the table, which showed only as vague shadow half-way between my eyes and the unseen floor. As the Child ran under the table, the steel prongs of my pitchfork glimmered with a violet, fluctuating light. A little way off, there showed high up in the gloom, the vaguely shining outline of the other fork, so I knew the inspector had it raised in his hand, ready. There was no doubt but that he saw something. On the table, the metal of the five lanterns shone with the same strange glow; and about each lantern there was a little cloud of absolute blackness, where the phenomenon that is light to our natural eyes, came through the fittings; and in this complete darkness, the metal of each lantern showed plain, as might a cat's-eye in a nest of black cotton wool.

"Just beyond the table, the Child paused again, and stood, seeming to oscillate a little upon its feet, which gave the impression that it was lighter and vaguer than a thistle-down; and yet, in the same moment, another part of me seemed to know that it was to me, as something that might be beyond thick, invisible glass, and subject to conditions and forces that I was unable to comprehend.

"The Child was looking back again, and my gaze went the same way. I stared across the cellar, and saw the cage hanging clear in the violet light, every wire and tie outlined with its glimmering; above it there was a little space of gloom, and then the dull shining of the iron pulley which I had screwed into the ceiling.

"I stared in a bewildered way 'round the cellar; there were thin lines of vague fire crossing the floor in all directions; and suddenly I remembered the piano wire that the landlord and I had stretched. But there was nothing else to be seen, except that near the table there were indistinct glimmerings of light, and at the far end the outline of a dull glowing revolver, evidently in the detective's pocket. I remember a sort of subconscious satisfaction, as I settled the point in a queer automatic fashion. On the table, near to me, there was a little shapeless collection of the light; and this I knew, after an instant's consideration, to be the steel portions of my watch.

"I had looked several times at the Child, and 'round at the cellar, whilst I was decided these trifles; and had found it still in that attitude of hiding from something. But now, suddenly, it ran clear away into the distance, and was nothing more than a slightly deeper colored nucleus far away in the strange colored atmosphere.

"The landlord gave out a queer little cry, and twisted over against me, as if to avoid something. From the inspector there came a sharp breathing sound, as if he had been suddenly drenched with cold water. Then suddenly the violet color went out of the night, and I was conscious of the nearness of something monstrous and repugnant.

"There was a tense silence, and the blackness of the cellar seemed absolute, with only the faint glow about each of the lanterns on the table. Then, in the darkness and the silence, there came a faint tinkle of water from the well, as if something were rising noiselessly out of it, and the water running back with a gentle tinkling. In the same instant, there came to me a sudden waft of the awful smell.

"I gave a sharp cry of warning to the inspector, and loosed the rope. There came instantly the sharp splash of the cage entering the water; and then, with a stiff, frightened movement, I opened the shutter of my lantern, and shone the light at the cage, shouting to the others to do the same.

"As my light struck the cage, I saw that about two feet of it projected from the top of the well, and there was something protruding up out of the water, into the cage. I stared, with a feeling that I recognized the thing; and then, as the other lanterns were opened, I saw that it was a leg of mutton. The thing was held by a brawny fist and arm, that rose out of the water. I stood utterly bewildered, watching to see what was coming. In a moment there rose into view a great bearded face, that I felt for one quick instant was the face of a drowned man, long dead. Then the face opened at the mouth part, and spluttered and coughed. Another big hand came into view, and wiped the water from the eyes, which blinked rapidly, and then fixed themselves into a stare at the lights.

"From the detective there came a sudden shout:—

"'Captain Tobias!' he shouted, and the inspector echoed him; and instantly burst into loud roars of laughter.

"The inspector and the detective ran across the cellar to the cage; and I followed, still bewildered. The man in the cage was holding the leg of mutton as far away from him, as possible, and holding his nose.

"'Lift thig dam trap, quig!' he shouted in a stifled voice; but the inspector and the detective simply doubled before him, and tried to hold their noses, whilst they laughed, and the light from their lanterns went dancing all over the place.

"'Quig! quig!' said the man in the cage, still holding his nose, and trying to speak plainly.

"Then Johnstone and the detective stopped laughing, and lifted the cage. The man in the well threw the leg across the cellar, and turned swiftly to go down into the well; but the officers were too quick for him, and had him out in a twinkling. Whilst they held him, dripping upon the floor, the inspector jerked his thumb in the direction of the offending leg, and the landlord, having harpooned it with one of the pitchforks, ran with it upstairs and so into the open air.

"Meanwhile, I had given the man from the well a stiff tot of whisky; for which he thanked me with a cheerful nod, and having emptied the glass at a draft, held his hand for the bottle, which he finished, as if it had been so much water.

"As you will remember, it was a Captain Tobias who had been the previous tenant; and this was the very man, who had appeared from the well. In the course of the talk that followed, I learned the reason for Captain Tobias leaving the house; he had been wanted by the police for smuggling. He had undergone imprisonment; and had been released only a couple of weeks earlier.

"He had returned to find new tenants in his old home. He had entered the house through the well, the walls of which were not continued to the bottom (this I will deal with later); and gone up by a little stairway in the cellar wall, which opened at the top through a panel beside my mother's bedroom. This panel was opened, by revolving the left doorpost of the bedroom door, with the result that the bedroom door always became unlatched, in the process of opening the panel.

"The captain complained, without any bitterness, that the panel had warped, and that each time he opened it, it made a cracking noise. This had been evidently what I mistook for raps. He would not give his reason for entering the house; but it was pretty obvious that he had hidden something, which he wanted to get. However, as he found it impossible to get into the house without the risk of being caught, he decided to try to drive us out, relying on the bad reputation of the house, and his own artistic efforts as a ghost. I must say he succeeded. He intended then to rent the house again, as before; and would then, of course have plenty of time to get whatever he had hidden. The house suited him admirably; for there was a passage—as he showed me afterward—connecting the dummy well with the crypt of the church beyond the garden wall; and these, in turn, were connected with certain caves in the cliffs, which went down to the beach beyond the church.

"In the course of his talk, Captain Tobias offered to take the house off my hands; and as this suited me perfectly, for I was about stalled with it, and the plan also suited the landlord, it was decided that no steps should be taken against him; and that the whole business should be hushed up.

"I asked the captain whether there was really anything queer about the house; whether he had ever seen anything. He said yes, that he had twice seen a Woman going about the house. We all looked at one another, when the captain said that. He told us she never bothered him, and that he had only seen her twice, and on each occasion it had followed a narrow escape from the Revenue people.

"Captain Tobias was an observant man; he had seen how I had placed the mats against the doors; and after entering the rooms, and walking all about them, so as to leave the foot-marks of an old pair of wet woollen slippers everywhere, he had deliberately put the mats back as he found them.

"The maggot which had dropped from his disgusting leg of mutton had been an accident, and beyond even his horrible planning. He was hugely delighted to learn how it had affected us.

"The moldy smell I had noticed was from the little closed stairway, when the captain opened the panel. The door slamming was also another of his contributions.

"I come now to the end of the captain's ghost play; and to the difficulty of trying to explain the other peculiar things. In the first place, it was obvious there was something genuinely strange in the house; which made itself manifest as a Woman. Many different people had seen this Woman, under differing circumstances, so it is impossible to put the thing down to fancy; at the same time it must seem extraordinary that I should have lived two years in the house, and seen nothing; whilst the policeman saw the Woman, before he had been there twenty minutes; the landlord, the detective, and the inspector all saw her.

"I can only surmise that fear was in every case the key, as I might say, which opened the senses to the presence of the Woman. The policeman was a highly-strung man, and when he became frightened, was able to see the Woman. The same reasoning applies all 'round. I saw nothing, until I became really frightened; then I saw, not the Woman; but a Child, running away from Something or Someone. However, I will touch on that later. In short, until a very strong degree of fear was present, no one was affected by the Force which made Itself evident, as a Woman. My theory explains why some tenants were never aware of anything strange in the house, whilst others left immediately. The more sensitive they were, the less would be the degree of fear necessary to make them aware of the Force present in the house.

"The peculiar shining of all the metal objects in the cellar, had been visible only to me. The cause, naturally I do not know; neither do I know why I, alone, was able to see the shining."

"The Child," I asked. "Can you explain that part at all? Why you didn't see the Woman, and why they didn't see the Child. Was it merely the same Force, appearing differently to different people?"

"No," said Carnacki, "I can't explain that. But I am quite sure that the Woman and the Child were not only two complete and different entities; but even they were each not in quite the same planes of existence.

"To give you a root idea, however, it is held in the Sigsand MS. that a child 'stillborn' is 'Snatyched back bye thee Haggs.' This is crude; but may yet contain an elemental truth. Yet, before I make this clearer, let me tell you a thought that has often been made. It may be that physical birth is but a secondary process; and that prior to the possibility, the Mother Spirit searches for, until it finds, the small Element—the primal Ego or child's soul. It may be that a certain waywardness would cause such to strive to evade capture by the Mother Spirit. It may have been such a thing as this, that I saw. I have always tried to think so; but it is impossible to ignore the sense of repulsion that I felt when the unseen Woman went past me. This repulsion carries forward the idea suggested in the Sigsand MS., that a stillborn child is thus, because its ego or spirit has been snatched back by the 'Hags.' In other words, by certain of the Monstrosities of the Outer Circle. The thought is inconceivably terrible, and probably the more so because it is so fragmentary. It leaves us with the conception of a child's soul adrift half-way between two lives, and running through Eternity from Something incredible and inconceivable (because not understood) to our senses.

"The thing is beyond further discussion; for it is futile to attempt to discuss a thing, to any purpose, of which one has a knowledge so fragmentary as this. There is one thought, which is often mine. Perhaps there is a Mother Spirit—"

"And the well?" said Arkwright. "How did the captain get in from the other side?"

"As I said before," answered Carnacki. "The side walls of the well did not reach to the bottom; so that you had only to dip down into the water, and come up again on the other side of the wall, under the cellar floor, and so climb into the passage. Of course, the water was the same height on both sides of the walls. Don't ask me who made the well entrance or the little stairway; for I don't know. The house was very old, as I have told you; and that sort of thing was useful in the old days."

"And the Child," I said, coming back to the thing which chiefly interested me. "You would say that the birth must have occurred in that house; and in this way, one might suppose that the house to have become en rapport, if I can use the word in that way, with the Forces that produced the tragedy?"

"Yes," replied Carnacki. "This is, supposing we take the suggestion of the Sigsand MS., to account for the phenomenon."

"There may be other houses—" I began.

"There are," said Carnacki; and stood up.

"Out you go," he said, genially, using the recognized formula. And in five minutes we were on the Embankment, going thoughtfully to our various homes.

CHAPTER 6
THE THING INVISIBLE

Carnacki had just returned to Cheyne Walk, Chelsea. I was aware of this interesting fact by reason of the curt and quaintly worded postcard which I was rereading, and by which I was requested to present myself at his house not later than seven o'clock on that evening. Mr. Carnacki had, as I and the others of his strictly limited circle of friends knew, been away in Kent for the past three weeks; but beyond that, we had no knowledge. Carnacki was genially secretive and curt, and spoke only when he was ready to speak. When this stage arrived, I and his three other friends—Jessop, Arkright, and Taylor—would receive a card or a wire, asking us to call. Not one of us ever willingly missed, for after a thoroughly sensible little dinner Carnacki would snuggle down into his big armchair, light his pipe, and wait whilst we arranged ourselves comfortably in our accustomed seats and nooks. Then he would begin to talk.

Upon this particular night I was the first to arrive and found Carnacki sitting, quietly smoking over a paper. He stood up, shook me firmly by the hand, pointed to a chair, and sat down again, never having uttered a word.

For my part, I said nothing either. I knew the man too well to bother him with questions or the weather, and so took a seat and a cigarette. Presently the three others turned up and after that we spent a comfortable and busy hour at dinner.

Dinner over, Carnacki snugged himself down into his great chair, as I have said was his habit, filled his pipe and puffed for awhile, his gaze directed thoughtfully at the fire. The rest of us, if I may so express it, made ourselves cozy, each after his own particular manner. A minute or so later Carnacki began to speak, ignoring any preliminary remarks, and going straight to the subject of the story we knew he had to tell:

"I have just come back from Sir Alfred Jarnock's place at Burton-tree, in South Kent," he began, without removing his gaze from the fire. "Most extraordinary things have been happening down there lately and Mr. George Jarnock, the eldest son, wired to ask me to run over and see whether I could help to clear matters up a bit. I went.

"When I got there, I found that they have an old Chapel attached to the castle which has had quite a distinguished reputation for being what is popularly termed 'haunted.' They have been rather proud of this, as I managed to discover, until quite lately when something very disagreeable occurred, which served to remind them that family ghosts are not always content, as I might say, to remain purely ornamental.

"It sounds almost laughable, I know, to hear of a long-respected supernatural phenomenon growing unexpectedly dangerous; and in this case, the tale of the haunting was considered as little more than an old myth, except after nightfall, when possibly it became more plausible seeming.

"But however this may be, there is no doubt at all but that what I might term the Haunting Essence which lived in the place, had become suddenly dangerous—deadly dangerous too, the old butler being nearly stabbed to death one night in the Chapel, with a peculiar old dagger.

"It is, in fact, this dagger which is popularly supposed to 'haunt' the Chapel. At least, there has been always a story handed down in the family that this dagger would attack any enemy who should dare to venture into the Chapel, after nightfall. But, of course, this had been taken with just about the same amount of seriousness that people take most ghost tales, and that is not usually of a worryingly real nature. I mean that most people never quite know how much or how little they believe of matters ab-human or ab-normal, and generally they never have an opportunity to learn. And, indeed, as you are all aware, I am as big a skeptic concerning the truth of ghost tales as any man you are likely to meet; only I am what I might term an unprejudiced skeptic. I am not given to either believing or disbelieving things 'on principle,' as I have found many idiots prone to be, and what is more, some of them not ashamed to boast of the insane fact. I view all reported 'hauntings' as unproven until I have examined into them, and I am bound to admit that ninety-nine cases in a hundred turn out to be sheer bosh and fancy. But the hundredth! Well, if it were not for the hundredth, I should have few stories to tell you—eh?

"Of course, after the attack on the butler, it became evident that there was at least 'something' in the old story concerning the dagger, and I found everyone in a half belief that the queer old weapon did really strike the butler, either by the aid of some inherent force, which I found them peculiarly unable to explain, or else in the hand of some invisible thing or monster of the Outer World!

"From considerable experience, I knew that it was much more likely that the butler had been 'knifed' by some vicious and quite material human!

"Naturally, the first thing to do, was to test this probability of human agency, and I set to work to make a pretty drastic examination of the people who knew most about the tragedy.

"The result of this examination, both pleased and surprised me, for it left me with very good reasons for belief that I had come upon one of those extraordinary rare 'true manifestations' of the extrusion of a Force from the Outside. In more popular phraseology—a genuine case of haunting.

"These are the facts: On the previous Sunday evening but one, Sir Alfred Jarnock's household had attended family service, as usual, in the Chapel. You see, the Rector goes over to officiate twice each Sunday, after concluding his duties at the public Church about three miles away.

"At the end of the service in the Chapel, Sir Alfred Jarnock, his son Mr. George Jarnock, and the Rector had stood for a couple of minutes, talking, whilst old Bellett the butler went 'round, putting out the candles.

"Suddenly, the Rector remembered that he had left his small prayer book on the Communion table in the morning; he turned, and asked the butler to get it for him before he blew out the chancel candles.

"Now I have particularly called your attention to this because it is important in that it provides witnesses in a most fortunate manner at an extraordinary moment. You see, the Rector's turning to speak to Bellett had naturally caused both Sir Alfred Jarnock and his son to glance in the direction of the butler, and it was at this identical instant and whilst all three were looking at him, that the old butler was stabbed—there, full in the candlelight, before their eyes.

"I took the opportunity to call early upon the Rector, after I had questioned Mr. George Jarnock, who replied to my queries in place of Sir Alfred Jarnock, for the older man was in a nervous and shaken condition as a result of the happening, and his son wished him to avoid dwelling upon the scene as much as possible.

"The Rector's version was clear and vivid, and he had evidently received the astonishment of his life. He pictured to me the whole affair—Bellett, up at the chancel gate, going for the prayer book, and absolutely alone; and then the blow, out of the Void, he described it; and the force prodigious—the old man being driven headlong into the body of the Chapel. Like the kick of a great horse, the Rector said, his benevolent old eyes bright and intense with the effort he had actually witnessed, in defiance of all that he had hitherto believed.

"When I left him, he went back to the writing which he had put aside when I appeared. I feel sure that he was developing the first unorthodox sermon that he had ever evolved. He was a dear old chap, and I should certainly like to have heard it.

"The last man I visited was the butler. He was, of course, in a frightfully weak and shaken condition, but he could tell me nothing that did not point to there being a Power abroad in the Chapel. He told the same tale, in every minute particle, that I had learned from the others. He had been just going up to put out the altar candles and fetch the Rector's book, when something struck him an enormous blow high up on the left breast and he was driven headlong into the aisle.

"Examination had shown that he had been stabbed by the dagger—of which I will tell you more in a moment—that hung always above the altar. The weapon had entered, fortunately some inches above the heart, just under the collarbone, which had been broken by the stupendous force of the blow, the dagger itself being driven clean through the body, and out through the scapula behind.

"The poor old fellow could not talk much, and I soon left him; but what he had told me was sufficient to make it unmistakable that no living person had been within yards of him when he was attacked; and, as I knew, this fact was verified by three capable and responsible witnesses, independent of Bellett himself.

"The thing now was to search the Chapel, which is small and extremely old. It is very massively built, and entered through only one door, which leads out of the castle itself, and the key of which is kept by Sir Alfred Jarnock, the butler having no duplicate.

"The shape of the Chapel is oblong, and the altar is railed off after the usual fashion. There are two tombs in the body of the place; but none in the chancel, which is bare, except for the tall candlesticks, and the chancel rail, beyond which is the undraped altar of solid marble, upon which stand four small candlesticks, two at each end.

"Above the altar hangs the 'waeful dagger,' as I had learned it was named. I fancy the term has been taken from an old vellum, which describes the dagger and its supposed abnormal properties. I took the dagger down, and examined it minutely and with method. The blade is ten inches long, two inches broad at the base, and tapering to a rounded but sharp point, rather peculiar. It is double-edged.

"The metal sheath is curious for having a crosspiece, which, taken with the fact that the sheath itself is continued three parts up the hilt of the dagger (in a most inconvenient fashion), gives it the appearance of a cross. That this is not unintentional is shown by an engraving of the Christ crucified upon one side, whilst upon the other, in Latin, is the inscription: 'Vengeance is Mine, I will Repay.' A quaint and rather terrible conjunction of ideas. Upon the blade of the dagger is graven in old English capitals:

I WATCH. I STRIKE.

ON THE BUTT of the hilt there is carved deeply a Pentacle.

"This is a pretty accurate description of the peculiar old weapon that has had the curious and uncomfortable reputation of being able (either of its own accord or in the hand of something invisible) to strike murderously any enemy of the Jarnock family who may chance to enter the Chapel after nightfall. I may tell you here and now, that before I left, I had very good reason to put certain doubts behind me; for I tested the deadliness of the thing myself.

"As you know, however, at this point of my investigation, I was still at that stage where I considered the existence of a supernatural Force unproven. In the meanwhile, I treated the Chapel drastically, sounding and scrutinizing the walls and floor, dealing with them almost foot by foot, and particularly examining the two tombs.

"At the end of this search, I had in a ladder, and made a close survey of the groined roof. I passed three days in this fashion, and by the evening of the third day I had proved to my entire satisfaction that there is no place in the whole of that Chapel where any living being could have hidden, and also that the only way of ingress and egress to and from the Chapel is through the doorway which leads into the castle, the door of which was always kept locked, and the key kept by Sir Alfred Jarnock himself, as I have told you. I mean, of course, that this doorway is the only entrance practicable to material people.

"Yes, as you will see, even had I discovered some other opening, secret or otherwise, it would not have helped at all to explain the mystery of the incredible attack, in a normal fashion. For the butler, as you know, was struck in full sight of the Rector, Sir Jarnock and his son. And old Bellett himself knew that no living person had touched him.... 'Out of the Void,' the Rector had described the inhumanly brutal attack. 'Out of the Void!' A strange feeling it gives one—eh?

"And this is the thing that I had been called in to bottom!

"After considerable thought, I decided on a plan of action. I proposed to Sir Alfred Jarnock that I should spend a night in the Chapel, and keep a constant watch upon the dagger. But to this, the old knight—a little, wizened, nervous man—would not listen for a moment. He, at least, I felt assured had no doubt of the reality of some dangerous supernatural Force a roam at night in the Chapel. He informed me that it had been his habit every evening to lock the Chapel door, so that no one might foolishly or heedlessly run the risk of any peril that it might hold at night, and that he could not allow me to attempt such a thing after what had happened to the butler.

"I could see that Sir Alfred Jarnock was very much in earnest, and would evidently have held himself to blame had he allowed me to make the experiment and any harm come to me; so I said nothing in argument; and presently, pleading the fatigue of his years and health, he said goodnight, and left me; having given me the impression of being a polite but rather superstitious, old gentleman.

"That night, however, whilst I was undressing, I saw how I might achieve the thing I wished, and be able to enter the Chapel after dark, without making Sir Alfred Jarnock nervous. On the morrow, when I borrowed the key, I would take an impression, and have a duplicate made. Then, with my private key, I could do just what I liked.

"In the morning I carried out my idea. I borrowed the key, as I wanted to take a photograph of the chancel by daylight. When I had done this I locked up the Chapel and handed the key to Sir Alfred Jarnock, having first taken an impression in soap. I had brought out the exposed plate—in its slide—with me; but the camera I had left exactly as it was, as I wanted to take a second photograph of the chancel that night, from the same position.

"I took the dark slide into Burtontree, also the cake of soap with the impress. The soap I left with the local ironmonger, who was something of a locksmith and promised to let me have my duplicate, finished, if I would call in two hours. This I did, having in the meanwhile found out a photographer where I developed the plate, and left it to dry, telling him I would call next day. At the end of the two hours I went for my key and found it ready, much to my satisfaction. Then I returned to the castle.

"After dinner that evening, I played billiards with young Jarnock for a couple of hours. Then I had a cup of coffee and went off to my room, telling him I was feeling awfully tired. He nodded and told me he felt the same way. I was glad, for I wanted the house to settle as soon as possible.

"I locked the door of my room, then from under the bed—where I had hidden them earlier in the evening—I drew out several fine pieces of plate armor, which I had removed from the armory. There was also a shirt of chain mail, with a sort of quilted hood of mail to go over the head.

"I buckled on the plate armor, and found it extraordinarily

uncomfortable, and over all I drew on the chain mail. I know nothing about armor, but from what I have learned since, I must have put on parts of two suits. Anyway, I felt beastly, clamped and clumsy and unable to move my arms and legs naturally. But I knew that the thing I was thinking of doing called for some sort of protection for my body. Over the armor I pulled on my dressing gown and shoved my revolver into one of the side pockets—and my repeating flashlight into the other. My dark lantern I carried in my hand.

"As soon as I was ready I went out into the passage and listened. I had been some considerable time making my preparations and I found that now the big hall and staircase were in darkness and all the house seemed quiet. I stepped back and closed and locked my door. Then, very slowly and silently I went downstairs to the hall and turned into the passage that led to the Chapel.

"I reached the door and tried my key. It fitted perfectly and a moment later I was in the Chapel, with the door locked behind me, and all about me the utter dree silence of the place, with just the faint showings of the outlines of the stained, leaded windows, making the darkness and lonesomeness almost the more apparent.

"Now it would be silly to say I did not feel queer. I felt very queer indeed. You just try, any of you, to imagine yourself standing there in the dark silence and remembering not only the legend that was attached to the place, but what had really happened to the old butler only a little while gone, I can tell you, as I stood there, I could believe that something invisible was coming toward me in the air of the Chapel. Yet, I had got to go through with the business, and I just took hold of my little bit of courage and set to work.

"First of all I switched on my light, then I began a careful tour of the place; examining every corner and nook. I found nothing unusual. At the chancel gate I held up my lamp and flashed the light at the dagger. It hung there, right enough, above the altar, but I remember thinking of the word 'demure,' as I looked at it. However, I pushed the thought away, for what I was doing needed no addition of uncomfortable thoughts.

"I completed the tour of the place, with a constantly growing awareness of its utter chill and unkind desolation—an atmosphere of cold dismalness seemed to be everywhere, and the quiet was abominable.

"At the conclusion of my search I walked across to where I had left my camera focused upon the chancel. From the satchel that I had put beneath the tripod I took out a dark slide and inserted it in the camera, drawing the shutter. After that I uncapped the lens, pulled out my flashlight apparatus, and pressed the trigger. There was an intense, brilliant flash, that made the whole of the interior of the Chapel jump into sight, and disappear as quickly. Then, in the light from my lantern, I inserted the shutter into the slide, and reversed the slide, so as to have a fresh plate ready to expose at any time.

"After I had done this I shut off my lantern and sat down in one of the pews near to my camera. I cannot say what I expected to happen, but I had an extraordinary feeling, almost a conviction, that something peculiar or horrible would soon occur. It was, you know, as if I knew.

"An hour passed, of absolute silence. The time I knew by the far-off, faint chime of a clock that had been erected over the stables. I was beastly cold, for the whole place is without any kind of heating pipes or furnace, as I had noticed during my search, so that the temperature was sufficiently uncomfortable to suit my frame of mind. I felt like a kind of human periwinkle encased in boilerplate and frozen with cold and funk. And, you know, somehow the dark about me seemed to press coldly against my face. I cannot say whether any of you have ever had the feeling, but if you have, you will know just how disgustingly unnerving it is. And then, all at once, I had a horrible sense that something was moving in the place. It was not that I could hear anything but I had a kind of intuitive knowledge that something had stirred in the darkness. Can you imagine how I felt?

"Suddenly my courage went. I put up my mailed arms over my face. I wanted to protect it. I had got a sudden sickening feeling that something was hovering over me in the dark. Talk about fright! I could have shouted if I had not been afraid of the noise.... And then, abruptly, I heard something. Away up the aisle, there sounded a dull clang of metal, as it might be the tread of a mailed heel upon the stone of the aisle. I sat immovable. I was fighting with all my strength to get back my courage. I could not take my arms down from over my face, but I knew that I was getting hold of the gritty part of me again. And suddenly I made a mighty effort and lowered my arms. I held my face up in the darkness. And, I tell you, I respect myself for the act, because I thought truly at that moment that I was going to die. But I think, just then, by the slow revulsion of feeling which had assisted my effort, I was less sick, in that instant, at the thought of having to die, than at the knowledge of the utter weak cowardice that had so unexpectedly shaken me all to bits, for a time.

"Do I make myself clear? You understand, I feel sure, that the sense of respect, which I spoke of, is not really unhealthy egotism; because, you see, I am not blind to the state of mind which helped me. I mean that if I had uncovered my face by a sheer effort of will, unhelped by any revulsion of feeling, I should have done a thing much more worthy of mention. But, even as it was, there were elements in the act, worthy of respect. You follow me, don't you?

"And, you know, nothing touched me, after all! So that, in a little while, I had got back a bit to my normal, and felt steady enough to go through with the business without any more funking.

"I daresay a couple of minutes passed, and then, away up near the chancel, there came again that clang, as though an armored foot stepped cautiously. By Jove! but it made me stiffen. And suddenly the thought came that the sound I heard might be the rattle of the dagger above the altar. It was not a particularly sensible notion, for the sound was far too heavy and resonant for such a cause. Yet, as can be easily understood, my reason was bound to submit somewhat to my fancy at such a time. I remember now, that the idea of that insensate thing becoming animate, and attacking me, did not occur to me with any sense of possibility or reality. I thought rather, in a vague way, of some invisible monster of outer space fumbling at the dagger. I remembered the old Rector's description of the attack on the butler.... of the void. And he had described the stupendous force of the blow as being 'like the kick of a great horse.' You can see how uncomfortably my thoughts were running.

"I felt 'round swiftly and cautiously for my lantern. I found it close to me, on the pew seat, and with a sudden, jerky movement, I switched on the light. I flashed it up the aisle, to and fro across the chancel, but I could see nothing to frighten me. I turned quickly, and sent the jet of light darting across and across the rear end of the Chapel; then on each side of me, before and behind, up at the roof and down at the marble floor, but nowhere was there any visible thing to put me in fear, not a thing that need have set my flesh thrilling; just the quiet Chapel, cold, and eternally silent. You know the feeling.

"I had been standing, whilst I sent the light about the Chapel, but now I pulled out my revolver, and then, with a tremendous effort of will, switched off the light, and sat down again in the darkness, to continue my constant watch.

"It seemed to me that quite half an hour, or even more, must have passed, after this, during which no sound had broken the intense stillness. I had grown less nervously tense, for the flashing of the light 'round the place had made me feel less out of all bounds of the normal—it had given me something of that unreasoned sense of safety that a nervous child obtains at night, by covering its head up with the bedclothes. This just about illustrates the completely human illogicalness of the workings of my feelings; for, as you know, whatever Creature, Thing, or Being it was that had made that extraordinary and horrible attack on the old butler, it had certainly not been visible.

"And so you must picture me sitting there in the dark; clumsy with armor, and with my revolver in one hand, and nursing my lantern, ready, with the other. And then it was, after this little time of partial relief from intense nervousness, that there came a fresh strain on me; for somewhere in the utter quiet of the Chapel, I thought I heard something. I listened, tense and rigid, my heart booming just a little in my ears for a moment; then I thought I heard it again. I felt sure that something had moved at the top of the aisle. I strained in the darkness, to hark; and my eyes showed me blackness within blackness, wherever I glanced, so that I took no heed of what they told me; for even if I looked at the dim loom of the stained window at the top of the chancel, my sight gave me the shapes of vague shadows passing noiseless and ghostly across, constantly. There was a time of almost peculiar silence, horrible to me, as I felt just then. And suddenly I seemed to hear a sound again, nearer to me, and repeated, infinitely stealthy. It was as if a vast, soft tread were coming slowly down the aisle.

"Can you imagine how I felt? I do not think you can. I did not move, any more than the stone effigies on the two tombs; but sat there, stiffened. I fancied now, that I heard the tread all about the Chapel. And then, you know, I was just as sure in a moment that I could not hear it—that I had never heard it.

"Some particularly long minutes passed, about this time; but I think my nerves must have quieted a bit; for I remember being sufficiently aware of my feelings, to realize that the muscles of my shoulders ached, with the way that they must have been contracted, as I sat there, hunching myself, rigid. Mind you, I was still in a disgusting funk; but what I might call the 'imminent sense of danger' seemed to have eased from around me; at any rate, I felt, in some curious fashion, that there was a respite—a temporary cessation of malignity from about me. It is impossible to word my feelings more clearly to you, for I cannot see them more clearly than this, myself.

"Yet, you must not picture me as sitting there, free from strain; for the nerve tension was so great that my heart action was a little out of normal control, the blood beat making a dull booming at times in my ears, with the result that I had the sensation that I could not hear acutely. This is a simply beastly feeling, especially under such circumstances.

"I was sitting like this, listening, as I might say with body and soul, when suddenly I got that hideous conviction again that something was moving in the air of the place. The feeling seemed to stiffen me, as I sat, and my head appeared to tighten, as if all the scalp had grown tense. This was so real, that I suffered an actual pain, most peculiar and at the same time intense; the whole head pained. I had a fierce desire to cover my face again with my mailed arms, but I fought it off. If I had given way then to that, I should simply have bunked straight out of the place. I sat and sweated coldly (that's the bald truth), with the 'creep' busy at my spine....

"And then, abruptly, once more I thought I heard the sound of that huge, soft tread on the aisle, and this time closer to me. There was an awful little silence, during which I had the feeling that something enormous was bending over toward me, from the aisle.... And then, through the booming of the blood in my ears, there came a slight sound from the place where my camera stood—a disagreeable sort of slithering sound, and then a sharp tap. I had the lantern ready in my left hand, and now I snapped it on, desperately, and shone it straight above me, for I had a conviction that there was something there. But I saw nothing. Immediately I flashed the light at the camera, and along the aisle, but again there was nothing visible. I wheeled 'round, shooting the beam of light in a great circle about the place; to and fro I shone it, jerking it here and there, but it showed me nothing.

"I had stood up the instant that I had seen that there was nothing in sight over me, and now I determined to visit the chancel, and see whether the dagger had been touched. I stepped out of the pew into the aisle, and here I came to an abrupt pause, for an almost invincible, sick repugnance was fighting me back from the upper part of the Chapel. A constant, queer prickling went up and down my spine, and a dull ache took me in the small of the back, as I fought with myself to conquer this sudden new feeling of terror and horror.

I tell you, that no one who has not been through these kinds of experiences, has any idea of the sheer, actual physical pain attendant upon, and resulting from, the intense nerve strain that ghostly fright sets up in the human system. I stood there feeling positively ill. But I got myself in hand, as it were, in about half a minute, and then I went, walking, I expect, as jerky as a mechanical tin man, and switching the light from side to side, before and behind, and over my head continually. And the hand that held my revolver sweated so much, that the thing fairly slipped in my fist. Does not sound very heroic, does it?

"I passed through the short chancel, and reached the step that led up to the small gate in the chancel rail. I threw the beam from my lantern upon the dagger. Yes, I thought, it's all right. Abruptly, it seemed to me that there was something wanting, and I leaned forward over the chancel gate to peer, holding the light high. My suspicion was hideously correct. The dagger had gone. Only the cross-shaped sheath hung there above the altar.

"In a sudden, frightened flash of imagination, I pictured the thing adrift in the Chapel, moving here and there, as though of its own volition; for whatever Force wielded it, was certainly beyond visibility. I turned my head stiffly over to the left, glancing frightenedly behind me, and flashing the light to help my eyes. In the same instant I was struck a tremendous blow over the left breast, and hurled backward from the chancel rail, into the aisle, my armor clanging loudly in the horrible silence. I landed on my back, and slithered along on the polished marble. My shoulder struck the corner of a pew front, and brought me up, half stunned. I scrambled to my feet, horribly sick and shaken; but the fear that was on me, making little of that at the moment. I was minus both revolver and lantern, and utterly bewildered as to just where I was standing. I bowed my head, and made a scrambling run in the complete darkness and dashed into a pew. I jumped back, staggering, got my bearings a little, and raced down the center of the aisle, putting my mailed arms over my face. I plunged into my camera, hurling it among the pews. I crashed into the font, and reeled back. Then I was at the exit. I fumbled madly in my dressing gown pocket for the key. I found it and scraped at the door, feverishly, for the keyhole. I found the keyhole, turned the key, burst the door open, and was into the passage. I slammed the door and leant hard against it, gasping, whilst I felt crazily again for the keyhole, this time to lock the door upon what was in the Chapel. I succeeded, and began to feel my way stupidly along the wall of the corridor. Presently I had come to the big hall, and so in a little to my room.

"In my room, I sat for a while, until I had steadied down something to the normal. After a time I commenced to strip off the armor. I saw then that both the chain mail and the plate armor had been pierced over the breast. And, suddenly, it came home to me that the Thing had struck for my heart.

"Stripping rapidly, I found that the skin of the breast over the heart had just been cut sufficiently to allow a little blood to stain my shirt, nothing more. Only, the whole breast was badly bruised and intensely painful. You can imagine what would have happened if I had not worn the armor. In any case, it is a marvel that I was not knocked senseless.

"I did not go to bed at all that night, but sat upon the edge, thinking, and waiting for the dawn; for I had to remove my litter before Sir Alfred Jarnock should enter, if I were to hide from him the fact that I had managed a duplicate key.

"So soon as the pale light of the morning had strengthened sufficiently to show me the various details of my room, I made my way quietly down to the Chapel. Very silently, and with tense nerves, I opened the door. The chill light of the dawn made distinct the whole place—everything seeming instinct with a ghostly, unearthly quiet. Can you get the feeling? I waited several minutes at the door, allowing the morning to grow, and likewise my courage, I suppose. Presently the rising sun threw an odd beam right in through the big, East window, making colored sunshine all the length of the Chapel. And then, with a tremendous effort, I forced myself to enter.

"I went up the aisle to where I had overthrown my camera in the darkness. The legs of the tripod were sticking up from the interior of a pew, and I expected to find the machine smashed to pieces; yet, beyond that the ground glass was broken, there was no real damage done.

"I replaced the camera in the position from which I had taken the previous photography; but the slide containing the plate I had exposed by flashlight I removed and put into one of my side pockets, regretting that I had not taken a second flash picture at the instant when I heard those strange sounds up in the chancel.

"Having tidied my photographic apparatus, I went to the chancel to recover my lantern and revolver, which had both—as you know—been knocked from my hands when I was stabbed. I found the lantern lying, hopelessly bent, with smashed lens, just under the pulpit. My revolver I must have held until my shoulder struck the pew, for it was lying there in the aisle, just about where I believe I cannoned into the pew corner. It was quite undamaged.

"Having secured these two articles, I walked up to the chancel rail to see whether the dagger had returned, or been returned, to its sheath above the altar. Before, however, I reached the chancel rail, I had a slight shock; for there on the floor of the chancel, about a yard away from where I had been struck, lay the dagger, quiet and demure upon the polished marble pavement. I wonder whether you will, any of you, understand the nervousness that took me at the sight of the thing. With a sudden, unreasoned action, I jumped forward and put my foot on it, to hold it there. Can you understand? Do you? And, you know, I could not stoop down and pick it up with my hands for quite a minute, I should think. Afterward, when I had done so, however, and handled it a little, this feeling passed away and my Reason (and also, I expect, the daylight) made me feel that I had been a little bit of an ass. Quite natural, though, I assure you! Yet it was a new kind of fear to me. I'm taking no notice of the cheap joke about the ass! I am talking about the curiousness of learning in that moment a new shade or quality of fear that had hitherto been outside of my knowledge or imagination. Does it interest you?

"I examined the dagger, minutely, turning it over and over in my hands and never—as I suddenly discovered—holding it loosely. It was as if I were subconsciously surprised that it lay quiet in my hands. Yet even this feeling passed, largely, after a short while. The curious weapon showed no signs of the blow, except that the dull color—of the blade was slightly brighter on the rounded point that had cut through the armor.

"Presently, when I had made an end of staring at the dagger, I went up the chancel step and in through the little gate. Then, kneeling upon the altar, I replaced the dagger in its sheath, and came outside of the rail again, closing the gate after me and feeling awarely uncomfortable because the horrible old weapon was back again in its accustomed place. I suppose, without analyzing my feelings very deeply, I had an unreasoned and only half-conscious belief that there was a greater probability of danger when the dagger hung in its five century resting place than when it was out of it! Yet, somehow I don't think this is a very good explanation, when I remember the demure look the thing seemed to have when I saw it lying on the floor of the chancel. Only I know this, that when I had replaced the dagger I had quite a touch of nerves and I stopped only to pick up my lantern from where I had placed it whilst I examined the weapon, after which I went down the quiet aisle at a pretty quick walk, and so got out of the place.

"That the nerve tension had been considerable, I realized, when I had locked the door behind me. I felt no inclination now to think of old Sir Alfred as a hypochondriac because he had taken such hyper-seeming precautions regarding the Chapel. I had a sudden wonder as to whether he might not have some knowledge of a long prior tragedy in which the dagger had been concerned.

"I returned to my room, washed, shaved and dressed, after which I read awhile. Then I went downstairs and got the acting butler to give me some sandwiches and a cup of coffee.

"Half an hour later I was heading for Burtontree, as hard as I could walk; for a sudden idea had come to me, which I was anxious to test. I reached the town a little before eight thirty, and found the local photographer with his shutters still up. I did not wait, but knocked until he appeared with his coat off, evidently in the act of dealing with his breakfast. In a few words I made clear that I wanted the use of his dark room immediately, and this he at once placed at my disposal.

"I had brought with me the slide which contained the plate that I had used with the flashlight, and as soon as I was ready I set to work to develop. Yet, it was not the plate which I had exposed, that I first put into the solution, but the second plate, which had been ready in the camera during all the time of my waiting in the darkness. You see, the lens had been uncapped all that while, so that the whole chancel had been, as it were, under observation.

"You all know something of my experiments in 'Lightless Photography,' that is, appreciating light. It was X-ray work that started me in that direction. Yet, you must understand, though I was attempting to develop this 'unexposed' plate, I had no definite idea of results—nothing more than a vague hope that it might show me something.

"Yet, because of the possibilities, it was with the most intense and absorbing interest that I watched the plate under the action of the developer. Presently I saw a faint smudge of black appear in the upper part, and after that others, indistinct and wavering of outline. I held the negative up to the light. The marks were rather small, and were almost entirely confined to one end of the plate, but as I have said, lacked definiteness. Yet, such as they were, they were sufficient to make me very excited and I shoved the thing quickly back into the solution.

"For some minutes further I watched it, lifting it out once or twice to make a more exact scrutiny, but could not imagine what the markings might represent, until suddenly it occurred to me that in one of two places they certainly had shapes suggestive of a cross hilted dagger. Yet, the shapes were sufficiently indefinite to make me careful not to let myself be overimpressed by the uncomfortable resemblance, though I must confess, the very thought was sufficient to set some odd thrills adrift in me.

"I carried development a little further, then put the negative into the hypo, and commenced work upon the other plate. This came up nicely, and very soon I had a really decent negative that appeared similar in every respect (except for the difference of lighting) to the negative I had taken during the previous day. I fixed the plate, then having washed both it and the 'unexposed' one for a few minutes under the tap, I put them into methylated spirits for fifteen minutes, after which I carried them into the photographer's kitchen and dried them in the oven.

"Whilst the two plates were drying the photographer and I made an enlargement from the negative I had taken by daylight. Then we did the same with the two that I had just developed, washing them as quickly as possible, for I was not troubling about the permanency of the prints, and drying them with spirits.

"When this was done I took them to the window and made a thorough examination, commencing with the one that appeared to show shadowy daggers in several places. Yet, though it was now enlarged, I was still unable to feel convinced that the marks truly represented anything abnormal; and because of this, I put it on one side, determined not to let my imagination play too large a part in constructing weapons out of the indefinite outlines.

"I took up the two other enlargements, both of the chancel, as you will remember, and commenced to compare them. For some minutes I examined them without being able to distinguish any difference in the scene they portrayed, and then abruptly, I saw something in which they varied. In the second enlargement—the one made from the flashlight negative—the dagger was not in its sheath. Yet, I had felt sure it was there but a few minutes before I took the photograph.

"After this discovery I began to compare the two enlargements in a very different manner from my previous scrutiny. I borrowed a pair of calipers from the photographer and with these I carried out a most methodical and exact comparison of the details shown in the two photographs.

"Suddenly I came upon something that set me all tingling with excitement. I threw the calipers down, paid the photographer, and walked out through the shop into the street. The three enlargements I took with me, making them into a roll as I went. At the corner of the street I had the luck to get a cab and was soon back at the castle.

"I hurried up to my room and put the photographs away; then I went down to see whether I could find Sir Alfred Jarnock; but Mr. George Jarnock, who met me, told me that his father was too unwell to rise and would prefer that no one entered the Chapel unless he were about.

"Young Jarnock made a half apologetic excuse for his father; remarking that Sir Alfred Jarnock was perhaps inclined to be a little over careful; but that, considering what had happened, we must agree that the need for his carefulness had been justified. He added, also, that even before the horrible attack on the butler his father had been just as particular, always keeping the key and never allowing the door to be unlocked except when the place was in use for Divine Service, and for an hour each forenoon when the cleaners were in.

"To all this I nodded understandingly; but when, presently, the young man left me I took my duplicate key and made for the door of the Chapel. I went in and locked it behind me, after which I carried out some intensely interesting and rather weird experiments. These proved successful to such an extent that I came out of the place in a perfect fever of excitement. I inquired for Mr. George Jarnock and was told that he was in the morning room.

"'Come along,' I said, when I had found him. 'Please give me a lift. I've something exceedingly strange to show you.'

"He was palpably very much puzzled, but came quickly. As we strode along he asked me a score of questions, to all of which I just shook my head, asking him to wait a little.

"I led the way to the Armory. Here I suggested that he should take one side of a dummy, dressed in half plate armor, whilst I took the other. He nodded, though obviously vastly bewildered, and together we carried the thing to the Chapel door. When he saw me take out my key and open the way for us he appeared even more astonished, but held himself in, evidently waiting for me to explain. We entered the Chapel and I locked the door behind us, after which we carted the armored dummy up the aisle to the gate of the chancel rail where we put it down upon its round, wooden stand.

"'Stand back!' I shouted suddenly as young Jarnock made a movement to open the gate. 'My God, man! you mustn't do that!'

"Do what?" he asked, half-startled and half-irritated by my words and manner.

"One minute," I said. "Just stand to the side a moment, and watch."

He stepped to the left whilst I took the dummy in my arms and turned it to face the altar, so that it stood close to the gate. Then, standing well away on the right side, I pressed the back of the thing so that it leant forward a little upon the gate, which flew open. In the same instant, the dummy was struck a tremendous blow that hurled it into the aisle, the armor rattling and clanging upon the polished marble floor.

"Good God!" shouted young Jarnock, and ran back from the chancel rail, his face very white.

"Come and look at the thing," I said, and led the way to where the dummy lay, its armored upper limbs all splayed adrift in queer contortions. I stooped over it and pointed. There, driven right through the thick steel breastplate, was the 'waeful dagger.'

"Good God!" said young Jarnock again. "Good God! It's the dagger! The thing's been stabbed, same as Bellett!"

"Yes," I replied, and saw him glance swiftly toward the entrance of the Chapel. But I will do him the justice to say that he never budged an inch.

"Come and see how it was done," I said, and led the way back to the chancel rail. From the wall to the left of the altar I took down a long, curiously ornamented, iron instrument, not unlike a short spear. The sharp end of this I inserted in a hole in the left-hand gatepost of the chancel gateway. I lifted hard, and a section of the post, from the floor upward, bent inward toward the altar, as though hinged at the bottom. Down it went, leaving the remaining part of the post standing. As I bent the movable portion lower there came a quick click and a section of the floor slid to one side, showing a long, shallow cavity, sufficient to enclose the post. I put my weight to the lever and hove the post down into the niche. Immediately there was a sharp clang, as some catch snicked in, and held it against the powerful operating spring.

I went over now to the dummy, and after a few minute's work managed to wrench the dagger loose out of the armor. I brought the old weapon and placed its hilt in a hole near the top of the post where it fitted loosely, the point upward. After that I went again to the lever and gave another strong heave, and the post descended about a foot, to the bottom of the cavity, catching there with another clang. I withdrew the lever and the narrow strip of floor slid back, covering post and dagger, and looking no different from the surrounding surface.

Then I shut the chancel gate, and we both stood well to one side. I took the spear-like lever, and gave the gate a little push, so that it opened. Instantly there was a loud thud, and something sang through the air, striking the bottom wall of the Chapel. It was the dagger. I showed Jarnock then that the other half of the post had sprung back into place, making the whole post as thick as the one upon the right-hand side of the gate.

"There!" I said, turning to the young man and tapping the divided post. "There's the 'invisible' thing that used the dagger, but who the deuce is the person who sets the trap?" I looked at him keenly as I spoke.

"My father is the only one who has a key," he said. "So it's practically impossible for anyone to get in and meddle."

I looked at him again, but it was obvious that he had not yet reached out to any conclusion.

"See here, Mr. Jarnock," I said, perhaps rather curter than I should have done, considering what I had to say. "Are you quite sure that Sir Alfred is quite balanced—mentally?"

"He looked at me, half frightenedly and flushing a little. I realized then how badly I put it.

"'I—I don't know,' he replied, after a slight pause and was then silent, except for one or two incoherent half remarks.

"'Tell the truth,' I said. 'Haven't you suspected something, now and again? You needn't be afraid to tell me.'

"'Well,' he answered slowly, 'I'll admit I've thought Father a little —a little strange, perhaps, at times. But I've always tried to think I was mistaken. I've always hoped no one else would see it. You see, I'm very fond of the old guvnor.'

"I nodded.

"'Quite right, too,' I said. 'There's not the least need to make any kind of scandal about this. We must do something, though, but in a quiet way. No fuss, you know. I should go and have a chat with your father, and tell him we've found out about this thing.' I touched the divided post.

"Young Jarnock seemed very grateful for my advice and after shaking my hand pretty hard, took my key, and let himself out of the Chapel. He came back in about an hour, looking rather upset. He told me that my conclusions were perfectly correct. It was Sir Alfred Jarnock who had set the trap, both on the night that the butler was nearly killed, and on the past night. Indeed, it seemed that the old gentleman had set it every night for many years. He had learnt of its existence from an old manuscript book in the Castle library. It had been planned and used in an earlier age as a protection for the gold vessels of the ritual, which were, it seemed, kept in a hidden recess at the back of the altar.

"This recess Sir Alfred Jarnock had utilized, secretly, to store his wife's jewelry. She had died some twelve years back, and the young man told me that his father had never seemed quite himself since.

"I mentioned to young Jarnock how puzzled I was that the trap had been set before the service, on the night that the butler was struck; for, if I understood him aright, his father had been in the habit of setting the trap late every night and unsetting it each morning before anyone entered the Chapel. He replied that his father, in a fit of temporary forgetfulness (natural enough in his neurotic condition), must have set it too early and hence what had so nearly proved a tragedy.

"That is about all there is to tell. The old man is not (so far as I could learn), really insane in the popularly accepted sense of the word. He is extremely neurotic and has developed into a hypochon-driac, the whole condition probably brought about by the shock and sorrow resultant on the death of his wife, leading to years of sad broodings and to overmuch of his own company and thoughts. Indeed, young Jarnock told me that his father would sometimes pray for hours together, alone in the Chapel." Carnacki made an end of speaking and leant forward for a spill.

"But you've never told us just how you discovered the secret of the divided post and all that," I said, speaking for the four of us.

"Oh, that!" replied Carnacki, puffing vigorously at his pipe. "I found—on comparing the—photos, that the one—taken in the—daytime, showed a thicker left-hand gatepost, than the one taken at night by the flashlight. That put me on to the track. I saw at once that there might be some mechanical dodge at the back of the whole queer business and nothing at all of an abnormal nature. I examined the post and the rest was simple enough, you know.

"By the way," he continued, rising and going to the mantelpiece, "you may be interested to have a look at the so-called 'waeful dagger.' Young Jarnock was kind enough to present it to me, as a little memento of my adventure."

He handed it 'round to us and whilst we examined it, stood silent before the fire, puffing meditatively at his pipe.

"Jarnock and I made the trap so that it won't work," he remarked after a few moments. "I've got the dagger, as you see, and old Bellett's getting about again, so that the whole business can be hushed up, decently. All the same I fancy the Chapel will never lose its reputation as a dangerous place. Should be pretty safe now to keep valuables in."

"There's two things you haven't explained yet," I said. "What do you think caused the two clangey sounds when you were in the Chapel in the dark? And do you believe the soft tready sounds were real, or only a fancy, with your being so worked up and tense?"

"Don't know for certain about the clangs," replied Carnacki.

"I've puzzled quite a bit about them. I can only think that the spring which worked the post must have 'given' a trifle, slipped you know, in the catch. If it did, under such a tension, it would make a bit of a ringing noise. And a little sound goes a long way in the middle of the night when you're thinking of 'ghostesses.' You can understand that—eh?"

"Yes," I agreed. "And the other sounds?"

"Well, the same thing—I mean the extraordinary quietness— may help to explain these a bit. They may have been some usual enough sound that would never have been noticed under ordinary conditions, or they may have been only fancy. It is just impossible to say. They were disgustingly real to me. As for the slithery noise, I am pretty sure that one of the tripod legs of my camera must have slipped a few inches: if it did so, it may easily have jolted the lens cap off the baseboard, which would account for that queer little tap which I heard directly after."

"How do you account for the dagger being in its place above the altar when you first examined it that night?" I asked. "How could it be there, when at that very moment it was set in the trap?"

"That was my mistake," replied Carnacki. "The dagger could not possibly have been in its sheath at the time, though I thought it was. You see, the curious cross-hilted sheath gave the appearance of the complete weapon, as you can understand. The hilt of the dagger protrudes very little above the continued portion of the sheath—a most inconvenient arrangement for drawing quickly!" He nodded sagely at the lot of us and yawned, then glanced at the clock.

"Out you go!" he said, in friendly fashion, using the recognized formula. "I want a sleep."

We rose, shook him by the hand, and went out presently into the night and the quiet of the Embankment, and so to our homes.

CHAPTER 7

THE HAUNTED JARVEE

'Seen anything of Carnacki lately?' I asked Arkright when we met in the City.

'No,' he replied. 'He's probably off on one of his jaunts. We'll be having a card one of these days inviting us to No. 472, Cheyne Walk, and then we'll hear all about it. Queer chap that.'

He nodded, and went on his way. It was some months now since we four - Jessop, Arkright, Taylor and myself - had received the usual summons to drop in at No. 472 and hear Carnacki's story of his latest case. What talks they were! Stories of all kinds and true in every word, yet full of weird and extraordinary incidents that held one silent and awed until he had finished.

Strangely enough, the following morning brought me a curtly worded card telling me to be at No. 472 at seven o'clock promptly. I was the first to arrive, Jessop and Taylor soon followed and just before dinner was announced Arkright came in.

Dinner over, Carnacki as usual passed round his smokes, snuggled himself down luxuriously in his favourite armchair and went straight to the story we knew he had invited us to hear.

'I've been on a trip in one of the real old-time sailing ships,' he said without any preliminary remarks. 'The Jarvee, owned by my old friend Captain Thompson. I went on the voyage primarily for my health, but I picked on the old Jarvee because Captain Thompson had often told me there was something queer about her. I used to ask him up here whenever he came ashore and try to get him to tell me more about it, you know; but the funny thing was he never could tell me anything definite concerning her queerness. He seemed always to know but when it came to putting his knowledge into words it was as if he found that the reality melted out of it. He would end up usually by saying that you saw things and then he would wave his hands vaguely, but further than that he never seemed able to pass on the knowledge of something strange which he had noticed about the ship, except odd outside details.

'"Can't keep men in her no-how," he often told me. "They get frightened and they see things and they feel things. An' I've lost a power o' men out of her. Fallen from aloft, you know. She's getting a bad name." And then he'd shake his head very solemnly.

'Old Thompson was a brick in every way. When I got aboard I found that he had given me the use of a whole empty cabin opening off my own as my laboratory and workshop. He gave the carpenter orders to fit up the empty cabin with shelves and other conveniences according to my directions and in a couple of days I had all the apparatus, both mechanical and electric with which I had conducted my other ghost-hunts, neatly and safely stowed away, for I took a great deal of gear with me as I intended to interest myself by examining thoroughly into the mystery about which the captain was at once so positive and so vague.

'During the first fortnight out I followed my usual methods of making a thorough and exhaustive search. This I did with the most scrupulous care, but found nothing abnormal of any kind in the whole vessel. She was an old wooden ship and I took care to sound and measure every casement and bulkhead, to examine every exit from the holds and to seal all the hatches. These and many other precautions I took, but at the end of the fortnight I had neither seen anything nor found anything.

'The old barque was just, to all seeming, a healthy, average old-timer jogging along comfortably from one port to another. And save for an indefinable sense of what I could now describe as "abnormal peace" about the ship I could find nothing to justify the old captain's solemn and frequent assurances that I would see soon enough for myself. This he would say often as we walked the poop together; afterwards stopping to take a long, expectant, half-fearful look at the immensity of the sea around.

'Then on the eighteenth day something truly happened. I had been pacing the poop as usual with old Thompson when suddenly he stopped and looked up at the mizzen royal which had just begun to flap against the mast. He glanced at the wind-vane near him, then ruffled his hat back and stared at the sea.

'"Wind's droppin', mister. There'll be trouble tonight," he said. "D'you see yon?" And he pointed away to windward.

'"What?" I asked, staring with a curious little thrill that was due to more than curiosity. "Where?"

'"Right off the beam," he said. "Comin' from under the sun."

'"I don't see anything," I explained after a long stare at the wide-spreading silence of the sea that was already glassing into a dead calm surface now that the wind had died.

'"Yon shadow fixin'," said the old man, reaching for his glasses.

'He focussed them and took a long look, then passed them across to me and pointed with his finger. "Just under the sun," he repeated. "Comin' towards us at the rate o' knots." He was curiously calm and matter-of-fact and yet I felt that a certain excitement had him in the throat; so that I took the glasses eagerly and stared according to his directions.

'After a minute I saw it - a vague shadow upon the still surface of the sea that seemed to move towards us as I stared. For a moment I gazed fascinated, yet ready every moment to swear that I saw nothing and in the same instant to be assured that there was truly something out there upon the water, apparently coming towards the ship.

'"It's only a shadow, captain," I said at length.

'"Just so, mister," he replied simply. "Have a look over the stern to the norrard." He spoke in the quietest way, as a man speaks who is sure of all his facts and who is facing an experience he has faced before, yet who salts his natural matter-of-factness with a deep and constant excitement.

'At the captain's hint I turned about and directed the glasses to the northward. For a while I searched, sweeping my aided vision to and fro over the greying arc of the sea.

'Then I saw the thing plain in the field of the glass - a vague something, a shadow upon the water and the shadow seemed to be moving towards the ship.

'"That's queer," I muttered with a funny little stirring at the back of my throat.

'"Now to the west'ard, mister," said the captain, still speaking in his peculiar level way.

'I looked to the westward and in a minute I picked up the thing - a third shadow that seemed to move across the sea as I watched it.

'"My God, captain," I exclaimed, "what does it mean?"

'"That's just what I want to know, mister," said the captain. "I've seen 'em before and thought sometimes I must be going mad. Some-times they're plain an' sometimes they're scarce to be seen, an' sometimes they're like livin' things, an' sometimes they're like nought at all but silly fancies. D' you wonder I couldn't name 'em proper to you?"

'I did not answer for I was staring now expectantly towards the south along the length of the barque. Afar off on the horizon my glasses picked up something dark and vague upon the surface of the sea, a shadow it seemed which grew plainer.

'"My God! " I muttered again. "This is real. This--" I turned again to the eastward.

'"Comin' in from the four points, ain't they," said Captain Thompson and he blew his whistle.

'"Take them three r'yals off her," he told the mate, "an' tell one of the boys to shove lanterns up on the sherpoles. Get the men down smart before dark," he concluded as the mate moved off to see the orders carried out.

'"I'm sendin' no men aloft to-night," he said to me. "I've lost enough that way."

'"They may be only shadows, captain, after all," I said, still looking earnestly at that far-off grey vagueness on the eastward sea. "Bit of mist or cloud floating low." Yet though I said this I had no belief that it was so. And as for old Captain Thompson, he never took the trouble to answer, but reached for his glasses which I passed to him.

'"Gettin' thin an' disappearin' as they come near," he said presently. "I know, I've seen 'em do that oft an' plenty before. They'll be close round the ship soon but you nor me won't see them, nor no one else, but they'll be there. I wish 'twas mornin'. I do that!"

'He had handed the glasses back to me and I had been staring at each of the oncoming shadows in turn. It was as Captain Thompson had said. As they drew nearer they seemed to spread and thin out and presently to become dissipated into the grey of the gloaming so that I could easily have imagined that I watched merely four little portions of grey cloud, expanding naturally into impalpableness and invisibility.

'"Wish I'd took them t'gallants off her while I was about it," remarked the old man presently. "Can't think to send no one off the decks to-night, not unless there's real need." He slipped away from me and peered at the aneroid in the skylight. "Glass steady, anyhow," he muttered as he came away, seeming more satisfied.

'By this time the men had all returned to the decks and the night was down upon us so that I could watch the queer, dissolving shadows which approached the ship.

'Yet as I walked the poop with old Captain Thompson, you can imagine how I grew to feel. Often I found myself looking over my shoulder with quick, jerky glances; for it seemed to me that in the curtains of gloom that hung just beyond the rails there must be a vague, incredible thing looking inboard.

'I questioned the captain in a thousand ways, but could get little out of him beyond what I knew. It was as if he had no power to convey to another the knowledge which he possessed and I could ask no one else, for every other man in the ship was newly signed on, including the mates, which was in itself a significant fact.

'"You'll see for yourself, mister," was the refrain with which the captain parried my questions, so that it began to seem as if he almost feared to put anything he knew into words. Yet once, when I had jerked round with a nervous feeling that something was at my back he said calmly enough: "Naught to fear, mister, whilst you're in the light and on the decks." His attitude was extraordinary in the way in which he accepted the situation. He appeared to have no personal fear.

'The night passed quietly until about eleven o'clock when suddenly and without one atom of warning a furious squall burst on the vessel. There was something monstrous and abnormal in the wind; it was as if some power were using the elements to an infernal purpose. Yet the captain met the situation calmly. The helm was put down and the sails shaken while the three t'gallants were lowered. Then the three upper topsails. Yet still the breeze roared over us, almost drowning the thunder which the sails were making in the night.

'"Split 'em to ribbons!" the captain yelled in my ear above the noise of the wind. "Can't help it. I ain't sendin' no men aloft to-night unless she seems like to shake the sticks out of her. That's what bothers me."

'For nearly an hour after that, until eight bells went at midnight, the wind showed no signs of easing but breezed up harder than ever. And all the while the skipper and I walked the poop, he ever and again peering up anxiously through the darkness at the banging and thrashing sails.

'For my part I could do nothing except stare round and round at the extraordinarily dark night in which the ship seemed to be embedded solidly. The very feel and sound of the wind gave me a sort of constant horror, for there seemed to be an unnaturalness rampant in the atmosphere. But how much this was the effect of my over-strung nerves and excited imagination, I cannot say. Certainly, in all my experience I had never come across anything just like what I felt and endured through that peculiar squall.

'At eight bells when the other watch came on deck the captain was forced to send all hands aloft to make the canvas fast, as he had begun to fear that he would actually lose his masts if he delayed longer. This was done and the barque snugged right down.

'Yet, though the work was done successfully, the captain's fears were justified in a sufficiently horrible way, for as the men were beginning to make their way in off the wards there was a loud crying and shouting aloft and immediately afterwards a crash down on the main deck, followed instantly by a second crash.

'"My God! Two of 'em!" shouted the skipper as he snatched a lamp from the forrard binnacle. Then down on to the main deck. It was as he had said. Two of the men had fallen, or - as the thought came to me - been thrown from aloft and were lying silent on the deck. Above us in the darkness I heard a few vague shouts followed by a curious quiet, save for the constant blast of the wind whose whistling and howling in the rigging seemed but to accentuate the complete and frightened silence of the men aloft. Then I was aware that the men were coming down swiftly and presently one after the other came with a quick leap out of the rigging and stood about the two fallen men with odd exclamations and questions which always merged off instantly into new silence.

'And all the time I was conscious of a most extraordinary sense of oppression and frightened distress and fearful expectation, for it seemed to me, standing there near the dead in that unnatural wind that a power of evil filled all the night about the ship and that some fresh horror was imminent.

'The following morning there was a solemn little service, very rough and crude, but undertaken with a nice reverence and the two men who had fallen were tilted off from a hatch-cover and plunged suddenly out of sight. As I watched them vanish in the deep blue of the water an idea came to me and I spent part of the afternoon talking it over with the captain, after which I passed the rest of the time until sunset was upon us in arranging and fitting up a part of my electrical apparatus. Then I went on deck and had a good look round. The evening was beautifully calm and ideal for the experiment which I had in mind, for the wind had died away with a peculiar suddenness after the death of the two men and all that day the sea had been like glass.

'To a certain extent I believed that I comprehended the primary cause of the vague but peculiar manifestations which I had witnessed the previous evening and which Captain Thompson believed implicitly to be intimately connected with the death of the two sailormen.

'I believed the origin of the happenings to lie in a strange but perfectly understandable cause, i.e., in that phenomenon known technically as "attractive vibrations." Harzam, in his monograph on "Induced Hauntings," points out that such are invariably produced by "induced vibrations," that is, by temporary vibrations set up by some outside cause.

'This is somewhat abstruse to follow out in a story of this kind, but it was on a long consideration of these points that I had resolved to make experiments to see whether I could not produce a counter or "repellent" vibration, a thing which Harzam had succeeded in producing on three occasions and in which I have had a partial success once, failing only because of the imperfectness of the apparatus I had aboard.

'As I have said, I can scarcely follow the reasoning further in a brief record such as this, neither do I think it would be of interest to you who are interested only in the startling and weird side of my investigations. Yet I have told you sufficient to show you the germ of my reasonings and to enable you to follow intelligently my hopes and expectations in sending out what I hoped would prove "repellent" vibrations.

'Therefore it was that when the sun had descended to within ten degrees of the visible horizon the captain and I began to watch for the appearance of the shadows. Presently, under the sun, I discovered the same peculiar appearance of a moving greyness which I had seen on the preceding night and almost immediately Captain Thompson told me that he saw the same to the south.

'To the north and east we perceived the same extraordinary thing and I at once set my electric apparatus at work, sending out the strange repelling force to the dim, far shadows of mystery which moved steadily out of the distance towards the vessel.

'Earlier in the evening the captain had snugged the barque right down to her topsails, for as he said, until the calm went he would risk nothing. According to him it was always during calm weather that the extraordinary manifestations occurred. In this case he was certainly justified, for a most tremendous squall struck the ship in the middle watch, taking the fore upper topsail right out of the ropes.

'At the time when it came I was lying down on a locker in the saloon, but I ran up on to the poop as the vessel canted under the enormous force of the wind. Here I found the air pressure tremendous and the noise of the squall stunning. And over it all and through it all I was conscious of something abnormal and threatening that set my nerves uncomfortably acute. The thing was not natural.

'Yet, despite the carrying away of the topsail, not a man was sent aloft.

'"Let 'em all go!" said old Captain Thompson. "I'd have shortened her down to the bare sticks if I'd done all I wanted!"

'About two a.m. the squall passed with astonishing suddenness and the night showed clear above the vessel. From then onward I paced the poop with the skipper, often pausing at the break to look along the lighted main deck. It was on one of these occasions that I saw something peculiar. It was like a vague flitting of an impossible shadow between me and the whiteness of the well-scrubbed decks. Yet, even as I stared, the thing was gone and I could not say with surety that I had seen anything.

'"Pretty plain to see, mister," said the captain's voice at my elbow. "I've only seen that once before an' we lost half of the hands that trip. We'd better be at 'ome, I'm thinkin'. It'll end in scrappin' her, sure."

'The old man's calmness bewildered me almost as much as the confirmation his remark gave that I had really seen something abnormal floating between me and the deck eight feet below us.

'"Good lord, Captain Thompson," I exclaimed, "this is simply infernal! "

'"Just that," he agreed. "I said, mister, you'd see if you'd wait. And this ain't the half. You wait till you sees 'em looking like little black clouds all over the sea round the ship and movin' steady with the ship. All the same, I ain't seen 'em aboard but the once. Guess we're in for it.'

'"How do you mean?" I asked. But though I questioned him in every way I could get nothing satisfactory out of him.

'"You'll see, mister. You wait an' see. She's a queer un." And that was about the extent of his further efforts and methods of enlightening me.

'From then on through the rest of the watch I leaned over the break of the poop, staring down at the maindeck and odd whiles taking quick glances to the rear. The skipper had resumed his steady pacing of the poop, but now and again he would come to a pause beside me and ask calmly enough whether I had seen any more of "them there."

'Several times I saw the vagueness of something drifting in the lights of the lanterns and a sort of wavering in the air in this place and that, as if it might be an attenuated something having movement, that was half-seen for a moment and then gone before my brain could record anything definite.

'Towards the end of the watch, however, both the captain and I saw something very extraordinary. He had just come beside me and was leaning over the rail across the break. "Another of 'em there," he remarked in his calm way, giving me a gentle nudge and nodding his head towards the port side of the maindeck, a yard or two to our left.

'In the place he had indicated there was a faint, dull shadowy spot seeming suspended about a foot above the deck. This grew more visible and there was movement in it and a constant, oily-seeming whirling from the centre outwards. The thing expanded to several feet across, with the lighted planks of the deck showing vaguely through. The movement from the centre outwards was now becoming very distinct, till the whole strange shape blackened and grew more dense, so that the deck below was hidden.

'Then as I stared with the most intense interest there went a thinning movement over the thing and almost directly it had dissolved so that there was nothing more to be seen than a vague rounded shape of shadow, hovering and convoluting dimly between us and the deck below. This gradually thinned out and vanished and we were both of us left staring down at a piece of the deck where the planking and pitched seams showed plain and distinct in the light from the lamps that were now hung nightly on the sherpoles.

'"Mighty queer that, mister," said the captain meditatively as he fumbled for his pipe. "Mighty queer." Then he lit his pipe and began again his pacing of the poop.

'The calm lasted for a week with the sea like glass and every night without warning there was a repetition of the extraordinary squall, so that the captain had everything made fast at dusk and waited patiently for a trade wind.

'Each evening I experimented further with my attempts to set up "repellent" vibrations, but without result. I am not sure whether I ought to say that my meddling produced no result; for the calm gradually assumed a more unnatural permanent aspect whilst the sea looked more than ever like a plain of glass, bulged anon with the low oily roll of some deep swell. For the rest, there was by day a silence so profound as to give a sense of unrealness, for never a sea-bird hove in sight whilst the movement of the vessel was so slight as scarce to keep up the constant creak, creak of spars and gear, which is the ordinary accompaniment of a calm.

'The sea appeared to have become an emblem of desolation and freeness, so that it seemed to me at last that there was no more any known world, but just one great ocean going on for ever into the far distances in every direction. At night the strange squalls assumed a far greater violence so that sometimes it seemed as if the very spars would be ripped and twisted out of the vessel, yet fortunately no harm came in that wise.

'As the days passed I became convinced at last that my experiments were producing very distinct results, though the opposite to those which I hoped to produce, for now at each sunset a sort of grey cloud resembling light smoke would appear far away in every quarter almost immediately upon the commencement of the vibrations, with the effect that I desisted from any prolonged attempt and became more tentative in my experiments.

'At last, however, when we had endured this condition of affairs for a week, I had a long talk with old Captain Thompson and he agreed to let me carry out a bold experiment to its conclusion. It was to keep the vibrations going steadily at full power from a little before sunset until the dawn and to take careful notes of the results.

'With this in view, all was made ready. The royal and t'gallant yards were sent down, all the sails stowed and everything about the decks made fast. A sea anchor was rigged out over the bows and a long line of cable veered away. This was to ensure the vessel coming head to wind should one of those strange squalls strike us from any quarter during the night.

'Late in the afternoon the men were sent into the fo'c'sle and told that they might please themselves and turn in or do anything they

liked, but that they were not to come on deck during the night whatever happened. To ensure this the port and starboard doors were
padlocked. Afterwards I made the first and the eighth signs of the
Saaamaaa Ritual opposite each door-post, connecting them with
triple lines crossed at every seventh inch. You've dipped deeper into
the science of magic than I have, Arkright, and you will know what
that means. Following this I ran a wire entirely around the outside of
the fo'c'sle and connected it up with my machinery, which I had
erected in the sail-locker aft.

'"In any case," I explained to the captain, "they run practically no
risk other than the general risk which we may expect in the form of a
terrific storm-burst. The real danger will be to those who are 'meddling.' The 'path of the vibrations' will make a kind of 'halo' round
the apparatus. I shall have to be there to control and I'm willing to
risk it, but you'd better get into your cabin and the three mates must
do the same."

'This the old captain refused to do and the three mates begged to
be allowed to stay and "see the fun." I warned them very seriously
that there might be a very disagreeable and unavoidable danger, but
they agreed to risk it and I can tell you I was not sorry to have their
companionship.

'I set to work then, making them help where I needed help, and
so presently I had all my gear in order. Then I led my wires up
through the skylight from the cabin and set the vibrator dial and
trembler-box level, screwing them solidly down to the poop-deck, in
the clear space that lay between the foreside of the skylight and the
lid of the sail locker.

'I got the three mates and the captain to take their places close
together and I warned them not to move whatever happened. I set
to work then, alone, and chalked a temporary pentacle about the
whole lot of us, including the apparatus. Afterwards I made haste to
get the tubes of my electric pentacle fitted all about us, for it was
getting on to dusk. As soon as this was done I switched on the
current into the vacuum tubes and immediately the pale sickly glare

shone dull all about us, seeming cold and unreal in the last light of the evening.

'Immediately afterwards I set the vibrations beating out into all space and then I took my seat beside the control board. Here I had a few words with the others, warning them again whatever they might hear or see not to leave the pentacle, if they valued their lives. They nodded to this and I knew that they were fully impressed with the possibility of the unknown danger that we were meddling with.

'Then we settled down to watch. We were all in our oilskins, for I expected the experiment to include some very peculiar behaviour on the part of the elements and so we were ready to face the night. One other thing I was careful to do and that was to confiscate all matches so that no one should forgetfully light his pipe, for the light rays are "paths" to certain of the Forces.

'With a pair of marine glasses I was staring round at the horizon. All around, but miles away in the greying of the evening, there seemed to be a strange, vague darkening of the surface of the sea. This became more distinct and it seemed to me presently that it might be a slight, low-lying mist far away about the ship. I watched it very intently and the captain and the three mates were doing likewise through their glasses.

'"Coming in on us at the rate o' knots, mister," said the old man in a low voice. "This is what I call playin' with 'ell. I only hope it'll all come right." That was all he said and afterwards there was absolute silence from him and the others through the strange hours that followed.

'As the night stole down upon the sea we lost sight of the peculiar incoming circle of mist and there was a period of the most intense and oppressive silence to the five of us, sitting there watchful and quiet within the pale glow of the electric pentacle.

'A while later there came a sort of strange, noiseless lightning. By noiseless I mean that while the flashes appeared to be near at hand and lit up all the vague sea around, yet there was no thunder; neither, so it appeared to me, did there seem to be any reality in the flashes. This is a queer thing to say but it describes my impressions. It was as if I saw a representation of lightning rather than the physical electricity itself. No, of course, I am not pretending to use the word in its technical sense.

'Abruptly a strange quivering went through the vessel from end to end and died away. I looked fore and aft and then glanced at the four men who stared back at me with a sort of dumb and half-frightened wonder, but no one said anything. About five minutes passed with no sound anywhere except the faint buzz of the apparatus and nothing visible anywhere except the noiseless lightning which came down, flash after flash, lighting the sea all around the vessel.

'Then a most extraordinary thing happened. The peculiar quivering passed again through the ship and died away. It was followed immediately by a kind of undulation of the vessel, first fore and aft and then from side to side. I can give you no better illustration of the strangeness of the movement on that glass-like sea than to say that it was just such a movement as might have been given her had an invisible giant hand lifted her and toyed with her, canting her this way and that with a certain curious and rather sickening rhythm of movement. This appeared to last about two minutes, so far as I can guess, and ended with the ship being shaken up and down several times, after which there came again the quivering and then quietness.

'A full hour must have passed during which I observed nothing except that twice the vessel was faintly shaken and the second time this was followed by a slight repetition of the curious undulations. This, however, lasted but a few seconds and afterwards there was only the abnormal and oppressive silence of the night, punctured time after time by these noiseless flashes of lightning. All the time I did my best to study the appearance of the sea and atmosphere around the ship.

'One thing was apparent, that the surrounding wall of vagueness had drawn in more upon the ship, so that the brightest flashes now showed me no more than about a clear quarter of a mile of ocean around us, after which the sight was just lost in trying to penetrate a kind of shadowy distance that yet had no depth in it, but which still lacked any power to arrest the vision at any particular point so that one could not know definitely whether there was anything there or not, but only that one's sight was limited by some phenomenon which hid all the distant sea. Do I make this clear?

'The strange, noiseless lightning increased in vividness and the flashes began to come more frequently. This went on till they were almost continuous, so that all the near sea could be watched with scarce an intermission. Yet the brightness of the flashes seemed to have no power to dull the pale light of the curious detached glows that circled in silent multitudes about us.

'About this time I became aware of a strange sense of breathlessness. Each breath seemed to be drawn with difficulty and presently with a sense of positive distress. The three mates and the captain were breathing with curious little gasps and the faint buzz of the vibrator seemed to come from a great distance away. For the rest there was such a silence as made itself known like a dull, numbing ache upon the brain.

'The minutes passed slowly and then, abruptly, I saw something new. There were grey things floating in the air about the ship which were so vague and attenuated that at first I could not be sure that I saw anything, but in a while there could be no doubt that they were there.

'They began to show plainer in the constant glare of the quiet lightning and growing darker and darker they increased visibly in size. They appeared to be but a few feet above the level of the sea and they began to assume humped shapes.

'For quite half an hour, which seemed indefinitely longer, I watched those strange humps like little hills of blackness floating just above the surface of the water and moving round and round the vessel with a slow, everlasting circling that produced on my eyes the feeling that it was all a dream.

'It was later still that I discovered still another thing. Each of those great vague mounds had begun to oscillate as it circled round about us. I was conscious at the same time that there was communicated to the vessel the beginning of a similar oscillating movement, so very slight at first that I could scarcely be sure she so much as moved.

'The movement of the ship grew with a steady oscillation, the bows lifting first and then the stern, as if she were pivoted amidships. This ceased and she settled down on to a level keel with a series of queer jerks as if her weight were being slowly lowered again to the buoying of the water.

'Suddenly there came a cessation of the extraordinary lightning and we were in an absolute blackness with only the pale sickly glow of the electric pentacle above us and the faint buzz of the apparatus seeming far away in the night. Can you picture it all? The five of us there, tense and watchful and wondering what was going to happen.

'The thing began gently - a little jerk upward of the starboard side of the vessel, then a second jerk, then a third and the whole ship was canted distinctly to port. It continued in a kind of slow rhythmic tilting with curious timed pauses between the jerks and suddenly, you know, I saw that we were in absolute danger, for the vessel was being capsized by some enormous Force in the utter silence and blackness of that night.

'"My God, mister, stop it!" came the captain's voice, quick and very hoarse. "She'll be gone in a moment! She'll be gone !"

'He had got on to his knees and was staring round and gripping at the deck. The three mates were also gripping at the deck with their palms to stop them from sliding down the violent slope. In that moment came a final tilting of the side of the vessel and the deck rose up almost like a wall. I snatched at the lever of the vibrator and switched it over.

'Instantly the angle of the deck decreased as the vessel righted several feet with a jerk. The righting movement continued with little rhythmic jerks until the ship was once more on an even keel.

'And even as she righted I was aware of an alteration in the tenseness of the atmosphere and a great noise far off to starboard. It was the roaring of wind. A huge flash of lightning was followed by others and the thunder crashed continually overhead. The noise of the wind to starboard rose to a loud screaming and drove towards us through the night. Then the lightning ceased and the deep roll of the thunder was lost in the nearer sound of the wind which was now within a mile of us and making a most hideous, bellowing scream. The shrill howling came at us out of the dark and covered every other sound. It was as if all the night on that side were a vast cliff, sending down high and monstrous echoes upon us. This is a queer thing to say, I know, but it may help you to get the feeling of the thing; for that just describes exactly how it felt to me at the time - that queer, echoing, empty sense above us in the night, yet all the emptiness filled with sound on high. Do you get it? It was most extraordinary and there was a grand something about it all as if one had come suddenly upon the steeps of some monstrous lost world.

'Then the wind rushed out at us and stunned us wit its sound and force and fury. We were smothered and half-stunned. The vessel went over on to her port side merely from pressure of the wind on her naked spars and side. The whole night seemed one yell and the foam roared and snowed over us in countless tons. I have never known anything like it. We were all splayed about the poop, holding on to anything we could, while the pentacle was smashed to atoms so that we were in complete darkness. The storm-burst had come down on us.

'Towards morning the storm calmed and by evening we were running before a fine breeze; yet the pumps had to be kept going steadily for we had sprung a pretty bad leak, which proved so serious that we had to take to the boats two days later. However, we were picked up that night so that we had only a short time of it. As for the Jarvee, she is now safely at the bottom of the Atlantic, where she had better remain for ever.

Carnacki came to an end and tapped out his pipe.

'But you haven't explained,' I remonstrated. 'What made her like that? What made her different from other ships? Why did those shadows and things come to her? What's your idea?'

'Well,' replied Carnacki, 'in my opinion she was a focus. That is a technical term which I can best explain by saying that she possessed the "attractive vibration" that is the power to draw to her any psychic waves in the vicinity, much in the way of a medium. The way in which the "vibration" is acquired - to use a technical term again - is, of course, purely a matter for supposition. She may have developed it during the years, owing to a suitability of conditions or it may have been in her ("of her" is a better term) from the very day her keel was laid. I mean the direction in which she lay the condition of the atmosphere, the state of the "electric tensions," the very blows of the hammers and the accidental combining of materials suited to such an end - all might tend to such a thing. And this is only to speak of the known. The vast unknown it is vain to speculate upon in a brief chatter like this.

'I would like to remind you here of that idea of mine that certain forms of so-called "hauntings" may have their cause in the "attractive vibrations." A building or a ship - just as I have indicated - may develop "vibrations," even as certain materials in combination under the proper conditions will certainly develop an electric current.

'To say more in a talk of this scope is useless. I am more inclined to remind you of the glass which will vibrate to a certain note struck upon a piano and to silence all your worrying questions with that simple little unanswered one: What is electricity? When we've got that clear it will be time to take the next step in a more dogmatic fashion. We are but speculating on the coasts of a strange country of mystery. In this case, I think the next best step for you all will be home and bed.'

And with this terse ending, in the most genial way possible, Carnacki ushered us out presently on to the quiet chill of the Embankment, replying heartily to our various good-nights.

CHAPTER 8

THE FIND

In response to Carnacki's usual card of invitation to dinner I arrived in good time at Cheyne Walk to find Arkright, Taylor and Jessop already there, and a few minutes later we were seated round the dining table.

We dined well as usual, and as nearly always happened at these gatherings Carnacki talked on every subject under the sun but the one on which we had all expectations. It was not until we were all seated comfortably in our respective armchairs that he began.

'A very simple case,' he told us, puffing at his pipe. 'Quite a simple bit of mental analysis. I had been talking one day to Jones of Malbrey and Jones, the editors of the Bibliophile and Book Table, and he mentioned having come across a book called the Dumpley's Acrostics. Now the only known copy of this book is in the Caylen Museum. This second copy which had been picked up by a Mr. Ludwig appeared to be genuine. Both Malbrey and Jones pronounced it to be so, and that, to anyone knowing their reputation, would pretty well settle it.

'I heard all about the book from my old friend Van Dyll, the Dutchman who happened to be at the Club for lunch.

'"What do you know about a book called Dumpley's Acrostics?' I asked him.

'"You might as well ask me what I know of your city of London, my friend," he replied. "I know all there is to know which is very little. There was but one copy of that extraordinary book printed, and that copy is now in the Caylen Museum."

'"Exactly what I had thought," I told him.

'"The book was written by John Dumpley," he continued, "and presented to Queen Elizabeth on her fortieth birthday. She had a passion for word-play of that kind - which is merely literary gymnastics but was raised by Dumpley to an extraordinary height of involved and scandalous punning in which those unsavoury tales of those at Court are told with a wit and pretended innocence that is incredible in its malicious skill.

'"The type was distributed and the manuscript burnt immediately after printing that one copy which was for the Queen. The book was presented to her by Lord Welbeck who paid John Dumpley twenty English guineas and twelve sheep each year with twelve firkins of Miller Abbott's ale to hold his tongue. Lord Welbeck wished to be thought the author of the book, and undoubtedly he had supplied Dumpley with the very scandalous and intimate details of famous Court personages about whom the book is written.

'"He had his own name put in the place of Dumpley's; for though it was not a matter for much pride for a well born man to write well in those days, still a good wit such as the Acrostics was deemed to be was a thing for high praise at the Court."

'"I'd no idea it was as famous as you say," I told him.

'"It has a great fame among a few," replied Van Dyll, "because it is at the same time unique and of a value both historic and intrinsic. There are collectors today who would give their souls if a second copy might be discovered. But that's impossible."

'"The impossible seems to have been achieved," I said. "A second copy is being offered for sale by a Mr. Ludwig. I have been asked to make a few investigations. Hence my inquiries."

'Van Dyll almost exploded.

'"Impossible ! " he roared. "It's another fraud!"

'Then I fired my shell.

'"Messrs. Malbrey and Jones have pronounced it unmistakably genuine," I said, "and they are, as you know, above suspicion. Also Mr. Ludwig's account of how he bought the book at a 'dump' sale in the Charing Cross Road seems quite straight and above-board. He got it at Bentloes, and I've just been up there. Mr. Bentloes says it is quite possible though not probable. And anyway, he's mighty sick about it. I don't wonder, either !"

'Van Dyll got to his feet.

'"Come on round to Malbrey and Jones," he said excitedly, and we went straight off to the offices of the bibliophile where Dyll is well-known.

'"What's all this about?" he called out almost before he got into the Editors' private room. "What's all this about the Dumpley's Acrostics, eh? Show it to me. Where is it?"

'"It's that newly discovered copy of the Acrostics the Professor is asking for," I explained to Mr. Malbrey who was at his desk. "He's somewhat upset at the news I've just given him."

'Probably to no other men in England, except its lawful owner, would Malbrey have handed the discovered volume on so brief a notice. But Van Dyll is among the great ones when it comes to bibliology, and Malbrey merely wheeled round in his office chair and opened a large safe. From this he took a volume wrapped about with tissue paper, and standing up he handed it ceremoniously to Professor Dyll.

'Van Dyll literally snatched it from him, tore off the paper and ran to the window to have a better light. There for nearly an hour, while we watched in silence, he examined the book, using a magnifying glass as he studied type, paper, and binding.

'At last he sat back and brushed his hand across his forehead.

'"Well?" we all asked.

'"It appears to be genuine," he said. "Before pronouncing finally upon it, however, I should like to have the opportunity of comparing it with the authentic copy in the Caylen Museum."

'Mr. Malbrey rose from his seat and closed his desk.

'"I shall be delighted to come with you now, Professor," he said. "We shall be only too pleased to have your opinion in the next issue of the Bibliophile which we are making a special Dumpley number, for the interest aroused by this find will be enormous among collectors.'

'When we all arrived at the Museum, Van Dyll sent in his name to the chief librarian and we were all invited into his private room. Here the Professor stated the facts and showed him the book he had brought along with him.

'The librarian was tremendously interested, and after a brief examination of the copy expressed his opinion that it was apparently genuine, but he would like to compare it with the authentic copy.

'This he did and the three experts compared the book with the Museum copy for considerably over an hour, during which time I listened keenly and jotted down from time to time in my notebook my own conclusions.

'The verdict of all three was finally unanimous that the newly found copy of the Acrostics was undoubtedly genuine and printed at the same time and from the same type as the Museum copy.

'"Gentlemen," I said, "as I am working in the interests of Messrs. Malbrey and Jones, may I ask two questions? First, I should like to ask the librarian whether the Museum copy has ever been lent out of the Museum."

'"Certainly not," replied the librarian. "Rare editions are never loaned, and are rarely even handled except in the presence of an attendant."

'"Thanks," I said. "That ought to settle things pretty well. The other question I wish to ask is why were you all so convinced before that there was but one copy in existence?"

'"Because," said the librarian, "as both Mr. Malbrey and Professor Dyll could tell you, Lord Welbeck states in his private Memoirs that only one copy was printed. He appears to have been determined upon this, apparently to enhance the value of his gift to the Queen. He states clearly that he had the one copy printed, and that the printing was done entirely in his presence at the House of Pennywell, Printers of Lamprey Court. You can see the name at the beginning of the book. He also personally superintended the distribution of the type and burnt the manuscript and even the proof-pulls, as he says. Indeed, so precise and unmistakable are his statements on these points that I should always refuse to consider the authenticity of any 'found' copy unless it could stand such a drastic test as this one has been put through. But here is the copy," he went on, "unmistakably genuine, and we have to take the evidence of our senses rather than the evidence of Lord Welbeck's statement. The finding of this book is a kind of literary thunderbolt. It will make some commotion in the collecting dove-cotes if I'm not mistaken!"

'"What should you estimate its possible value at?" I asked him.

'He shrugged his shoulders.

'"Impossible to say," he answered. "If I were a rich man I would gladly give a thousand pounds to possess it. Professor Dyll there, being more fortunately endowed with worldly wealth, would prob-ably outbid me unmercifully! I expect if Messrs. Malbrey and Jones do not buy it soon it will go across to America in the wake of half the treasures of the earth."

'We separated then and went our various ways. I returned here, had a cup of tea and sat down for a good long think, for I wasn't at all satisfied in my mind that everything was as plain and aboveboard as it seemed.

'"Now," I said to myself, "let's have a little plain and unbiased reasoning applied, and see what comes of the test."

'"First of all there is the apparently incontrovertible statement in Lord Welbeck's Memoirs that there was only one copy of the Acros-tics printed. That titled gentleman evidently took extraordinary pains to see that no second copy of the book was printed, and the very proofs he burned. Also this copy is no conglomeration of collected printer's proofs, for the examination the three experts have given it quite preclude that idea. All this points then to what I might term 'Certainty Number One,' that only one copy was printed.

'"But now - come to the next step, a second copy has been proved today to exist. That is Certainty Number Two. And the two make that impossibility - a paradox. Therefore, though of the two certainties I may be bound in the end to accept the second, yet equally I cannot accept the complete smashing of the plain statement made in Lord Welbeck's private Memoirs. There seems to be more in this than meets the eye."'

Carnacki puffed thoughtfully at his pipe for a few minutes before he resumed his story.

'In the next few days,' he continued, 'by simple methods of deduction and a matter-of-fact following of the dues that were thereby indicated, I had laid bare as cunningly planned a little drama of clever crime as I have ever met with.

'I got into communication with Scotland Yard, my clients Messrs. Malbrey and Jones, Ralph Ludwig the owner of the find, and Mr. Notts the librarian. I arranged for a detective from the Yard to meet us all at the offices of the Bibliophile and Book Table, and I managed to persuade Notts to bring along with him the Museum copy of the Acrostics.

'In this way I had my stage set, with all the characters involved, in that little bookish office of the hundred-year-old Collectors' Weekly.

'The meeting was for three in the afternoon, and when they had all arrived I asked them to listen to me for a few minutes.

'"Gentlemen," I said, "I should like you to follow me a little in a line of reasoning which I wish to indicate to you. Two days ago Mr. Ludwig brought to this office a copy of a book of which only one copy was supposed to be extant. An examination of his find by three experts, perhaps the three greatest experts in England, proved it to be undoubtedly genuine. That is fact number one. Fact number two is that there were the very best reasons for supposing there could not be two original copies of this particular book in existence.

'"Now we were forced, by the experts' opinion, into accepting the first fact as indubitable. But there still remained to explain away the second fact, that is, the good reason for supposing that only one copy of this book was originally printed.

'"I found that although I was forced to accept the fact of the finding of the second copy, yet I could not see how to explain away the good reason I have mentioned. Therefore, not feeling that my reason was satisfied I followed the line of investigation which unsatisfied reason indicated. I went to the Caylen Museum and asked questions.

'"I had already learned from Mr. Notts that rare editions were never loaned. And an examination of the registers showed that the Acrostics had been referred to only three times by three different people in the last two years, and then, as I knew, always in the presence of an attendant. This seemed proof enough that I was hunting a mare's nest; but reason still asserted that there were more things not explained. So I went home and thought it all out again.

'"One deduction remained from all my hours of thinking. That was that the three different men who had examined the book within the last two years could be the only line of explanation left to me. I had found out their names - Charles, Noble and Waterfield. My meditations suggested a handwriting expert, and the two of us visited the Museum register with the result that I found my reason had not led me astray. The expert pronounced the handwriting of the three men to be the handwriting of one and the same person.

'"My next step was simple. I came here to the office with the expert and asked if I could be shown any handwriting of Mr. Ralph Ludwig. I could, and the expert assured me that Mr. Ludwig was the man who had written the three different signatures in the register of the Museum.

'"The next step is deduction on my part and is indicated by reasoning as the only possible lines on which Mr. Ludwig could have worked. I can only suppose that he must have come across a dummy copy of the Acrostics in some way or other, possibly in the bundle of books he says he picked up at Bentloes' sale. This blank-paper dummy of the book would be made up by the printers and book-binders so as to enable Lord Welbeck to see how the Acrostics would bind up and bulk. The method is common in the publishing trade, as you know. The binding may be exactly a duplicate of what the finished article will be but the inside is nothing but blank paper of the same thickness and quality as that on which the book will be printed. In this way a publisher can see beforehand just how the book will look.

'"I am quite convinced that I have described the first step in Mr. Ludwig's ingenious little plot. He made only three visits to the Museum and as you will see in a minute, if he had not been provided with a facsimile in binding of the Acrostics on his first visit, he could not have carried out his plot under four. Moreover, unless I am mistaken in my psychology of the incident it was through becoming possessed of this particular dummy copy that he thought out this scheme. Is that not so, Mr. Ludwig?" I asked him. But he refused to reply to my question, and sat there looking very crestfallen.

'"Well, gentlemen," I went on, "the rest is plain sailing. He went the first time to the Museum to study their copy, after which he deftly replaced it with the dummy one he had brought in with him. The attendant took the copy - which was externally identical with the original and replaced it in its case. This was, of course, the one big risk in Mr. Ludwig's little adventure. A smaller risk was that someone should call and ask for the Acrostics before he could replace it with the original, for this was what he meant to do, and which he did after he had photographed each page. Isn't that so, Mr. Ludwig?" I asked him; but he still refused to open his mouth.

'"This," I resumed, "accounts for his second visit when he returned the original and started to print on a handpress the photo-graphic blocks which he had prepared. Once the pages were bound up in the dummy he went back to the Museum and exchanged the copies, this time taking away for keeps the Museum copy and leaving the very excellently printed dummy in its place. Each time, as you know, he used a new name and a new handwriting, and probably disguises of some kind; for he had no wish to be connected with the Museum copy. That is all I have to tell you; but I hardly think Mr. Ludwig will care to deny my story, eh, Mr. Ludwig?"'

Carnacki knocked out the ashes of his, pipe as he finished.

'I can't imagine what he stole it for,' said Arkright. 'He could surely never have hoped to sell it.'

'No, that's true,' Carnacki replied. 'Certainly not in the open market. He would have to sell it to some unscrupulous collector who would, of course, knowing it was stolen, give him next to nothing for it, and might in the end hand him over to the police. But don't you see if he could so arrange that the Museum still had its copy he might sell his own without fear in the open market to the highest bidder, as an authentic second copy which had come to light. He had sense to know that his copy would be mercilessly challenged and examined, and that is why he made his third exchange, and finally left his dummy, printed as exactly like the original as was possible, and took away with him the authentic copy.'

'But the two books were bound to be compared,' I argued.

'Quite true, but the copy at the Museum would not be so suspiciously examined. Everyone considered that book beyond suspicion. If the three experts had given the same attention to the false copy in the Museum which they thought all the time was the original, I don't suppose for a moment this little story would have been told. It's a very good example of the way people take things for granted. Out you go!' he said, genially, which was his usual method of dismissing us. And a few minutes later we were out on the Embankment.

CHAPTER 9

THE HOG

Wealth had finished dinner and Carnacki had drawn his big chair up to the fire, and started his pipe.

Jessop, Arkright, Taylor and I had each of us taken up our favourite positions, and waited for Carnacki to begin.

'What I'm going to tell you about happened in the next room,' he said, after drawing at his pipe for a while. 'It has been a terrible experience. Doctor Witton first brought the case to my notice. We'd been chatting over a pipe at the Club one night about an article in the Lancet, and Witton mentioned having just such a similar case in a man called Bains. I was interested at once. It was one of those cases of a gap or flaw in a man's protection barrier, I call it. A failure to be what I might term efficiently insulated - spiritually - from the outer monstrosities.

'From what I knew of Witton, I knew he'd be no use. You all know Witton. A decent sort, hard-headed, practical, stand-no-kind-of-nonsense sort of man, all right at his own job when that job's a fractured leg or a broken collarbone; but he'd never have made anything of the Bains case.'

For a space Carnacki puffed meditatively at his pipe, and we waited for him to go on with his tale.

'I told Witton to send Bains to me,' he resumed, 'and the following Saturday he came up. A little sensitive man. I liked him as soon as I set eyes on him. After a bit, I got him to explain what was troubling him, and questioned him about what Doctor Witton had called his "dreams."

'"They're more than dreams," he said, "they're so real that they're actual experiences to me. They're simply horrible. And yet there's nothing very definite in them to tell you about. They generally come just as I am going off to sleep. I'm hardly over before suddenly I seem to have got down into some deep, vague place with some inexplicable and frightful horror all about me. I can never understand what it is, for I never see anything, only I always get a sudden knowledge like a warning that I have got down into some terrible place - a sort of hellplace I might call it, where I've no business ever to have wandered; and the warning is always insistent - even imperative - that I must get out, get out, or some enormous horror will come at me."

'"Can't you pull yourself back?" I asked him. "Can't you wake up?"

'"No," he told me. "That's just what I can't do, try as I will. I can't stop going along this labyrinth-of-hell as I call it to myself, towards some dreadful unknown Horror. The warning is repeated, ever so strongly - almost as if the live me of my waking moments was awake and aware. Something seems to warn me to wake up, that whatever I do I must wake, wake, and then my consciousness comes suddenly alive and I know that my body is there in the bed, but my essence or spirit is still down there in that hell, wherever it is, in a danger that is both unknown and inexpressible; but so overwhelming that my whole spirit seems sick with terror.

' "I keep saying to myself all the time that I must wake up," he continued, "but it is as if my spirit is still down there, and as if my consciousness knows that some tremendous invisible Power is fighting against me. I know that if I do not wake then, I shall never wake up again, but go down deeper and deeper into some stupendous horror of soul destruction. So then I fight. My body lies in the bed there, and pulls. And the power down there in that labyrinth exerts itself too so that a feeling of despair, greater than any I have ever known on this earth, comes on me. I know that if I give way and cease to fight, and do not wake, then I shall pass out - out to that monstrous Horror which seems to be silently calling my soul to destruction.

'"Then I make a final stupendous effort," he continued, "and my brain seems to fill my body like the ghost of my soul. I can even open my eyes and see with my brain, or consciousness, out of my own eyes. I can see the bedclothes, and I know just how I am lying in the bed; yet the real me is down in that hell in terrible danger. Can you get me?" he asked.

'"Perfectly," I replied.

'"Well, you know," he went on, "I fight and fight. Down there in that great pit my very soul seems to shrink back from the call of some brooding horror that impels it silently a little further, always a little further round a visible corner, which if I once pass I know I shall never return again to this world. Desperately I fight brain and consciousness fighting together to help it. The agony is so great that I could scream were it not that I am rigid and frozen in the bed with fear.

'"Then, just when my strength seems almost gone, soul and body win, and blend slowly. And I lie there worn out with this terrible extraordinary fight. I have still a sense of a dreadful horror all about me, as if out of that horrible place some brooding monstrosity had followed me up, and hangs still and silent and invisible over me, threatening me there in my bed. Do I make it clear to you?" he asked. "It's like some monstrous Presence."

' "Yes," I said. "I follow you."

'The man's forehead was actually covered with sweat, so keenly did he live again through the horrors he had experienced.

'After a while he continued:

'"Now comes the most curious part of the dream or whatever it is," he said. "There's always a sound I hear as I lie there exhausted in the bed. It comes while the bedroom is still full of the sort of atmosphere of monstrosity that seems to come up with me when I get out of that place. I hear the sound coming up out of that enormous depth, and it is always the noise of pigs - pigs grunting, you know. It's just simply dreadful. The dream is always the same. Sometimes I've had it every single night for a week, until I fight not to go to sleep; but, of course, I have to sleep sometimes. I think that's how a person might go mad, don't you?" he finished.

'I nodded, and looked at his sensitive face. Poor beggar ! He had been through it, and no mistake.

'"Tell me some more," I said. "The grunting - what does it sound like exactly?"

'"It's just like pigs grunting," he told me again. "Only much more awful. There are grunts, and squeals and pighowls, like you hear when their food is being brought to them at a pig farm. You know those large pig farms where they keep hundreds of pigs. All the grunts, squeals and howls blend into one brutal chaos of sound - only it isn't a chaos. It all blends in a queer horrible way. I've heard it. A sort of swinish clamouring melody that grunts and roars and shrieks in chunks of grunting sounds, all tied together with squealings and shot through with pig howls. I've sometimes thought there was a definite beat in it; for every now and again there comes a gargantuan GRUNT, breaking through the million pig-voiced roaring - a stupendous GRUNT that comes in with a beat. Can you understand me? It seems to shake everything.... It's like a spiritual earthquake. The howling, squealing, grunting, rolling clamour of swinish noise coming up out of that place, and then the monstrous GRUNT rising up through it all, an ever-recurring beat out of the depth - the voice of the swine-mother of monstrosity beating up from below through that chorus of mad swine-hunger.... It's no use! I can't explain it. No one ever could. It's just terrible! And I'm afraid you're saying to yourself that I'm in a bad way; that I want a change or a tonic; that I must buck up or I'll land myself in a madhouse. If only you could understand ! Doctor Witton seemed to half understand, I thought; but I know he's only sent me to you as a sort of last hope. He thinks I'm booked for the asylum. I could tell it."

'"Nonsense!" I said. "Don't talk such rubbish. You're as sane as I am. Your ability to think clearly what you want to tell me, and then to transmit it to me so well that you compel my mental retina to see something of what you have seen, stands sponsor for your mental balance.

'"I am going to investigate your case, and if it is what I suspect, one of those rare instances of a 'flaw' or 'gap' in your protective barrier (what I might call your spiritual insulation from the Outer Monstrosities) I've no doubt we can end the trouble. But we've got to go properly into the matter first, and there will certainly be danger in doing so."

'"I'll risk it," replied Bains. "I can't go on like this any longer."

' "Very well," I told him. "Go out now, and come back at five o'clock. I shall be ready for you then. And don't worry about your sanity. You're all right, and we'll soon make things safe for you again. Just keep cheerful and don't brood about it."'

—— 2 ——

'I PUT in the whole afternoon preparing my experimenting room, across the landing there, for his case. When he returned at five o'clock I was ready for him and took him straight into the room.

'It gets dark now about six-thirty, as you know, and I had just nice time before it grew dusk to finish my arrangements. I prefer always to be ready before the dark comes.

'Bains touched my elbow as we walked into the room.

' "There's something I ought to have told you," he said, looking rather sheepish. "I've somehow felt a bit ashamed of it."

' "Out with it," I replied.

'He hesitated a moment, then it came out with a jerk.

' "I told you about the grunting of the pigs," he said. "Well, I grunt too. I know it's horrible. When I lie there in bed and hear those sounds after I've come up, I just grunt back as if in reply. I can't stop myself. I just do it. Something makes me. I never told Doctor Witton that. I couldn't. I'm sure now you think me mad," he concluded.

'He looked into my face, anxious and queerly ashamed.

'"It's only the natural sequence of the abnormal events, and I'm glad you told me," I said, slapping him on the back. "It follows logically on what you had already told me. I have had two cases that in some way resembled yours."

'"What happened?" he asked me. "Did they get better?"

'"One of them is alive and well today, Mr. Bains," I replied. "The other man lost his nerve, and fortunately for all concerned, he is dead."

'I shut the door and locked it as I spoke, and Bains stared round, rather alarmed, I fancy, at my apparatus.

'"What are you going to do?" he asked. "Will it be a dangerous experiment?"

'"Dangerous enough," I answered, "if you fail to follow my

instructions absolutely in everything. We both run the risk of never leaving this room alive. Have I your word that I can depend on you to obey me whatever happens?"

'He stared round the room and then back at me.

'"Yes," he replied. And, you know, I felt he would prove the right kind of stuff when the moment came.

'I began now to get things finally in train for the night's work. I told Bains to take off his coat and his boots. Then I dressed him entirely from head to foot in a single thick rubber combination-over-all, with rubber gloves, and a helmet with ear-flaps of the same material attached.

'I dressed myself in a similar suit. Then I began on the next stage of the night's preparations.

'First I must tell you that the room measures thirty-nine feet by thirty-seven, and has a plain board floor over which is fitted a heavy, half-inch rubber covering.

'I had cleared the floor entirely, all but the exact centre where I had placed a glass-legged, upholstered table, a pile of vacuum tubes and batteries, and three pieces of special apparatus which my experiment required.

'"Now Bains," I called, "come and stand over here by this table. Don't move about. I've got to erect a protective 'barrier' round us, and on no account must either of us cross over it by even so much as a hand or foot, once it is built."

'We went over to the middle of the room, and he stood by the glass-legged table while I began to fit the vacuum tubing together round us.

'I intended to use the new spectrum "defense" which I have been perfecting lately. This, I must tell you, consists of seven glass vacuum circles with the red on the outside, and the colour circles lying inside it, in the order of orange, yellow, green, blue, indigo and violet.

'The room was still fairly light, but a slight quantity of dusk seemed to be already in the atmosphere, and I worked quickly.

'Suddenly, as I fitted the glass tubes together I was aware of some vague sense of nerve-strain, and glancing round at Bains who was standing there by the table I noticed him staring fixedly before him. He looked absolutely drowned in uncomfortable memories.

'"For goodness' sake stop thinking of those horrors," I called out to him. "I shall want you to think hard enough about them later; but in this specially constructed room it is better not to dwell on things of that kind till the barriers are up. Keep your mind on anything normal or superficial - the theatre will do - think about that last piece you saw at the Gaiety. I'll talk to you in a moment."

'Twenty minutes later the "barrier" was completed all round us, and I connected up the batteries. The room by this time was greying with the coming dusk, and the seven differently coloured circles shone out with extraordinary effect, sending out a cold glare.

'"By Jove! " cried Bains, "that's very wonderful - very wonderful!"

'My other apparatus which I now began to arrange consisted of a specially made camera, a modified form of phonograph with ear-pieces instead of a horn, and a glass disk composed of many fathoms of glass vacuum tubes arranged in a special way. It had two wires leading to an electrode constructed to fit round the head.

'By the time I had looked over and fixed up these three things, night had practically come, and the darkened room shone most strangely in the curious upward glare of the seven vacuum tubes.

'"Now, Bains," I said, "I want you to lie on this table. Now put your hands down by your sides and lie quiet and think. You've just got two things to do," I told him. "One is to lie there and concentrate your thoughts on the details of the dream you are always having, and the other is not to move off this table whatever you see or hear, or whatever happens, unless I tell you. You understand, don't you?"

'"Yes," he answered, "I think you may rely on me not to make a fool of myself. I feel curiously safe with you somehow."

' "I'm glad of that," I replied. "But I don't want you to minimize the possible danger too much. There may be horrible danger. Now, just let me fix this band on your head," I added, as I adjusted the electrode. I gave him a few more instructions, telling him to concentrate his thoughts particularly upon the noises he heard just as he was waking, and I warned him again not to let himself fall asleep. "Don't talk," I said, "and don't take any notice of me. If you find I disturb your concentration keep your eyes closed."

'He lay back and I walked over to the glass disk arranging the camera in front of it on its stand in such a way that the lens was opposite the centre of the disk.

'I had scarcely done this when a ripple of greenish light ran across the vacuum tubes of the disk. This vanished, and for maybe a minute there was complete darkness. Then the green light rippled once more across it - rippled and swung round, and began to dance in varying shades from a deep heavy green to a rank ugly shade; back and forward, back and forward.

'Every half second or so there shot across the varying greens a flicker of yellow, an ugly, heavy repulsive yellow, and then abruptly there came sweeping across the disk a great beat of muddy red. This died as quickly as it came, and gave place to the changing greens shot through by the unpleasant and ugly yellow hues. About every seventh second the disk was submerged, and the other colours momentarily blotted out by the great beat of heavy, muddy red which swept over everything.

' "He's concentrating on those sounds," I said to myself, and I felt queerly excited as I hurried on with my operations. I threw a word over my shoulder to Bains.

'"Don't get scared, whatever happens," I said. "You're all right!"

'I proceeded now to operate my camera. It had a long roll of specially prepared paper ribbon in place of a film or plates. By turning the handle the roll passed through the machine exposing the ribbon.

'It took about five minutes to finish the roll, and during ail that time the green lights predominated; but the dull heavy beat of muddy red never ceased to flow across the vacuum tubes of the disk at every seventh second. It was like a recurrent beat in some unheard and somehow displeasing melody.

'Lifting the exposed spool of paper ribbon out of the camera I laid it horizontally in the two "rests" that I had arranged for it on my modified gramaphone. Where the paper had been acted upon by the varying coloured lights which had appeared on the disk, the prepared surface had risen in curious, irregular little waves.

'I unrolled about a foot of the ribbon and attached the loose end to an empty spool-roller (on the opposite side of the machine) which I had geared to the driving clockwork mechanism of the gramo-phone. Then I took the diaphragm and lowered it gently into place above the ribbon. Instead of the usual needle the diaphragm was fitted with a beautifully made metal-filament brush, about an inch broad, which just covered the whole breadth of the ribbon. This fine and fragile brush rested lightly on the prepared surface of the paper, and when I started the machine the ribbon began to pass under the brush, and as it passed, the delicate metal-filament "bristles" followed every minute inequality of those tiny, irregular wave-like excrescences on the surface.

'I put the ear-pieces to my ears, and instantly I knew that I had succeeded in actually recording what Bains had heard in his sleep. In fact, I was even then hearing "mentally" by means of his effort of memory. I was listening to what appeared to be the faint, far-off squealing and grunting of countless swine. It was extraordinary, and at the same time exquisitely horrible and vile. It frightened me, with a sense of my having come suddenly and unexpectedly too near to something foul and most abominably dangerous.

'So strong and imperative was this feeling that I twitched the ear-pieces out of my ears, and sat a while staring round the room trying to steady my sensations back to normality.

'The room looked strange and vague in the dull glow of light from the circles, and I had a feeling that a taint of monstrosity was all about me in the air. I remembered what Bains had told me of the feeling he'd always had after coming up out of "that place" - as if some horrible atmosphere had followed him up and filled his bedroom. I understood him perfectly now - so much so that I had mentally used almost his exact phrase in explaining to myself what I felt.

'Turning round to speak to him I saw there was something curious about the centre of the "defense."

'Now, before I tell you fellows any more I must explain that there are certain, what I call "focussing", qualities about this new "defense" I've been trying.

'The Sigsand manuscript puts it something like this: "Avoid diversities of colour; nor stand ye within the barrier of the colour lights; for in colour hath Satan a delight. Nor can he abide in the Deep if ye adventure against him armed with red purple. So be warned. Neither forget that in blue, which is God's colour in the Heavens, ye have safety."

'You see, from that statement in the Sigsand manuscript I got my first notion for this new "defense" of mine. I have aimed to make it a "defense" and yet have "focussing" or "drawing" qualities such as the Sigsand hints at. I have experimented enormously, and I've proved that reds and purples - the two extreme colours of the spectrum - are fairly dangerous; so much so that I suspect they actually "draw" or "focus" the outside forces. Any action or "meddling" on the part of the experimentalist is tremendously enhanced in its effect if the action is taken within barriers composed of these colours, in certain proportions and tints.

'In the same way blue is distinctly a "general defense." Yellow appears to be neutral, and green a wonderful protection within limits. Orange, as far as I can tell, is slightly attractive and indigo is dangerous by itself in a limited way, but in certain combinations with the other colours it becomes a very powerful "defense". I've not yet discovered a tenth of the possibilities of these circles of mine. It's a kind of colour organ upon which I seem to play a tune of colour combinations that can be either safe or infernal in its effects. You know I have a keyboard with a separate switch to each of the colour circles.

'Well, you fellows will understand now what I felt when I saw the curious appearance of the floor in the middle of the "defense." It looked exactly as if a circular shadow lay, not just on the floor, but a few inches above it. The shadow seemed to deepen and blacken at the centre even while I watched it. It appeared to be spreading from the centre outwardly, and all the time it grew darker.

'I was watchful, and not a little puzzled; for the combination of lights that I had switched on approximated a moderately safe "general defense." Understand, I had no intention of making a focus until I had learnt more. In fact, I meant that first investigation not to go beyond a tentative inquiry into the kind of thing I had got to deal with.

'I knelt down quickly and felt the floor with the palm of my hand, but it was quite normal to the feel, and that reassured me that there was no Saaaiti mischief abroad; for that is a form of danger which can involve, and make use of, the very material of the "defense" itself. It can materialize out of everything except fire.

'As I knelt there I realized all at once that the legs of the table on which Bains lay were partly hidden in the ever blackening shadow, and my hands seemed to grow vague as I felt at the floor.

'I got up and stood away a couple of feet so as to see the phenomenon from a little distance. It struck me then that there was something different about the table itself. It seemed unaccountably lower.

'"It's the shadow hiding the legs," I thought to myself. "This promises to be interesting; but I'd better not let things go too far."

'I called out to Bains to stop thinking so hard. "Stop concentrating for a bit," I said; but he never answered, and it occurred to me suddenly that the table appeared to be still lower.

'"Bains," I shouted, "stop thinking a moment." Then in a flash I realized it. "Wake up, man! Wake up!" I cried.

'He had fallen over asleep - the very last thing he should have done; for it increased the danger twofold. No wonder I had been getting such good results! The poor beggar was worn out with his sleepless nights. He neither moved nor spoke as I strode across to him.

'"Wake up!" I shouted again, shaking him by the shoulder.

'My voice echoed uncomfortably round the big empty room; and Bains lay like a dead man.

'As I shook him again I noticed that I appeared to be standing up to my knees in the circular shadow. It looked like the mouth of a pit. My legs, from the knees downwards, were vague. The floor under my feet felt solid and firm when I stamped on it; but all the same I had a feeling that things were going a bit too far, so striding across to the switchboard I switched on the "full defense."

'Stepping back quickly to the table I had a horrible and sickening shock. The table had sunk quite unmistakably. Its top was within a couple of feet of the floor, and the legs had that fore-shortened appearance that one sees when a stick is thrust into water. They looked vague and shadowy in the peculiar circle of dark shadows which had such an extraordinary resemblance to the black mouth of a pit. I could see only the top of the table plainly with Bains lying motionless on it; and the whole thing was going down, as I stared, into that black circle.'

—— 3 ——

'THERE WAS NOT a moment to lose, and like a flash I caught Bains round his neck and body and lifted him clean up into my arms off the table. And as I lifted him he grunted like a great swine in my ear.

'The sound sent a thrill of horrible funk through me. It was just as though I held a hog in my arms instead of a human. I nearly dropped him. Then I held his face to the light and stared down at him. His eyes were half opened, and he was looking at me apparently as if he saw me perfectly.

'Then he grunted again. I could feel his small body quiver with the sound.

'I called out to him. "Bains," I said, "can you hear me?"

'His eyes still gazed at me; and then, as we looked at each other, he grunted like a swine again.

'I let go one hand, and hit him across the cheek, a stinging slap.

'"Wake up, Bains!" I shouted. "Wake up!" But I might have hit a corpse. He just stared up at me. And. suddenly I bent lower and looked into his eyes more closely. I never saw such a fixed, intelligent, mad horror as I saw there. It knocked out all my sudden disgust. Can you understand?

'I glanced round quickly at the table. It stood there at its normal height; and, indeed, it was in every way normal. The curious shadow that had somehow suggested to me the black mouth of the pit had vanished. I felt relieved; for it seemed to me that I had entirely broken up any possibility of a partial "focus" by means of the full "defense" which I had switched on.

'I laid Bains on the floor, and stood up to look round and consider what was best to do. I dared not step outside of the barriers, until any "dangerous tensions" there might be in the room had been dissipated. Nor was it wise, even inside the full "defense," to have him sleeping the kind of sleep he was in; not without certain preparations having been made first, which I had not made.

'I can tell you, I felt beastly anxious. I glanced down at Bains, and had a sudden fresh shock; for the peculiar circular shadow was forming all round him again, where he lay on the floor. His hands and face showed curiously vague, and distorted, as they might have looked through a few inches of faintly stained water. But his eyes were somehow clear to see. They were staring up, mute and terrible, at me, through that horrible darkening shadow.

'I stopped, and with one quick lift, tore him up off the floor into my arms, and for the third time he grunted like a swine, there in my arms. It was damnable.

'I stood up, in the barrier, holding Bains, and looked about the room again; then back at the floor. The shadow was still thick round about my feet, and I stepped quickly across to the other side of the table. I stared at the shadow, and saw that it had vanished; then I glanced down again at my feet, and had another shock; for the shadow was showing faintly again, all round where I stood.

'I moved a pace, and watched the shadow become invisible; and then, once more, like a slow stain, it began to grow about my feet.

'I moved again, a pace, and stared round the room, meditating a break for the door. And then, in that instant, I saw that this would be certainly impossible; for there was something indefinite in the atmosphere of the room - something that moved, circling slowly about the barrier.

'I glanced down at my feet, and saw that the shadow had grown thick about them. I stepped a pace to the right, and as it disappeared, I stared again round the big room and somehow it seemed tremendously big and unfamiliar. I wonder whether you can understand.

'As I stared I saw again the indefinite something that floated in the air of the room. I watched it steadily for maybe a minute. It went twice completely round the barrier in that time. And, suddenly, I saw it more distinctly. It looked like a small puff of black smoke.

'And then I had something else to think about; for all at once I was aware of an extraordinary feeling of vertigo, and in the same moment, a sense of sinking - I was sinking bodily. I literally sickened as I glanced down, for I saw in that moment that I had gone down, almost up to my thighs into what appeared to be actually the shadowy, but quite unmistakable, mouth of a pit. Do you under stand? I was sinking down into this thing, with Bains in my arms.

'A feeling of furious anger came over me, and I swung my right boot forward with a fierce kick. I kicked nothing tangible, for I went clean through the side of the shadowy thing, and fetched up against the table, with a crash. I had come through something that made all my skin creep and tingle - an invisible, vague something which resembled an electric tension. I felt that if it had been stronger, I might not have been able to charge through as I had. I wonder if I make it clear to you?

'I whirled round, but the beastly thing had gone; yet even as I stood there by the table, the slow greying of a circular shadow began to form again about my feet.

'I stepped to the other side of the table, and leaned against it for a moment: for I was shaking from head to foot with a feeling of extraordinary horror upon me, that was in some way, different from any kind of horror I have ever felt. It was as if I had in that one moment been near something no human has any right to be near, for his soul's sake. And abruptly, I wondered whether I had not felt just one brief touch of the horror that the rigid Bains was even then enduring as I held him in my arms.

'Outside of the barrier there were now several of the curious little clouds. Each one looked exactly like a little puff of black smoke. They increased as I watched them, which I did for several minutes; but all the time as I watched, I kept moving from one part to another of the "defense", so as to prevent the shadow forming round my feet again.

'Presently, I found that my constant changing of position had resolved into a slow monotonous walk round and round, inside the "defense"; and all the time I had to carry the unnaturally rigid body of poor Bains.

'It began to tire me; for though he was small, his rigidity made him dreadfully awkward and tiring to hold, as you can understand; yet I could not think what else to do; for I had stopped shaking him, or trying to wake him, for the simple reason that he was as wide awake as I was mentally; though but physically inanimate, through one of those partial spiritual disassociations which he had tried to explain to me.

'Now I had previously switched out the red, orange, yellow and green circles, and had on the full defense of the blue end of the spectrum - I knew that one of the repelling vibrations of each of the three colours: blue, indigo and violet were beating out protectingly into space; yet they were proving insufficient, and I was in the position of having either to take some desperate action to stimulate Bains to an even greater effort of will than I judged him to be making, or else to risk experimenting with fresh combinations of the defensive colours.

'You see, as things were at that moment, the danger was increasing steadily; for plainly, from the appearance of the air of the room outside the barrier, there were some mighty dangerous tensions generating. While inside the danger was also increasing; the steady recurrence of the shadow proving that the "defense" was insufficient.

'In short, I feared that Bains in his peculiar condition was literally a "doorway" into the "defense"; and unless I could wake him or find out the correct combinations of circles necessary to set up stronger repelling vibrations against that particular danger, there were very ugly possibilities ahead. I felt I had been incredibly rash not to have foreseen the possibility of Bains falling asleep under the hypnotic effect of deliberately paralleling the associations of sleep.

'Unless I could increase the repulsion of the barriers or wake him there was every likelihood of having to chose between a rush for the door - which the condition of the atmosphere outside the barrier showed to be practically impossible - or of throwing him outside the barrier, which, of course, was equally not possible.

'All this time I was walking round and round inside the barrier, when suddenly I saw a new development of the danger which threatened us. Right in the centre of the "defense" the shadow had formed into an intensely black circle, about a foot wide.

'This increased as I looked at it. It was horrible to see it grow. It crept out in an ever widening circle till it was quite a yard across.

'Quickly I put Bains on the floor. A tremendous attempt was evidently going to be made by some outside force to enter the "defense", and it was up to me to make a final effort to help Bains to "wake up." I took out my lancet, and pushed up his left coat sleeve.

'What I was going to do was a terrible risk, I knew, for there is no doubt that in some extraordinary fashion blood attracts.

'The Sigsand mentions it particularly in one passage which runs something like this: "In blood there is the Voice which calleth through all space. Ye Monsters in ye Deep hear, and hearing, they lust. Likewise hath it a greater power to reclaim backward ye soul that doth wander foolish adrift from ye body in which it doth have natural abiding. But woe unto him that doth spill ye blood in ye deadly hour; for there will be surely Monsters that shall hear ye Blood Cry."

'That risk I had to run. I knew that the blood would call to the outer forces; but equally I knew that it should call even more loudly to that portion of Bains' "Essence" that was adrift from him, down in those depths.

'Before lancing him, I glanced at the shadow. It had spread out until the nearest edge was not more than two feet away from Bains' right shoulder; and the edge was creeping nearer, like the blackening edge of burning paper, even while I stared. The whole thing had a less shadowy, less ghostly appearance than at any time before. And it looked simply and literally like the black mouth of a pit.

'"Now, Bains," I said, "pull yourself together, man. Wake up!" And at the same time as I spoke to him, I used my lancet quickly but superficially.

'I watched the little red spot of blood well up, then trickle round his wrist and fall to the floor of the "defense". And in the moment that it fell the thing that I had feared happened. There was a sound like a low peal of thunder in the room, and curious deadly-looking flashes of light rippled here and there along the floor outside the barrier.

'Once more I called to him, trying to speak firmly and steadily as I saw that the horrible shadowy circle had spread across every inch of the floor space of the centre of the "defense", making it appear as if both Bains and I were suspended above an unutterable black void - the black void that stared up at me out of the throat of that shadowy pit. And yet, all the time I could feel the floor solid under my knees as I knelt beside Bains holding his wrist.

' "Bains!" I called once more, trying not to shout madly at him. "Bains, wake up! Wake up, man! Wake up!"

'But he never moved, only stared up at me with eyes of quiet horror that seemed to be looking at me out of some dreadful eternity.'

—— 4 ——

'By this time the shadow had blackened all around us, and I felt that strangely terrible vertigo coming over me again. Jumping to my feet I caught up Bains in my arms and stepped over the first of the protective circles - the violet, and stood between it and the indigo circle, holding Bains as close to me as possible so as to prevent any portion of his helpless body from protruding outside the indigo and blue circles.

'From the black shadowy mouth which now filled the whole of the centre of the "defense" there came a faint sound - not near but seeming to come up at me out of unknown abysses. Very, very faint and lost it sounded, but I recognised it as unmistakably the infinitely remote murmur of countless swine.

'And that same moment Bains, as if answering the sound, grunted like a swine in my arms.

'There I stood between the glass vacuum tubes of the circles, gazing dizzily into that black shadowy pit-mouth, which seemed to drop sheer into hell from below my left elbow.

'Things had gone so utterly beyond all that I had thought of, and it had all somehow come about so gradually and yet so suddenly, that I was really a bit below my natural self. I felt mentally paralyzed, and could think of nothing except that not twenty feet away was the door and the outer natural world; and here was I face to face with some unthought-of danger, and all adrift, what to do to avoid it.

'You fellows will understand this better when I tell you that the bluish glare from the three circles showed me that there were now hundreds and hundreds of those small smoke-like puffs of black cloud circling round and round outside the barrier in an unvarying, unending procession.

'And all the time I was holding the rigid body of Bains in my arms, trying not to give way to the loathing that got me each time he grunted. Every twenty or thirty seconds he grunted, as if in answer to the sounds which were almost too faint for my normal hearing. I can tell you, it was like holding something worse than a corpse in my arms, standing there balanced between physical death on the one side and soul destruction on the other.

'Abruptly, from out of the deep that lay so close that my elbow and shoulder overhung it, there came again a hint, marvelously faint murmur of swine, so utterly far away that the sound was as remote as a lost echo.

'Bains answered it with a pig-like squeal that set every fibre in me protesting in sheer human revolt, and I sweated coldly from head to foot. Pulling myself together I tried to pierce down into the mouth of the great shadow when, for the second time, a low peel of thunder sounded in the room, and every joint in my body seemed to jolt and burn.

'In turning to look down the pit I had allowed one of Bains' heels to protrude for a moment slightly beyond the blue circle, and a fraction of the "tension" outside the barrier had evidently discharged through Bains and me. Had I been standing directly inside the "defense" instead of being "insulated" from it by the violet circle, then no doubt things might have been much more serious. As it was, I had, psychically, that dreadful soiled feeling which the healthy human always experiences when he comes too closely in contact with certain Outer Monstrosities. Do you fellows remember how I had just the same feeling when the Hand came too near me in the "Gateway" case?

'The physical effects were sufficiently interesting to mention; for Bains left boot had been ripped open, and the leg of his trousers was charred to the knee, while all around the leg were numbers of bluish marks in the form of irregular spirals.

'I stood there holding Bains, and shaking from head to foot. My head ached and each joint had a queer numbish feeling; but my physical pains were nothing compared with my mental distress. I felt that we were done! I had no room to turn or move for the space between the violet circle which was the innermost, and the blue circle which was the outermost of those in use was thirty-one inches, including the one inch of the indigo circle. So you see I was forced to stand there like an image, fearing each moment lest I should get another shock, and quite unable to think what to do.

'I daresay five minutes passed in this fashion. Bains had not grunted once since the "tension" caught him, and for this I was just simply thankful; though at first I must confess I had feared for a moment that he was dead.

'No further sounds had come up out of the black mouth to my left, and I grew steady enough again to begin to look about me, and think a bit. I leant again so as to look directly down into the shadowy pit. The edge of the circular mouth was now quite defined, and had a curious solid look, as if it were formed out of some substance like black glass.

'Below the edge, I could trace the appearance of solidity for a considerable distance, though in a vague sort of way. The centre of this extraordinary phenomenon was simple and unmitigated blackness - an utter velvety blackness that seemed to soak the very light out of the room down into it. I could see nothing else, and if anything else came out of it except a complete silence, it was the atmosphere of frightening suggestion that was affecting me more and more every minute.

'I turned away slowly and carefully, so as not to run any risks of allowing either Bains or myself to expose any part of us over the blue circle. Then I saw that things outside of the blue circle had developed considerably; for the odd, black puffs of smoke-like cloud had increased enormously and blent into a great, gloomy, circular wall of tufted cloud, going round and round and round eternally, and hiding the rest of the room entirely from me.

'Perhaps a minute passed, while I stared at this thing; and then, you know, the room was shaken slightly. This shaking lasted for three or four seconds, and then passed; but it came again in about half a minute, and was repeated from time to time. There was a queer oscillating quality in the shaking, that made me think suddenly of that Jarvee Haunting case. You remember it?

'There came again the shaking, and a ripple of deadly light seemed to play round the outside of the barrier; and then, abruptly, the room was full of a strange roaring - a brutish enormous yelling, grunting storm of swine-sounds.

'They fell away into a complete silence, and the rigid Bains grunted twice in my arms, as if answering. Then the storm of swine noise came again, beating up in a gigantic riot of brute sound that roared through the room, piping, squealing, grunting, and howling. And as it sank with a steady declination, there came a single gargantuan grunt out of some dreadful throat of monstrousness, and in one beat, the crashing chorus of unknown millions of swine came thundering and raging through the room again.

'There was more in that sound than mere chaos - there was a mighty devilish rhythm in it. Suddenly, it swept down again into a multitudinous swinish whispering and minor gruntings of unthink-able millions; and then with a rolling deafening bellow of sound came the single vast grunt. And, as if lifted upon it the swine roar of the millions of the beasts beat up through the room again; and at every seventh second, as I knew well enough without the need of the watch on my wrist, came the single storm beat of the great grunt out of the throat of unknowable monstrosity - and in my arms, Bains, the human, grunted in time to the swine melody - a rigid grunting monster there in my two arms.

'I tell you from head to foot I shook and sweated. I believe I prayed; but if I did I don't know what I prayed. I have never before felt or endured just what I felt, standing there in that thirty-one-inch space, with that grunting thing in my arms, and the hell melody beating up out of the great Deeps: and to my right, "tensions" that would have torn me into a bundle of blazing tattered flesh, if I had jumped out over the barriers.

'And then, with an effect like a clap of unexpected thunder, the vast storm of sound ceased; and the room was full of silence and an unimaginable horror.

'This silence continued. I want to say something which may sound a bit silly; but the silence seemed to trickle round the room. I don't know why I felt it like that; but my words give you just what I seemed to feel, as I stood there holding the softly grunting body of Bains.

'The circular, gloomy wall of dense black cloud enclosed the barrier as completely as ever, and moved round and round and round, with a slow, "eternal" movement. And at the back of that black wall of circling cloud, a dead silence went trickling round the room, out of my sight. Do you understand at all?...

'IT SEEMED to me to show very clearly the state of almost insane mental and psychic tension I was enduring.... The way in which my brain insisted that the silence was trickling round the room, interests me enormously; for I was either in a state approximating a phase of madness, or else I was, psychically, tuned to some abnormal pitch of awareness and sensitiveness in which silence had ceased to be an abstract quality, and had become to me a definite concrete element, much as (to use a stupidly crude illustration), the invisible moisture of the atmosphere becomes a visible and concrete element when it becomes deposited as water. I wonder whether this thought attracts you as it does me?

'And then, you know, a slow awareness grew in me of some further horror to come. This sensation or knowledge or whatever it should be named, was so strong that I had a sudden feeling of suffocation.... I felt that I could bear no more; and that if anything else happened, I should just pull out my revolver and shoot Bains through the head, and then myself, and so end the whole dreadful business.

'This feeling, however, soon passed; and I felt stronger and more ready to face things again. Also, I had the first, though still indefinite, idea of a way in which to make things a bit safer; but I was too dazed to see how to "shape" to help myself efficiently.

'And then a low, far-off whining stole up into the room, and I knew that the danger was coming. I leant slowly to my left, taking care not to let Bains' feet stick over the blue circle, and stared down into the blackness of the pit that dropped sheer into some Unknown, from under my left elbow.

'The whining died; but far down in the blackness, there was something - just a remote luminous spot. I stood in a grim silence for maybe ten long minutes, and looked down at the thing. It was increasing in size all the time, and had become much plainer to see; yet it was still lost in the far, tremendous Deep.

'Then, as I stood and looked, the low whining sound crept up to me again, and Bains, who had lain like a log in my arms all the time, answered it with a long animallike whine, that was somehow newly abominable.

'A very curious thing happened then; for all around the edge of the pit, that looked so peculiarly like black glass, there came a sudden, luminous glowing. It came and went oddly, smouldering queerly round and round the edge in an opposite direction to the circling of the wall of black, tufted cloud on the outside of the barrier.

'This peculiar glowing finally disappeared, and, abruptly, out of the tremendous Deep, I was conscious of a dreadful quality or "atmosphere" of monstrousness that was coming up out of the pit. If I said there had been a sudden waft of it, this would very well describe the actuality of it; but the spiritual sickness of distress that it caused me to feel, I am simply stumped to explain to you. It was something that made me feel I should be soiled to the very core of me, if I did not beat it off from me with my will.

'I leant sharply away from the pit towards the outer of the burning circles. I meant to see that no part of my body should over-hang the pit whilst that disgusting power was beating up out of the unknown depths.

'And thus it was, facing so rigidly away from the centre of the "defense", I saw presently a fresh thing; for there was something, many things, I began to think, on the other side of the gloomy wall that moved everlastingly around the outside of the barrier.

'The first thing I noticed was a queer disturbance of the ever circling cloud-wall. This disturbance was within eighteen inches of the floor, and directly before me. There was a curious, "puddling" action in the misty wall; as if something were meddling with it. The area of this peculiar little disturbance could not have been more than a foot across, and it did not remain opposite to me; but was taken round by the circling of the wall.

'When it came past me again, I noticed that it was bulging slightly inwards towards me: and as it moved away from me once more, I saw another similar disturbance, and then a third and a fourth, all in different parts of the slowly whirling black wall; and all of them were no more than about eighteen inches from the floor.

'When the first one came opposite me again, I saw that the slight bulge had grown into a very distinct protuberance towards me.

'All around the moving wall, there had now come these curious swellings. They continued to reach inwards, and to elongate; and all the time they kept in a constant movement.

'Suddenly, one of them broke, or opened, at the apex, and there protruded through, for an instant, the tip of a pallid, but unmistakable snout. It was gone at once, but I had seen the thing distinctly; and within a minute, I saw another one poke suddenly through the wall, to my right, and withdraw as quickly. I could not look at the base of the strange, black, moving circle about the barrier without seeing a swinish snout peep through momentarily, in this place or that.

'I stared at these things in a very peculiar state of mind. There was so great a weight of the abnormal about me, before and behind and every way, that to a certain extent it bred in me a sort of antidote to fear. Can you understand? It produced in me a temporary dazedness in which things and the horror of things became less real. I stared at them, as a child stares out from a fast train at a quickly passing night-landscape, oddly hit by the furnaces of unknown industries. I want you to try to understand.

'In my arms Bains lay quiet and rigid; and my arms and back ached until I was one dull ache in all my body; but I was only partly conscious of this when I roused momentarily from my psychic to my physical awaredness, to shift him to another position, less intolerable temporarily to my tired arms and back.

'There was suddenly a fresh thing - a low but enormous, solitary grunt came rolling, vast and brutal into the room. It made the still body of Bains quiver against me, and he grunted thrice in return, with the voice of a young pig.

'High up in the moving wall of the barrier, I saw a fluffing out of the black tufted clouds; and a pig's hoof and leg, as far as the knuckle, came through and pawed a moment. This was about nine or ten feet above the floor. As it gradually disappeared I heard a low grunting from the other side of the veil of clouds which broke out suddenly into a diafaeon of brute-sound, grunting, squealing and swine-howling; all formed into a sound that was the essential melody of the brute - a grunting, squealing howling roar that rose, roar by roar, howl by howl and squeal by squeal to a crescendo of horrors - the bestial growths, longings, zests and acts of some grotto of hell.... It is no use, I can't give it to you. I get dumb with the failure of my command over speech to tell you what that grunting, howling, roaring melody conveyed to me. It had in it something so inexplicably below the horizons of the soul in its monstrousness and fearfulness that the ordinary simple fear of death itself, with all its attendant agonies and terrors and sorrows, seemed like a thought of something peaceful and infinitely holy compared with the fear of those unknown elements in that dreadful roaring melody. And the sound was with me inside the room - there right in the room with me. Yet I seemed not to be aware of confining walls, but of echoing spaces of gargantuan corridors. Curious! I had in my mind those two words - gargantuan corridors.

As the rolling chaos of swine melody beat itself away on every side, there came booming through it a single grunt, the single recurring grunt of the HOG; for I knew now that I was actually and without any doubt hearing the beat of monstrosity, the HOG.

'In the Sigsand the thing is described something like this: "Ye Hogge which ye Almighty alone hath power upon. If in sleep or in ye hour of danger ye hear the voice of ye Hogge, cease ye to meddle. For ye Hogge doth be of ye outer Monstrous Ones, nor shall any human come nigh him nor continue meddling when ye hear his voice, for in ye earlier life upon the world did the Hogge have power, and shall again in ye end. And in that ye Hogge had once a power upon ye earth, so doth he crave sore to come again. And dreadful shall be ye harm to ye soul if ye continue to meddle, and to let ye beast come nigh. And I say unto all, if ye have brought this dire danger upon ye, have memory of ye cross, for of all sign hath ye Hogge a horror."

'There's a lot more, but I can't remember it all and that is about the substance of it.

'There was I holding Bains who was all the time howling that dreadful grunt out with the voice of a swine. I wonder I didn't go mad. It was, I believe, the antidote of dazedness produced by the strain which helped me through each moment.

'A minute later, or perhaps five minutes, I had a sudden new sensation, like a warning cutting through my dulled feelings. I turned my head; but there was nothing behind me, and bending over to my left I seemed to be looking down into that black depth which fell away sheer under my left elbow. At that moment the roaring bellow of swine-noise ceased and I seemed to be staring down into miles of black aether at something that hung there - a pallid face floating far down and remote - a great swine face.

'And as I gazed I saw it grow bigger. A seemingly motionless, pallid swine-face rising upward out of the depth. And suddenly I realized that I was actually looking at the Hog.'

'FOR PERHAPS A FULL minute I stared down through the darkness at that thing swimming like some far-off, deadwhite planet in the stupendous void. And then I simply woke up bang, as you might say, to the possession of my faculties. For just a certain over-degree of strain had brought about the dumbly helpful anesthesia of dazedness, so this sudden overwhelming supreme fact of horror produced, in turn, its reaction from inertness to action. I passed in one moment from listlessness to a fierce efficiency.

'I knew that I had, through some accident, penetrated beyond all previous "bounds", and that I stood where no human soul had any right to be, and that in but a few of the puny minutes of earth's time I might be dead.

'Whether Bains had passed beyond the "lines of retraction" or not, I could not tell. I put him down carefully but quickly on his side, between the inner circles - that is, the violet circle and the indigo circle - where he lay grunting slowly. Feeling that the dreadful moment had come I drew out my automatic. It seemed best to make sure of our end before that thing in the depth came any nearer: for once Bains in his present condition came within what I might term the "inductive forces" of the monster, he would cease to be human. There would happen, as in that case of Aster who stayed outside the pentacles in the Black Veil Case, what can only be described as a pathological, spiritual change - literally in other words, soul destruction.

'And then something seemed to be telling me not to shoot. This sounds perhaps a bit superstitious; but I meant to kill Bains in that moment, and what stopped me was a distinct message from the outside.

'I tell you, it sent a great thrill of hope through me, for I knew that the forces which govern the spinning of the outer circle were intervening. But the very fact of the intervention proved to me afresh the enormous spiritual peril into which we had stumbled; for that inscrutable Protective Force only intervenes between the human soul and the Outer Monstrosities.

'The moment I received that message I stood up like a flash and turned towards the pit, stepping over the violet circle slap into the mouth of darkness. I had to take the risk in order to get at the switch board which lay on the glass shelf under the table top in the centre. I could not shake free from the horror of the idea that I might fall down through that awful blackness. The floor felt solid enough under me; but I seemed to be walking on nothing above a black void, like an inverted starless night, with the face of the approaching Hog rising up from far down under my feet - a silent, incredible thing out of the abyss - a pallid, floating swine-face, framed in enormous blackness.

'Two quick, nervous strides took me to the table standing there in the centre with its glass legs apparently resting on nothing. I grabbed out the switch board, sliding out the vulcanite plate which carried the switch-control of the blue circle. The battery which fed this circle was the right-hand one of the row of seven, and each battery was marked with the letter of its circle painted on it, so that in an emergency I could select any particular battery in a moment.

'As I snatched up the B switch I had a grim enough warning of the unknown dangers that I was risking in that short journey of two steps; for that dreadful sense of vertigo returned suddenly and for one horrible moment I saw everything through a blurred medium as if I were trying to look through water.

'Below me, far away down between my feet I could see the Hog which, in some peculiar way, looked different dearer and much nearer, and enormous. I felt it had got nearer to me all in a moment. And suddenly I had the impression I was descending bodily.

'I had a sense of a tremendous force being used to push me over the side of that pit, but with every shred of will power I had in me I hurled myself into the smoky appearance that hid everything and reached the violet circle where Bains lay in front of me.

'Here I crouched down on my heels, and with my two arms out before me I slipped the nails of each forefinger under the vulcanite base of the blue circle, which I lifted very gently so that when the base was far enough from the floor I could push the tips of my fingers underneath. I took care to keep from reaching farther under than the inner edge of the glowing tube which rested on the two-inch-broad foundation of vulcanite.

'Very slowly I stood upright, lifting the side of the blue circle with me. My feet were between the indigo and the violet circles, and only the blue circle between me and sudden death; for if it had snapped with the unusual strain I was putting upon it by lifting it like that, I knew that I should in all probability go west pretty quickly.

'So you fellows can imagine what I felt like. I was conscious of a disagreeable faint prickling that was strongest in the tips of my fingers and wrists, and the blue circle seemed to vibrate strangely as if minute particles of something were impinging upon it in countless millions. Along the shining glass tubes for a couple of feet on each side of my hands a queer haze of tiny sparks boiled and whirled in the form of an extraordinary halo.

'Stepping forward over the indigo circle I pushed the blue circle out against the slowly moving wall of black cloud causing a ripple of tiny pale flashes to curl in over the circle. These flashes ran along the vacuum tube until they came to the place where the blue circle crossed the indigo, and there they flicked off into space with sharp cracks of sound.

'As I advanced slowly and carefully with the blue circle a most extraordinary thing happened, for the moving wall of cloud gave from it in a great belly of shadow, and appeared to thin away from before it. Lowering my edge of the circle to the floor I stepped over Bains and right into the mouth of the pit, lifting the other side of the circle over the table. It creaked as if it were about to break in half as I lifted it, but eventually it came over safely.

'When I looked again into the depth of that shadow I saw below me the dreadful pallid head of the Hog floating in a circle of night. It struck me that it glowed very slightly - just a vague luminosity. And quite near - comparatively. No one could have judged distances in that black void.

'Picking up the edge of the blue circle again as I had done before, I took it out further till it was half clear of the indigo circle. Then I picked up Bains and carried him to that portion of the floor guarded by the part of the blue circle which was clear of the "defense". Then I lifted the circle and started to move it forward as quickly as I dared, shivering each time the joints squeaked as the whole fabric of it groaned with the strain I was putting upon it. And all the time the moving wall of tufted clouds gave from the edge of the blue circle, bellying away from it in a marvelous fashion as if blown by an unheard wind.

'From time to time little flashes of light had begun to flick in over the blue circle, and I began to wonder whether it would be able to hold out the "tension" until I had dragged it clear of the defense.

'Once it was clear I hoped the abnormal stress would cease from about us, and concentrate chiefly around the "defense" again, and the attractions of the negative "tension."

'Just then I heard a sharp tap behind me, and the blue circle jarred somewhat, having now ridden completely over the violet and indigo circles, and dropped clear on to the floor. The same instant there came a low rolling noise as of thunder, and a curious roaring. The black circling wall had thinned away from around us and the room showed clearly once more, yet nothing was to be seen except that now and then a peculiar bluish flicker of light would ripple across the floor.

'Turning to look at the "defense" I noticed it was surrounded by the circling wall of black cloud, and looked strangely extraordinary seen from the outside. It resembled a slightly swaying squat funnel of whirling black mist reaching from the floor to the ceiling, and through it I could see glowing, sometimes vague and sometimes plain, the indigo and violet circles. And then as I watched, the whole room seemed suddenly filled with an awful presence which pressed upon me with a weight of horror that was the very essence of spiritual deathliness.

'Kneeling there in the blue circle by Bains, my initiative faculties stupefied and temporarily paralyzed, I could form no further plan of escape, and indeed I seemed to care for nothing at the moment. I felt I had already escaped from immediate destruction and I was strung up to an amazing pitch of indifference to any minor horrors.

'Bains all this while had been quietly lying on his side. I rolled him over and looked closely at his eyes, taking care on account of his condition not to gaze into them; for if he had passed beyond the "line of retraction" he would be dangerous. I mean, if the "wandering" part of his essence had been assimilated by the Hog, then Bains would be spiritually accessible and might be even then no more than the outer form of the man, charged with radiation of the monstrous ego of the Hog, and therefore capable of what I might term for want of a more exact phrase, a psychically infective force; such force being more readily transmitted through the eyes than any other way, and capable of producing a brain storm of an extremely dangerous character.

'I found Bains, however, with both eyes with an extraordinary distressed interned quality; not the eyeballs, remember, but a reflex action transmitted from the "mental eye" to the physical eye, and giving to the physical eye an expression of thought instead of sight. I wonder whether I make this clear to you?

'Abruptly, from every part of the room there broke out the noise of those hoofs again, making the place echo with the sound as if a thousand swine had started suddenly from an absolute immobility into a mad charge. The whole riot of animal sound seemed to heave itself in one wave towards the oddly swaying and circling funnel of black cloud which rose from floor to ceiling around the violet and indigo circles.

'As the sounds ceased I saw something was rising up through the middle of the "defense". It rose with a slow steady movement. I saw it pale and huge through the swaying, whirling funnel of cloud - a monstrous pallid snout rising out of that unknowable abyss.... It rose higher like a huge pale mound. Through a thinning of the cloud curtain I saw one small eye.... I shall never see a pig's eye again without feeling something of what I felt then. A pig's eye with a sort of hell-light of vile understanding shining at the back of it.'

—— 6 ——

"AND THEN SUDDENLY A DREADFUL terror came over me, for I saw the beginning of the end that I had been dreading all along - I saw through the slow whirl of the cloud curtains that the violet circle had begun to leave the floor. It was being taken up on the spread of the vast snout.

'Straining my eyes to see through the swaying funnel of clouds I saw that the violet circle had melted and was running down the pale sides of the snout in streams of violet-colored fire. And as it melted there came a change in the atmosphere of the room. The black funnel shone with a dull gloomy red, and a heavy red glow filled the room.

'The change was such as one might experience if one had been looking through a protective glass at some light and the glass had been suddenly removed. But there was a further change that I realized directly through my feelings. It was as if the horrible presence in the room had come closer to my own soul. I wonder if I am making it at all clear to you. Before, it had oppressed me somewhat as a death on a very gloomy and dreary day beats down upon one's spirit. But now there was a savage menace, and the actual feeling of a foul thing close up against me. It was horrible, simply horrible.

'And then Bains moved. For the first time since he went to sleep the rigidity went out of him, and rolling suddenly over on to his stomach he fumbled up in a curious animallike fashion, on to his hands and feet. Then he charged straight across the blue circle towards the thing in the "defense".

'With a shriek I jumped to pull him back; but it was not my voice that stopped him. It was the blue circle. It made him give back from it as though some invisible hand had jerked him backwards. He threw up his head like a hog, squealing with the voice of a swine, and started off round the inside of the blue circle. Round and round it he went, twice attempting to bolt across it to the horror in that swaying funnel of cloud. Each time he was thrown back, and each time he squealed like a great swine, the sounds echoing round the room in a horrible fashion as though they came from somewhere a long way off.

'By this time I was fairly sure that Bains had indeed passed the "line of retraction", and the knowledge brought a fresh and more hopeless horror and pity to me, and a grimmer fear for myself. I knew that if it were so, it was not Bains I had with me in the circle but a monster, and that for my own last chance of safety I should have to get him outside of the circle.

'He had ceased his tireless running round and round, and now lay on his side grunting continually and softly in a dismal kind of way. As the slowly whirling clouds thinned a little I saw again that pallid face with some clearness. It was still rising, but slowly, very slowly, and again a hope grew in me that it might be checked by the "defense". Quite plainly I saw that the horror was looking at Bains, and at that moment I saved my own life and soul by looking down. There, close to me on the floor was the thing that looked like Bains, its hands stretched out to grip my ankles. Another second, and I should have been tripped outwards. Do you realize what that would have meant?

'It was no time to hesitate. I simply jumped and came down crash with my knees on top of Bains. He lay quiet enough after a short struggle; but I took off my braces and lashed his hands up behind him. And I shivered with the very touch of him, as though I was touching something monstrous.

'By the time I had finished I noticed that the reddish glow in the room had deepened quite considerably, and the whole room was darker. The destruction of the violet circle had reduced the light perceptibly; but the darkness that I am speaking of was something more than that. It seemed as if something now had come into the atmosphere of the room - a sort of gloom, and in spite of the shining of the blue circle and the indigo circle inside the funnel of cloud, there was now more red light than anything else.

'Opposite me the huge, cloud-shrouded monster in the indigo circle appeared to be motionless. I could see its outline vaguely all the time, and only when the cloud funnel thinned could I see it plainly _ a vast, snouted mound, faintly and whitely luminous, one gargantuan side turned towards me, and near the base of the slope a minute slit out of which shone one whitish eye.

'Presently through the thin gloomy red vapour I saw something that killed the hope in me, and gave me a horrible despair; for the indigo circle, the final barrier of the defense, was being slowly lifted into the air - the Hog had begun to rise higher. I could see its dreadful snout rising upwards out of the cloud. Slowly, very slowly, the snout rose up, and the indigo circle went up with it.

'In the dead stillness of that room I got a strange sense that all eternity was tense and utterly still as if certain powers knew of this horror I had brought into the world.... And then I had an awareness of something coming... something from far, far away. It was as if some hidden unknown part of my brain knew it. Can you under-stand? There was somewhere in the heights of space a light that was coming near. I seemed to hear it coming. I could just see the body of Bains on the floor, huddled and shapeless and inert. Within the swaying veil of cloud the monster showed as a vast pale, faintly luminous mound, hugely snouted - an infernal hillock of monstros-ity, pallid and deadly amid the redness that hung in the atmosphere of the room.

'Something told me that it was making a final effort against the help that was coming. I saw the indigo circle was now some inches from the floor, and every moment I expected to see it flash into streams of indigo fire running down the pale slopes of the snout. I could see the circle beginning to move upward at a perceptible speed. The monster was triumphing.

'Out in some realm of space a low continuous thunder sounded. The thing in the great heights was coming fast, but it could never come in time. The thunder grew from a low, far mutter into a deep steady rolling of sound.... It grew louder and louder, and as it grew I saw the indigo circle, now shining through the red gloom of the room, was a whole foot off the floor. I thought I saw a faint splutter of indigo light.... The final circle of the barrier was beginning to melt.

'That instant the thunder of the thing in flight which my brain heard so plainly, rose into a crashing, a worldshaking bellow of speed, making the room rock and vibrate to an immensity of sound. A strange flash of blue flame ripped open the funnel of cloud momentarily from top to base, and I saw for one brief instant the pallid monstrosity of the Hog, stark and pale and dreadful.

'Then the sides of the funnel joined again hiding the thing from me as the funnel became submerged quickly into a dome of silent blue light - God's own colour! All at once it seemed the cloud had gone, and from floor to ceiling of the room, in awful majesty, like a living Presence, there appeared that dome of blue fire banded with three rings of green light at equal distances. There was no sound or movement, not even a flicker, nor could I see anything in the light: for looking into it was like looking into the cold blue of the skies. But I felt sure that there had come to our aid one of those inscrutable forces which govern the spinning of the outer circle, for the dome of blue light, banded with three green bands of silent fire, was the outward or visible sign of an enormous force, undoubtedly of a defensive nature.

'Through ten minutes of absolute silence I stood there in the blue circle watching the phenomenon. Minute by minute I saw the heavy repellent red driven out of the room as the place lightened quite noticeably. And as it lightened, the body of Bains began to resolve out of a shapeless length of shadow, detail by detail, until I could see the braces with which I had lashed his wrists together.

'And as I looked at him his body moved slightly, and in a weak but perfectly sane voice he said:

'"I've had it again! My God! I've had it again!"'

'I KNELT DOWN QUICKLY by his side and loosened the braces from his wrists, helping him to turn over and sit up. He gripped my arm a little crazily with both hands.

'"I went to sleep after all," he said. "And I've been down there again. My God! It nearly had me. I was down in that awful place and it seemed to be just round a great corner, and I was stopped from coming back. I seemed to have been fighting for ages and ages. I felt I was going mad. Mad! I've been nearly down into a hell. I could hear you calling down to me from some awful height. I could hear your voice echoing along yellow passages. They were yellow. I know they were. And I tried to come and I couldn't."

'"Did you see me?" I asked him when he stopped, gasping.

'"No," he answered, leaning his head against my shoulder. "I tell you it nearly got me that time. I shall never dare go to sleep again as long as I live. Why didn't you wake me?"

'"I did," I told him. "I had you in my arms most of the time. You kept looking up into my eyes as if you knew I was there."

'"I know," he said. "I remember now; but you seemed to be up at the top of a frightful hole, miles and miles up from me, and those horrors were grunting and squealing and howling, and trying to catch me and keep me down there. But I couldn't see anything - only the yellow walls of those passages. And all the time there was something round the corner."

'"Anyway, you're safe enough now," I told him. "And I'll guarantee you shall be safe in the future."

'The room had grown dark save for the light from the blue circle. The dome had disappeared, the whirling funnel of black cloud had gone, the Hog had gone, and the light had died out of the indigo circle. And the atmosphere of the room was safe and normal again as

I proved by moving the switch, which was near me, so as to lessen the defensive power of the blue circle and enable me to "feel" the outside tension. Then I turned to Bains.

'"Come along," I said. "We'll go and get something to eat, and have a rest."

'But Bains was already sleeping like a tired child, his head pillowed on his hand. "Poor little devil!" I said as I picked him up in my arms. "Poor little devil!"

'I walked across to the main switchboard and threw over the current so as to throw the "V" protective pulse out of the four walls and the door; then I carried Bains out into the sweet wholesome normality of everything. It seemed wonderful, coming out of that chamber of horrors, and it seemed wonderful still to see my bedroom door opposite, wide open, with the bed looking so soft and white as usual - so ordinary and human. Can you chaps understand?

'I carried Bains into the room and put him on the couch; and then it was I realized how much I'd been up against, for when I was getting myself a drink I dropped the bottle and had to get another.

'After I had made Bains drink a glass I laid him on the bed.

'"Now," I said, "look into my eyes fixedly. Do you hear me? You are going off to sleep safely and soundly, and if anything troubles you, obey me and wake up. Now, sleep - sleep - sleep! "

'I swept my hands down over his eyes half a dozen times, and he fell over like a child. I knew that if the danger came again he would obey my will and wake up. I intend to cure him, partly by hypnotic suggestion, partly by a certain electrical treatment which I am getting Doctor Witton to give him.

'That night I slept on the couch, and when I went to look at Bains in the morning I found him still sleeping, so leaving him there I went into the test room to examine results. I found them very surprising.

'Inside the room I had a queer feeling, as you can imagine. It was extraordinary to stand there in that curious bluish light from the "treated" windows, and see the blue circle lying, still glowing, where I had left it; and further on, the "defense", lying circle within circle, all "out"; and in the centre the glass-legged table standing where a few hours before it had been submerged in the horrible monstrosity of the Hog. I tell you, it all seemed like a wild and horrible dream as I stood there and looked. I have carried out some curious tests in there before now, as you know, but I've never come nearer to a catastrophe.

'I left the door open so as not to feel shut in, and then I walked over to the "defense". I was intensely curious to see what had happened physically under the action of such a force as the Hog. I found unmistakable signs that proved the thing had been indeed a Saaitii manifestation, for there had been no psychic or physical illusion about the melting of the violet circle. There remained nothing of it except a ring of patches of melted glass. The gutta base had been fused entirely, but the floor and everything was intact. You see, the Saaitii forms can often attack and destroy, or even make use of, the very defensive material used against them.

'Stepping over the outer circle and looking closely at the indigo circle I saw that it was melted clean through in several places. Another fraction of time and the Hog would have been free to expand as an invisible mist of horror and destruction into the atmosphere of the world. And then, in that very moment of time, salvation had come. I wonder if you can get my feelings as I stood there staring down at the destroyed barrier.'

Carnacki began to knock out his pipe which is always a sign that he has ended his tale, and is ready to answer any questions we may want to ask.

Taylor was first in. 'Why didn't you use the Electric Pentacle as well as your new spectrum circles?' he asked.

'Because,' replied Carnacki, 'the pentacle is simply "defensive" and I wished to have the power to make a "focus" during the early part of the experiment, and then, at the critical moment, to change the combination of the colours so as to have a "defense" against the results of the "focus". You follow me.

'You see,' he went on, seeing we hadn't grasped his meaning, 'there can be no "focus" within a pentacle. It is just of a "defensive" nature. Even if I had switched the current out of the electric pentacle I should still have had to contend with the peculiar and undoubtedly "defensive" power that its form seems to exert, and this would have been sufficient to "blur" the focus.

'In this new research work I'm doing, I'm bound to use a "focus" and so the pentacle is barred. But I'm not sure it matters. I'm convinced this new spectrum "defense" of mine will prove absolutely invulnerable when I've learnt how to use it; but it will take me some time. This last case has taught me something new. I had never thought of combining green with blue; but the three bands of green in the blue of that dome has set me thinking. If only I knew the right combinations! It's the combinations I've got to learn. You'll understand better the importance of these combinations when I remind you that green by itself is, in a very limited way, more deadly than red itself - and red is the danger colour of all.'

'Tell us, Carnacki,' I said, 'what is the Hog? Can you? I mean what kind of monstrosity is it? Did you really see it, or was it all some horrible, dangerous kind of dream? How do you know it was one of the outer monsters? And what is the difference between that sort of danger and the sort of thing you saw in the Gateway of the Monster case? And what.... ?'

'Steady! ' laughed Carnacki. 'One at a time! I'll answer all your questions; but I don't think I'll take them quite in your order. For instance, speaking about actually seeing the Hog, I might say that, speaking generally, things seen of a "ghostly" nature are not seen with the eyes; they are seen with the mental eye which has this psychic quality, not always developed to a useable state, in addition to its "normal" duty of revealing to the brain what our physical eyes record.

'You will understand that when we see "ghostly" things it is often the "mental" eye performing simultaneously the duty of revealing to the brain what the physical eye sees as well as what it sees itself. The two sights blending their functions in such a fashion gives us the impression that we are actually seeing through our physical eyes the whole of the "sight" that is being revealed to the brain.

'In this way we get an impression of seeing with our physical eyes both the material and the immaterial parts of an "abnormal" scene; for each part being received and revealed to the brain by machinery suitable to the particular purpose appears to have equal value of reality that is, it appears to be equally material. Do you follow me?'

We nodded our assent, and Carnacki continued:

'In the same way, were anything to threaten our psychic body we should have the impression, generally speaking, that it was our physical body that had been threatened, because our psychic sensations and impressions would be super-imposed upon our physical, in the same way that our psychic and our physical sight are super-imposed.

'Our sensations would blend in such a way that it would be impossible to differentiate between what we felt physically and what we felt psychically. To explain better what I mean. A man may seem to himself, in a "ghostly" adventure, to fall actually. That is, to be falling in a physical sense; but all the while it may be his psychic entity, or being - call it what you will - that is falling. But to his brain there is presented the sensation of falling all together. Do you get me?

'At the same time, please remember that the danger is none the less because it is his psychic body that falls. I am referring to the sensation I had of falling during the time of stepping across the mouth of that pit. My physical body could walk over it easily and feel the floor solid under me; but my psychic body was in very real danger of falling. Indeed, I may be said to have literally carried my psychic body over, held within me by the pull of my lifeforce. You see, to my psychic body the pit was as real and as actual as a coal pit would have been to my physical body. It was merely the pull of my life-force which prevented my psychic body from falling out of me, rather like a plummet, down through the everlasting depths in obedience to the giant pull of the monster.

'As you will remember, the pull of the Hog was too great for my life-force to withstand, and, psychically, I began to fall. Immediately on my brain was recorded a sensation identical with that which would have been recorded on it had my actual physical body been falling. It was a mad risk I took, but as you know, I had to take it to get to the switch and the battery. When I had that physical sense of falling and seemed to see the black misty sides of the pit all around me, it was my mental eye recording upon the brain what it was seeing. My psychic body had actually begun to fall and was really below the edge of the pit but still in contact with me. In other words my physical magnetic and psychic "haloes" were still mingled. My physical body was still standing firmly upon the floor of the room, but if I had not each time by effort or will forced my physical body across to the side, my psychic body would have fallen completely out of "contact" with me, and gone like some ghostly meteorite, obedient to the pull of the Hog.

'The curious sensation I had of forcing myself through an obstructing medium was not a physical sensation at all, as we understand that word, but rather the psychic sensation of forcing my entity to re-cross the "gap" that had already formed between my falling psychic body now below the edge of the pit and my physical body standing on the floor of the room. And that "gap" was full of a force that strove to prevent my body and soul from rejoining. It was a terrible experience. Do you remember how I could still see with my brain through the eyes of my psychic body, though it had already fallen some distance out of me? That is an extraordinary thing to remember.

'However, to get ahead, all "ghostly" phenomena are extremely diffuse in a normal state. They become actively physically dangerous in all cases where they are concentrated. The best off-hand illustration I can think of is the all-familiar electricity - a force which, by the way, we are too prone to imagine we understand because we've named and harnessed it, to use a popular phrase. But we don't understand it at all! It is still a complete fundamental mystery. Well, electricity when diffused is an "imagined and unpictured something", but when concentrated it is sudden death. Have you got me in that?

'Take, for instance, that explanation, as a very, very crude sort of illustration of what the Hog is. The Hog is one of those million-mile-long clouds of "nebulosity" lying in the Outer Circle. It is because of this that I term those clouds of force the Outer Monsters.

'What they are exactly is a tremendous question to answer. I sometimes wonder whether Dodgson there realizes just how impossible it is to answer some of his questions,' and Carnacki laughed.

'But to make a brief attempt at it. There is around this planet, and presumably others, of course, circles of what I might call "emanations". This is an extremely light gas, or shall I say ether. Poor ether, it's been hard worked in its time!

'Go back one moment to your school-days, and bear in mind that at one time the earth was just a sphere of extremely hot gases. These gases condensed in the form of materials and other "solid" matters; but there are some that are not yet solidified - air, for instance. Well, we have an earth-sphere of solid matter on which to stamp as solidly as we like; and round about that sphere there lies a ring of gases the constituents of which enter largely into all life, as we understand life - that is, air.

'But this is not the only circle of gas which is floating round us. There are, as I have been forced to conclude, larger and more attenuated "gas" belts lying, zone on zone, far up and around us. These compose what I have called the inner circles. They are surrounded in turn by a circle or belt of what I have called, for want of a better word, "emanations".

'This circle which I have named the Outer Circle can not lie less than a hundred thousand miles off the earth, and has a thickness which I have presumed to be anything between five and ten million miles. I believe, but I cannot prove, that it does not spin with the earth but in the opposite direction, for which a plausible cause might be found in the study of the theory upon which a certain electrical machine is constructed.

'I have reason to believe that the spinning of this, the Outer Circle, is disturbed from time to time through causes which are quite unknown to me, but which I believe are based in physical phenomena. Now, the Outer Circle is the psychic circle, yet it is also physical. To illustrate what I mean I must again instance electricity, and say that just as electricity discovered itself to us as something quite different from any of our previous conceptions of matter, so is the Psychic or Outer Circle different from any of our previous conceptions of matter. Yet it is none the less physical in its origin, and in the sense that electricity is physical, the Outer or Psychic Circle is physical in its constituents. Speaking pictorially it is, physically, to the Inner Circle what the Inner Circle is to the upper strata of the air, and what the air - as we know that intimate gas - is to the waters and the waters to the solid world. You get my line of suggestion?'

We all nodded, and Carnacki resumed.

'Well, now let me apply all this to what I am leading up to. I suggest that these million-mile-long clouds of monstrosity with float in the Psychic or Outer Circle, are bred of the elements of that circle. They are tremendous psychic forces, bred out of its elements just as an octopus or shark is bred out of the sea, or a tiger or any other physical force is bred out of the elements of its earth-and-air surroundings.

'To go further, a physical man is composed entirely from the constituents of earth and air, by which terms I include sunlight and water and "condiments"! In other words without earth and air he could not BE! Or to put it another way, earth and air breed within themselves the materials of the body and the brain, and therefore, presumably, the machine of intelligence.

'Now apply this line of thought to the Psychic or Outer Circle which though so attenuated that I may crudely presume it to be approximate to our conception of aether, yet contains all the elements for the production of certain phases of force and intelligence. But these elements are in a form as little like matter as the emanations of scent are like the scent itself. Equally, the force-and-intelligence-producing capacity of the Outer Circle no more approximates to the life-and-intelligence- producing capacity of the earth and air than the results of the Outer Circle constituents resemble the results of earth and air. I wonder whether I make it clear.

'And so it seems to me we have the conception of a huge psychic world, bred out of the physical, lying far outside of this world and completely encompassing it, except for the doorways about which I hope to tell you some other evening. This enormous psychic world of the Outer Circle "breeds'- if I may use the term, its own psychic forces and intelligences, monstrous and otherwise, just as this world produces its own physical forces and intelligences - beings, animals, insects, etc., monstrous and otherwise.

'The monstrosities of the Outer Circle are malignant towards all that we consider most desirable, just in the same way a shark or a tiger may be considered malignant, in a physical way, to all that we consider desirable. They are predatory - as all positive force is predatory. They have desires regarding us which are incredibly more dreadful to our minds when comprehended than an intelligent sheep would consider our desires towards its own carcass. They plunder and destroy to satisfy lusts and hungers exactly as other forms of existence plunder and destroy to satisfy their lusts and hungers. And the desire of these monsters is chiefly, if not always, for the psychic entity of the human.

'But that's as much as I can tell you tonight. Some evening I want to tell you about the tremendous mystery of the Psychic Doorways. In the meantime, have I made things a bit clearer to you, Dodgson?'

'Yes, and no,' I answered. 'You've been a brick to make the attempt, but there are still about ten thousand other things I want to know.'

Carnacki stood up. 'Out you go!' he said using the recognized formula in friendly fashion. 'Out you go! I want a sleep.'

And shaking him by the hand we strolled out on to the quiet Embankment.

BOOK TWO
OTHER STRANGE PHENOMENA

CHAPTER 10

THE GODDESS OF DEATH

It was in the latter end of November when I reached Themesworth to find the little town almost in a panic. In answer to my half-jesting inquiry as to whether the French were attempting to land, I was told a harrowing tale of some restless statute that had a habit of running amuck among the worthy townspeople. Nearly a dozen had already fallen victims, the first having been pretty Sally Morgan, the town belle.

These and other matters I learnt. Wherever I went it was the same story. "Good Heavens! what ignorance, what superstition!" This I thought, imagining that they were the dupes of some murderous rogue. Afterwards I was to change my mind. I gathered that the tragedies had all happened in some park near by, where, during the day, this Walking Marble rested innocently enough upon its pedestal.

Though I scouted the story of the walking statue, I was greatly interested in the matter. Already it had come to me to look into it and show these benighted people how mistaken they had been; besides, the thing promised some excitement. As I strolled through the town I laughed, picturing to myself the absurdity of some people believing in a walking marble statute. Pooh! What fools there are! Arriving at my hotel, I was pleased to learn from my landlord that my old friend and schoolmate, William Turner, had been staying there for some time.

That evening while I was at dinner he burst into my room, and was delighted at seeing me.

"I've suppose you've heard of the town bogey by now?" he said presently, dropping his voice. "It's a dangerous enough bogey, and we're all puzzled to explain how on earth it has escaped detection so long. Of course," he went on, "this story about the walking statue is all rubbish, though it's surprising what a number of people believe it."

"What do you say to trying our hands at catching it?" I said. "There would be a little excitement, and we should be doing the town a public benefit."

Will smiled. "I'm game if you are, Herton—we could take a stroll in the park to-night, if you like; perhaps we might see something."

"Right," I answered heartily. "What time do you propose going?"

Will pulled out his watch. "It's half-past eight now; shall we say eleven o'clock? It ought to be late enough then."

I assented and invited him to join me at my wine. He did so, and we passed the time away very pleasantly in reminiscences of old times.

"What about weapons?" I asked presently. "I suppose it will be advisable to take something in that line?"

For answer Will unbuttoned his coat, and I saw the gleam of a brace of pistols. I nodded, and, going to my trunk, opened it and showed him a couple of beautiful little pistols I often carried. Having loaded them, I put them in my side pockets. Shortly afterwards, eleven chimed, and getting into our cloaks, we left the house.

It was very cold, and a wintry wind moaned through the night. As we entered the park, we involuntarily kept closer together.

Somehow, my desire for adventure seemed to be ebbing away, and I wanted to get out from the place, and into the lighted streets.

"We'll just have a look at the statue," said Will; "then home and to bed."

A few minutes later we reached a little clearing among the bushes.

"Here we are," Will whispered. "I wish the moon would come out a moment; it would enable us to get a glance at the thing." He peered into the gloom on our right. "I'm hanged," he muttered, "if I can see it at all!"

Glancing to our left, I noticed that the path now led along the edge of a steep slope, at the bottom of which, some considerable distance below us, I caught the gleam of water.

"The park lake," Will explained in answer to a short query on my part. "Beastly deep too!

He turned away, and we both gazed into the dark gap among the bushes.

A moment afterwards the clouds cleared for an instant, and a ray of light struck down full upon us, lighting up the little circle of bushes and showing the clearing plainly. It was only a momentary gleam, but quite sufficient. There stood a pedestal great and black; but there was no statue upon it!

Will gave a quick gasp, and for a minute we stood stupidly; then we commenced to retrace our steps hurriedly. Neither of us spoke. As we moved we granted fearfully from side to side. Nearly half the return journey was accomplished, when, happening to look behind me, I saw in the dim shadows to my left the bushes part, and a huge, white, carven face, crowned with black, suddenly protrude.

I gave a sharp cry and reeled backwards. Will turned. "Oh, mercy upon us!" I heard him shout, and he started to run.

The Thing came out of the shadow. It looked like a giant. I stood rooted; then it came towards me, and I turned and ran. In the hands I had seen something that looked like a twisted cloth. Will was some dozen yards ahead. Behind, silent and vast, ran that awful being.

We neared the park entrance. I looked over my shoulder. It was gaining on us rapidly. Onwards we tore. A hundred yards further lay the gates; and safety in the lighted streets. Would we do it? Only fifty yards to go, and my chest seemed bursting. The distance shortened. The gates were close to. ...We were through. Down the street we ran; then turned to look. It had vanished.

"Thank Heaven!" I gasped, panting heavily.

A minute later Will said: "What a blue funk we've been in." I said nothing. We were making towards the hotel. I was bewildered and wanted to get by myself to think.

Next morning, while I was sitting dejectedly at breakfast, Will came in. We looked at one another shamefacedly. Will sat down. Presently he spoke:

"What cowards we are!"

I said nothing. It was too true; and the knowledge weighed on me like lead.

"Look here!" and Will spoke sharply and sternly. "We've got to go through with this matter to the end, if only for our own sakes."

I glanced at him eagerly. His determined tone seemed to inspire me with fresh hope and courage.

"What we've got to do first," he continued, "is to give that marble god a proper overhauling, and make sure no one has been playing tricks with us—perhaps it's possible to move it in some way."

I rose from the table, and went to the window. It had snowed heavily the preceding day, and the ground was covered with an even layer of white. As I looked out, a sudden idea came to me, and I turned quickly to Will.

"The snow!" I cried. "It will show the footprints, if there are any."

Will stared, puzzled.

"Round the statue," I explained, "if we go at once."

He grasped my meaning, and stood up. A few minutes later we were striding out briskly for the Park. A sharp walk brought us to the place. As we came in sight, I gave a cry of astonishment. The pedestal was occupied by a figure, identical with the thing that had chased us the night before. There it stood, erect and rigid, its sightless eyes glaring into space.

Will's face wore a look of expectation.

"See," he said, "it's back again. It cannot have managed that by itself, and we shall see by the footprints how many scoundrels there are in the affair."

He moved forward across the snow. I followed. Reaching the pedestal, we made a careful examination of the ground; but to our utter perplexity the snow was undisturbed. Next, we turned our attention to the figure itself, and though Will, who had seen it often before, searched carefully, he could find nothing amiss.

This it must be remembered, was my first sight of it, for—now that my mind was rational—I would not admit, even to myself, that what we had seen in the darkness was anything more than a masquerade, intended to lead people to the belief that it was the dead marble they saw walking.

Seen in the broad daylight, the thing looked what it was, a marble statue, intended to represent some deity. Which, I could not tell; and when I asked Will he shook his head.

In height it might have been eight feet, or perhaps a trifle under. The face was large—as indeed was the whole figure—and in expression cruel to the last degree. sion cruel to the last degree.

Above his brow was a large, strangely shaped headdress, carved out of some jet-black substance. The body was carved from a single block of milk-white marble, and draped gracefully and plainly in a robe confined at the waist by a narrow black girdle. The arms drooped loosely by the sides, and in the right hand hung a twisted cloth of a similar hue to the girdle. The left was empty and half gripped.

Will had always spoken of the statue as a god. Now, however, as my eyes ran over the various details, a doubt formed itself in my mind, and I suggested to Will that he was possibly mistaken as to the intended sex of the image.

For a moment he looked interested; then remarked gloomily that he didn't see it mattered much whether the thing was a man-god or a woman-god. The point was, had it the power to come off its pedestal or not?

I looked at him reproachfully.

"Surely you are not really going to believe that silly superstition?" I expostulated.

He shook his head moodily. "No, but can you or anyone else explain away last night's occurrences in any ordinary manner?"

To this there was no satisfactory reply, so I held my tongue.

"Pity," remarked Will presently, "that we know so little about this god. And the one man who might have enlightened us dead and gone—goodness knows where!"

"Who's that?" I queried.

"Oh, of course. I was forgetting, you don't know! Well, it's the way: For some years an old Indian colonel, called Whigman, lived here. He was a queer old stick, and absolutely refused to have anything to do with anybody. In fact, with the exception of an old Hindoo serving-man, he saw no one. About nine months ago he and his servant were found brutally murdered—strangled, so the doctors said. And now comes the most surprising part of it all. In his will he had left the whole of his huge estate to the citizens of Themesworth to be used as a park."

"Strangled, I think you said?" and I looked at Will questioningly.

He glanced at me a moment absently, then the light of comprehension flashed across his face. He looked startled. "Jove! You don't mean that?"

"I do though, old chap. The murder of these others has in every case been accomplished by strangling—their bodies, so you've told me, have shown that much. Then there are other things that point to my theory being the right one."

"What! you really think that the Colonel met his death at the same hands as---?"

He did not finish.

I nodded assent.

"Well, if you are correct, what about the length of time between them and Sally Morgan's murder—seven months, isn't it—and not a soul hurt all that time, and now--" He threw up his arms with an expressive gesture.

"Heaven knows!" I replied, "I don't."

For some length of time we discussed the matter in all its bearings, but without arriving at any satisfactory conclusion.

On our way back to town Will showed me a tiny piece of white marble which he had surreptitiously chipped from the statue. I examined it closely. Yes, it was marble, and somehow the certainty of that seemed to give us more confidence.

"Marble is marble," Will said, "and it's ridiculous to suppose anything else." I did not attempt to deny this.

During the next few days we paid visits to the park, but without result. The statue remained as we had left it.

A week passed. Then, one morning early, before the dawn, we were roused by a frightful scream, followed by a cry of deepest agony. It ended in a murmuring gurgle, and all was silent.

Without hesitation, we seized pistols, and with lighted candles rushed from our rooms to the great entrance door. This we hurriedly opened. Outside, the night was very quiet. It had been snowing and the ground was covered with a sheet of white.

For a moment we saw nothing. Then we distinguished the form of a woman lying across the steps leading up to the door. Running out, we seized her and carried her into the hall. There we recognized her as one of the waitresses of the hotel. Will turned back her collar and exposed the throat, showing a livid weal round it.

He was very serious, and his voice trembled, though not with fear, as he spoke to me. "We must dress and follow the tracks; there is no time to waste." He smiled gravely. "I don't think we shall do the running away this time."

At this moment the landlord appeared. On seeing the girl, and hearing our story, he seemed thunderstruck with fear and amazement, and could do nothing save wring his hands helplessly. Leaving him with the body, we went to our rooms and dressed quickly; then down again into the hall, where we found a crowd of fussy women-folk around the poor victim.

In the taproom I heard voices, and pushing my way in, discovered several of the serving men discussing the tragedy in excited tones. As they turned at my entrance, I called to them to know who would volunteer to accompany us. At once a strongly-built young fellow stepped forward, followed, after a slight hesitation, by two older men. Then, as we had sufficient for our purpose, I told them to get heavy sticks and bring lanterns.

As soon as they were ready we sallied out: Will and I first, the others following and keeping well together. The night was not particularly dark—the snow seemed to lighten it. At the bottom of High Street one of the men gave a short gasp, and pointed ahead.

There, dimly seen, and stealing across the snow with silent strides, was a giant form draped in white. Signing to the men to keep quiet, we ran quickly forward, the snow muffling our footsteps. We neared it rapidly. Suddenly Will stumbled and fell forward on his face, one of his pistols going off with the shock.

Instantly the Thing ahead looked round, and next moment was bounding from us in great leaps. Will was on his feet in a second, and, with a muttered curse at his own clumsiness, joined in the chase again. Through the park gates it went, and we followed hard. As we got nearer, I could plainly see the black headdress, and in the right hand there was a dark something; but what struck me most was the enormous size of the thing; it was certainly quite as tall as the marble goddess.

On we went. We were within a hundred feet of it when it stopped dead and turned towards us, and never shall I forget the fear that chilled me, for there, from head to foot, perfect in every detail, stood the marble goddess. At the movement, we had brought up standing; but now I raised a pistol and fired. That seemed to break the spell, and like one man we leapt forward. As we did so, the thing circled like a flash, and resumed its flight at a speed that bade fair to leave us behind in short time.

Then the thought came to me to head it off. This I did by sending the three men round to the right-hand side of the park lake, while Will and I continued the pursuit. A minute later, the monster disappeared around a bend in the path; but this troubled me little, as I felt convinced that it would blunder right into the arms of the men, and they would turn it back, and then—ah! then this mystery and horror would be solved.

On we ran. A minute, perhaps, passed. All at once I heard a hoarse cry ahead followed by a loud scream, which ceased suddenly. With fear plucking at my heart, I spurted forward, Will close behind. Round the corner we burst, and I saw the two men bending over something on the ground.

"Have you got it?" I shouted excitedly. The men turned quickly, and, seeing me, beckoned hurriedly. A moment later I was with them, and kneeling alongside a silent form. Alas! it was the brave young fellow who had been the first to volunteer. His neck seemed to be broken. Standing up, I turned to the men for an explanation.

"It was this way, sir; Johnson, that's him," nodding to the dead man, "he was smarter on his legs than we be, and he got ahead. Just before we reached him we heard him shout. We was close behind, and I don't think it could ha' been half a minute before we was up and found him."

"Did you see anything---" I hesitated. I felt sick. Then I continued, "anything of That—you know what I mean?"

"Yes, sir; leastways, my mate did. He saw it run across to those bushes an'--"

"Come on, Will," I cried, without waiting to hear more; and throwing the light of our lanterns ahead of us, we burst into the shrubberies. Scarcely had we gone a dozen paces when the light struck full upon a towering figure. There was a crash, and my lantern was smashed all to pieces. I was thrown to the ground, and something slid through the bushes. Springing to the edge, we were just in time to catch sight of it running in the direction of the lake. Simultaneously we raised our pistols and fired. As the smoke cleared away, I saw the Thing bound over the railings into the water. A faint splash was borne to our ears, then—silence.

Hurriedly we ran to the spot, but could see nothing.

"Perhaps we hit it," I ventured.

"You forget," laughed Will hysterically, "marble won't float."

"Don't talk rubbish," I answered angrily. Yet I felt that I would have given something to know what it was really.

For some minutes we waited; then, as nothing came to view, we moved away towards the gate—the mean going on ahead, carrying their dead comrade. Our way lead past the little clearing where the statue stood. It was still dark when we reached it.

"Look, Herton, look!" Will's voice rose to a shriek. I turned sharply. I had been lost momentarily in perplexing thought. Now, I saw that we were right opposite the place of the marble statue, and Will was shining the light of the lantern in its direction; but it showed me nothing save the pedestal, bare and smooth.

I glanced at Will. The lantern was shaking visibly in his grasp. Then I looked towards the pedestal again in a dazed manner. I stepped up to it and passed my hand slowly over the top. I felt very queer.

After that, I walked round it once or twice, No use! there was no mistake this time. My eyes showed me nothing, save that vacant place, where, but a few hours previously, had stood the massive marble.

Silently we left the spot. The men had preceded us with their sad burden. Fortunately, in the dim light, they had failed to note the absence of the goddess.

Dawn was breaking as in mournful procession we entered the town. Already the news seemed to have spread, and quite a body of the town people escorted us to the hotel.

During the day a number of men went up to the park, armed with hammers, intending to destroy the statue, but returned later silent and awestruck, declaring that it had disappeared bodily, only the great altar remaining.

I was feeling unwell. The shock thoroughly upset me, and a sense of helplessness assailed me.

About midnight, feeling worn out, I went to bed. It was late on the following morning when I woke with a start. An idea had some to me, and, rising, I dressed quickly and went downstairs. In the bar I found the landlord, and to him I applied for information as to where the library of the late Colonel Whigman had been removed.

He scratched his head a moment reflectively.

"I couldn't rightly say, sir; but I know Mr. Jepson, the town clerk, will be able to, and I daresay he wouldn't mind telling you anything you might want to know."

Having inquired where I was likely to meet this official, I set off, and in a short while found myself chatting to a pleasant, ruddy-faced man of about forty.

"The late colonel's library!" he said genially, "certainly, come this way, Sir Horton," and he ushered me into a long room, lined with books.

What I wanted was to find if the colonel had left among his library any diary or written record of his life in India. For a couple of hours I searched persistently. Then, just as I was giving up hope, I found it—a little green-backed book, filled with closely-written and crabbed writing.

Opening it, I found staring me in the face, a rough pen-and-ink sketch of—the marble goddess.

The following pages I read eagerly. They told a strange story of how, while engaged in the work of exterminating Thugs, the colonel and his men had found a large idol of white marble, quite unlike any Indian Deity the colonel had ever seen.

After a full description—in which I recognized once more the statue in Bungalow Park—there was some reference to an exciting skirmish with the priests of the temple, in which the colonel had a narrow escape from death at the hands of the high priest, "who was a most enormous man and mad with fury."

Finally, having obtained possession, they found among other things that the Deity of the temple was another—and, to Europeans, unknown—form of Kali, the Goddess of Death. The temple itself being a sort of Holy of Holies of Thugdom, where they carried on their brutal and disgusting rites.

After this, the diary went on to say that, loath to destroy the idol, the colonel brought it back with him from Calcutta, having first demolished the temple in which it had been found.

Later, he found occasion to ship it off to England. Shortly after this his life was attempted, and, his time of service being up, he came home.

Here it ended, and yet I was no nearer to the solution than I had been when first I opened the book.

Standing up, I placed it on the table; then, as I reached for my hat, I noticed on the floor a half-sheet of paper, which had evidently fallen from the diary as I read. Stooping, I picked it up. It was soiled, and in parts illegible; but what I saw there filled me with astonishment. Here, at last, in my hands, I held the key to the horrible mystery that surrounded us!

Hastily I crumpled the paper into my pocket, and, opening the door, rushed from the room. Reaching the hotel, I bounded upstairs to where Will sat reading.

"I've found it out! I've found it out!" I gasped. Will sprang from his seat, his eyes blazing with excitement. I seized him by the arm and, without stopping to explain, dragged him hatless into the street.

"Come on," I cried.

As we ran through the streets people looked up wonderingly, and many joined in the race.

At last we reached the open space and the open pedestal. Here I paused a moment to gain breath. Will looked at me curiously. The crowd formed round in a semi-circle, at some little distance.

Then without a word I stepped up to the altar, and, stooping, reached up under it. There was a loud click, and I sprang back sharply. Something rose from the center of the pedestal with a slow, stately movement. For a second no one spoke; then a great cry of fear came from the crowd: "The image! The image!" and some began to run. There was another click and Kali, the Goddess of Death, stood fully revealed.

Again I stepped up to the altar. The crowd watched me breathlessly and the timid ceased to fly. For a moment I fumbled. Then one side of the pedestal swung back. I held up my hand for silence. Someone procured a lantern, which I lit and lowered through the opening. It went down some ten feet, then rested on the earth beneath. I peered down, and as my eyes became accustomed to the darkness, I made out a square-shaped pit in the ground directly below the pedestal.

Will came to my side and looked over my shoulder.

"We must get a ladder," he said. I nodded, and he sent a man for one. When it came we pushed it through until it rested firmly; then after a final survey, we climbed cautiously down.

I remember feeling surprised at the size of the place. It was as big as a good-sized room. At this moment, as I stood glancing round, Will called to me. His voice denoted great perplexity. Crossing over, I found him staring at a litter of things which strewed the ground: tins, bottles, cans, rubbish, a bucket with some water in it, and, further on, a kind of rude bed.

"Someone's been living here!" and he looked at me blankly. "It wasn't---" he began, then hesitated. "It wasn't that after all," and he indicated with his head.

"No," I replied, "It wasn't that."

I assented. Will's face was a study. Then he seemed to grasp the full significance of the fact, and a great look of relief crossed his features.

A moment later I made a discovery. On the left side in the far corner was a low curved entrance, like a small tunnel. On the opposite side was a similar opening. Lowering the lantern, I looked into the right-hand one, but could see nothing. By stooping somewhat we could walk along it, which we did for some distance, until it ended in a heap of stones and earth. Returning to the hollow under the pedestal, we tried the other, and, after a little, noticed that it trended steadily downwards.

"It seems to be going in the direction of the lake," I remarked; "we had better be careful."

A few feet further on the tunnel broadened and heightened considerably, and I saw a faint glimmer, which, on reaching, proved to be water.

"Can't get any further," Will cried. "You were right. We have got down to the level of the lake."

"But what on earth was this tunnel designed for?" I asked, glancing around. "You see it reaches below the surface of the lake."

"Goodness knows," Will answered. I expect it was one of those secret passages made centuries ago—most likely in Crowell's time. You see, Colonel Whigman's was a very old place, built I can't say how long ago. It belonged once to an old baron. However, there is nothing here; we might as well go."

"Just a second, Will," I said, the recollection of the statue's wild leap into the lake at the moment recurring to me.

I stooped and held the lantern close over the water which blocked our further progress.

As I did so I thought I saw something of an indistinct whiteness floating a few inches beneath the surface. Involuntarily my left hand took a firmer grip of the lantern, and the fingers of my right hand opened out convulsively.

What was it I saw? I could feel myself becoming as icy cold as the water itself. I glanced at Will. He was standing disinterestedly a little behind me. Evidently he had, so far, seen nothing.

Again, I looked, and a horrible sensation of fear and awe crept over me as I seemed to see, staring up at me, the face of Kali, the goddess of Death.

"See, Will!" I said quickly. "Is it fancy?"

Following the direction of my grimace, he peered down into the gloomy water, then started back with a cry.

"What is it Herton? I seemed to see a face like---"

"Take the lantern, Will." I said, as a sudden inspiration came to me: "I've an idea what it is"; and leaning forward, I plunged my arms in up to the elbows, and grasped something cold and hard. I shuddered, but held on, and pulled, and slowly up from the water rose a vast white face, which came away in my hands. It was a huge mask—an exact facsimile of the features of the statue above us.

Thoroughly shaken, we retreated to the pedestal with our trophy, and from thence up the ladder into the blessed daylight.

Here, to a crowd of eager listeners, we told our story; and so left it.

Little remains to be told.

Workmen were sent down, and from the water they drew forth the dead body of an enormous Hindoo, draped from head to foot in white. In the body were a couple of bullet wounds. Our fire had been true that night, and he had evidently died trying to enter the pedestal through the submerged opening of the passage.

Who we was, or where he came from, no one could explain.

Afterwards, among the colonel's papers, we found a reference to the High Priest which led us to suppose that it was he, who, in vengeance for the sacrilege against his appalling deity, had, to such terrible purpose, impersonated Kali, the Goddess of Death.

CHAPTER II

THE BAUMOFF EXPLOSIVE

D ally, Whitlaw and I were discussing the recent stupendous explosion which had occurred in the vicinity of Berlin. We were marveling concerning the extraordinary period of darkness that had followed, and which had aroused so much newspaper comment, with theories galore.

The papers had got hold of the fact that the War Authorities had been experimenting with a new explosive, invented by a certain chemist, named Baumoff, and they referred to it constantly as "The New Baumoff Explosive".

We were in the Club, and the fourth man at our table was John Stafford, who was professionally a medical man, but privately in the Intelligence Department. Once or twice, as we talked, I had glanced at Stafford, wishing to fire a question at him; for he had been acquainted with Baumoff. But I managed to hold my tongue; for I knew that if I asked out pointblank, Stafford (who's a good sort, but a bit of an ass as regards his almost ponderous code-of-silence) would be just as like as not to say that it was a subject upon which he felt he was not entitled to speak.

Oh, I know the old donkey's way; and when he had once said

that, we might just make up our minds never to get another word out of him on the matter as long as we lived. Yet, I was satisfied to notice that he seemed a bit restless, as if he were on the itch to shove in his oar; by which I guessed that the papers we were quoting had got things very badly muddled indeed, in some way or other, at least as regarded his friend Baumoff. Suddenly, he spoke:

"What unmitigated, wicked piffle!" said Stafford, quite warm. "I tell you it is wicked, this associating of Baumoff's name with war inventions and such horrors. He was the most intensely poetical and earnest follower of the Christ that I have ever met; and it is just the brutal Irony of Circumstance that has attempted to use one of the products of his genius for a purpose of Destruction. But you'll find they won't be able to use it, in spite of their having got hold of Baumoff's formula. As an explosive it is not practicable. It is, shall I say, too impartial; there is no way of controlling it.

"I know more about it, perhaps, than any man alive; for I was Baumoff's greatest friend, and when he died, I lost the best comrade a man ever had. I need make no secret about it to you chaps. I was 'on duty' in Berlin, and I was deputed to get in touch with Baumoff. The government had long had an eye on him; he was an Experimental Chemist, you know, and altogether too jolly clever to ignore. But there was no need to worry about him. I got to know him, and we became enormous friends; for I soon found that he would never turn his abilities towards any new war-contrivance; and so, you see, I was able to enjoy my friendship with him, with a comfy conscience — a thing our chaps are not always able to do in their friendships. Oh, I tell you, it's a mean, sneaking, treacherous sort of business, ours; though it's necessary; just as some odd man, or other, has to be a hangsman. There's a number of unclean jobs to be done to keep the Social Machine running!

"I think Baumoff was the most enthusiastic intelligent believer in Christ that it will be ever possible to produce. I learned that he was compiling and evolving a treatise of most extraordinary and convincing proofs in support of the more inexplicable things concerning the life and death of Christ. He was, when I became acquainted with him, concentrating his attention particularly upon endeavoring to show that the Darkness of the Cross, between the sixth and the ninth hours, was a very real thing, possessing a tremendous significance. He intended at one sweep to smash utterly all talk of a timely thunderstorm or any of the other more or less inefficient theories which have been brought forward from time to time to explain the occurrence away as being a thing of no particular significance.

"Baumoff had a pet aversion, an atheistic Professor of Physics, named Hautch, who — using the 'marvelous' element of the life and death of Christ, as a fulcrum from which to attack Baumoff's theories — smashed at him constantly, both in his lectures and in print. Particularly did he pour bitter unbelief upon Baumoff"s upholding that the Darkness of the Cross was anything more than a gloomy hour or two, magnified into blackness by the emotional inaccuracy of the Eastern mind and tongue.

"One evening, some time after our friendship had become very real, I called on Baumoff, and found him in a state of tremendous indignation over some article of the Professor's which attacked him brutally; using his theory of the Significance of the 'Darkness', as a target. Poor Baumoff! It was certainly a marvelously clever attack; the attack of a thoroughly trained, well-balanced Logician. But Baumoff was something more; he was Genius. It is a title few have any rights to; but it was his!

"He talked to me about his theory, telling me that he wanted to show me a small experiment, presently, bearing out his opinions. In his talk, he told me several things that interested me extremely. Having first reminded me of the fundamental fact that light is conveyed to the eye through the means of that indefinable medium, named the Æther. He went a step further, and pointed out to me that, from an aspect which more approached the primary, Light was a vibration of the Æther, of a certain definite number of waves per second, which possessed the power of producing upon our retina the sensation which we term Light.

"To this, I nodded; being, as of course is everyone, acquainted with so well-know1n a statement. From this, he took a quick, mental stride, and told me that an ineffably vague, but measurable, darkening of the atmosphere (greater or smaller according to the personality-force of the individual) was always evoked in the immediate vicinity of the human, during any period of great emotional stress.

"Step by step, Baumoff showed me how his research had led him to the conclusion that this queer darkening (a million times too subtle to be apparent to the eye) could be produced only through something which had power to disturb or temporally interrupt or break up the Vibration of Light. In other words, there was, at any time of unusual emotional activity, some disturbance of the Æther in the immediate vicinity of the person suffering, which had some effect upon the Vibration of Light, interrupting it, and producing the aforementioned infinitely vague darkening.

"'Yes?' I said, as he paused, and looked at me, as if expecting me to have arrived at a certain definite deduction through his remarks. 'Go on.'

"'Well,' he said, 'don't you see, the subtle darkening around the person suffering, is greater or less, according to the personality of the suffering human. Don't you?'

"'Oh!' I said, with a little gasp of astounded comprehension, 'I see what you mean. You — you mean that if the agony of a person of ordinary personality can produce a faint disturbance of the Æther, with a consequent faint darkening, then the Agony of Christ, possessed of the Enormous Personality of the Christ, would produce a terrific disturbance of the Æther, and therefore, it might chance, of the Vibration of Light, and that this is the true explanation of the Darkness of the Cross; and that the fact of such an extraordinary and apparently unnatural and improbable Darkness having been recorded is not a thing to weaken the Marvel of Christ. But one more unutterably wonderful, infallible proof of His God-like power? Is that it? Is it? Tell me?'

"Baumoff just rocked on his chair with delight, beating one fist into the palm of his other hand, and nodding all the time to my summary. How he loved to be understood; as the Searcher always craves to be understood.

"'And now,' he said, 'I'm going to show you something.'

"He took a tiny, corked test-tube out of his waistcoat pocket, and emptied its contents (which consisted of a single, grey-white grain, about twice the size of an ordinary pin's head) on to his dessert plate. He crushed it gently to powder with the ivory handle of a knife, then damped it gently, with a single minim of what I supposed to be water, and worked it up into a tiny patch of grey-white paste. He then took out his gold tooth-pick, and thrust it into the flame of a small chemist's spirit lamp, which had been lit since dinner as a pipe-lighter. He held the gold tooth-pick in the flame, until the narrow, gold blade glowed white hot.

"'Now look!' he said, and touched the end of the tooth-pick against the infinitesimal patch upon the dessert plate. There came a swift little violet flash, and suddenly I found that I was staring at Baumoff through a sort of transparent darkness, which faded swiftly into a black opaqueness. I thought at first this must be the complementary effect of the flash upon the retina. But a minute passed, and we were still in that extraordinary darkness.

"'My Gracious! Man! What is it?' I asked, at last.

"His voice explained then, that he had produced, through the medium of chemistry, an exaggerated effect which simulated, to some extent, the disturbance in the Æther produced by waves thrown off by any person during an emotional crisis or agony. The waves, or vibrations, sent out by his experiment produced only a partial simulation of the effect he wished to show me — merely the temporary interruption of the Vibration of Light, with the resulting darkness in which we both now sat.

"'That stuff,' said Baumoff, 'would be a tremendous explosive, under certain conditions.'

I heard him puffing at his pipe, as he spoke, but instead of the glow of the pipe shining out visible and red, there was only a faint glare that wavered and disappeared in the most extraordinary fashion.

"'My Goodness!' I said, 'when's this going away?' And I stared across the room to where the big kerosene lamp showed only as a faintly glimmering patch in the gloom; a vague light that shivered and flashed oddly, as though I saw it through an immense gloomy depth of dark and disturbed water.

" It's all right,' Baumoff's voice said from out of the darkness. 'It's going now; in five minutes the disturbance will have quieted, and the waves of light will flow off evenly from the lamp in their normal fashion. But, whilst we're waiting, isn't it immense, eh?'

"'Yes,' I said. 'It's wonderful; but it's rather unearthly, you know.'

"'Oh, but I've something much finer to show you,' he said. 'The real thing. Wait another minute. The darkness is going. See! You can see the light from the lamp now quite plainly. It looks as if it were submerged in a boil of waters, doesn't it? that are growing clearer and clearer and quieter and quieter all the time.'

"It was as he said; and we watched the lamp, silently, until all signs of the disturbance of the light-carrying medium had ceased. Then Baumoff faced me once more.

"'Now,' he said. 'You've seen the somewhat casual effects of just crude combustion of that stuff of mine. I'm going to show you the effects of combusting it in the human furnace, that is, in my own body; and then, you'll see one of the great wonders of Christ's death reproduced on a miniature scale.'

"He went across to the mantelpiece, and returned with a small, 120 minim glass and another of the tiny, corked test-tubes, containing a single grey-white grain of his chemical substance. He uncorked the test-tube, and shook the grain of substance into the minim glass, and then, with a glass stirring-rod, crushed it up in the bottom of the glass, adding water, drop by drop as he did so, until there were sixty minims in the glass.

"'Now!' he said, and lifting it, he drank the stuff. 'We will give it thirty-five minutes,' he continued; 'then, as carbonization proceeds, you will find my pulse will increase, as also the respiration, and presently there will come the darkness again, in the subtlest, strangest fashion; but accompanied now by certain physical and psychic phenomena, which will be owing to the fact that the vibrations it will throw off, will be blent into what I might call the emotional-vibrations, which I shall give off in my distress. These will be enormously intensified, and you will possibly experience an extraordinarily interesting demonstration of the soundness of my more theoretical reasonings. I tested it by myself last week' (He waved a bandaged finger at me), 'and I read a paper to the Club on the results. They are very enthusiastic, and have promised their co-operation in the big demonstration I intend to give on next Good Friday — that's seven weeks off, to-day.'

"He had ceased smoking; but continued to talk quietly in this fashion for the next thirty-five minutes. The Club to which he had referred was a peculiar association of men, banded together under the presidentship of Baumoff himself, and having for their appellation the title of — so well as I can translate it — 'The Believers And Provers Of Christ'. If I may say so, without any thought of irreverence, they were, many of them, men fanatically crazed to uphold the Christ. You will agree later, I think, that I have not used an incorrect term, in describing the bulk of the members of this extraordinary club, which was, in its way, well worthy of one of the religio-maniacal extrudences which have been forced into temporary being by certain of the more religiously-emotional minded of our cousins across the water.

"Baumoff looked at the clock; then held out his wrist to me. 'Take my pulse,' he said, 'it's rising fast. Interesting data, you know.'

"I nodded, and drew out my watch. I had noticed that his respirations were increasing; and I found his pulse running evenly and strongly at 105. Three minutes later, it had risen to 175, and his respirations to 41. In a further three minutes, I took his pulse again, and found it running at 203, but with the rhythm regular. His respirations were then 49. He had, as I knew, excellent lungs, and his heart was sound. His lungs, I may say, were of exceptional capacity, and there was at this stage no marked dyspnoea. Three minutes later I found the pulse to be 227, and the respiration 54.

"'You've plenty of red corpuscles, Baumoff!' I said. 'But I hope you're not going to overdo things.'

"He nodded at me, and smiled; but said nothing. Three minutes later, when I took the last pulse, it was 233, and the two sides of the heart were sending out unequal quantities of blood, with an irregular rhythm. The respiration had risen to 67 and was becoming shallow and ineffectual, and dyspnoea was becoming very marked. The small amount of arterial blood leaving the left side of the heart betrayed itself in the curious bluish and white tinge of the face.

"'Baumoff!' I said, and began to remonstrate; but he checked me, with a queerly invincible gesture.

"'It's all right!' he said, breathlessly, with a little note of impatience. 'I know what I'm doing all the time. You must remember I took the same degree as you in medicine.'

"It was quite true. I remembered then that he had taken his M.D. in London; and this in addition to half a dozen other degrees in different branches of the sciences in his own country. And then, even as the memory reassured me that he was not acting in ignorance of the possible danger, he called out in a curious, breathless voice:

"'The Darkness! It's beginning. Take note of every single thing. Don't bother about me. I'm all right!'

"I glanced swiftly round the room. It was as he had said. I perceived it now. There appeared to be an extraordinary quality of gloom growing in the atmosphere of the room. A kind of bluish gloom, vague, and scarcely, as yet, affecting the transparency of the atmosphere to light.

"Suddenly, Baumoff did something that rather sickened me. He drew his wrist away from me, and reached out to a small metal box, such as one sterilizes a hypodermic in. He opened the box, and took out four rather curious looking drawing-pins, I might call them, only they had spikes of steel fully an inch long, whilst all around the rim of the heads (which were also of steel) there projected downward, parallel with the central spike, a number of shorter spikes, maybe an eighth of an inch long.

"He kicked off his pumps; then stooped and slipped his socks off, and I saw that he was wearing a pair of linen inner-socks.

"'Antiseptic!' he said, glancing at me. 'Got my feet ready before you came. No use running unnecessary risks.' He gasped as he spoke. Then he took one of the curious little steel spikes.

"'I've sterilized them,' he said; and therewith, with deliberation, he pressed it in up to the head into his foot between the second and third branches of the dorsal artery.

"'For God's sake, what are you doing!' I said, half rising from my chair.

"'Sit down!' he said, in a grim sort of voice. 'I can't have any interference. I want you simply to observe; keep note of everything. You ought to thank me for the chance, instead of worrying me, when you know I shall go my own way all the time.'

"As he spoke, he had pressed in the second of the steel spikes up to the hilt in his left instep, taking the same precaution to avoid the arteries. Not a groan had come from him; only his face betrayed the effect of this additional distress.

"'My dear chap!' he said, observing my upsetness. 'Do be sensible. I know exactly what I'm doing. There simply must be distress, and the readiest way to reach that condition is through physical pain.' His speech had becomes a series of spasmodic words, between gasps, and sweat lay in great clear drops upon his lip and forehead. He slipped off his belt and proceeded to buckle it round both the back of his chair and his waist; as if he expected to need some support from falling.

"'It's wicked!' I said. Baumoff made an attempt to shrug his heaving shoulders, that was, in its way, one of the most piteous things that I have seen, in its sudden laying bare of the agony that the man was making so little of.

"He was now cleaning the palms of his hands with a little sponge, which he dipped from time to time in a cup of solution. I knew what he was going to do, and suddenly he jerked out, with a painful attempt to grin, an explanation of his bandaged finger. He had held his finger in the flame of the spirit lamp, during his previous experiment; but now, as he made clear in gaspingly uttered words, he wished to simulate as far as possible the actual conditions of the great scene that he had so much in mind. He made it so clear to me that we might expect to experience something very extraordinary, that I was conscious of a sense of almost superstitious nervousness.

"'I wish you wouldn't, Baumoff!' I said.

"'Don't — be — silly!' he managed to say. But the two latter words were more groans than words; for between each, he had thrust home right to the heads in the palms of his hands the two remaining steel spikes. He gripped his hands shut, with a sort of spasm of savage determination, and I saw the point of one of the spikes break through the back of his hand, between the extensor tendons of the second and third fingers. A drop of blood beaded the point of the spike. I looked at Baumoff's face; and he looked back steadily at me.

"'No interference,' he managed to exclaim. 'I've not gone through all this for nothing. I know — what — I'm doing. Look — it's coming. Take note — everything!'

"He relapsed into silence, except for his painful gasping. I realized that I must give way, and I stared round the room, with a peculiar commingling of an almost nervous discomfort and a stirring of very real and sober curiosity.

"'Oh,' said Baumoff, after a moment's silence, 'something's going to happen. I can tell. Oh, wait — till I — I have my — big demonstration. I'll show that brute Hautch."

"I nodded; but I doubt that he saw me; for his eyes had a distinctly in-turned look, the iris was rather relaxed. I glanced away round the room again; there was a distinct occasional breaking up of the light-rays from the lamp, giving a coming-and-going effect.

"The atmosphere of the room was also quite plainly darker — heavy, with an extraordinary sense of gloom. The bluish tint was unmistakably more in evidence; but there was, as yet, none of that opacity which we had experienced before, upon simple combustion, except for the occasional, vague coming-and-going of the lamp-light.

"Baumoff began to speak again, getting his words out between gasps. 'Th' — this dodge of mine gets the — pain into the — the — right place. Right association of — of ideas — emotions — for — best — results. You follow me? Parallelizing things — as — much as — possible. Fixing whole attention — on the — the death scene — '

"He gasped painfully for a few moments. 'We demonstrate truth of — of The Darkening; but — but there's psychic effect to be — looked for, through — results of parallelization of — conditions. May have extraordinary simulation of — the actual thing. Keep note. Keep note.' Then, suddenly, with a clear, spasmodic burst: 'My God, Stafford, keep note of everything. Something's going to happen. Something — wonderful — Promise not — to bother me. I know — what I'm doing.'

"Baumoff ceased speaking, with a gasp, and there was only the labour of his breathing in the quietness of the room. As I stared at him, halting from a dozen things I needed to say, I realized suddenly that I could no longer see him quite plainly; a sort of wavering in the atmosphere, between us, made him seem momentarily unreal. The whole room had darkened perceptibly in the last thirty seconds; and as I stared around, I realized that there was a constant invisible swirl in the fast-deepening, extraordinary blue gloom that seemed now to permeate everything. When I looked at the lamp, alternate flashings of light and blue — darkness followed each other with an amazing swiftness.

"'My God!' I heard Baumoff whispering in the half-darkness, as if to himself, 'how did Christ bear the nails!'

"I stared across at him, with an infinite discomfort, and an irritated pity troubling me; but I knew it was no use to remonstrate now. I saw him vaguely distorted through the wavering tremble of the atmosphere. It was somewhat as if I looked at him through convolutions of heated air; only there were marvelous waves of blue-blackness making gaps in my sight. Once I saw his face clearly, full of an infinite pain, that was somehow, seemingly, more spiritual than physical, and dominating everything was an expression of enormous resolution and concentration, making the livid, sweat-damp, agonized face somehow heroic and splendid.

"And then, drenching the room with waves and splashes of opaqueness, the vibration of his abnormally stimulated agony finally broke up the vibration of Light. My last, swift glance round, showed me, as it seemed, the invisible aether boiling and eddying in a tremendous fashion; and, abruptly, the flame of the lamp was lost in an extraordinary swirling patch of light, that marked its position for several moments, shimmering and deadening, shimmering and deadening; until, abruptly, I saw neither that glimmering patch of light, nor anything else. I was suddenly lost in a black opaqueness of night, through which came the fierce, painful breathing of Baumoff.

"A full minute passed; but so slowly that, if I had not been counting Baumoff's respirations, I should have said that it was five. Then Baumoff spoke suddenly, in a voice that was, somehow, curiously changed — a certain toneless note in it:

"'My God!' he said, from out of the darkness, 'what must Christ have suffered!'

"It was in the succeeding silence, that I had the first realization that I was vaguely afraid; but the feeling was too indefinite and unfounded, and I might say subconscious, for me to face it out. Three minutes passed, whilst I counted the almost desperate respirations that came to me through the darkness. Then Baumoff began to speak again, and still in that peculiarly altering voice:

"'By Thy Agony and Bloody Sweat,' he muttered. Twice he repeated this. It was plain indeed that he had fixed his whole attention with tremendous intensity, in his abnormal state, upon the death scene.

"The effect upon me of his intensity was interesting and in some ways extraordinary. As well as I could, I analyzed my sensations and emotions and general state of mind, and realized that Baumoff was producing an effect upon me that was almost hypnotic.

"Once, partly because I wished to get my level by the aid of a normal remark, and also because I was suddenly newly anxious by a change in the breath sounds, I asked Baumoff how he was. My voice going with a peculiar and really uncomfortable blankness through that impenetrable blackness of opacity.

"He said: 'Hush! I'm carrying the Cross.' And, do you know, the effect of those simple words, spoken in that new, toneless voice, in that atmosphere of almost unbearable tenseness, was so powerful that, suddenly, with eyes wide open, I saw Baumoff clear and vivid against that unnatural darkness, carrying a Cross. Not, as the picture is usually shown of the Christ, with it crooked over the shoulder; but with the Cross gripped just under the cross-piece in his arms, and the end trailing behind, along rocky ground. I saw even the pattern of the grain of the rough wood, where some of the bark had been ripped away; and under the trailing end there was a tussock of tough wire-grass, that had been uprooted by the lowing end, and dragged and ground along upon the rocks, between the end of the Cross and the rocky ground. I can see the thing now, as I speak. Its vividness was extraordinary; but it had come and gone like a flash, and I was sitting there in the darkness, mechanically counting the respirations; yet unaware that I counted.

"As I sat there, it came to me suddenly — the whole entire marvel of the thing that Baumoff had achieved. I was sitting there in a darkness which was an actual reproduction of the miracle of the Darkness of the Cross. In short, Baumoff had, by producing in himself an abnormal condition, developed an Energy of Emotion that must have almost, in its effects, paralleled the Agony of the Cross. And in so doing, he had shown from an entirely new and wonderful point, the indisputable truth of the stupendous personality and the enormous spiritual force of the Christ. He had evolved and made practical to the average understanding a proof that would make to live again the reality of that wonder of the world — CHRIST. And for all this, I had nothing but admiration of an almost stupefied kind.

"But, at this point, I felt that the experiment should stop. I had a strangely nervous craving for Baumoff to end it right there and then, and not to try to parallel the psychic conditions. I had, even then, by some queer aid of sub-conscious suggestion, a vague reaching-out-towards the danger of "monstrosity" being induced, instead of any actual knowledge gained.

"'Baumoff!' I said. 'Stop it.'"

"But he made no reply, and for some minutes there followed a silence, that was unbroken, save by his gasping breathing. Abruptly, Baumoff said, between his gasps: 'Woman — behold — thy — son. ' He muttered this several times, in the same uncomfortably toneless voice in which he had spoken since the darkness became complete.

"'Baumoff.' I said again. 'Baumoff! Stop it.' " And as I listened for his answer, I was relieved to think that his breathing was less shallow. The abnormal demand for oxygen was evidently being met, and the extravagant call upon the heart's efficiency was being relaxed.

"'Baumoff!' I said, once more. 'Baumoff! Stop it!'"

"And, as I spoke, abruptly, I thought the room was shaken a little.

"Now, I had already as you will have realized, been vaguely conscious of a peculiar and growing nervousness. I think that is the word that best describes it, up to this moment. At this curious little shake that seemed to stir through the utterly dark room, I was suddenly more than nervous. I felt a thrill of actual and literal fear;

yet with no sufficient cause of reason to justify me; so that, after sitting very tense for some long minutes, and feeling nothing further, I decided that I needed to take myself in hand, and keep a firmer grip upon my nerves. And then, just as I had arrived at this more comfortable state of mind, the room was shaken again, with the most curious and sickening oscillatory movement, that was beyond all comfort of denial.

"'My God!' I whispered. And then, with a sudden effort of courage, I called: 'Baumoff! For God's sake stop it."

"You've no idea of the effort it took to speak aloud into that darkness; and when I did speak, the sound of my voice set me afresh on edge. It went so empty and raw across the room; and somehow, the room seemed to be incredibly big. Oh, I wonder whether you realize how beastly I felt, without my having to make any further effort to tell you.

"And Baumoff never answered a word; but I could hear him breathing, a little fuller; though still heaving his thorax painfully, in his need for air. The incredible shaking of the room eased away; and there succeeded a spasm of quiet, in which I felt that it was my duty to get up and step across to Baumoff's chair. But I could not do it. Somehow, I would not have touched Baumoff then for any cause whatever. Yet, even in that moment, as now I know, I was not aware that I was afraid to touch Baumoff.

"And then the oscillations commenced again. I felt the seat of my trousers slide against the seat of my chair, and I thrust out my legs, spreading my feet against the carpet, to keep me from sliding off one way or the other on to the floor. To say I was afraid, was not to describe my state at all. I was terrified. And suddenly, I had comfort, in the most extraordinary fashion; for a single idea literally glazed into my brain, and gave me a reason to which to cling. It was a single line:

"'Æther, the soul of iron and sundry stuffs' which Baumoff had once taken as a text for an extraordinary lecture on vibrations, in the earlier days of our friendship. He had formulated the suggestion that, in embryo, Matter was, from a primary aspect, a localized vibration, traversing a closed orbit. These primary localized vibrations were inconceivably minute. But were capable, under certain conditions, of combining under the action of keynote-vibrations into secondary vibrations of a size and shape to be determined by a multitude of only guessable factors. These would sustain their new form, so long as nothing occurred to disorganize their combination or depreciate or divert their energy — their unity being partially determined by the inertia of the still Æther outside of the closed path which their area of activities covered. And such combination of the primary localized vibrations was neither more nor less than matter. Men and worlds, aye! and universes.

"And then he had said the thing that struck me most. He had said, that if it were possible to produce a vibration of the Æther of a sufficient energy, it would be possible to disorganize or confuse the vibration of matter. That, given a machine capable of creating a vibration of the Æther of a sufficient energy, he would engage to destroy not merely the world, but the whole universe itself, including heaven and hell themselves, if such places existed, and had such existence in a material form.

"I remember how I looked at him, bewildered by the pregnancy and scope of his imagination. And now his lecture had come back to me to help my courage with the sanity of reason. Was it not possible that the Æther disturbance which he had produced, had sufficient energy to cause some disorganization of the vibration of matter, in the immediate vicinity, and had thus created a miniature quaking of the ground all about the house, and so set the house gently a-shake?

"And then, as this thought came to me, another and a greater, flashed into my mind. 'My God!' I said out loud into the darkness of the room. It explains one more mystery of the Cross, the disturbance of the Æther caused by Christ's Agony, disorganized the vibration of matter in the vicinity of the Cross, and there was then a small local earthquake, which opened the graves, and rent the veil, possibly by disturbing its supports. And, of course, the earthquake was an effect, and not a cause, as belittlers of the Christ have always insisted.

"'Baumoff!' I called. 'Baumoff, you've proved another thing. Baumoff! Baumoff! Answer me. Are you all right?'

"Baumoff answered, sharp and sudden out of the darkness; but not to me:

"'My God!' he said. 'My God!' His voice came out at me, a cry of veritable mental agony. He was suffering, in some hypnotic, induced fashion, something of the very agony of the Christ Himself.

"'Baumoff!" I shouted, and forced myself to my feet. I heard his chair clattering, as he sat there and shook. 'Baumoff!'

"An extraordinary quake went across the floor of the room, and I heard a creaking of the woodwork, and something fell and smashed in the darkness. Baumoff's gasps hurt me; but I stood there. I dared not go to him. I knew then that I was afraid of him — of his condition, or something I don't know what. But, oh, I was horribly afraid of him.

"'Bau — ' I began, but suddenly I was afraid even to speak to him. And I could not move. Abruptly, he cried out in a tone of incredible anguish:

"'Eloi, Eloi, lama sabachthani!'But the last word changed in his mouth, from his dreadful hypnotic grief and pain, to a scream of simply infernal terror.

"And, suddenly, a horrible mocking voice roared out in the room, from Baumoff's chair: 'Eloi, Eloi, lama sabachthani!'

"Do you understand, the voice was not Baumoff's at all. It was not a voice of despair; but a voice sneering in an incredible, bestial, monstrous fashion. In the succeeding silence, as I stood in an ice of fear, I knew that Baumoff no longer gasped. The room was absolutely silent, the most dreadful and silent place in all this world. Then I bolted; caught my foot, probably in the invisible edge of the hearth-rug, and pitched headlong into a blaze of internal brain-stars. After which, for a very long time, certainly some hours, I knew nothing of any kind.

"I came back into this Present, with a dreadful headache oppressing me, to the exclusion of all else. But the Darkness had dissipated. I rolled over on to my side, and saw Baumoff and forgot even the pain in my head. He was leaning forward towards me: his eyes wide open, but dull. His face was enormously swollen, and there was, somehow, something beastly about him. He was dead, and the belt about him and the chair-back, alone prevented him from falling forward on to me. His tongue was thrust out of one corner of his mouth. I shall always remember how he looked. He was leering, like a human-beast, more than a man.

"I edged away from him, across the floor; but I never stopped looking at him, until I had got to the other side of the door, and closed between us. Of course, I got my balance in a bit, and went back to him; but there was nothing I could do.

"Baumoff died of heart-failure, of course, obviously! I should never be so foolish as to suggest to any sane jury that, in his extraordinary, self-hypnotized, defenseless condition, he was "entered" by some Christ-apeing Monster of the Void. I've too much respect for my own claim to be a common-sensible man, to put forward such an idea with seriousness! Oh, I know I may seem to speak with a jeer; but what can I do but jeer at myself and all the world, when I dare not acknowledge, even secretly to myself, what my own thoughts are. Baumoff did, undoubtedly die of heart-failure; and, for the rest, how much was I hypnotized into believing. Only, there was over by the far wall, where it had been shaken down to the floor from a solidly fastened-up bracket, a little pile of glass that had once formed a piece of beautiful Venetian glassware. You remember that I heard something fall, when the room shook. Surely the room did shake? Oh, I must stop thinking. My head goes round.

"The explosive the papers are talking about. Yes, that's Baumoff's; that makes it all seem true, doesn't it? They had the darkness at Berlin, after the explosion. There is no getting away from that. The Government know only that Baumoff's formulae is capable of producing the largest quantity of gas, in the shortest possible time. That, in short, it is ideally explosive. So it is; but I imagine it will prove an explosive, as I have already said, and as experience has proved, a little too impartial in its action for it to create enthusiasm on either side of a battlefield. Perhaps this is but a mercy, in disguise; certainly a mercy, if Baumoff's theories as to the possibility of disorganizing matter, be anywhere near to the truth.

"I have thought sometimes that there might be a more normal explanation of the dreadful thing that happened at the end. Baumoff may have ruptured a blood-vessel in the brain, owing to the enormous arterial pressure that his experiment induced; and the voice I heard and the mockery and the horrible expression and leer may have been nothing more than the immediate outburst and expression of the natural "obliqueness" of a deranged mind, which so often turns up a side of a man's nature and produces an inversion of character, that is the very complement of his normal state. And certainly, poor Baumoff's normal religious attitude was one of marvelous reverence and loyalty towards the Christ.

"Also, in support of this line of explanation, I have frequently observed that the voice of a person suffering from mental derangement is frequently wonderfully changed, and has in it often a very repellant and inhuman quality. I try to think that this explanation fits the case. But I can never forget that room. Never."

CHAPTER 12
THE VOICE IN THE NIGHT

It was a dark, starless night. We were becalmed in the Northern Pacific. Our exact position I do not know; for the sun had been hidden during the course of a weary, breathless week, by a thin haze which had seemed to float above us, about the height of our mastheads, at whiles descending and shrouding the surrounding sea.

With there being no wind, we had steadied the tiller, and I was the only man on deck. The crew, consisting of two men and a boy, were sleeping forward in their den, while Will—my friend, and the master of our little craft—was aft in his bunk on the port side of the little cabin.

Suddenly, from out of the surrounding darkness, there came a hail:

"Schooner, ahoy!"

The cry was so unexpected that I gave no immediate answer, because of my surprise.

It came again—a voice curiously throaty and inhuman, calling from somewhere upon the dark sea away on our port broadside:

"Schooner, ahoy!"

"Hullo!" I sung out, having gathered my wits somewhat. "What are you? What do you want?"

"You need not be afraid," answered the queer voice, having probably noticed some trace of confusion in my tone. "I am only an old—man."

The pause sounded odd, but it was only afterward that it came back to me with any significance.

"Why don't you come alongside, then?" I queried somewhat snappishly; for I liked not his hinting at my having been a trifle shaken.

"I—I—can't. It wouldn't be safe. I——" The voice broke off, and there was silence.

"What do you mean?" I asked, growing more and more astonished. "What's not safe? Where are you?"

I listened for a moment; but there came no answer. And then, a sudden indefinite suspicion, of I knew not what, coming to me, I stepped swiftly to the binnacle and took out the lighted lamp. At the same time, I knocked on the deck with my heel to waken Will. Then I was back at the side, throwing the yellow funnel of light out into the silent immensity beyond our rail. As I did so, I heard a slight muffled cry, and then the sound of a splash, as though someone had dipped oars abruptly. Yet I cannot say with certainty that I saw anything; save, it seemed to me, that with the first flash of the light there had been something upon the waters, where now there was nothing.

"Hullo, there!" I called. "What foolery is this?"

But there came only the indistinct sounds of a boat being pulled away into the night.

Then I heard Will's voice from the direction of the after scuttle:

"What's up, George?"

"Come here, Will!" I said.

"What is it?" he asked, coming across the deck.

I told him the queer thing that had happened. He put several questions; then, after a moment's silence, he raised his hands to his lips and hailed:

"Boat, ahoy!"

From a long distance away there came back to us a faint reply, and my companion repeated his call. Presently, after a short period of silence, there grew on our hearing the muffled sound of oars, at which Will hailed again.

This time there was a reply: "Put away the light."

"I'm damned if I will," I muttered; but Will told me to do as the voice bade, and I shoved it down under the bulwarks.

"Come nearer," he said, and the oar strokes continued. Then, when apparently some half dozen fathoms distant, they again ceased.

"Come alongside!" exclaimed Will. "There's nothing to be frightened of aboard here."

"Promise that you will not show the light?"

"What's to do with you," I burst out, "that you're so infernally afraid of the light?"

"Because—" began the voice, and stopped short.

"Because what?" I asked quickly.

Will put his hand on my shoulder. "Shut up a minute, old man," he said, in a low voice. "Let me tackle him."

He leaned more over the rail.

"See here, mister," he said, "this is a pretty queer business, you coming upon us like this, right out in the middle of the blessed Pacific. How are we to know what sort of a hanky-panky trick you're up to? You say there's only one of you. How are we to know, unless we get a squint at you—eh? What's your objection to the light, anyway?"

As he finished, I heard the noise of the oars again, and then the voice came; but now from a greater distance, and sounding extremely hopeless and pathetic.

"I am sorry—sorry! I would not have troubled you, only I am hungry, and—so is she."

The voice died away, and the sound of the oars, dipping irregularly, was borne to us.

"Stop!" sang out Will. "I don't want to drive you away. Come back! We'll keep the light hidden, if you don't like it."

He turned to me:

"It's a damned queer rig, this; but I think there's nothing to be afraid of?"

There was a question in his tone, and I replied.

"No, I think the poor devil's been wrecked around here, and gone crazy."

The sound of the oars drew nearer.

"Shove that lamp back in the binnacle," said Will; then he leaned over the rail and listened. I replaced the lamp and came back to his side. The dipping of the oars ceased some dozen yards distant.

"Won't you come alongside now?" asked Will in an even voice. "I have had the lamp put back in the binnacle."

"I—I cannot," replied the voice. "I dare not come nearer. I dare not even pay you for the— the provisions."

"That's all right," said Will, and hesitated. "You're welcome to as much grub as you can take—" Again he hesitated.

"You are very good!" exclaimed the voice. "May God, Who understands everything, reward you—" It broke off huskily.

"The—the lady?" said Will abruptly. "Is she—"

"I have left her behind upon the island," came the voice.

"What island?" I cut in.

"I know not its name," returned the voice. "I would to God—" it began, and checked itself as suddenly.

"Could we not send a boat for her?" asked Will at this point.

"No!" said the voice, with extraordinary emphasis. "My God! No!" There was a moment's pause; then it added, in a tone which seemed a merited reproach:

"It was because of our want I ventured—because her agony tortured me."

"I am a forgetful brute!" exclaimed Will. "Just wait a minute, whoever you are, and I will bring you up something at once."

In a couple of minutes he was back again, and his arms were full of various edibles. He paused at the rail.

"Can't you come alongside for them?" he asked.

"No—I dare not," replied the voice, and it seemed to me that in its tones I detected a note of stifled craving—as though the owner hushed a mortal desire. It came to me then in a flash that the poor old creature out there in the darkness was suffering for actual need for that which Will held in his arms; and yet, because of some unintelligible dread, refraining from dashing to the side of our schooner and receiving it. And with the lightning-like conviction there came the knowledge that the Invisible was not mad, but sanely facing some intolerable horror.

"Damn it, Will!" I said, full of many feelings, over which predominated a vast sympathy. "Get a box. We must float off the stuff to him in it."

This we did, propelling it away from the vessel, out into the darkness, by means of a boat hook. In a minute a slight cry from the Invisible came to us, and we knew that he had secured the box.

A little later he called out a farewell to us, and so heartful a blessing, that I am sure we were the better for it. Then, without more ado, we heard the ply of oars across the darkness.

"Pretty soon off," remarked Will, with perhaps just a little sense of injury.

"Wait," I replied. "I think somehow he'll come back. He must have been badly needing that food."

"And the lady," said Will. For a moment he was silent; then he continued:

"It's the queerest thing ever I've tumbled across since I've been fishing."

"Yes," I said, and fell to pondering.

And so the time slipped away—an hour, another, and still Will stayed with me; for the queer adventure had knocked all desire for sleep out of him.

The third hour was three parts through when we heard again the sound of oars across the silent ocean.

"Listen!" said Will, a low note of excitement in his voice.

"He's coming, just as I thought," I muttered.

The dipping of the oars grew nearer, and I noted that the strokes were firmer and longer. The food had been needed.

They came to a stop a little distance off the broadside, and the queer voice came again to us through the darkness:

"Schooner, ahoy!"

"That you?" asked Will.

"Yes," replied the voice. "I left you suddenly, but—but there was great need."

"The lady?" questioned Will.

"The—lady is grateful now on earth. She will be more grateful soon in—in heaven."

Will began to make some reply, in a puzzled voice; but became confused, and broke off short. I said nothing. I was wondering at the curious pauses, and, apart from my wonder, I was full of a great sympathy.

The voice continued:

"We—she and I, have talked, as we shared the result of God's tenderness and yours—"

Will interposed; but without coherence.

"I beg of you not to—to belittle your deed of Christian charity this night," said the voice. "Be sure that it has not escaped His notice."

It stopped, and there was a full minute's silence. Then it came again:

"We have spoken together upon that which—which has befallen us. We had thought to go out, without telling anyone of the terror which has come into our—lives. She is with me in believing that tonight's happenings are under a special ruling, and that it is God's wish that we should tell to you all that we have suffered since—since—"

"Yes?" said Will softly.

"Since the sinking of the Albatross."

"Ah!" I exclaimed involuntarily. "She left Newcastle for 'Frisco some six months ago, and hasn't been heard of since."

"Yes" answered the voice. "But some few degrees to the North of the line, she was caught in a terrible storm, and dismasted. When the day came, it was found that she was leaking badly, and, presently, it falling to a calm, the sailors took to the boats, leaving—leaving a young lady—my fiancée—and myself upon the wreck.

"We were below, gathering together a few of our belongings, when they left. They were entirely callous, through fear, and when we came up upon the decks, we saw them only as small shapes afar off upon the horizon. Yet we did not despair, but set to work and constructed a small raft. Upon this we put such few matters as it would hold, including a quantity of water and some ship's biscuit. Then, the vessel being very deep in the water, we got ourselves onto the raft and pushed off.

"It was later, when I observed that we seemed to be in the way of some tide or current, which bore us from the ship at an angle; so that in the course of three hours, by my watch, her hull became invisible to our sight, her broken masts remaining in view for a somewhat longer period. Then, towards evening, it grew misty, and so through the night. The next day we were still encompassed by the mist, the weather remaining quiet.

"For four days we drifted through this strange haze, until, on the evening of the fourth day, there grew upon our ears the murmur of breakers at a distance. Gradually it became plainer, and, somewhat after midnight, it appeared to sound upon either hand at no very great space. The raft was raised upon a swell several times, and then we were in smooth water, and the noise of the breakers was behind.

"When the morning came, we found that we were in a sort of great lagoon; but of this we noticed little at the time; for close before us, through the enshrouding mist, loomed the hull of a large sailing vessel. With one accord, we fell upon our knees and thanked God, for we thought that here was an end to our perils. We had much to learn.

"The raft drew near to the ship, and we shouted on them to take us aboard; but none answered. Presently the raft touched against the side of the vessel, and seeing a rope hanging downward, I seized it and began to climb. Yet I had much ado to make my way up, because of a kind of grey, lichenous fungus that had seized upon the rope, and which blotched the side of the ship lividly.

"I reached the rail and clambered over it, onto the deck. Here I saw that the decks were covered, in great patches, with grey masses, some of them rising into nodules several feet in height; but at the time I thought less of this matter than of the possibility of there being people aboard the ship. I shouted; but none answered. Then I went to the door below the poop deck. I opened it, and peered in. There was a great smell of staleness, so that I knew in a moment that nothing living was within, and with the knowledge, I shut the door quickly; for I felt suddenly lonely.

"I went back to the side where I had scrambled up. My—my sweetheart was still sitting quietly upon the raft. Seeing me look down, she called up to know whether there were any aboard of the ship. I replied that the vessel had the appearance of having been long deserted, but that if she would wait a little I would see whether there was anything in the shape of a ladder by which she could ascend to the deck. Then we would make a search through the vessel together. A little later, on the opposite side of the decks, I found a rope side ladder. This I carried across, and a minute afterwards she was beside me.

"Together we explored the cabins and apartments in the after part of the ship; but nowhere was there any sign of life. Here and there, within the cabins themselves, we came across odd patches of that queer fungus; but this, as my sweetheart said, could be cleansed away.

"In the end, having assured ourselves that the after portion of the vessel was empty, we picked our ways to the bows, between the ugly grey nodules of that strange growth; and here we made a further search, which told us that there was indeed none aboard but ourselves.

"This being now beyond any doubt, we returned to the stern of the ship and proceeded to make ourselves as comfortable as possible. Together we cleared out and cleaned two of the cabins; and after that I made examination whether there was anything eatable in the ship. This I soon found was so, and thanked God in my heart for His goodness. In addition to this I discovered the whereabouts of the fresh-water pump, and having fixed it, I found the water drinkable, though somewhat unpleasant to the taste.

"For several days we stayed aboard the ship, without attempting to get to the shore. We were busily engaged in making the place habitable. Yet even thus early we became aware that our lot was even less to be desired than might have been imagined; for though, as a first step, we scraped away the odd patches of growth that studded the floors and walls of the cabins and saloon, yet they returned almost to their original size within the space of twenty-four hours, which not only discouraged us but gave us a feeling of vague unease.

"Still we would nor admit ourselves beaten, so set to work afresh, and not only scraped away the fungus but soaked the places where it had been with carbolic, a can-full of which I had found in the pantry. Yet, by the end of the week the growth had returned in full strength, and, in addition, it had spread to other places, as though our touching it had allowed germs from it to travel elsewhere.

"On the seventh morning, my sweetheart woke to find a small patch of it growing on her pillow, close to her face. At that, she came to me, as soon as she could get her garments upon her. I was in the galley at the time lighting the fire for breakfast.

" 'Come here, John,' she said, and led me aft. When I saw the thing upon her pillow I shuddered, and then and there we agreed to go right out of the ship and see whether we could not fare to make ourselves more comfortable ashore.

"Hurriedly we gathered together our few belongings, and even among these I found that the fungus had been at work, for one of her shawls had a little lump of it growing near one edge. I threw the whole thing over the side without saying anything to her.

"THE RAFT WAS STILL ALONGSIDE, but it was too clumsy to guide, and I lowered down a small boat that hung across the stern, and in this we made our way to the shore. Yet, as we drew near to it, I became gradually aware that here the vile fungus, which had driven us from the ship, was growing riot. In places it rose into horrible, fantastic mounds, which seemed almost to quiver, as with a quiet life, when the wind blew across them. Here and there it took on the forms of vast fingers, and in others it just spread out flat and smooth and treacherous. Odd places, it appeared as grotesque stunted trees, seeming extraordinarily kinked and gnarled—the whole quaking vilely at times.

"At first, it seemed to us that there was no single portion of the surrounding shore which was not hidden beneath the masses of the hideous lichen; yet, in this, I found we were mistaken; for somewhat later, coasting along the shore at a little distance, we descried a smooth white patch of what appeared to be fine sand, and there we landed. It was not sand. What it was I do not know. All that I have observed is that upon it the fungus will not grow; while everywhere else, save where the sand-like earth wanders oddly, path-wise, amid the grey desolation of the lichen, there is nothing but that loathsome greyness.

"It is difficult to make you understand how cheered we were to find one place that was absolutely free from the growth, and here we deposited our belongings. Then we went back to the ship for such things as it seemed to us we should need. Among other matters, I managed to bring ashore with me one of the ship's sails, with which I constructed two small tents, which, though exceedingly rough-shaped, served the purposes for which they were intended. In these we lived and stored our various necessities, and thus for a matter of some four weeks all went smoothly and without particular unhappiness. Indeed, I may say with much happiness—for—for we were together.

"It was on the thumb of her right hand that the growth first showed. It was only a small circular spot, much like a little grey mole. My God! how the fear leaped to my heart when she showed me the place. We cleansed it, between us, washing it with carbolic and water. In the morning of the following day she showed her hand to me again. The grey warty thing had returned. For a little while we looked at one another in silence. Then, still wordless, we started again to remove it. In the midst of the operation she spoke suddenly.

" 'What's that on the side of your face, dear?' Her voice was sharp with anxiety. I put my hand up to feel.

" 'There! Under the hair by your ear. A little to the front a bit.' My finger rested upon the place, and then I knew.

" 'Let us get your thumb done first,' I said. And she submitted, only because she was afraid to touch me until it was cleansed. I finished washing and disinfecting her thumb, and then she turned to my face. After it was finished we sat together and talked awhile of many things; for there had come into our lives sudden, very terrible thoughts. We were, all at once, afraid of something worse than death. We spoke of loading the boat with provisions and water and making our way out onto the sea; yet we were helpless, for many causes, and—and the growth had attacked us already. We decided to stay. God would do with us what was His will. We would wait.

"A month, two months, three months passed and the places grew somewhat, and there had come others. Yet we fought so strenuously with the fear that its headway was but slow, comparatively speaking.

"Occasionally we ventured off to the ship for such stores as we needed. There we found that the fungus grew persistently. One of the nodules on the main deck soon became as high as my head.

"We had now given up all thought or hope of leaving the island.

We had realized that it would be unallowable to go among healthy humans, with the things from which we were suffering.

"With this determination and knowledge in our minds we knew that we should have to husband our food and water; for we did not know, at that time, but that we should possibly live for many years.

"This reminds me that I have told you that I am an old man. Judged by years this is not so. But—but—"

He broke off; then continued somewhat abruptly:

"As I was saying, we knew that we should have to use care in the matter of food. But we had no idea then how little food there was left of which to take care. It was a week later that I made the discovery that all the other bread tanks—which I had supposed full—were empty, and that (beyond odd tins of vegetables and meat, and some other matters) we had nothing on which to depend, but the bread in the tank which I had already opened.

"After learning this I bestirred myself to do what I could, and set to work at fishing in the lagoon; but with no success. At this I was somewhat inclined to feel desperate until the thought came to me to try outside the lagoon, in the open sea.

"Here, at times, I caught odd fish, but so infrequently that they proved of but little help in keeping us from the hunger which threatened. It seemed to me that our deaths were likely to come by hunger, and not by the growth of the thing which had seized upon our bodies.

"We were in this state of mind when the fourth month wore out. Then I made a very horrible discovery. One morning, a little before midday, I came off from the ship with a portion of the biscuits which were left. In the mouth of her tent I saw my sweetheart sitting, eating something.

" 'What is it, my dear?' I called out as I leaped ashore. Yet, on hearing my voice, she seemed confused, and, turning, slyly threw something toward the edge of the little clearing. It fell short, and a vague suspicion having arisen within me, I walked across and picked it up. It was a piece of the grey fungus.

"As I went to her with it in my hand, she turned deadly pale; then a rose red.

"I felt strangely dazed and frightened.

" 'My dear! My dear!' I said, and could say no more. Yet at my words she broke down and cried bitterly. Gradually, as she calmed, I got from her the news that she had tried it the preceding day, and—and liked it. I got her to promise on her knees not to touch it again, however great our hunger. After she had promised, she told me that the desire for it had come suddenly, and that, until the moment of desire, she had experienced nothing toward it but the most extreme repulsion.

"Later in the day, feeling strangely restless and much shaken with the thing which I had discovered, I made my way along one of the twisted paths—formed by the white, sand-like substance—which led among the fungoid growth. I had, once before, ventured along there; but not to any great distance. This time, being involved in perplexing thought, I went much farther than hitherto.

"Suddenly I was called to myself by a queer hoarse sound on my left. Turning quickly I saw that there was movement among an extraordinarily shaped mass of fungus, close to my elbow. It was swaying uneasily, as though it possessed life of its own. Abruptly, as I stared, the thought came to me that the thing had a grotesque resemblance to the figure of a distorted human creature. Even as the fancy flashed into my brain, there was a slight, sickening noise of tearing, and I saw that one of the branchlike arms was detaching itself from the surrounding grey masses, and coming toward me. The head of the thing—a shapeless grey ball, inclined in my direction. I stood stupidly, and the vile arm brushed across my face. I gave out a frightened cry, and ran back a few paces. There was a sweetish taste upon my lips where the thing had touched me. I licked them, and was immediately filled with an inhuman desire. I turned and seized a mass of the fungus. Then more, and—more. I was insatiable. In the midst of devouring, the remembrance of the morning's discovery swept into my mazed brain. It was sent by God. I dashed the fragment I held to the ground. Then, utterly wretched and feeling a dreadful guiltiness, I made my way back to the little encampment.

"I think she knew, by some marvelous intuition which love must have given, so soon as she set eyes on me. Her quiet sympathy made it easier for me, and I told her of my sudden weakness, yet omitted to mention the extraordinary thing which had gone before. I desired to spare her all unnecessary terror.

"But, for myself, I had added an intolerable knowledge, to breed an incessant terror in my brain; for I doubted not but that I had seen the end of one of these men who had come to the island in the ship in the lagoon; and in that monstrous ending I had seen our own.

"Thereafter we kept from the abominable food, though the desire for it had entered into our blood. Yet our drear punishment was upon us; for, day by day, with monstrous rapidity, the fungoid growth took hold of our poor bodies. Nothing we could do would check it materially, and so—and so—we who had been human became—Well, it matters less each day. Only—only we had been man and maid!

"And day by day the fight is more dreadful, to withstand the hunger-lust for the terrible lichen.

"A week ago we ate the last of the biscuit, and since that time I have caught three fish. I was out here fishing tonight when your schooner drifted upon me out of the mist. I hailed you. You know the rest, and may God, out of His great heart, bless you for your goodness to a—a couple of poor outcast souls."

There was the dip of an oar—another. Then the voice came again, and for the last time, sounding through the slight surrounding mist, ghostly and mournful.

"God bless you! Good-bye!"

"Good-bye," we shouted together hoarsely, our hearts full of many emotions.

I glanced about me. I became aware that the dawn was upon us.

The sun flung a stray beam across the hidden sea; pierced the mist dully, and lit up the receding boat with a gloomy fire. Indistinctly I saw something nodding between the oars. I thought of a sponge—a great, grey nodding sponge— The oars continued to ply. They were grey—as was the boat—and my eyes searched a moment vainly for the conjunction of hand and oar. My gaze flashed back to the—head. It nodded forward as the oars went backward for the stroke. Then the oars were dipped, the boat shot out of the patch of light, and the—the thing went nodding into the mist.

CHAPTER 13

THE DERELICT

"It's the material," said the old ship's doctor — "the material plus the conditions — and, maybe," he added slowly, "a third factor — yes, a third factor; but there, there ——" He broke off his half-meditative sentence and began to charge his pipe.

"Go on, doctor," we said encouragingly, and with more than a little expectancy. We were in the smoke-room of the Sand-a-lea, running across the North Atlantic; and the doctor was a character. He concluded the charging of his pipe, and lit it; then settled himself, and began to express himself more fully.

"The material," he said with conviction, "is inevitably the medium of expression of the life-force — the fulcrum, as it were; lacking which it is unable to exert itself, or, indeed, to express itself in any form or fashion that would be intelligible or evident to us. So potent is the share of the material in the production of that thing which we name life, and so eager the life-force to express itself, that I am convinced it would, if given the right conditions, make itself manifest even through so hopeless seeming a medium as a simple block of sawn wood; for I tell you, gentlemen, the life-force is both as fiercely urgent and as indiscriminate as fire — the destructor; yet which some are now growing to consider the very essence of life rampant. There is a quaint seeming paradox there," he concluded, nodding his old grey head.

"Yes, doctor," I said. "In brief, your argument is that life is a thing, state, fact, or element, call it what you like, which requires the material through which to manifest itself, and that given the material, plus the conditions, the result is life. In other words, that life is an evolved product, manifested through matter and bred of conditions — eh?"

"As we understand the word," said the old doctor. "Though, mind you, there may be a third factor. But, in my heart, I believe that it is a matter of chemistry — conditions and a suitable medium; but given the conditions, the brute is so almighty that it will seize upon anything through which to manifest itself. It is a force generated by conditions; but, nevertheless, this does not bring us one iota nearer to its explanation, any more than to the explanation of electricity or fire. They are, all three, of the outer forces — monsters of the void. Nothing we can do will create any one of them, our power is merely to be able, by providing the conditions, to make each one of them manifest to our physical senses. Am I clear?"

"Yes, doctor, in a way, you are," I said. "But I don't agree with you, though I think I understand you. Electricity and fire are both what I might call natural things, but life is an abstract something — a kind of all-permeating wakefulness. Oh, I can't explain it! Who could? But it s spiritual, not just a thing bred out of a condition, like fire, as you say, or electricity. It's a horrible thought of yours. Life's a kind of spiritual mystery ——"

"Easy, my boy!" said the old doctor, laughing gently to himself. "Or else I may be asking you to demonstrate the spiritual mystery of life of the limpet, or the crab, shall we say." He grinned at me with ineffable perverseness. "Anyway," he continued, "as I suppose you've all guessed, I've a yarn to tell you in support of my impression that life is no more a mystery or a miracle than fire or electricity. But, please to remember, gentlemen, that because we've succeeded in naming and making good use of these two forces, they're just as much mysteries, fundamentally as ever. And, anyway, the thing I'm going to tell you won't explain the mystery of life, but only give you one of my pegs on which I hang my feeling that life is as I have said, a force made manifest through conditions — that is to say, natural chemistry — and that it can take for its purpose and need, the most incredible and unlikely matter; for without matter it cannot come into existence — it cannot become manifest ——"

"I don't agree with you, doctor," I interrupted. "Your theory would destroy all belief in life after death. It would ——"

"Hush, sonny," said the old man, with a quiet little smile of comprehension. "Hark to what I've to say first; and, anyway, what objection have you to material life after death? And if you object to a material framework, I would still have you remember that I am speaking of life, as we understand the word in this our life. Now do be a quiet lad, or I'll never be done:

"It was when I was a young man, and that is a good many years ago, gentlemen. I had passed my examinations, but was so run down with overwork that it was decided that I had better take a trip to sea. I was by no means well off, and very glad in the end to secure a nominal post as doctor in the sailing passenger clipper running out to China.

"The name of the ship was the Bheospse, and soon after I had got all my gear aboard she cast off, and we dropped down the Thames, and next day were well away out in the Channel.

"The captain's name was Gannington, a very decent man, though quite illiterate. The first mate, Mr. Berlies, was a quiet, sternish, reserved man, very well-read. The second mate, Mr. Selvern, was, perhaps, by birth and upbringing, the most socially cultured of the three, but he lacked the stamina and indomitable pluck of the two others. He was more of a sensitive, and emotionally and even mentally, the most alert man of the three.

"On our way out, we called at Madagascar, where we landed some of our passengers; then we ran eastward, meaning to call at

North-West Cape; but about a hundred degrees east we encountered very dreadful weather, which carried away all our sails, and sprung the jib-boom and foret'gallantmast.

"The storm carried us northward for several hundred miles, and when it dropped us finally, we found ourselves in a very bad state. The ship had been strained, and had taken some three feet of water through her seams; the maintopmast had been sprung, in addition to the jib-boom and foret'gallantmast, two of our boats had gone, as also one of the pigsties, with three fine pigs, these latter having been washed overboard but some half-hour before the wind began to ease, which it did very quickly, though a very ugly sea ran for some hours after.

"The wind left us just before dark, and when morning came it brought splendid weather — a calm, mildly undulating sea, and a brilliant sun, with no wind. It showed us also that we were not alone, for about two miles away to the westward was another vessel, which Mr. Selvern, the second mate, pointed out to me.

"'That's a pretty rum-looking, packet, doctor,' he said, and handed me his glass.

"I looked through it at the other vessel, and saw what he meant; at least, I thought I did.

"'Yes, Mr. Selvern,' I said. 'She's got a pretty old-fashioned look about her.'

"He laughed at me in his pleasant way.

"'It's easy to see you're not a sailor, doctor,' he remarked. 'There's a dozen rum things about her. She's a derelict, and has been floating round, by the look of her, for many a score of years. Look at the shape of her counter, and the bows and cutwater. She's as old as the hills, as you might say, and ought to have gone down to Davy Jones a good while ago. Look at the growths on her, and the thickness of her standing rigging; that's all salt encrustations, I fancy, if you notice the white colour. She's been a small barque; but, don't you see, she's not a yard left aloft. They've all dropped out of the slings; everything rotted away; wonder the standing rigging hasn't gone, too. I wish the old man would let us take the boat and have a look at her. She'd be well worth it.'

"'There seemed little chance, however, of this, for all hands were turned to and kept hard at it all day long repairing the damage to the masts and gear; and this took a long while, as you may think. Part of the time I gave a hand heaving on one of the deck capstans, for the exercise was good for my liver. Old Captain Gannington approved, and I persuaded him to come along and try some of the same medicine, which he did; and we got very chummy over the job.

"We got talking about the derelict, and he remarked how lucky we were not to have run full tilt on to her in the darkness, for she lay right away to leeward of us, according, to the way that we had been drifting in the storm. He also was of the opinion that she had a strange look about her, and that she was pretty old; but on this latter point he plainly had far less knowledge than the second mate, for he was, as I have said, an illiterate man, and knew nothing of seacraft beyond what experience had taught him. He lacked the book knowl-edge which the second mate had of vessels previous to his day, which it appeared the derelict was.

"'She's an old 'un, doctor,' was the extent of observations in this direction.

"Yet, when I mentioned to him that it would be interesting to go aboard and give her a bit of an overhaul, he nodded his head as if the idea had been already in his mind and accorded with his own incli-nations.

"'When the work's over, doctor,' he said. 'Can't spare the men now, ye know. Got to get all shipshape an' ready as smart as we can. But, we'll take my gig, an' go off in the second dog-watch. The glass is steady, an' it'll be a bit of gam for us.'

"That evening, after tea, the captain gave orders to clear the gig and get her overboard. The second mate was to come with us, and the skipper gave him word to see that two or three lamps were put into the boat, as it would soon fall dark. A little later we were pulling across the calmness of the sea with a crew of six at the oars, and making very good speed of it.

"Now, gentlemen, I have detailed to you with great exactness all the facts, both big and little, so that you can follow step by step each incident in this extraordinary affair, and I want you now to pay the closest attention. I was sitting in the stern-sheets with the second mate and the captain, who was steering, and as we drew nearer and nearer to the stranger I studied her with an ever-growing attention, as, indeed, did Captain Gannington and the second mate. She was, as you know, to the west-ward of us, and the sunset was making a great flame of red light to the back of her, so that she showed a little blurred and indistinct by reason of the halation of the light, which almost defeated the eye in any attempt to see her rotting spars and standing rigging, submerged, as they were, in the fiery glory of the sunset.

"It was because of this effect of the sunset that we had come quite close, comparatively, to the derelict before we saw that she was all surrounded by a sort of curious scum, the colour of which was difficult to decide upon by reason of the red light that was in the atmosphere, but which afterwards we discovered to be brown. This scum spread all about the old vessel for many hundreds of yards in a huge, irregular patch, a great stretch of which reached out to the eastward, upon the starboard side of the boat some score or so fathoms away.

"'Queer stuff,' said Captain Gannington, leaning to the side and looking over. 'Something in the cargo as 'as gone rotten, and worked out through 'er seams.'

"'Look at her bows and stern,' said the second mate. 'Just look at the growth on her!'

"There were, as he said, great clumpings of strange-looking sea-fungi under the bows and the short counter astern. From the stump of her jib-boom and her cutwater great beards of rime and marine growths hung downward into the scum that held her in. Her blank starboard side was presented to us — all a dead, dirtyish white, streaked and mottled vaguely with dull masses of heavier colour.

"'There's a steam or haze rising off her,' said the second mate, speaking again. 'You can see it against the light. It keeps coming and going. Look!'

"I saw then what he meant — a faint haze or steam, either suspended above the old vessel or rising from her. And Captain Gannington saw it also.

"'Spontaneous combustion!' he exclaimed. 'We'll 'ave to watch when we lift the 'atches, 'nless it's some poor devil that's got aboard of 'er. But that ain't likely.'

"We were now within a couple of hundred yards of the old derelict, and had entered into the brown scum. As it poured off the lifted oars I heard one of the men mutter to himself, 'Dam' treacle!' And, indeed, it was not something unlike it. As the boat continued to forge nearer and nearer to the old ship the scum grew thicker and thicker, so that, at last, it perceptibly slowed us.

"'Give way, lads! Put some beef to it!' sang out Captain Gannington. And thereafter there was no sound except the panting of the men and the faint, reiterated suck, suck of the sullen brown scum upon the oars as the boat was forced ahead. As we went, I was conscious of a peculiar smell in the evening air, and whilst I had no doubt that the puddling of the scum by the oars made it rise, I could give no name to it; yet, in a way, it was vaguely familiar.

"We were now very close to the old vessel, and presently she was high about us against the dying light. The captain called out then to 'in with the bow oars and stand by with the boat-hook,' which was done.

"'Aboard there! Ahoy! Aboard there! Ahoy!' shouted Captain Gannington; but there came no answer, only the dull sound his voice going lost into the open sea, each time he sung out.

"'Ahoy! Aboard there! Ahoy!' he shouted time after time, but there was only the weary silence of the old hulk that answered us; and, somehow as he shouted, the while that I stared up half expectantly at her, a queer little sense of oppression, that amounted almost to nervousness, came upon me. It passed, but I remember how I was suddenly aware that it was growing dark. Darkness comes fairly rapidly in the tropics, though not so quickly as many fiction writers seem to think; but it was not that the coming dusk had perceptibly deepened in that brief time of only a few moments, but rather that my nerves had made me suddenly a little hypersensitive. I mention my state particularly, for I am not a nervy man normally, and my abrupt touch of nerves is significant, in the light of what happened.

"'There's no one on board there!' said Captain Gannington. 'Give way, men!' For the boat's crew had instinctively rested on their oars, as the captain hailed the old craft. The men gave way again; and then the second mate called out excitedly, 'Why, look there, there's our pigsty! See, it's got Bheospse painted on the end. It's drifted down here and the scum's caught it. What a blessed wonder!'

"It was, as he had said, our pigsty that had been washed overboard in the storm; and most extraordinary to come across it there.

"'We'll tow it off with us, when we go,' said the captain, and shouted to the crew to get down to their oars; for they were hardly moving the boat, because the scum was so thick, close in around the old ship, that it literally clogged the boat from moving. I remember that it struck me, in a half-conscious sort of way, as curious that the pigsty, containing our three dead pigs, had managed to drift in so far unaided, whilst we could scarcely manage to force the boat in, now that we had come right into the scum. But the thought passed from my mind, for so many things happened within the next few minutes.

"The men managed to bring the boat in alongside, within a couple of feet of the derelict, and the man with the boat-hook hooked on.

"''Ave ye got 'old there, forward?' asked Captain Gannington.

"'Yessir!' said the bowman; and as he spoke there came a queer noise of tearing.

"'What's that?' asked the Captain.

"'It's tore, sir. Tore clean away!' said the man, and his tone showed that he had received something of a shock.

"'Get a hold again, then!' said Captain Gannington irritably. 'You don't s'pose this packet was built yesterday! Shove the hook into the main chains' The man did so gingerly, as you might say, for it seemed to me, in the growing dusk, that he put no strain on to the hook, though, of course there was no need — you see the boat could not go very far of herself, in the stuff in which she was imbedded. I remember thinking this, also as I looked up at the bulging side of the old vessel. Then I heard Captain Gannington's voice:

"'Lord, but she s old! An' what a colour, doctor! She don't half want paint, do she? Now then, somebody, one of them oars.' An oar was passed to him, and he leant it up against the ancient, bulging side; then he paused, and called to the second mate to light a couple of the lamps, and stand by to pass them up, for darkness had settled down now upon the sea.

"The second mate lit two of the lamps, and told one of the men to light a third, and keep it handy in the boat; then he stepped across, with a lamp in each hand, to where Captain Gannington stood by the oar against the side of the ship.

"'Now, my lad,' said the captain to the man who had pulled stroke, 'up with you, an' we'll pass ye up the lamps.'

"The man jumped to obey, caught the oar, and put his weight upon it; and as he did so, something seemed to give way a little.

"'Look!' cried out the second mate, and pointed, lamp in hand. 'It's sunk in!'

"This was true. The oar had made quite an indentation into the bulging, somewhat slimy side of the old vessel.

"'Mould, I reckon,' said Captain Gannington, bending towards the derelict to look. Then to the man:

"'Up you go, my lad, and be smart! Don't stand there waitin'!'

"At that the man, who had paused a moment as he felt the oar give beneath his weight began to shin' up, and in a few seconds he was aboard, and leant out over the rail for the lamps. These were passed up to him, and the captain called to him to steady the oar. Then Captain Gannington went, calling to me to follow, and after me the second mate.

"As the captain put his face over the rail, he gave a cry of astonishment.

"'Mould, by gum! Mould — tons of it. Good lord!'

"As I heard him shout that I scrambled the more eagerly after him, and in a moment or two I was able to see what he meant — everywhere that the light from the two lamps struck there was nothing but smooth great masses and surfaces of a dirty white coloured mould. I climbed over the rail, with the second mate close behind, and stood upon the mould covered decks. There might have been no planking beneath the mould, for all that our feet could feel. It gave under our tread with a spongy, puddingy feel. It covered the deck furniture of the old ship, so that the shape of each article and fitment was often no more than suggested through it.

"Captain Gannington snatched a lamp from the man and the second mate reached for the other. They held the lamps high, and we all stared. It was most extraordinary, and somehow most abominable. I can think of no other word, gentlemen, that so much describes the predominant feeling that affected me at the moment.

"'Good lord!' said Captain Gannington several times. 'Good lord!' But neither the second mate nor the man said anything, and, for my part I just stared, and at the same time began to smell a little at the air, for there was a vague odor of something half familiar, that somehow brought to me a sense of half-known fright.

"I turned this way and that, staring, as I have said. Here and there the mould was so heavy as to entirely disguise what lay beneath, converting the deck-fittings into indistinguishable mounds of mould all dirty-white and blotched and veined with irregular, dull, purplish markings.

"There was a strange thing about the mould which Captain Gannington drew attention to — it was that our feet did not crush into it and break the surface, as might have been expected, but merely indented it.

"'Never seen nothin' like it before! Never!' said the captain after having stooped with his lamp to examine the mould under our feet. He stamped with his heel, and the mould gave out a dull, puddingy sound. He stooped again, with a quick movement, and stared, holding the lamp close to the deck. 'Blest if it ain't a reg'lar skin to it!'

"The second mate and the man and I all stooped and looked at it. The second mate progged it with his forefinger, and I remember I rapped it several times with my knuckles, listening to the dead sound it gave out, and noticing the close, firm texture of the mould.

"'Dough!' the second mate. 'It's just like blessed dough! Pouf!' He stood up with a quick movement. 'I could fancy it stinks a bit,' he said.

"As he said this I knew, suddenly, what the familiar thing was in the vague odor that hung about us — it was that the smell had something animal-like in it; something of the same smell, only heavier, that you would smell in any place that is infested with mice. I began to look about with a sudden very real uneasiness. There might be vast numbers of hungry rats aboard. They might prove exceedingly dangerous, if in a starving condition; yet, as you will understand, somehow I hesitated to put forward my idea as a reason for caution, it was too fanciful.

"Captain Gannington had begun to go aft along the mould-covered main-deck with the second mate, each of them holding their lamps high up, so as to cast a good light about the vessel. I turned quickly and followed them, the man with me keeping close to my heels, and plainly uneasy. As we went, I became aware that there was a feeling of moisture in the air, and I remembered the slight mist, or smoke, above the hulk, which had made Captain Gannington suggest spontaneous combustion in explanation.

"And always, as we went, there was that vague, animal smell; suddenly I found myself wishing we were well away from the old vessel.

"Abruptly, after a few paces, the captain stopped and pointed at a row of mould-hidden shapes on each side of the maindeck. 'Guns,' he said. 'Been a privateer in the old days, I guess — maybe worse! We'll 'ave a look below, doctor; there may be something worth touchin'. She's older than I thought. Mr. Selvern thinks she's about two hundred years old; but I scarce think it.'

"We continued our way aft, and I remember that I found myself walking as lightly and gingerly as possible, as if I were subconsciously afraid of treading through the rotten, mould-hid decks. I think the others had a touch of the same feeling, from the way that they walked. Occasionally the soft stuff would grip our heels, releasing them with a little sullen suck.

"The captain forged somewhat ahead of the second mate; and I know that the suggestion he had made himself, that perhaps there might be something below worth carrying away, had stimulated his imagination. The second mate was, however, beginning to feel somewhat the same way that I did; at least I have that impression. I think, if it had not been for what I might truly describe as Captain Gannington's sturdy courage, we should all of us have just gone back over the side very soon, for there was most certainly an unwholesome feeling abroad that made one feel queerly lacking in pluck; and you will soon see that this feeling was justified.

"Just as the captain reached the few mould-covered steps leading up on to the short half-poop, I was suddenly aware that the feeling of moisture in the air had grown very much more definite. It was perceptible now, intermittently, as a sort of thin, moist, fog-like vapour, that came and went oddly, and seemed to make the decks a little indistinct to the view, this time and that. Once an odd puff of it beat up suddenly from somewhere, and caught me in the face, carrying a queer, sickly, heavy odour with it that somehow frightened me strangely with a suggestion of a waiting and half-comprehended danger.

"We had followed Captain Gannington up the three mould covered steps, and now went slowly along the raised after-deck. By the mizzenmast Captain Gannington paused, and held his lantern near to it. 'My word, mister,' he said to the second mate, 'it's fair thickened up with mould! Why, I'll g'antee it's close on four foot thick.' He shone the light down to where it met the deck. 'Good lord!' he said. 'Look at the sea-lice on it!' I stepped up, and it was as he had said; the sea-lice were thick upon it, some of them huge, not less than the size of large beetles, and all a clear, colourless shade, like water, except where there were little spots of grey on them.

"'I've never seen the like of them, 'cept on a live cod,' said Captain Gannington, in an extremely puzzled voice. 'My word! But they're whoppers!' Then he passed on; but a few paces farther aft he stopped again, and held his lamp near to the mould-hidden deck.

"'Lord bless me, doctor,' he called out, in a low voice, 'did ye ever see the like of that? Why, it's a foot long, if it's a hinch!'

"I stooped over his shoulder, and saw what he meant; it was a clear, colourless creature about a foot long, and about eight inches high, with a curved back that was extraordinarily narrow. As we stared, all in a group, it gave a queer little flick, and was gone.

"'Jumped!' said the captain. 'Well, if that ain't a giant of all the sea-lice that ever I've seen. I guess it's jumped twenty foot clear.' He straightened his back, and scratched his head a moment, swinging the lantern this way and that with the other hand, and staring about us. 'Wot are they doin' aboard 'ere?' he said. 'You'll see 'em — little things — on fat cod an' such-like. I'm blowed, doctor, if I understand.'

"He held his lamp towards a big mound of the mould that occupied part of the after portion of the low poop-deck, a little foreside of where there came a two-foot high 'break' to a kind of second and loftier poop, that ran away aft to the taffrail. The mound was pretty big, several feet across, and more than a yard high. Captain Gannington walked up to it.

"'I reck'n this's the scuttle,' he remarked, and gave it a heavy kick. The only result was a deep indentation into the huge, whiteish hump of mould, as if he had driven his foot into a mass of some doughy substance. Yet I am not altogether correct in saying that this was the only result, for a certain other thing happened. From the place made by the captain's foot there came a sudden gush of a purplish fluid, accompanied by a peculiar smell, that was, and was not, half familiar. Some of the mould-like substance had stuck to the toe of the captain's boot, and from this likewise there issued a sweat, as it were, of the same colour.

"'Well?' said Captain Gannington, in surprise, and drew back his foot to make another kick at the hump of mould. But he paused at an exclamation from the second mate:

"'Don't sir,' said the second mate.

"I glanced at him, and the light from Captain Gannington's lamp showed me that his face had a bewildered, half-frightened look, as if he were suddenly and unexpectedly half afraid of something, and as if his tongue had given away his sudden fright, without any intention on his part to speak. The captain also turned and stared at him.

"'Why, mister?' he asked, in a somewhat puzzled voice, through which there sounded just the vaguest hint of annoyance. 'We've got to shift this muck, if we're to get below.'

"I looked at the second mate, and it seemed to me that, curiously enough he was listening less to the captain than to some other sound. Suddenly he said, in a queer voice, 'Listen, everybody!'

"Yet we heard nothing, beyond the faint murmur of the men talking together in the boat alongside.

"'I don't, hear nothing,' said Captain Gannington, after a short pause. 'Do you, doctor?'

"'No,' I said.

"'Wot was it you thought you heard?' the captain, turning again to the second mate. But the second mate shook his head in a curious, almost irritable way, as if the captain's question interrupted his listening. Captain Gannington stared a moment at him, then held his lantern up and glanced about him almost uneasily. I know I felt a queer sense of strain. But the light showed nothing beyond the greyish dirty-white of the mould in all directions.

"'Mister Selvern,' said the captain, at last, looking at him, 'don't get fancying, things. Get hold of your bloomin' self. Ye know ye heard nothin'?'

"'I'm quite sure I heard something, sir,' said the second mate. 'I seemed to hear ——' He broke off sharply, and appeared to listen with an almost painful intensity.

"'What did it sound like?' I asked.

"'It's all right, doctor,' said Captain Gannington, laughing gently. 'Ye can give him a tonic when we get back. I'm goin' to shift this stuff.' He drew back, and kicked for the second time at the ugly mass which he took to hide the companionway. The result of his kick was startling, for the whole thing wobbled sloppily, like a mound of unhealthy-looking jelly.

"He drew his foot out of it quickly, and took a step backward, staring, and holding his lamp towards it. 'By gum,' he said, and it was plain that he was generally startled, 'the blessed thing's gone soft!'

"The man had run back several steps from the suddenly flaccid mound, and looking horribly frightened. Though of what, I am sure he had not the least idea. The second mate stood where he was, and stared. For my part, I know I had a most hideous uneasiness upon me. The captain continued to hold his light towards the wobbling mound and stare.

"'It's gone squashy all through,' he said. 'There's no scuttle there. There's no bally woodwork inside that lot! Phoo! What a rum smell!'

"He walked round to the after side of the strange mound, to see whether there might be some signs of an opening, into the hull at the back of the great heap of mould-stuff. And then:

"'Listen!' said the second mate again, in the strangest sort of voice.

"Captain Gannington straightened himself upright, and there succeeded a pause of the most intense quietness, in which there was not even the hum of talk from the men alongside in the boat. We all heard it — a kind of dull, soft thud, thud, thud, thud, somewhere in the hull under us, yet so vague as to make me half doubtful I heard it, only that the others did so, too.

"Captain Gannington turned suddenly to where the man stood.

"'Tell them ——' he began. But the fellow cried out something, and pointed. There had come a strange intensity into his somewhat unemotional face, so that the captain's glance followed his action instantly. I stared also as you may think. It was the great mound at which the man was pointing. I saw what he meant. From the two gapes made in the mould-like stuff by Captain Gannington's boot, the purple fluid was jetting out in a queerly regular fashion, almost as if it were being forced out by a pump. My word! But I stared! And even as I stared a larger jet squirted out, and splashed as far as the man, spattering his boots and trouser legs.

"The fellow had been pretty nervous before, in a stolid, ignorant sort of way, and his funk had been growing steadily; but at this he simply let out a yell, and turned about to run. He paused an instant, as if a sudden fear of the darkness that held the decks, between him and the boat, had taken him. He snatched at the second mate's lantern, tore it out of his hand, and plunged heavily away over the vile stretch of mould.

"Mr. Selvern, the second mate, said not a word; he was just staring, staring at the strange-smelling twin-streams of dull purple that were jetting out from the wobbling mound. Captain Gannington, however, roared an order to the man to come back, but the man plunged on and on across the mould, his feet seeming to be clogged by the stuff, as if it had grown suddenly soft. He zigzagged as he ran, the lantern swaying, in wild circles as he wrenched his feet free with a constant plop, plop; and I could hear his frightened gasps even from where I stood.

"'Come back with that lamp!' roared the captain again; but still the man took no notice.

"And Captain Gannington was silent an instant, his lips working in a queer, inarticulate fashion, as if he were stunned momentarily by the very violence of his anger at the man's insubordination. And in the silence I heard the sounds again — thud, thud, thud, thud! Quite distinctly now, beating, it seemed suddenly to me, right down under my feet, but deep.

"I stared down at the mould on which I was standing, with a quick, disgusting sense of the terrible all about me; then I looked at the captain, and tried to say something, without appearing frightened. I saw that he had turned again to the mound, and all the anger had gone out of his face. He had his lamp out towards the mound, and was listening. There was another moment of absolute silence, at least, I knew that I was not conscious of any sound at all in all the world, except that extraordinary thud, thud, thud, thud, down somewhere in the huge bulk under us.

"The captain shifted his feet with a sudden, nervous movement, and as he lifted them the mould went plop, plop! He looked quickly at me, trying to smile, as if he were not thinking anything very much about it.

"'What do you make of it, doctor?' he said.

"'I think ——' I began. But the second mate interrupted with a single word, his voice pitched a little high, in a tone that made us both stare instantly at him.

"'Look!' he said, and pointed at the mound. The thing was all of a slow quiver. A strange ripple ran outward from it, along the deck, like you will see a ripple run inshore out of a calm sea. It reached a mound a little foreside of us, which I had supposed to be the cabin skylight, and in a moment the second mound sank nearly level with the surrounding decks, quivering floppily in a most extraordinary fashion. A sudden quick tremor took the mould right under the second mate, and he gave out a hoarse little cry, and held his arms out on each side of him, to keep his balance. The tremor in the mould spread, and Captain Gannington swayed, and spread out his feet with a sudden curse of fright. The second mate jumped across to him, and caught him by the wrist.

"'The boat, sir!' he said, saying the very thing that I had lacked the pluck to say. 'For God's sake ——'

"But he never finished, for a tremendous hoarse scream cut off his words. They hove themselves round and looked. I could see without turning. The man who had run from us was standing in the waist of the ship, about a fathom from the starboard bulwarks. He was swaying from side to side, and screaming, in a dreadful fashion. He appeared to be trying to lift his feet, and the light from his swaying lantern showed an almost incredible sight. All about him the mould was in active movement. His feet had sunk out of sight. The stuff appeared to be lapping at his legs and abruptly his bare flesh showed. The hideous stuff had rent his trouser-leg away as if it were paper. He gave out a simply sickening scream, and, with a vast effort, wrenched one leg free. It was partly destroyed. The next instant he pitched face downward, and the stuff heaped itself upon him, as if it were actually alive, with a dreadful, severe life. It was simply infernal. The man had gone from sight. Where he had fallen was now a writhing, elongated mound, in constant and horrible increase, as the mould appeared to move towards it in strange ripples from all sides.

"Captain Gannington and the second mate were stone silent, in amazed and incredulous horror, but I had begun to reach towards a grotesque and terrific conclusion, both helped and hindered by my professional training.

"From the men in the boat alongside there was a loud shouting. and I saw two of their faces appear suddenly above the rail. They showed clearly a moment in the light from the lamp which the man had snatched from Mr. Selvern; for, strangely enough, this lamp was standing upright and unharmed on the deck, a little way foreside of that dreadful, elongated, growing mound, that still swayed and writhed with an incredible horror. The lamp rose and fell on the passing ripples of the mould, just — for all the world — as you will see a boat rise and fall on little swells. It is of some interest to me now, psychologically, to remember how that rising and falling lantern brought home to me more than anything the incomprehensible dreadful strangeness of it all.

"The men's faces disappeared with sudden yells, as if they had slipped, or been suddenly hurt; and there was a fresh uproar of shouting from the boat. The men were calling to us to come away — to come away. In the same instant I felt my left boot drawn suddenly and forcibly downward, with a horrible, painful grip. I wrenched it free, with a yell of angry fear. Forward of us, I saw that the vile surface was all amove, and abruptly I found myself shouting in a queer, frightened voice, 'The boat, captain! The boat, captain!'

"Captain Gannington stared round at me, over his right shoulder, in a peculiar, dull way, that told me he was utterly dazed with bewilderment and the incomprehensibleness of it all. I took a quick, clogged, nervous step towards him, and gripped his arm, and shook it fiercely. 'The boat!' I shouted at him. 'The boat! For God's sake, tell the men to bring the boat aft!'

"Then the mound must have drawn his feet down, for abruptly he bellowed fiercely with terror, his momentary apathy giving place to furious energy. His thickset, vastly muscular body doubled and writhed with his enormous effort, and he struck out madly dropping the lantern. He tore his feet free, something ripping as he did so. The reality and necessity of the situation had come upon him brutishly real, and he was roaring to the men in the boat, 'Bring the boat aft! Bring 'er aft! Bring 'er aft!' The second mate and I were shouting the same thing madly.

"'For God's sake, be smart, lads!' roared the captain, and stooped quickly for his lamp, which still burned. His feet were gripped again, and he hove them out, blaspheming breathlessly, aud leaping a yard high with his effort. Then he made a run for the side, wrenching his feet free at each step. In the same instant the second mate cried out something, and grabbed at the captain.

"'It's got hold of my feet! It's got hold of my feet!' he screamed. His feet, had disappeared up to his boot-tops, and Captain Gannington caught him round the waist with his powerful left arm, gave a mighty heave, and the next instant had him free; but both his boot-soles had gone. For my part, I jumped madly from foot to foot, to avoid the plucking of the mould; and suddenly I made a run for the ship's side. But before I could get there, a queer gape came in the mould between us and the side, at least a couple of feet wide, and how deep I don't know. It closed up in an instant, and all the mould where the cape had been vent into a sort of flurry of horrible ripplings, so that I ran back from it; for I did not dare to put my foot upon it. Then the captain was shouting to me:

"'Aft, doctor! Aft, doctor! This way, doctor! Run!' I saw then that he had passed me, and was up on the after raised portion of the poop. He had the second mate, thrown like a sack, all loose and quiet, over his left shoulder; for Mr. Selvern had fainted, and his long legs flogged limp and helpless against the captain's massive knees as he ran. I saw, with a queer, unconscious noting of minor details, how the torn soles of the second mate's boots flapped and jigged as the captain staggered aft.

"'Boat ahoy! Boat ahoy! Boat ahoy!' shouted the captain; and then I was beside him, shouting also. The men were answering with loud yells of encouragement, and it was plain they were working desperately to force the boat aft through the thick scum about the ship.

"We reached the ancient, mould-hid taffrail, and slewed about breathlessly in the half-darkness to see what was happening. Captain Gannington had left his lantern by the big mound when he picked up the second mate; and as we stood, gasping we discovered suddenly that all the mould between us and the light was full of movement. Yet, the part on which we stood, for about six or eight feet forward of us, was still firm.

"Every couple of seconds we shouted to the men to hasten, and they kept on calling to us that they would be with us in an instant. And all the time we watched the deck of that dreadful hulk, feeling, for my part, literally sick with mad suspense, and ready to jump overboard into that filthy scum all about us.

"Down somewhere in the huge bulk of the ship there was all the time that extraordinary dull, ponderous thud, thud, thud, thud growing ever louder. I seemed to feel the whole hull of the derelict, beginning to quiver and thrill with each dull beat. And to me, with the grotesque and hideous suspicion of what made that noise, it was at once the most dreadful and incredible sound I have ever heard.

"As we waited desperately for the boat, I scanned incessantly so much of the grey white bulk as the lamp showed. The whole of the decks seemed to be in strange movement. Forward of the lamp, I could see indistinctly the moundings of the mould swaying and nodding hideously beyond the circle of the brightest rays. Nearer, and full in the glow of the lamp, the mound which should have indicated the skylight, was swelling steadily. There were ugly, purple veinings on it, and as it swelled, it seemed to me that the veinings and mottlings on it were becoming plainer, rising as though embossed upon it, like you will see the veins stand out on the body of a powerful, full-blooded horse. It was most extraordinary. The mound that we had supposed to cover the companionway had sunk flat with the surrounding mould, and I could not see that it jetted out any more of the purplish fluid.

"A quaking movement of the mound began away forward of the lamp, and came flurrying away aft towards us, and at the sight of that I climbed up on to the spongy-feeling taffrail, and yelled afresh for the boat. The men answered with a shout, which told me they were nearer, but the beastly scum was so thick that it was evidently a fight to move the boat at all. Beside me, Captain Gannington was shaking the second mate furiously, and the man stirred and began to moan. The captain shook him again, 'Wake up! Wake up, mister!' he shouted.

"The second mate staggered out of the captain's arms, and collapsed suddenly, shrieking: 'My feet! Oh, God! My feet!' The captain and I lugged him off the mound, and got him into a sitting position upon the taffrail, where he kept up a continual moaning.

"'Hold 'im, doctor,' said the captain. And whilst I did so, he ran forward a few yards, and peered down over the starboard quarter rail. 'For God's sake, be smart, lads! Be smart! Be smart!' he shouted down to the men, and they answered him, breathless, from close at hand, yet still too far away for the boat to be any use to us on the instant.

"I was holding the moaning, half-unconscious officer, and staring forward along the poop decks. The flurrying of the mould was coming aft, slowly and noiselessly. And then, suddenly, I saw something closer:

"'Look out, captain!' I shouted. And even as I shouted, the mould near to him gave a sudden, peculiar slobber. I had seen a ripple stealing towards him through the mould. He gave an enormous, clumsy leap, and landed near to us on the sound part of the mould, but the movement followed him. He turned and faced it, swearing fiercely. All about his feet there came abruptly little gapings, which made horrid sucking noises. 'Come back, captain!' I yelled. 'Come back, quick!' As I shouted, a ripple came at his feet — lipping at them; and he stamped insanely at it, and leaped back, his boot torn half off his foot. He swore madly with pain and anger, and jumped swiftly for the taffrail.

"'Come on, doctor! Over we go!' he called. Then he remembered the filthy scum, and hesitated, and roared out desperately to the men to hurry. I stared down, also.

"'The second mate?' I said.

"'I'll take charge doctor,' said Captain Gannington, and caught hold of Mr. Selvern. As he spoke, I thought I saw something beneath us, outlined against the scum. I leaned out over the stern, and peered. There was something under the port-quarter.

"'There's something down there, captain!' I called, and pointed in the darkness. He stooped far over, and stared.

"'A boat, by gum! A boat!' he yelled, and began to wriggle swiftly along the taffrail, dragging the second mate after him. I followed. 'A boat it is, sure!' he exclaimed a few moments later, and, picking up the second mate clear of the rail, he hove him down into the boat, where he fell with a crash into the bottom.

"'Over ye go, doctor!' he yelled at me, and pulled me bodily off the rail and dropped me after the officer. As he did so, I felt the whole of the ancient, spongy rail give a peculiar, sickening quiver, and begin to wobble. I fell on to the second mate, and the captain came after, almost in the same instant, but, fortunately, he landed clear of us, on to the fore thwart, which broke under his weight, with a loud crack and splintering of wood.

"'Thank God!' I heard him mutter. 'Thank God! I guess that was a mighty near thing to going to Hades.'

"He struck a match, just as I got to my feet, and between us we got the second mate straightened out on one of the after fore-and-aft thwarts. We shouted to the men in the boat, telling them where we were, and saw the light of their lantern shining round the starboard counter of the derelict. They called back to us to tell us they were doing their best, and then, whilst we waited, Captain Gannington struck another match, and began to overhaul the boat we had dropped into. She was a modern, two-bowed boat, and on the stern there was painted 'Cyclone, Glasgow.' She was in pretty fair condition, and had evidently drifted into the scum and been held by it.

"Captain Gannington struck several matches, and went forrard towards the derelict. Suddenly he called to me, and I jumped over the thwarts to him. 'Look, doctor,' he said, and I saw what he meant — a mass of bones up in the bows of the boat. I stooped over them, and looked; there were the bones of at least three people, all mixed together in an extraordinary fashion, and quite clean and dry. I had a sudden thought concerning the bones, but I said nothing, for my thought was vague in some ways, and concerned the grotesque and incredible suggestion that had come to me as to the cause of that ponderous, dull thud, thud, thud thud, that beat on so infernally within the hull, and was plain to hear even now that we had got off the vessel herself. And all the while, you know, I had a sick, horrible mental picture of that frightful, wriggling mound aboard the hulk.

"As Captain Gannington struck a final match, I saw something that sickened me and the captain saw it in the same instant. The match went out, and he fumbled clumsily for another, and struck it.

We saw the thing again. We had not been mistaken. A great lip of grey-white was protruding in over the edge of the boat — a great lappet of the mould was coming stealthily towards us — a live mass of the very hull itself! And suddenly Captain Gannington yelled out in so many words the grotesque and incredible thing I was thinking: 'She's alive!'

"I never heard such a sound of comprehension and terror in a man's voice. The very horrified assurance of it made actual to me the thing that before had only lurked in my subconscious mind. I knew he was right; I knew that the explanation my reason and my training both repelled and reached towards was the true one. Oh, I wonder whether anyone can possibly understand our feelings in that moment? The unmitigated horror of it and the incredibleness!

"As the light of the match burned up fully, I saw that the mass of living matter coming towards us was streaked and veined with purple, the veins standing out, enormously distended. The whole thing quivered continuously to each ponderous thud, thud, thud, thud, of that gargantuan organ that pulsed within the huge grey-white bulk. The flame of the match reached the captain's fingers, and there came to me a little sickly whiff of burned flesh, but he seemed unconscious of any pain. Then the flame went out in a brief sizzle, yet at the last moment I had seen an extraordinary raw look become visible upon the end of that monstrous, protruding lappet. It had become dewed with a hideous, purplish sweat. And with the darkness there came a sudden charnel-like stench.

"I heard the matchbox split in Captain Gannington's hands as he wrenched it open. Then he swore, in a queer frightened voice, for he had come to the end of his matches. He turned clumsily in the dark- ness, and tumbled over the nearest thwart, in his eagerness to get to the stern of the boat; and I after him. For we knew that thing was coming towards us through the darkness, reaching over that piteous mingled heap of human bones all jumbled together in the bows. We shouted madly to the men, and for answer saw the bows of the boat emerge dimly into view round the starboard counter of the derelict.

"'Thank God!' I gasped out. But Captain Gannington roared to them to show a light. Yet this they could not do, for the lamp had just been stepped on in their desperate efforts to force the boat round to us.

"'Quick! Quick!' I shouted.

"'For God's sake, be smart, men!' roared the captain.

"And both of us faced the darkness under the port-counter, out of which we knew — but could not see — the thing was coming to us.

"'An oar! Smart, now — pass me an oar!' shouted the captain; and reached out his hands through the gloom towards the on-coming boat. I saw a figure stand up in the bows, and hold something out to us across the intervening yards of scum. Captain Gannington swept his hands through the darkness, and encountered it.

"'I've got it! Let go there!' he said, in a quick, tense voice.

"In the same instant the boat we were in was pressed over suddenly to starboard by some tremendous weight. Then I heard the captain shout, 'Duck y'r head, doctor!' And directly afterwards he swung the heavy, fourteen-foot oar round his head, and struck into the darkness. There came a sudden squelch, and he struck again, with a savage grunt of fierce energy. At the second blow the boat righted with a slow movement, and directly afterwards the other boat bumped gently into ours.

"Captain Gannington dropped the oar, and, springing across to the second mate, hove him up off the thwart, and pitched him with knee and arms clear in over the bows among the men; then he shouted to me to follow, which I did, and he came after me, bringing the oar with him. We carried the second mate aft, and the captain shouted to the men to back the boat a little; then they got her bows clear of the boat we had just left, and so headed out through the scum for the open sea.

"'Where's Tom 'Arrison?' gasped one of the men, in the midst of his exertions. He happened to be Tom Harrison's particular chum, and Captain Gannington answered him briefly enough:

"'Dead! Pull! Don't talk!'"

"Now, difficult as it had been to force the boat through the scum to our rescue, the difficulty to get clear seemed tenfold. After some five minutes pulling, the boat seemed hardly to have moved a fathom, if so much, and a quite dreadful fear took me afresh, which one of the panting men put suddenly into words, 'It's got us!' he gasped out. 'Same as poor Tom!' It was the man who had inquired where Harrison was.

"'Shut y'r mouth an' pull!' roared the captain. And so another few minutes passed. Abruptly, it seemed to me that the dull, ponderous thud, thud, thud, thud came more plainly through the dark, and I stared intently over the stern. I sickened a little, for I could almost swear that the dark mass of the monster was actually nearer — that it was coming nearer to us through the darkness. Captain Gannington must have had the same thought, for, after a brief look into the darkness, he jumped forward, and began to double-bank the stroke-oar.

"'Get forward under the oars, doctor,' he said to me rather breathlessly. 'Get in the bows, an' see if you can't free the stuff a bit round the bows.'

"I did as he told me, and a minute later I was in the bows of the boat, puddling the scum from side to side, and trying to break up the viscid, clinging muck. A heavy almost animal-like smell rose off it, and all the air seemed full of the deadening, heavy smell. I shall never find words to tell anyone on earth the whole horror of it all — the threat that seemed to hang in the very air around us, and but a little astern that incredible thing, coming, as I firmly believed, nearer, and scum holding us, like half-melted glue.

"The minutes passed in a deadly, eternal fashion, and I kept staring back astern into the darkness but never ceasing to puddle that filthy scum, striking at it and switching it from side to side until I sweated.

"Abruptly Captain Gannington sang out: 'We're gaining, lads. Pull!' And I felt the boat forge ahead perceptibly, as they gave way with renewed hope and energy. There was soon no doubt of it, for presently that hideous thud, thud, thud, thud had grown quite dim and vague somewhere astern and I could no longer see the derelict, for the night had come down tremendously dark and all the sky was thick, overset with heavy clouds. As we drew nearer and nearer to the edge of the scum, the boat moved more and more perceptibly, until suddenly we emerged with a clean, sweet, fresh sound into the open sea.

"'Thank God!' I said aloud, and drew in the boathook, and made my way aft again to where Captain Gannington now sat once more at the tiller. I saw him looking anxiously up at the sky and across to where the lights of our vessel burned, and again he would seem to listen intently, so that I found myself listening also.

"'What's that, Captain?' I said sharply; for it seemed to me that I heard a sound far astern, something, between a queer whine and a low whistling. 'What's that?'

"'It's wind, doctor.' he said in a low voice. 'I wish to God we were aboard.' Then to the men: 'Pull! Put y'r backs into it, or ye'll never put y'r teeth through good bread again!' The men obeyed nobly, and we reached the vessel safely, and had the boat safely stowed before the storm came, which it did in a furious white smother out of the west. I could see it for some minutes beforehand, tearing the sea in the gloom into a wall of phosphorescent foam; and as it came nearer, that peculiar whining, piping sound grew louder and louder, until it was like a vast steam whistle rushing towards us. And when it did come, we got it very heavy indeed, so that the morning showed us nothing but a welter of white seas, with that grim derelict many a score of miles away in the smother, lost as utterly as our hearts could wish to lose her.

"When I came to examine the second mate's feet, I found them in a very extraordinary condition. The soles of them had the appearance of having been partly digested. I know of no other word that so exactly describes their condition, and the agony the man suffered must have been dreadful.

"Now," concluded the doctor, "that is what I call a case in point. If we could know exactly what the old vessel had originally been loaded with, and the juxtaposition of the various articles of her cargo, plus the heat and time she had endured, plus one or two other only guessable quantities, we should have solved the chemistry of the life-force, gentlemen. Not necessarily the origin, mind you; but, at least, we should have taken a big step on the way. I've often regretted that gale, you know — in a way, that is, in a way. It was a most amazing discovery, but at the same time I had nothing but thankfulness to be rid of it. A most amazing chance. I often think of the way the monster woke out of its torpor. And that scum! The dead pigs caught in i! I fancy that was a grim kind of a net, gentlemen. It caught many things. It ——"

The old doctor sighed and nodded.

"If I could have had her bill of lading," he said, his eyes full of regret. "If —— It might have told me something to help. But, anyway ——" He began to fill his pipe again. "I suppose," he ended, looking round at us gravely, "I s'pose we humans are an ungrateful lot of beggars at the best! But — but, what a chance? What a, chance, eh?"

CHAPTER 14

DEMONS OF THE SEA

"Come out on deck and have a look, Darkly!" Jepson cried, rushing into the half deck. "The Old Man says there's been a submarine earthquake, and the sea's all bubbling and muddy!"

Obeying the summons of Jepson's excited tone, I followed him out. It was as he had said; the everlasting blue of the ocean was mottled with splotches of a muddy hue, and at times a large bubble would appear, to burst with a loud "pop." Aft, the skipper and the three mates could be seen on the poop, peering at the sea through their glasses. As I gazed out over the gently heaving water, far off to windward something was hove up into the evening air. It appeared to be a mass of seaweed, but fell back into the water with a sullen plunge as though it were something more substantial. Immediately after this strange occurrence, the sun set with tropical swiftness, and in the brief afterglow things assumed a strange unreality.

The crew were all below, no one but the mate and the helmsman remaining on the poop. Away forward, on the topgallant forecastle head the dim figure of the man on lookout could be seen, leaning against the forestay. No sound was heard save the occasional jingle of a chain sheet, of the flog of the steering gear as a small swell passed under our counter. Presently the mate's voice broke the silence, and, looking up, I saw that the Old Man had come on deck, and was talking with him. From the few stray words that could be overheard, I knew they were talking of the strange happenings of the day.

Shortly after sunset, the wind, which had been fresh during the day, died down, and with its passing the air grew oppressively hot. Not long after two bells, the mate sung out for me, and ordered me to fill a bucket from overside and bring it to him. When I had carried out his instructions, he placed a thermometer in the bucket.

"Just as I thought," he muttered, removing the instrument and showing it to the skipper; "ninety-nine degrees. Why, the sea's hot enough to make tea with! "

"Hope it doesn't get any hotter," growled the latter; "if it does, we shall all be boiled alive."

At a sign from the mate, I emptied the bucket and replaced it in the rack, after which I resumed my former position by the rail. The Old Man and the mate walked the poop side by side. The air grew hotter as the hours passed and after a long period of silence broken only by the occasional "pop" of a bursting gas bubble, the moon arose. It shed but a feeble light, however, as a heavy mist had arisen from the sea, and through this, the moonbeams struggled weakly. The mist, we decided, was due to the excessive heat of the sea water; it was a very wet mist, and we were soon soaked to the skin. Slowly the interminable night wore on, and the sun arose, looking dim and ghostly through the mist that rolled and billowed about the ship. From time to time we took the temperature of the sea, although we found but a slight increase therein. No work was done, and a feeling as of something impending pervaded the ship.

The fog horn was kept going constantly, as the lookout peered through the wreathing mists. The captain walked the poop in company with the mates, and once the third mate spoke and pointed out into the clouds of fog. All eyes followed his gesture; we saw what was apparently a black line, which seemed to cut the whiteness of the billows. It reminded us of nothing so much as an enormous cobra standing on its tail. As we looked it vanished. The grouped mates were evidently puzzled; there seemed to be a difference of opinion among them. Presently as they argued, I heard the second mate's voice:

"That's all rot," he said. "I've seen things in fog before, but they've always turned out to be imaginary."

The third shook his head and made some reply I could not overhear, but no further comment was made. Going below that afternoon, I got a short sleep, and on coming on deck at eight bells, I found that the steam still held us; if anything, it seemed to be thicker than ever. Hansard, who had been taking the temperatures during my watch below, informed me that the sea was three degrees hotter, and that the Old Man was getting into a rare old state. At three bells I went forward to have a look over the bows, and a chin with Stevenson, whose lookout it was. On gaining the forecastle head, I went to the side and looked down into the water. Stevenson came over and stood beside me.

"Rum go, this," he grumbled.

He stood by my side for a time in silence; we seemed to be hypnotized by the gleaming surface of the sea. Suddenly out of the depths, right before us, there arose a monstrous black face. It was like a frightful caricature of a human countenance. For a moment we gazed petrified; my blood seemed to suddenly turn to ice water; I was unable to move. With a mighty effort of will, I regained my self-control and, grasping Stevenson's arm, I found I could do no more than croak, my powers of speech seemed gone. "Look!" I gasped. "Look!"

Stevenson continued to stare into the sea, like a man turned to stone. He seemed to stoop further over, as if to examine the thing more closely. "Lord," he exclaimed, "it must be the devil himself!"

As though the sound of his voice had broken a spell, the thing disappeared. My companion looked at me, while I rubbed my eyes, thinking that I had been asleep, and that the awful vision had been a frightful nightmare. One look at my friend, however, disabused me of any such thought. His face wore a puzzled expression.

"Better go aft and tell the Old Man," he faltered.

I nodded and left the forecastle head, making my way aft like one in a trance. The skipper and the mate were standing at the break of the poop, and running up the ladder I told them what we had seen.

"Bosh!" sneered the Old Man. "You've been looking at your own ugly reflection in the water."

Nevertheless, in spite of his ridicule, he questioned me closely. Finally he ordered the mate forward to see it he could see anything. The latter, however, returned in a few moments, to report that nothing unusual could be seen. Four bells were struck, and we were relieved for tea. Coming on deck afterward, I found the men clustered together forward. The sole topic of conversation with them was the thing that Stevenson and I had seen.

"I suppose, Darkly, it couldn't have been a reflection by any chance, could it?" one of the older men asked.

"Ask Stevenson," I replied as I made my way aft.

At eight bells, my watch came on deck again, to find that nothing further had developed. But, about an hour before midnight, the mate, thinking to have a smoke, sent me to his room for a box of matches with which to light his pipe. It took me no time to clatter down the brass-treaded ladder, and back to the poop, where I handed him the desired article. Taking the box, he removed a match and struck it on the heel of his boot. As he did so, far out in the night a muffled screaming arose. Then came a clamor as of hoarse braying, like an ass but considerably deeper, and with a horribly suggestive human note running through it.

"Good God! Did you hear that, Darkly?" asked the mate in awed tones.

"Yes, sir," I replied, listening—and scarcely noticing his question —for a repetition of the strange sounds. Suddenly the frightful bellowing broke out afresh. The mate's pipe fell to the deck with a clatter.

"Run for'ard!" he cried. "Quick, now, and see if you can see anything."

With my heart in my mouth, and pulses pounding madly I raced forward. The watch were all up on the forecastle head, clustered around the lookout. Each man was talking and gesticulating wildly. They became silent, and turned questioning glances toward me as I shouldered my way among them.

"Have you seen anything?" I cried.

Before I could receive an answer, a repetition of the horrid sounds broke out again, profaning the night with their horror. They seemed to have definite direction now, in spite of the fog that enveloped us. Undoubtedly, too, they were nearer. Pausing a moment to make sure of their bearing, I hastened aft and reported to the mate. I told him that nothing could be seen, but that the sounds apparently came from right ahead of us. On hearing this he ordered the man at the wheel to let the ship's head come off a couple of points. A moment later a shrill screaming tore its way through the night, followed by the hoarse braying sounds once more.

"It's close on the starboard bow!" exclaimed the mate, as he beckoned the helmsman to let her head come off a little more. Then, singing out for the watch, he ran forward, slacking the lee braces on the way. When he had the yards trimmed to his satisfaction on the new course, he returned to the poop and hung far out over the rail listening intently. Moments passed that seemed like hours, yet the silence remained unbroken. Suddenly the sounds began again, and so close that it seemed as though they must be right aboard of us. At this time I noticed a strange booming note mingled with the brays. And once or twice there came a sound that can only be described as a sort of "gug, gug." Then would come a wheezy whistling, for all the world like an asthmatic person breathing.

All this while the moon shone wanly through the steam, which seemed to me to be somewhat thinner. Once the mate gripped me by the shoulder as the noises rose and fell again. They now seemed to be coming from a point broad on our beam. Every eye on the ship was straining into the mist, but with no result. Suddenly one of the men cried out, as something long and black slid past us into the fog astern. From it there rose four indistinct and ghostly towers, which resolved themselves into spars and ropes, and sails.

"A ship! It's a ship!" we cried excitedly. I turned to Mr. Gray; he, too, had seen something, and was staring aft into the wake. So ghostlike, unreal, and fleeting had been our glimpse of the stranger, that we were not sure that we had seen an honest, material ship, but thought that we had been vouchsafed a vision of some phantom vessel like the Flying Dutchman. Our sails gave a sudden flap, the clew irons flogging the bulwarks with hollow thumps. The mate glanced aloft.

"Wind's dropping," he growled savagely. "We shall never get out of this infernal place at this gait!"

Gradually the wind fell until it was a flat calm. No sound broke the deathlike silence save the rapid patter of the reef points, as she gently rose and fell on the light swell. Hours passed, and the watch was relieved and I then went below. At seven bells we were called again, and as I went along the deck to the galley, I noticed that the fog seemed thinner, and the air cooler. When eight bells were struck I relieved Hansard at coiling down the ropes. From him I learned that the steam had begun to clear about four bells, and that the temperature of the sea had fallen ten degrees.

In spite of the thinning mist, it was not until about a half an hour later that we were able to get a glimpse of the surrounding sea. It was still mottled with dark patches, but the bubbling and popping had ceased. As much of the surface of the ocean as could be seen had a peculiarly desolate aspect. Occasionally a wisp of steam would float up from the nearer sea, and roll undulatingly across its silent surface, until lost in the vagueness that still held the hidden horizon. Here and there columns of steam rose up in pillars, which gave me the impression that the sea was hot in patches. Crossing to the starboard side and looking over, I found that conditions there were similar to those to port. The desolate aspect of the sea filled me with an idea of chilliness, although the air was quite warm and muggy. From the break of the poop the mate called to me to get his glasses.

When I had done this, he took them from me and walked to the taffrail. Here he stood for some moments polishing them with his handkerchief. After a moment he raised them to his eyes, and peered long and intently into the mist astern. I stood for some time staring at the point on which the mate had focused his glasses. Presently something shadowy grew upon my vision. Steadily watching it, I distinctly saw the outlines of a ship take form in the fog.

"See!" I cried, but even as I spoke, a lifting wraith of mist disclosed to view a great four-masted bark lying becalmed with all sails set, within a few hundred yards of our stern. As though a curtain had been raised, and then allowed to fall, the fog once more settled down, hiding the strange bark from our sight. The mate was all excitement, striding with quick, jerky steps, up and down the poop, stopping every few moments to peer through his glasses at the point where the four-master had disappeared in the fog. Gradually, as the mists dispersed again, the vessel could be seen more plainly, and it was then that we got an inkling of the cause of the dreadful noises during the night.

For some time the mate watched her silently, and as he watched the conviction grew upon me that in spite of the mist, I could detect some sort of movement on board of her. After some time had passed, the doubt became a certainty, and I could also see a sort of splashing in the water alongside of her. Suddenly the mate put his glasses on top of the wheel box and told me to bring him the speaking trumpet. Running to the companionway, I secured the trumpet and was back at his side.

The mate raised it to his lips, and taking a deep breath, sent a hail across the water that should have awakened the dead. We waited tensely for a reply. A moment later a deep, hollow mutter came from the bark; higher and louder it swelled, until we realized that we were listening to the same sounds we had heard the night before. The mate stood aghast at this answer to his hail; in a voice barely more than a hushed whisper, he bade me call the Old Man. Attracted by the mate's hail and its unearthly reply, the watch had all come aft and were clustered in the mizzen rigging in order to see better.

After calling the captain, I returned to the poop, where I found the second and third mates talking with the chief. All were engaged in trying to pierce the clouds of mist that half hid our strange consort and to arrive at some explanation of the strange phenomena of the past few hours. A moment later the captain appeared carrying his telescope. The mate gave him a brief account of the state of affairs and handed him the trumpet. Giving me the telescope to hold, the captain hailed the shadowy bark. Breathlessly we all listened, when again, in answer to the Old Man's hail, the frightful sounds rose on the still morning air. The skipper lowered the trumpet and stood with an expression of astonished horror on his face.

"Lord!" he exclaimed. "What an ungodly row!"

At this, the third, who had been gazing through his binoculars, broke the silence.

"Look," he exclaimed. "There's a breeze coming up astern." At his words the captain looked up quickly, and we all watched the ruffling water.

"That packet yonder is bringing the breeze with her," said the skipper. "She'll be alongside in half an hour!"

Some moments passed, and the bank of fog had come to within a hundred yards of our taffrail. The strange vessel could be distinctly seen just inside the fringe of the driving mist wreaths. After a short puff, the wind died completely, but as we stared with hypnotic fascination, the water astern of the stranger ruffled again with a fresh catspaw. Seemingly with the flapping of her sails, she drew slowly up to us. As the leaden seconds passed, the big four-master approached us steadily. The light air had now reached us, and with a lazy lift of our sails, we, too, began to forge slowly through that weird sea. The bark was now within fifty yards of our stern, and she was steadily drawing nearer, seeming to be able to outfoot us with ease.

As she came on she luffed sharply, and came up into the wind with her weather leeches shaking.

I looked toward her poop, thinking to discern the figure of the man at the wheel, but the mist coiled around her quarter, and objects on the after end of her became indistinguishable. With a rattle of chain sheets on her iron yards, she filled away again. We meanwhile had gone ahead, but it was soon evident that she was the better sailor, for she came up to us hand over fist. The wind rapidly freshened and the mist began to drift away before it, so that each moment her spars and cordage became more plainly visible. The skipper and the mates were watching her intently when an almost simultaneous exclamation of fear broke from them.

"My God!"

And well they might show signs of fear, for crawling about the bark's deck were the most horrible creatures I had ever seen. In spite of their unearthly strangeness there was something vaguely familiar about them. Then it came to me that the face that Stevenson and I had seen during he night belonged to one of them. Their bodies had something of the shape of a seal's, but of a dead, unhealthy white. The lower part of the body ended in a sort of double-curved tail on which they appeared to be able to shuffle about. In place of arms, they had two long, snaky feelers, at the ends of which were two very humanlike hands, which were equipped with talons instead of nails. Fearsome indeed were these parodies of human beings!

Their faces, which, like their tentacles, were black, were the most grotesquely human things about them, and the upper jaw closed into the lower, after the manner of the jaws of an octopus. I have seen men among certain tribes of natives who had faces uncommonly like theirs, but yet no native I had ever seen could have given me the extraordinary feeling of horror and revulsion I experienced toward these brutal-looking creatures.

"What devilish beasts!" burst out the captain in disgust.

With this remark he turned to the mates, and as he did so, the expressions on their faces told me that they had all realized what the presence of these bestial-looking brutes meant. If, as was doubtless the case, these creatures had boarded the bark and destroyed her crew, what would prevent them from doing the same with us? We were a smaller ship and had a smaller crew, and the more I thought of it the less I liked it.

We could now see the name on the bark's bow with the naked eye. It read Scottish Heath, while on her boats we could see the name bracketed with Glasgow, showing that she hailed from that port. It was a remarkable coincidence that she should have a slant from just the quarter in which yards were trimmed, as before we saw her she must have been drifting around with everything "aback." But now in this light air she was able to run along beside us with no one at her helm. But steering herself she was, and although at times she yawed wildly, she never got herself aback. As we gazed at her we noticed a sudden movement on board of her, and several of the creatures slid into the water.

"See! See! They've spotted us. They're coming for us!" cried the mate wildly.

It was only too true, scores of them were sliding into the sea, letting themselves down by means of their long tentacles. On they came, slipping by scores and hundreds into the water, and swimming toward us in droves. The ship was making about three knots, otherwise they would have caught us in a very few minutes. But they persevered, gaining slowly but surely, and drawing nearer and nearer. The long, tentacle-like arms rose out of the sea in hundreds, and the foremost ones were already within a score of yards of the ship before the Old Man bethought himself to shout to the mates to fetch up the half dozen cutlasses that comprised the ship's armory. Then, turning to me, he ordered me to go down to his cabin and bring up the two revolvers out of the top drawer of the chart table, also a box of cartridges that was there.

When I returned with the weapons he loaded them and handed one to the mate. Meanwhile the pursuing creatures were coming steadily nearer, and soon half a dozen of the leaders were directly under our counter. Immediately the captain leaned over the rail and emptied his pistol into them, but without any apparent effect. He must have realized how puny and ineffectual his efforts were, for he did not reload his weapon.

Some dozens of the brutes had reached us, and as they did so, their tentacles rose into the air and caught our rail. I heard the third mate scream suddenly, and turning, I saw him dragged quickly to the rail, with a tentacle wrapped completely around him. Snatching a cutlass, the second mate hacked off the tentacle where it joined the body. A gout of blood splashed into the third mate's face, and he fell to the deck. A dozen more of those arms rose and wavered in the air, but they now seemed some yards astern of us. A rapidly widening patch of clear water appeared between us and the foremost of our pursuers, and we raised a wild shout of joy. The cause was soon apparent; for a fine fair wind had sprung up, and with the increase in its force, the Scottish Heath had got herself aback, while we were rapidly leaving the monsters behind us. The third mate rose to his feet with a dazed look, and as he did so something fell to the deck. I picked it up and found that it was the severed portion of the tentacle of the third's late adversary. With a grimace of disgust I tossed it into the sea, as I needed no reminder of that awful experience.

Three weeks later we anchored in San Francisco. There the captain made a full report of the affair to the authorities, with the result that a gunboat was despatched to investigate. Six weeks later she returned to report that she had been unable to find any signs, either of the ship herself or of the fearful creatures that had attacked her. And since then nothing, as far as I know, has ever been heard of the four-masted bark Scottish Heath, last seen by us in the possession of creatures that may rightly be called demons of the sea.

Whether she still floats, occupied by her hellish crew, or whether some storm has sent her to her last resting place beneath the waves is surely a matter of conjecture. Perchance on some dark, fog-bound night, a ship in that wilderness of waters may hear cries and sounds beyond those of the wailing of the winds. Then let them look to it, for it may be that the demons of the sea are near them.

www.ingramcontent.com/pod-product-compliance
Lightning Source LLC
Chambersburg PA
CBHW032338310726
48973CB00007B/1754